'There is a ...  the...

'A lovely debut – warm and engaging' Catherine Alliott

'Frazzled parents and grumpy children around the country share the same start to the day – the dreaded school run. If you're familiar with this scenario, Sophie King's debut will strike a chord with you . . . A great read' *Family Circle*

'An involving drama' *You*

'A funny new novel' *Mail on Sunday*

'A nice little page-turner' *Heat*

'This is an entertaining look at the trials of everyday life . . . It's one to pack alongside the beach towel' *Candis*

'The book is very entertaining and it's hard not to become involved. Any mum who has done the school run will identify with the everyday characters. I'd recommend it as a relaxing read' *Prima*

'. . . [An] irresistibly funny debut novel . . . This is a brilliantly observed book about how life's routines can be interrupted at any moment by tragedy, a hilarious incident or a new love coming into your life with a wallop' *V magazine*

Also by Sophie King

The School Run

About the author

Sophie King is a pseudonym for journalist Jane Bidder, who contributes regularly to national newspapers and women's magazines, including *Woman* and *The Times*. She also writes short stories for *Women's Weekly* and *My Weekly*. She was runner-up in the Harry Bowling Award in 2002 and the winner of the Romantic Novelists' Association's Elizabeth Goudge Award in 2004. Sophie King grew up in Harrow and now lives in Hertfordshire with her three children.

SOPHIE KING

Mums@Home

HODDER

Copyright © 2006 by Jane Bidder

First published in Great Britain in 2006 by Hodder & Stoughton
A division of Hodder Headline

The right of Jane Bidder to be identified as the Author
of the Work has been asserted by her in accordance with the
Copyright, Designs and Patents Act 1988.

A Hodder paperback

2

A CIP catalogue record for this title is
available from the British Library

0 340 83837 X

Typeset in Sabon by Palimpsest Book Production Limited,
Polmont, Stirlingshire

Printed and bound by Mackays of Chatham Ltd,
Chatham, Kent

Hodder Headline's policy is to use papers that are natural,
renewable and recyclable products and made from wood grown in
sustainable forests. The logging and manufacturing processes are
expected to conform to the environmental regulations of the
country of origin.

Hodder & Stoughton Ltd
A division of Hodder Headline
338 Euston Road
London NW1 3BH

This book is dedicated to:
Those friends who unpacked me/found the corkscrew/
made up my bed/bought me a torch to sleep with (the
nice thick rubber kind)/rang me back on my
mobile/understood when I didn't return messages/sent
me funny emails/taught me to laugh again.

They know who they are.

Also to my late mother Sally and my family: Bill,
William, Lucy, Giles, Daddy, Diane, Nancy and Beano.

This book is *not* dedicated to:
A certain child who downloaded a teenage site that
crippled my computer/cost me over £200/taught me
things I never knew/and caused me considerable
embarrassment at my friendly local computer shop.
(But I still love him.)

ACKNOWLEDGEMENTS

Special thanks to:
Betty Schwartz for booting me up.
Phil Patterson from Marjacq Scripts for helping me log on to the
wide world of publishing.
Sara Kinsella, my clever editor, for her perceptive attachments.
Isobel Akenhead for her sunny voice.
Carolyn Caughey for her warm and funny emails.
Dr Penny Stanway for her advice on medical matters.
The Romantic Novelists' Association and its online group, Romna.
Hazel Orme, my copyeditor – more astute than many a computer
dictionary.
Finally grateful thanks to Jamie Hodder-Williams.

AUGUST

1

This little bear can make your dreams come true by Christmas!
    Just send him to six friends and then make a wish. You'll also be automatically entered in a draw for a free trip to Paris, sponsored by Nappysacks.
    Do not delete this email or your wish won't come true!
    This has been brought to you by Mums@Home, a new website for parents. Check us out for news, views and tips.

'Georgiewhatareyoudoingonthecomputeratthistimeofnight?It's midnightforGod'ssakeandyou'vegottogetupearlytomorrow. You're meanttohavebeenasleephoursago.Backtobed NOW.Andifyoudothis againyou'rebannedfromthecomputerforaweek.'

Honestly, that child's addicted, thought Caroline despairingly. She had escorted her daughter back to bed, and returned to the screen. She couldn't be the only parent driven to distraction by her computer-mad kids, but what could you do? Change the password again? Last time she'd done that, she'd forgotten the new one, and had to wait hours for the helpline.

Under the desk Caroline snuggled her feet into her slippers. The trouble was that they all needed the Net: Georgie for homework (some teachers encouraged them to type their essays, even one-fingered), and herself for work, which was why she was sitting there now when everyone else (including Georgie, finally) was asleep.

If she was quick, she could wrap up the feature she should have finished at work today and go through her inbox.

This little bear can make your dreams come true by Christmas . . .

If only! This sort of stuff should have been filtered out into the junk box. To make it worse, her head was beginning to throb. Caroline delved into the deep pockets of her blue silk dressing-gown for the packet of paracetamol she always kept there, then knocked back a couple of tablets with a mug of tea-gone-cold.

Do not delete this email or your wish won't come true!

This was almost blackmail! Who were these Mums@Home, and how had they got hold of her address? She scanned the text. That explained it. It had come from Good Publicity, a service she often used as a journalist. It was quite useful, actually. If you needed case histories, you outlined the kind of person you needed to interview and why, then emailed it to Good Publicity, which sent it on to its client base of public-relations consultants seeking publicity for their clients. In return, they emailed journalists about new products and websites. Like this one.

Delete or save?

She watched her finger hovering as though it didn't belong to her. Mums@Home might be useful for her page. The sample tips, particularly the one about getting your children to bed, sounded quite good although the wish bit – accompanied by a spattering of hearts – suggested that the site, like so many, was run by an amateur.

An amateur who still believed in love.

Caroline sighed wistfully, automatically twisting her thin gold wedding ring up to the knuckle and down again. Bears, hearts and wishes belonged to the kind of birthday cards she could no longer bring herself to buy for Roger.

Make a wish . . . At this time of night, when she couldn't think clearly, she was almost tempted. The bear's eyes looked as though they really understood, rather like the white teddy she and Roger had given Annabel in the days when everything had seemed so simple. When she had been able to sleep at night instead of waking at three and thrashing around until daybreak. When she hadn't felt the compulsion to stay up late and check Roger's emails on the pretext of working.

This time, there'd been nothing in his inbox that seemed remotely suspicious. But, then, he wouldn't be so indiscreet. He never had been. It was she who had been stupidly naïve, unable to see the tell-tale signs.

'Can't you just forget it?' Roger had said, in the early days when he still allowed her to talk about it.

Make a wish.

Caroline ran her fingers through her fringe. She could make more than one. She could wish that Annabel would email from Thailand, that Ben would get his A-level grades and start communicating in non-grunt language, that Georgie would listen in class, instead of getting reports that Roger fumed at. And she could wish that they could go back two years. To unmuddied waters. To when Roger hadn't left a footprint that could never be wiped out.

Go on, murmured the bear. Send me.

Yeah, right, as Georgie would say. Who could she send it to, anyway, without them thinking she was one of those daft people who believed in stuff like this? It would need to be someone understanding, who'd known what she'd gone through.

Her sister Janie in Australia? Annabel, in case she bothered to check her mail at an Internet café? Her cousin, Linda, perhaps, who had just had a mastectomy? Zelda at work? Maybe Jeff.

Awkwardly, she scrolled down her address book, wishing she was as adept as Georgie, who would have lived online if not for Caroline's official cut-off time of nine p.m. For that generation, 'talking' on MSN was the equivalent of reading the Famous Five. But at least it wasn't an open-to-all chatroom. She and Roger had banned those. It was one of the few things they agreed on.

Send.

The computer pinged as it dispatched the arrow into cyberspace, briefly punctuating the silence of a sleeping house. Annabel's empty lilac-coloured bedroom, which still smelt faintly of her favourite Jean-Paul Gaultier scent – Caroline sometimes sprayed it to make herself feel her daughter was still there. Ben, fast asleep with his head under the pillow, in his room, which stank of sweat, and was crammed with CDs, textbooks and obscene posters on the wall – the kind you had to scrutinise before you realised that, yes, it really *was* what it looked like. Georgie, at the wrong end of her bed (restless like her mother), surrounded by cricket gear and teenage magazines. And Roger, sleeping the sound sleep of the unjust.

Feeling foolish, she began to whisper her wish, like a quiet chant. It felt soothing, like the prayers of her childhood, but now she really *must* go to bed or she'd never cope in the morning. Shivering (so much for summer nights), she padded down the corridor and slipped between the crisp lavender-sprayed cotton sheets.

Roger reached out for her in the dark, his hand tightening on her waist. Was he imagining, in his sleep, that she was someone else? Uncomfortably, she moved away.

Make your dreams come true!

Crazy! But anything was worth a try.

2

This little bear can make your dreams come true by Christmas!
    Just send him to six friends and then make a wish. You'll also be automatically entered in a draw for a free trip to Paris, sponsored by Nappysacks.
    Do not delete this email or your wish won't come true!
    This has been brought to you by Mums@Home, a new website for parents. Check us out for news, views and tips.

One of Susan's treats – as her friend Joy said, they had few enough – was to get up when Tabitha was still asleep and 'surf', as the techies called it. Still new to computers, Susan didn't see it as surfing; more like dipping her toe into the water of a world where she wasn't any different from other mothers – at a time when the house was peaceful enough for her to think clearly and simply be herself.

The website, which had been advertised on the centre's notice-board, looked intriguing. Mums@Home . . . It had a comforting ring to it, reminiscent of butterfly cakes with squidgy icing, *Blue Peter* and *The Archers*, her favourite radio programme.

This little bear can make your dreams come true . . . One simple wish that would change her life. Wave a magic wand and be in Happy Ever After Land, as shown on her very own screen saver, which came on automatically after a few minutes if she hadn't touched the keyboard or mouse. There it was: the photograph of Tabitha's christening, which she had copied on to the computer as a self-imposed daily penance: a reminder of what might have been. Herself, slim and smiling in her peacock-blue floaty Monsoon outfit, head nestled against Josh's broad shoulder. And in her arms, a cream lacy shawl that had belonged to her great-grandmother. Somewhere inside it, Tabitha lay sleeping peacefully. Not knowing any better. Blissfully in the dark, just as her parents had been. Susan moved the mouse to return to the bear and, as she did so, her arm knocked her thesaurus, so useful for crosswords, on to the floor. There was a little whimper from the room next door and Susan held her breath.

Don't wake up. Not yet. This was the only time she had to herself before a long day of nappies, feeding, mopping up rejected meals from the floor and hauling the wheelchair in and out of the bus.

Silence. But there *had* been a noise. Perhaps she ought to check Tabitha. But that might really wake her up. Besides, it was so reassuring sitting here, checking out different sites, glancing at the news headlines at the top of her home page and Googling whatever took her fancy – like holidays she couldn't possibly afford. In the old days, before Tabitha, she'd read proper books. Always had her nose in one, her dad used to say. But now there wasn't time so instead she surfed or 'read' her inbox.

Of course, you got some weirdos, like strangers trying to sell her Viagra or cosmetic surgery, or someone informing her she'd won a million quid in some dubious-sounding lottery. But it was exciting. Like opening a surprise parcel every day. Take this sample tip from Mums@Home: *You know the mesh bag that comes with Persil tablets? Keep it to store pound coins in.*

The computer had been her father's idea. 'It's not new. Someone was selling it at work,' he'd said brightly, when he arrived unexpectedly one weekend. 'But it'll do the job. We can email each other now and it will give you something to do.'

What he'd meant was that it would give her something *normal* to do, and he had been right. She avoided links with the numerous self-help groups for special-needs kids because that wasn't what she wanted. But the news items and their links got her brain cells working again – as did the online crosswords. On good days, even Tabitha could type at the keyboard in her own one-fingered way.

Briefly, she skimmed the home page again.

> Mums@Home is a new website for mums at home! Some of us work for money from home and some of us are full-time mums. We want to share chat, tips and experiences. If you'd like to join us, please register below.

An ordinary website for ordinary mums with ordinary kids! A website where she could 'talk' to people without seeing automatic pity in their eyes as they glanced down at Tabitha in her wheelchair. Susan got so fed up with talking to other 'disabled mums' at the centre. All they did was discuss their problems. There was a pre-school nursery for 'normal' kids there too – next to their bit – and she often envied the parents with young children who could already talk and walk better than Tabitha and her friends.

Maybe she *would* sign up for Mums@Home. Susan allowed the cursor to hover over the space for user name. But no. She was far too boring. Susan was the kind of woman who always replaced the loo roll before the last square ran out, who returned her library books on time, who never had anything interesting to talk about any more. That was what Josh had said before he left. And more.

She looked out of the window at the early-morning mist nudging the top of the rape fields, and breathed in their inimitable sweet smell. Pale colours were breaking out through the haze in an arc. A rainbow! Susan felt a prickle of childish excitement. That was it! 'Rainbow' suggested someone who was always smiling, never complaining. The kind of person she used to be and whom she wanted to be again – a woman who sprayed Nina Ricci into the dimples at the back of her knees, who never went out without her makeup and fitted effortlessly into a size ten. A girl, for that was what she felt like inside, despite everything, whose striking auburn hair was cut in a soft bob every five weeks instead of tied back with a scrunchie because she had neither time nor money for regular cuts.

That was *definitely* a whimper from next door. Hurry. Susan's fingers flew over the rest of the form. Details of children – names and ages. Hobbies. Send.

'Mummummum.'

'Coming, Tabs.' Susan jumped up, wincing as she knocked into the chair behind her, bruising her shin.

'MUMMUMMUMMUM . . .'

If she didn't hurry, the bed would be even wetter.

'MUMMUM.'

One wish. Susan closed her eyes tightly, as she had in childhood to pray. A teddy wish. A prayer. A scream. A shout. What was the difference? Paris . . . She'd always wanted to go to Paris. Josh – such a dreamer – had promised to take her one day. 'The Eiffel Tower,' he had crooned, in a lumpy bed during their honeymoon in wet Weston-super-Mare. 'That's where we'll go when we have the money.' She'd believed him.

'MUM!'

'I'm here, Tabitha. I'm here.'

She could smell her daughter from the doorway. 'It's all right, love. It's all right.' Holding her breath, she reached for the thick kitchen roll she kept in her room for this purpose. Where was the disinfectant? There. Almost empty.

'Don't worry, love. We'll have you clean and dry in no time.'

Puffing with the strain, Susan supported her daughter as they waddled together to the bathroom. A stand-up job in the bath except Tabitha didn't do stand-up very easily. Warm flannel over private parts that any other twelve-year-old would never have let her mother see. Over the last few months, she'd seen the shame in Tabitha's eyes when this happened. Her daughter was no fool: she knew all too well that she was different from others. Susan patted the last bits dry. 'See? All nice and clean again.'

'Smell, smell.' Tabitha was urgently pointing to the bathroom shelf.

'What do you want, love?'

'Smell, smell.' Tabitha's eyes were feverishly insistent.

'But you don't smell any more, love . . . Oh, I see.'

She wanted the cheap talcum powder that sat on the shelf along with other necessities, like incontinence pads. Powder that Josh had sent two Christmases ago, and Tabitha treated as reverently as if it were frankincense or myrrh.

'Just a bit, then.'

Susan shook some over her daughter and rubbed it in. Tabitha smiled toothily.

'We'll get you some of your medicine. OK?'

Tabitha grimaced. The poor kid hated the medicine their GP had prescribed for her loose tummies and Susan didn't blame her. It smelt horrible. It would also help if she could get the flipping top off. Child-proof, it said on the bottle. More like parent-proof. Susan tussled with the plastic lid and cursed softly as it came away, spilling the contents over her dressing-gown, the carpet and Tabitha's clean pyjamas. It was sticky too. The kind of stickiness that didn't always come out in the wash. She could have cried but Tabitha's wary eyes stopped her. It was at times like this that she needed someone else around: someone to help her put spilt medicine into perspective.

'See?' she said, forcing herself to sound bright. 'I've made a mess too!'

Tabitha's face relaxed.

'Down it goes,' said Susan, popping the spoon into her daughter's mouth. 'Good girl. Now I'll just mop up this mess and we'll have breakfast. OK?'

Swiftly, she washed her hands, which were always red and raw from being in water so much. Her ring finger remained misshapen from the pressure of her wedding band, even though she hadn't worn it for years. The bareness still startled her. In the distance, she could hear a tractor purring. In a minute, she'd turn on breakfast television, and maybe later she'd have a chance to explore the Mums@Home site.

'Ready for breakfast, love?' she said cheerfully.

Tabitha nodded.

Susan repressed the sigh that was fighting its way up her chest. Think of something nice. Thick wholemeal toast, oozing with butter and marmalade. Food. Meals. As Joy said, few pleasures came three times a day so they might as well make the most of it.

3

This little bear can make your dreams come true by Christmas!

DELETE, damn you. DELETE!

Mark's finger stabbed the button on his laptop, but nothing happened. The bloody thing had frozen and he knew why. Florrie had been downloading music from the Net again. Not only was it illegal but it also – according to the geek at the computer shop – introduced viruses that gradually crippled the machine: it got slower and slower until it ground to a halt.

That was probably why he was getting rubbish like this. Someone really should do something about the amount of junk mail that got through, despite so-called filters. The only reason he'd got up at this unearthly hour was to check his inbox in case someone had sent him something urgent for work, not to waste time on rubbish – but you had to open these things to make sure they weren't important. It only took a few seconds but they added up.

Turn the machine off, then on again. Pathetically simple but it often worked – and saved you queuing for the helpline. Sure enough, it was OK now.

Mark stared at the screen, rubbing his eyes and making a mental note to get them tested. What was Mums@Home anyway? Probably some self-help group that had bought his address from one of the countless mailing lists he was on. That was one of the problems with being a self-employed public-relations consultant.

13

You gave out your email address to all and sundry and ended up in address books across the world.

Do not delete this email or your wish won't come true. Mark snorted. He'd always hated Paris – at least since he and Hilary had had their honeymoon there.

He drained his coffee mug and rubbed the stubble on his chin. You wouldn't get a man writing stuff like that. Then again, you wouldn't get a man giving you suspicious looks at the kids' holiday club, which started – shit! – in precisely an hour and a half.

He had to log off soon – there was so much to do. Get the kids up. Make their packed lunches, providing there was bread in the freezer. Stop off on the way to holiday club to fill up with petrol. His own Inbox of Life was so full he'd have given anything to delete the lot. Apart from the kids, of course.

Mums@Home is a new website for mums at home! Some of us work for money from home and some of us are full-time mums. We want to share chat, tips and experiences. If you'd like to join us, please register below.

Mark nibbled his thumb, as he always did when he felt uncertain. He had so much to do but the email was difficult to ignore. Take the 'full-time mums' bit. Not 'dads'. Not even 'parents'. Typical! As though only a woman could do the job! Which was exactly what the parents at the kids' old school in London had probably thought when they'd cold-shouldered him every morning.

We want to share chat, tips and experiences.

He hesitated. It would be nice to do that with a faceless group of mums who wouldn't make judgements or, as had happened once in the school car park, an unexpected pass and, on another occasion, a comment from a father that might or might not have been racist, depending on the interpretation. He'd like to know how to deal with Florrie's moods, and whether it was relatively normal for an eleven-year-old to push other kids about or whether Ed really did need help, as that irate mother had complained to the holiday club last week . . . God, he could write a book about what he needed to know.

There was no one he could ask. Daphne, Hilary's mother, did her best but she was of a different generation. And now he was no longer in an office environment, he had no one to take out for a drink and pump for parental advice. Besides, he didn't know any other man who had full-time care of the kids.

If you'd like to join us, please register below.

He'd have to be a woman or it wouldn't work. Dishonest? Yes. But useful. And refreshingly anonymous.

User name? *Mimi*. A sort of derivative of his own, which meant it wasn't really cheating. Children's details? He'd be truthful about that or the advice wouldn't be pertinent. *Florrie, 12. Ed, 11.* Hobbies? *No time.* Work? *Home-based public-relations consultant with quirky sense of humour.*

Send.

Right. A quick flick through his other emails. Nothing that couldn't wait. Check out History. Nothing. That meant the kids had deleted the websites they were on last night, which also meant they probably weren't suitable. Mark did his best to check what they were on, usually by walking in unexpectedly, but otherwise he had to hope the NannyOnline system was up to Mary Poppins's standards.

SPYWARE SEARCH AND DESTROY. DO YOU WANT TO UPDATE?

Definitely. Awful how saddos with nothing better to do could penetrate your messages unless you had the right protection. A bit like sex. Not that he'd had much, recently.

Delete email wish from Mums@Home, even if it did bring bad luck, and wake up kids.

'Morning, Florrie, time to get up.'

There was a whiff of cheap scent as a half-dressed Florrie, in a little pale blue bra and pants set she'd bought last week, glowered at him. 'Dad, I've told you before. Knock first!'

She was right. Embarrassed, he turned his head away. 'Sorry but we're late.'

When had she started to get breasts? How did she know the bra fitted properly? He'd have to ask Daphne. She'd love that.

'Ed, are you up?' No dangers of bras here. Just legs and stale air. 'For Chrissake, Ed, don't kick! It hurts. And don't think you can hide under the duvet like that. It's time to get up.'

'Fuck off, Dad.'

His hand tightened on the doorknob. 'Don't talk to me like that!'

'Fuck off.'

In his day, 'language' had meant French. Nowadays kids seemed fluent in Obscenity. Angrily, Mark yanked open the striped blue and yellow curtains, which Hilary had put up in another life, letting in the morning sunlight. 'Right. You're banned from the computer tonight and for the rest of the week.'

'So?' Ed's spiky hedgehog hair, bearing the remnants of yesterday's gel, made him seem even more defiant.

Ignore him. It's a stage, gut instinct told him, for what it was worth. 'Give him a good smack,' was Daphne's view. Maybe Mums@Home could suggest a compromise.

Mark flung his son's jeans on to the bed. They were frayed and grubby at the hems, reminding him that he should have washed them ages ago. His own weren't much better, but working from home meant he didn't have to worry too much about that. 'I wish you'd behave for once. It would make my life so much easier. No wonder—' He stopped, appalled at what he'd been about to say in anger.

'No wonder what?' said Ed, from under the duvet.

'Nothing.'

'*What?*'

'No wonder we're late for holiday club,' said Mark.

'Don't want to go.'

'Well, I'm sorry but you have to. I've got to work. Now come on. And please, *please*, don't lose your temper with the other kids today or we'll both be in trouble again.'

Ed scowled.

When had his little boy started to do that? At what age did children's unlined faces develop frown lines?

'Dad!'

Florrie was calling him from the kitchen. A smell of burnt toast floated up to him.

'My legs are upstairs. I'll be down in a minute.'

If he could have divided himself into two, he could have got things done so much faster. It used to annoy him when Hilary said she only had one pair of hands, but now he knew what she'd meant.

'Ed?'

'What?'

'If you could make one wish, what would it be?'

'What are you on, Dad?'

'I'm serious, Ed.'

Something flickered in Ed's blue-green eyes and, for a second, Mark saw the little boy he had been.

'I'd wish Mum was here.'

Of course. Mark wrapped his arms round his son. 'She will be soon.'

'Get off, Dad.' Ed lashed out with his fists, just missing him. 'And get out of my room.'

Hurt, Mark moved away. 'Not till you turn that music down. What the hell is that rubbish?'

Ed's eyes flashed. 'My band, actually – Space Cadets.'

Mark gulped. Before they'd had to move here, Ed had belonged to a band with his London friends. He'd been happy then, had lived with his guitar strapped to his hip. They had made a tape, and Mark was going to help them send it to some music companies. (It might not get anywhere but the boys were so keen, it seemed wrong to dampen their enthusiasm.) Now he'd destroyed what had been possibly the last vestige of his son's confidence.

'It's only that it's a bit loud,' said Mark, hastily, in an attempt to repair the damage.

Ed turned away from him, face to the wall. 'You don't like it.'

'Well, the lyrics are quite rude, aren't they?'

'We put a Parents Advisory sticker on it,' mumbled Ed.

'Well, how about guitar lessons again, instead of the trumpet?' With any luck, it might be less invasive on the eardrums.

'No.'

'Why not?'

'Because I can't be arsed. Get out, Dad. *Please*.'

Suddenly there was a sound like a wardrobe crashing to the floor. Where did they get ring tones like that and how much had it cost? 'Your phone,' said Mark, wearily. 'I've told you before not to have it on at night next to you.'

He picked it up and Ed snatched it. 'Give it here.'

'OK, OK! I wasn't going to read your text messages. Now, change, will you?'

Permanently, he added silently. Not just out of your pyjamas but with a lobotomy on top. 'Then come down for breakfast.'

Ed put his head under the pillow. 'Not hungry.'

'You've got to eat or you won't get through the day.'

'How are you going to make me? Feed me like a baby or some spastic?' His voice was muffled.

'You know, Ed, today's politically correct term is "special needs". You and I are very lucky to have the use of all our limbs, and one day you might just realise it. And, in answer to your question, yes, maybe I will feed you, if that's what it takes to get breakfast down you.'

Mark knew he was descending to his son's level but he had a cousin, now in a home, who had never been able to walk or speak and his son's comments had disturbed him. He'd always tried to explain social compassion for others but it looked like he'd failed. Again.

'Dad. *Dad!*'

Florrie was yelling up the stairs now. Always yelling. Never coming to find him.

'What?'

'There are flames coming out of the toaster. *Quick!*'

4

This little bear can make your dreams come true by Christmas!

'*So* sweet! Do you hear that, Rose? One wish! But we need more than that, don't we, to make you the prettiest girl in the world? Especially if we're going to Paris!'

Lisa turned her belly stud three times to the right for luck and drew her knees up to her chest, clasping them with her arms because it was more comfortable that way. Eyes closed. Ready.

'I wish . . . that you'll have strawberry-blonde hair, like, that I can tint with pink streaks when you're older so everyone looks at us and says, "I can see you're mother and daughter!" I wish that you'll sleep well at night because we both need our beauty sleep. I wish that you'll be clever as well as beautiful because I want you to do better at school than me. I wish you'll always love me. I wish you'll be happy. And I wish you'll be healthy . . .'

She shivered at the thought of her baby being damaged like those poor kids at the centre. Touch wood. Quick. Maybe she shouldn't sit so near the screen. She ought to get one of those computer guards that were meant to deflect the rays but they cost enough.

Just send him to six friends and then make a wish.

Six? Blimey, that was a lot. Real friends stayed with you when something bad happened. Real friends didn't betray you.

She could send it to Mum, but she probably wouldn't reply. Lisa stroked her stomach lovingly. 'She won't be much of a nan, I'm afraid, love.'

There was Dad, but he might try to get some money out of her. True, he didn't know where she lived but it might be possible to track down someone's real address from their email.

Her heart quickened. She really mustn't worry herself – it might send bad vibes to the baby. Nasty thoughts could do that. It said so on Mums@Home.

It also said you should avoid germs if you were expecting. She was a bit worried about this keyboard, even though she'd cleaned it carefully. Wonder who'd had it before? She'd had a real stroke of luck, finding it on the tip like that. It had taken her three trips to get it all home and each time she'd been convinced that someone would nick the rest before she'd got back.

But they hadn't. Even better, it had all fitted together. Lisa hadn't thought she'd be able to do it but it hadn't been that difficult in the end. A bit like an electronic jigsaw, really. The hardest part was getting online but the man at the other end of the helpline had been really nice when she'd told him she was pregnant. His own wife had just given birth so he'd been ever so patient.

Lisa rubbed her hands with a baby wipe from the tub she kept by the computer. Nice smell. The kind that made you want to sniff it again. Summery. Babies' bottoms. Soft, brand-new skin, crying out to be kissed.

There had to be *someone* she could send the bear to. Impatiently, she scrolled down her address book. The billing department for her server. That could be one. And eBay, although she'd had to cut back after the last letter from her credit-card company. Maybe even Donald Duck – couldn't be his real name – who kept sending attachments that her virus system promptly quarantined.

Definitely not the doctor. She wasn't going back there again.

Send. Now all she had to do was wait for her wish to come true. Superstitious, her mum used to call her. But she had reason to be, didn't she?

Lisa continued to scroll down the page. She'd discovered Mums@Home through a magazine article that someone had pinned on the noticeboard at work. Some websites were boring or downright silly but this one had some good stuff on it. Like this:

MUMS@HOME THOUGHT FOR THE DAY
Misfortunes are opportunities wrapped in parcels.

Made her feel a whole lot better, that did. Lisa stroked her stomach tenderly. Sometimes she felt the baby – it *had* to be a girl – was trying to tell her something. 'OK, Rose. Why not? We'll log on. See what everyone else is doing, like.'

Enter user name. *Expectent Mum*. She was pleased with herself for having thought of that. It summed it up nicely. And the great thing about user names was that it was all totally anonymous so you could say exactly what you wanted.

Message Board.

Was there a message after yesterday's chat about epidurals? Yes! Earth Mother had replied!

From Earth Mother to Expectent Mum: If you don't want an epidural, put it in writing and give it to your consultant on your next antenatal visit. If they still give you one, you might be able to sue them.

Well, she never knew that! Earth Mother was *so* nice. Always asking if she was eating the right food – no one else had told her about soft cheese and pâté.

Lisa leaned back on her chair and stretched to get rid of the pins and needles in her toes. Sometimes you could sit for so long at the computer that you forgot how to move. But it was worth it. In fact, she didn't know how she'd managed before. It was like having a whole load of instant friends who were always there for you. It would be even better when she had her baby. Then she would always have someone to love her.

Lisa felt a warm glow run through her. 'You know what?' She addressed her stomach. 'I feel lucky today, Rose. Just like my horoscope said. And something tells me that we might just win that prize draw to Paris . . .'

Hi mum. Am sending you this so you can make a wish. R u ok? Sory about our arguement. Pleese write.

Dear Mr Summers, you have just performed an illegal operation.

Hi Mum and Dad,
Thailand is AMAZING! We've met so many incredible people. Only prob is that I'm running out of money. Any chance of a top-up?

Welcome to *The Archers* website! You are now going on a reality tour of Ambridge . . .

Mums@Home.co.uk
JOIN OUR DISCUSSIONS ON
Disciplining your kids. What's the best way? More of your news and views on epidurals.
Dating agencies: can single mums trust them?
Can you rewire a dead marriage?
TIP FROM MELINDA OF SOUTHSEA
Make a hand-puppet out of an old sock and get the puppet to 'talk' to your kids. It encourages them to do chores like clean teeth.

THOUGHT TO KEEP YOU SANE FROM MAD MUM
All things must pass. Good and bad.
CHUCKLE CORNER FROM ALI OF SLOUGH
Q: Are you sexually active?
A: No, I just lie there!

5

'More tea?'

Roger dabbed his mouth with kitchen roll, then carried his cereal bowl to the sink and carefully tipped the contents down the waste-disposal unit. 'No, thanks.'

He was so polite, thought Caroline, despairingly. Just like her, hovering with the teapot like a fifties housewife. Briefly, she caught sight of herself in the glass of the oven door. Funny how her image always seemed to belong to a stranger. The woman with shoulder-length blonde hair was more attractive than she felt inside. But the fear and uncertainty on her face, apparent in the oven's tinted glass, were hers, all right.

The fear forced her to put on her makeup before Roger got up, while the uncertainty made her uncomfortable about her small breasts, which had never recovered from feeding three children all those years ago. It was about then that Roger had stopped cupping his hands round them . . . Why, oh, why, hadn't she seen the warning signs?

Carefully, she began to unload the dishwasher, her back to him. It was so much easier to talk without eye-contact. Besides, she knew what he looked like. The mole on his neck, just below the collar. The upper lip that tightened when she said something that annoyed him. The thin line of black hair that ran down the centre of his chest, parting slightly above his navel. Had *that woman* run her tongue down it? Had he dug his nails into *her* skin with excitement as he had once with Caroline?

'Got anything interesting on today?' she asked nervously.

He was putting something into his briefcase and didn't bother to look up. 'Another meeting with Harris. That man's impossible.'

'Where?'

'Kingston.'

Kingston. Nowhere near Wembley. Unless he chose to go there when she wasn't aware of it and, God knows, he'd done that in the past.

'What about you?'

His coldness made her want to scream. Instead, she slid back the dishwasher drawer – too roughly: it stuck and she gave it a push to free it. 'Busy. It's conference day.'

'Don't do that. You'll break it.' He shoved past her. 'Look, all you have to do is ease it gently on to the runners. Don't be so impatient.'

'There's no need to snap.'

'I'm not.' He clicked his briefcase shut. 'Right. Better go or I'll miss the train.'

She glanced at the kitchen clock. She hadn't even got Georgie up yet. Just as well it was the holidays. She leaned towards him for a kiss. After his affair, they had begun to kiss properly again but now, almost through unspoken mutual agreement, they were back to cheeks. He smelt faintly of lemon.

'New aftershave?' It came out like an accusation.

'Yes.' He looked steadily at her, unsmiling. 'The one my mother gave me for my birthday. I'm off now. Bye.'

Why did he always make her feel as though it was *her* fault she was suspicious? And now she'd annoyed him – it was obvious from the way he'd said goodbye, and the way he strode down the path towards the gate. No turning back to wave. A tall, dark, good-looking man with a bulging briefcase, who seemed younger than his mid-forties in a soft grey pinstriped suit, as befitted an accountant. Very suitable, her mother had decreed after meeting him. Dependable.

The memory made her chest tighten as she raced up the stairs. She could hear the tell-tale series of pings that indicated her daughter was on MSN. 'Georgie! Will you get *off* that? You're going to be late and, besides, you can talk to your friends later.'

'I've got to check something, Mum. Have you got my kit ready?'

She had. Neatly pressed for the summer sports club, run by the school in the holidays, it was in Georgie's Adidas bag in the hall, next to her own dark-brown leather briefcase.

'What are you doing?'

'Seeing if there are any tickets left for The Wattevers.' Georgie's face was puckered in concentration and Caroline's heart leaped with love. It was worth putting up with all this awful stuff from Roger just to keep the children happy. They couldn't bear it, she was certain, if he went.

'Do you know that if you get picked to go on stage, they shave your hair?'

She shuddered at the thought of her daughter's beautiful hair being hacked at by some scissor-happy pop star. 'Then you're definitely not going. What about parental approval?'

'It's cool, Mum. You get to play their bass guitar too. Yes. *Yes!* There *are* some tickets. Can you get them for me, now, online?'

'Not now. There isn't time. Maybe later.'

'*Mum!*'

'Downstairs, please.'

Since when had parents pleaded with kids?

Reluctantly Georgie followed Caroline into the kitchen and sat down to breakfast, tearing at it with her knife and fork while she read last weekend's *Funday Times*.

'There's no need to stab your bacon. It's already dead.'

'You're so sad, Mum.'

'That's not very kind,' said Caroline, hurt. Like many modern parents, she'd encouraged the children to speak their minds and this was the result. Roger had often remarked that she had only herself to blame. 'More toast?'

'All right.'

'*Please.*'

'Please.'

Georgie was always hungry but she never put on weight, although she tried desperately – in her bid to become more of a heavyweight so she could be picked for the under-13 girls' rugby team next term.

'Don't turn on the television. I've got the radio on.'

'It's the holidays, Mum. Chill.'

Caroline silenced Wogan mid-sentence. She didn't want an argument on a work day – life was hectic enough already.

'Can I have some cereal?'

'You've just had a cooked breakfast.'

'So? It all goes down the same way. That's what Ben says about girls.'

Caroline continued unloading the dishwasher, wishing she'd done it the night before. So much to do. So little time. 'You don't want to believe everything he says.'

'Really?' Georgie frowned. 'Well, what do you think of this? You know that party Ben went to on Saturday night? He met some girl there and after he'd finished snogging her she said he'd kissed her ages ago at another party, and he couldn't even remember her.'

Caroline tried to remember the last time she'd been snogged. Probably at Ben's age. 'Well, if it was true, it wasn't very nice of him to forget.'

Georgie shovelled a final slice of toast, thickly coated with peanut butter, into her mouth. 'That's what I thought. God, I feel stuffed. I won't be able to run now. Mr Crapper makes us jog three times round the pitch even when we've got our periods.'

If she was that poor man, she'd definitely change her name. 'Don't say God and don't talk with your mouth full. And buck up or I'm going to miss the train.'

No point in waking Ben, who was still sleeping after finishing his A levels last month. He planned to wallow in post-traumatic sleep for an indefinite period of time, he'd informed his parents, during a rare sentence directed at them. Yes, he'd find a summer job ('Stop nagging, Dad') but not just yet.

'Ready?'

Georgie nodded as Caroline dabbed at the milk stain on her

daughter's previously pristine white T-shirt. 'Run and clean your teeth, then.'

'Did them before breakfast.'

'Then you need to do them again.'

'*Mum*, there isn't time.'

She was right. But a good mother (a not-so-stressed mother?) would insist. 'Upstairs now, pronto.'

A quick flick round the sink with a grubby dishcloth. Dash upstairs to drop a kiss on comatose Ben's cheek. Leave note for Mrs B, who was coming in, thank heavens, to sort out this mess. No time for the loo. Still a bit chilly today but not enough to wear tights. Besides, if she couldn't go barelegged in August, when could she? And her longish skirt covered most of her legs anyway. Once upon a time, in another life, Roger had told her she had a great pair of legs . . .

'Who are you playing today?' she asked Georgie, as they walked briskly down Broomfield Road towards the station.

'Greenway Seniors. We're going to crucify them.'

'*Georgie!* I've told you before, that's an inappropriate word.'

'Sorry,' said Georgie, happily. 'But I'm a teenager. I'm allowed to say whatever I like. Ben says so.'

'Well, I'm perimenopausal so maybe I can say what I like too.'

Georgie gave her one of her 'You're crazy, Mum' looks. 'Peri-what?'

'Nothing.'

'You're weird, Mum. There's Kirsty. Got to go. See you tonight.'

No kiss, and not even a wave when, five minutes later, Caroline was standing on the opposite platform where she could see her daughter chatting to her friends and steadily ignoring her. Her own train usually came first. Here it was. On time for a change. She picked up her briefcase and got in. The beauty of living at this end of the line was that there was usually a seat. She gazed at Georgie through the window and her daughter glanced up with the glimmer of a smile.

'Be careful,' Caroline mouthed through the glass. She still

couldn't help saying that to all of her children, even though, one by one, they were growing up and leaving. *Be careful.* It was like a mantra, a lifebelt in an uncertain world. So much might go wrong for them – they might be run over, bullied at school, pushed into drugs . . . find themselves without a father.

Caroline opened her laptop and groaned. The screen had frozen. Resigned, she turned it off and rebooted. If only, she mused, as the train passed terraced houses, an empty playground and a parade of shops, it was possible to do the same for her marriage . . .

An hour later, Caroline flashed her ID card at the security desk and got into the lift. Fourth floor. First set of swing doors on the left. Large open-plan office, studded with pale beech desks at which your knees virtually knocked your neighbour's. Screens already on. Coffee-machine bubbling. Karen's door firmly shut, which meant she was writing the Editor's Letter.

'Hi,' said Zelda, spinning round on her chair. 'Hope you got more sleep than I did. Aurora was up all bloody night. How the hell am I going to cope when number two arrives?'

Caroline dumped her case by her desk and helped herself to a glass of water. 'You'll manage. Just don't think too much about it in advance or you'll panic.'

'How did you cope with three?'

She hadn't – or what had happened wouldn't have. She could have been a nice stay-at-home mum and concentrated on keeping her husband happy. 'I think I'd have gone mad if I hadn't worked. I needed something to think about apart from the children. But there are times, to be honest, when I feel it's awfully selfish.'

'Nice one.'

'What?'

Zelda was tapping away at the keyboard without looking up at her streamlined flat screen – they'd all been issued with one recently. '"Are you a selfish mum?" We could put it up for conference.'

It wasn't bad, Caroline conceded. She and Zelda worked well as a team, which Karen, always astute, had spotted when Caroline had asked to go part-time and Zelda had got pregnant with Aurora. It had been Karen who had persuaded the powers-that-be that Zelda and Caroline should job-share. The result was that between them they edited the Parenting and Health pages for *Beautiful You* magazine. Caroline worked Mondays and Tuesdays, Zelda worked Wednesdays and Fridays, and they both came in on Thursdays for conference when the whole team thrashed out ideas for the next issue.

'Ready, everyone?' Karen put her head round the door of her office.

'Bloody hell! She's early,' muttered Zelda.

Caroline tried Roger's mobile. No reply. Zelda lived in Kingston. She'd know. 'Your mum's in Wembley, isn't she?'

'Yup. Why?'

'How long does it take you to get there?'

'Half an hour, maybe. Forty minutes. Come on – everyone else has gone in. Got your notes?'

She had. Organisation might not be her forte at home but work was different.

'Caroline, switch off your phone *now*. We've got to go in!'

Maybe, thought Caroline, studying Karen furtively as the editor dissected the beauty editor's ideas on non-surgical face lifts, it was easier not to be married. Karen was a single mum, an elegant, contented one. She had a younger boyfriend in advertising with whom she didn't live, and a nine-year-old son at an expensive private day school in London. She was always impeccably groomed with her hair cut in a spiky black style, and her clothes were generally from East. She had enough empathy with her staff to understand when things went wrong – not that she knew anything about Roger – and enough grit to demand action when it was needed.

Marriage would probably destroy her.

'Right. Moving on to Parenting.' Karen's nails – French-manicured – drummed on the pad in front of her. 'I want to get more relationship-y. This page is beginning to focus too much on the poor-little-me side of parenting. Don't you think, Zelda?'

'Depends how you see it, really.' Zelda glanced nervously across the pale beech conference table at Caroline. 'Actually, we've got a great idea here. "Are mums becoming selfish?"'

Karen pursed her impeccably lined lips. 'Exactly what I don't want. Anyway, *Just For You* did something similar last month. I want to help readers get through the impossible stuff that happens in their lives.'

'Like bad sex,' ventured the girl from Practicals. A titter ran round the table.

Caroline cleared her throat. 'What about "How to rewire your dead marriage"?' The Mums@Home discussion line – she'd spotted it after her laptop had unfrozen itself on the train – had ironic potential.

'I fancy "Infidelity",' mused Karen.

Caroline's mouth dried. 'What angle were you thinking of?'

'Did you see that new survey about marriage? No?' Her eyes narrowed with disapproval. 'Pity. One in four couples who have experienced infidelity are now trying again to make their relationship work compared with one in seven five years ago. I want you to find me three case histories who'll come clean. Yes, Zelda, identified with pics. Women who can say that their husband had an affair but are prepared to start again.'

'Men, too?' demanded Zelda, sharply.

'If you can get one.'

'I know this isn't my area,' drawled the beauty editor, 'but nowadays that just doesn't happen. My brother-in-law had an affair and my sister threw him out of the house before he could pack his iPod. Any self-respecting woman would do the same.'

'Not according to the marriage expert quoted in the survey.' Karen's fingers were drumming again. 'What do you think, Caroline?'

'I think it's going to be tough to find people who'll be identified,' she said quietly.

'Try the Net.' Karen tossed her hair dismissively. 'Find some self-help group. All kinds of idiots want to be in print. I don't need to tell you that. Pay them a hundred each. Two if you have to. There's got to be someone out there who'll talk.'

Caroline glanced at Zelda, whose face shone with unspoken sympathy. *Poor you. She didn't know or she wouldn't have suggested it. Are you all right?*

'Sorry.' Caroline stood up. 'I've just got to go to the loo. Back in a second.'

Karen frowned. Cloakroom rights were a no-no during conference.

Quickly, before she made a complete fool of herself, Caroline left the room. Through the open door, she could hear Zelda saying something about her not being well. All she needed was a few moments to compose herself and then she'd go back to acting – as she'd been doing for the past two years.

Caroline rinsed her face in the basin and quickly re-did her makeup. Better. But the problem remained. Even if she found someone stupid enough to be named, talking to her would bring back the pain. She'd like to confide in Zelda. In the early days, when she had barely been able to function in the office, she'd had to tell her that Roger had had an affair. But something had always held her back from revealing all the details. There was only one person who knew what had really happened.

'Jeff? It's me. Sorry, the reception's awful.'

She moved to the other side of the basin to improve the signal. A secretary came in from Cookery and Caroline tried to talk quietly.

'Look, sorry to bother you but I wondered if you were free for lunch this week? . . . No, of course I understand. Next week? . . . That would be lovely.'

6

Dating agencies: can single mums trust them? The question was still pounding round Susan's head. Why was it that everyone, including Mums@Home, presumed single mothers wanted another moron to stand in for the previous one? There were other things in life to think about. Such as why the Greenfields Centre bus was late.

As Tabitha howled with fury and stretched her face away, Susan wiped her daughter's mouth. Tabitha hated it and no bloody sock puppet, as Mums@Home had suggested, would make her feel better about it.

'Moremoremoremore.' Now her face was puckered with fury as she tried to reach for the remaining slice of cold toast on the table.

'No, darling, you can't have any more. You've already had four pieces and you know the bus sometimes makes you sick. It'll be here any minute. Do you want to look out for it?'

To her relief, the hot, bitter expression in Tabitha's eyes melted away and Susan wheeled her to the window. The changes in her nature, from fierce anger to childish delight, had become more marked in the last year. Dr Hill had said it was hormonal. At twelve, Tabitha was becoming a woman, with beautifully shaped breasts that were at odds with the rest of her crooked body, slumped in the chair. It wouldn't be long, Dr Hill had warned, before she'd have periods. One more thing to mop up.

'Can you see it yet?'

'Nnnnnnn.'

It was remarkable, the consultant had said, that Tabitha could speak in her own unique way. Many children with her problems were unable to. But Susan knew it was due to sheer determination, not luck. Since Tabitha was eighteen months old, when the diagnosis had been confirmed, she had battled crazily to teach her the skills that a 'normal' child would automatically learn. She'd spent hours, weeks, days and months repeating words to make them go in.

The crying shame of it was that Tabitha was naturally intelligent. She could point to words in magazines when Susan said them; she could type them on a keyboard, although it took an age. She was pretty, too, with her straight fair hair inherited from both her parents, and the sweet little snub nose that had made Susan think of the name Tabitha when she'd been born. Now the name suited her more than ever: different, unfathomable.

'Busbusbusbus!'

Tabitha was straining with excitement as the minibus pulled up outside the house. 'Mummummum, busbusbus!'

'I know, love. I'm coming.'

Susan took a quick look round the kitchen, with the handrail on the sides of the counters, to check she'd turned everything off. The flat in Pheasants Way had been purpose-built for those with special needs. It was a far cry from the pretty cottage she and Josh had bought before Tabitha's birth, but much more practical.

'Off we go, then! Whoops, nearly forgot your jumper. Better take that, hadn't we, in case it gets cold again?'

It was comforting to talk as though Tabitha might reply at any minute, thought Susan, as she hauled the wheelchair into the extra-wide hall and down the ramp. Its weight had cracked the slabs of the garden path and now, she noticed irritably, weeds were growing through them.

A group of faces stared out at them from the bus. Danny, who had Down's syndrome, was grinning broadly. He was Tabitha's special friend and his mother, Joy, liked to think that Susan was hers. Alan, only fifteen although he looked forty, ignored them as he picked his nose, carefully pressing his findings into the back of the blue-and-pink-flecked seat in front of him. Paula, with her large gold hoop earrings – a different pair for each day of the week – waved excitedly.

'Busbusbus!' screamed Tabitha, pounding the sides of the chair furiously with her fists. It was her sign to make Susan go faster. God, this chair was heavy. The driver normally came out to help her but this one was new. Inside the bus, she could see Danny's mother going up to the front and saying something to him. Reluctantly, or so it seemed, he lumbered down the steps. 'Need a hand, love?'

'What does it look like?' She hadn't meant to sound so sour but just as Tabitha had her highs and lows, so did Susan.

Together, she and the driver eased Tabitha out of the chair and up the steps. Flopping like a puppet with broken strings, she leaned on Susan, who had been taught how to take her daughter's weight by one of the instructors at the day centre. She was lucky, she'd been told (always lucky!), that Tabitha could manage a few steps. But what, Susan wanted to know, would happen when Tabitha grew even bigger and her mother was unable to take the weight? There were no answers to that one.

'Hiya,' said Joy, cheerfully. 'Morning, Tabs. That's right, you sit next to Danny. He's been dying to see you. Then Mum can sit next to me.'

Susan sank down gratefully. 'Thought he'd never get out to help.'

Joy rolled her eyes. 'Some people don't think.'

Susan didn't want to go down that road. 'Not thinking' was one of Joy's favourite topics. 'I know it's terrible,' she said quietly, as the bus began to move, 'but there are times when I can't wait for Tabitha to turn sixteen so she can go to the centre on her own in the holidays and I have some time to myself.'

Joy nodded. 'Me too. My bloody sister's always whining because her local holiday club won't take her kid until he's four. I told her she doesn't know how flipping lucky she is. Some people just don't think . . .'

Susan allowed Joy's words to wash over her as she stared out of the window. Rows and rows of fields punctuated by the odd satellite Bedfordshire village, sometimes with a shop and sometimes not. When she and Josh had moved out to the country, it had been with the express intention of giving their as-yet-unborn baby the chance to grow up in a safe, natural environment. There were times when she wondered if she should move back into a town or at least nearer to London where she had grown up. But it would mean starting all over again. Forging new networks. Finding another centre. Tabitha hated anything new.

'Here we are!' Joy said the same words every morning as though, one day, they might arrive somewhere different. She pulled out a powder compact and dabbed her nose. 'Do you think they'll take photographs?'

'Who?' In her head, Susan was still in London, walking round the familiar streets in the way Tabitha never would.

'The journalist. The lady who's coming from the radio station to do a piece. Didn't anyone tell you?'

'No. What does she want with us?'

Joy was still checking her reflection. 'You know. A general piece on why centres like this are important.'

Great, thought Susan. That was the last thing she needed – some nosy-parker asking personal questions. 'Come on, love,' she said to Tabitha. 'That's right. Lean on my shoulder. Not there. A bit higher.'

Somehow they got down the steps, her daughter frowning with concentration. If there was one thing they had in common, thought Susan, clinging to the rail, it was the desperate wish to be the same as everyone else.

'Go on, have one! Otherwise I'll feel bad.' Joy pushed the plate of biscuits almost into her lap. Slightly stale chocolate Digestives. Bourbons. Pink wafers. Comfort food to block out reality. Before Tabitha, Susan had been so slim, but afterwards it had seemed selfish and vain to take pride in her appearance. Tabitha's condition put the rest of life into context. Nothing else was important.

'That must be her,' hissed Joy. 'Over there.'

A small dark-haired girl was coming in, carrying a black box in each hand. Her crisp beige linen suit, the kind Susan might once have worn, immediately identified her from the others, who were in their usual jeans and T-shirts. No point in wearing anything nice when someone would slop something over it before the end of the day. The day-centre manager was talking to her earnestly, pointing out a couple of mothers who were hovering at the side of the room, hoping to be noticed and pretending not to be. It was like waiting to be picked for the school team.

Tabitha was engrossed in the jigsaw on the tray that fitted neatly on to the front of her wheelchair. She was amazing at jigsaws even though it took ages for her hands to close round the pieces and nudge them in. Heaven knows where she'd got that particular talent from. Susan could barely get her brain round the newspaper crossword. Tabitha could remember long strings of numbers too, even if she could hardly say them. Susan and she were working on writing them down but it was taking longer than Susan had hoped. Another year and they might achieve one to ten. With kids like these, a tiny step was a triumph.

Joy watched the reporter make her way to Alan, one of the manager's favourites. 'We won't get a look-in if that cow has her way.'

Susan was watching Tabitha's fingers painstakingly pick up a piece of jigsaw. She studied it intently, dropped it, then picked it up again. 'Why do you want to talk to her anyway?'

'It's our chance, isn't it? For a start we could get her to do something about statementing. We still haven't had a letter back from Social Services. Some people just don't think . . .'

Susan ate another Bourbon. And a third. Listlessly, she picked up one of the old magazines that someone had brought in, flicked through it and put it back on the chipped coffee-table. There was a poster on the wall of a foreign-looking place with a beach and hills behind it. The centre had several like it, stuck up with Blutack, each location unidentified and unattainable.

'She's coming,' hissed Joy.

The girl walked up to them boldly, smiling broadly. 'Susan?'

'Mrs Thomas, actually.'

It might be old-fashioned but she resented people who assumed they could call you by your first name when you didn't know them.

The expression on the journalist's face showed she had registered her mistake. 'I'm so sorry. I was told to ask for Susan.'

'I'm Joy. That's my boy over there, Danny. Got Down's, he has, and we're still waiting to hear about his statement.'

The journalist listened politely to Joy's diatribe. She had to give the girl credit, thought Susan. Many other people, herself included, would have cut in by now.

'That all sounds very unfortunate, Mrs, er . . .'

'Browne. That's with an *e* at the end. Aren't you going to turn on your microphone?'

The girl, who seemed incredibly young for a journalist even though it was the local station, nodded. 'In a minute. Actually, I was wondering if Mrs Thomas could spare me a few minutes. I need to get a mix of cases and I've already got a boy from the mum over there. I believe you have a daughter?'

Susan nodded. A childish part of her was pleased that she had scored one over Joy. 'Tabitha. Over there. Doing a jigsaw.'

'She seems very focused.'

'She is when she wants to do something.'

Joy's lips tightened. 'Quite stubborn at times, wouldn't you say, Susan?'

The journalist glanced around. 'Shall we find a quiet corner so that you can tell me what it's like to look after Tabitha?'

Susan laughed hoarsely. 'You'd need to live with us to appreciate that.'

The girl's eyes flickered with something between sympathy and curiosity. 'I'm sure, but at least we can make a start. Let's go over there, away from the noise.'

'It's OK. I'll keep an eye on Tabs.' Joy's voice was flat in the knowledge that she'd lost.

'Would you be able to interview my friend afterwards?' whispered Susan, as they settled into a pair of metal-framed chairs at the other end of the room. 'It would make her day, even if you didn't use it.'

The girl smiled at her. 'Why not? Now, tell me, Sus– Mrs Thomas, what did you do before Tabitha?'

She hadn't expected that. No one ever asked her about her life when it had been normal, and before she knew it, it had all come out. How she'd sold advertising space at the local newspaper. How she'd met Josh in the canteen and fallen in love in a way she had never thought possible. How she had finally got pregnant after four years of disappointment and moved to the country three months before the birth. How Tabitha's short labour had been such a shock. How . . .

'Would you like a tissue?'

And she'd *promised* herself she wouldn't cry. 'I'm sorry.' Crossly, Susan blew her nose. 'It's just that when I let myself think what my life could have been, I feel ridiculously sorry for myself and Tabitha.'

'Josh too?'

'No. Not him. But I don't want to talk about that.'

'That's OK. Now, tell me, Mrs Thomas, when did you first know something was wrong?'

'Susan. You can call me Susan. Not for months. She didn't feed particularly well but I thought that was me. And she didn't crawl. My doctor did some tests but said she was a late developer. Then, when she was just over a year, she had her second lot of injections.'

The girl drew a sharp breath. 'And you think that was responsible?'

Susan's nails dug into the palms of her hands. 'Tabitha started screaming about a week after the vaccination and she threw a high temperature. It came down after a day but I knew – my gut instinct told me – that something had happened to her.'

The girl was wide-eyed. 'What did you do?'

Susan laughed bitterly. 'I called out the GP but he said that a small number of children do react like that and that it was "normal" especially as she'd soon stopped crying and her temperature had come down reasonably fast. He assured me there was less than one in a million risk of a child getting meningitis or encephalitis due to the measles part of MMR. And that even these rarely caused brain damage. He also said there was no evidence that MMR causes autism.' She tried to swallow the lump in her throat. 'But by the time she was two, Tabitha still wasn't walking or talking.'

'You took her to a specialist?'

Susan nodded. 'He said there was a possibility she had been deprived of oxygen before, or during, the birth. But I couldn't see how. There was nothing in the notes to suggest it and, anyway, as I said, it had been a really fast birth. The consultant said that normally this kind of "cerebral palsy", as he called it, is caused by a long labour where the baby gets stuck and deprived of oxygen. He also said a really fast birth could cause brain damage too but he couldn't be certain if this had been the case with Tabitha. You'd be amazed at how many kids have an unexplained disability.'

She blew her nose. 'We had some other tests too, but they showed nothing. No one could find a particular reason for Tabitha's condition. Instead, there were all these possibilities. We've had so many medical advances over the last few years that we expect to know all the answers. But Tabitha and half the other kids here are living proof that we don't.'

The girl's eyes were filling with tears. 'And is there any hope for her?'

'Put it this way. We were told that she'd probably never walk, although she can, after a fashion. We were also told that she'd never talk, even though she can say enough for me to understand her.'

'It must have affected your relationship with your husband,' said the girl, sympathetically.

Susan looked up at the ceiling. It was dirty and there was a large cobweb in one corner. She'd learned long ago that it helped to concentrate on irrelevant things when the pain was particularly bad. 'Josh left soon after Tabitha was diagnosed.'

'That must have been terrible.'

'Yes,' she said slowly, remembering the gripping terror she'd felt when he'd shut the door behind him, leaving her with a small child. 'But by then I hated him.'

'Why?'

'Because he'd been in favour of her having the MMR in the first place. I hadn't been sure – I'd been scared by some of the stories in the papers about it – but he told me I was overreacting.'

The journalist's green-brown eyes were like a cat's. 'So it was his fault?'

'You could say that. Or you could say, like Josh did, that I'm just trying to pin the blame on someone.' She stood up. 'Look, I'm sorry, I don't want to talk any more. But my friend Joy is dying to tell you about her problems and she's got more of a story. You will let your listeners know how important the centre is to us all, won't you? It's open in the holidays as well as term-time, and it's got much smaller classes than the big one on the other side of town.'

Somehow Susan found her way to the loo. As she bolted the door behind her, she had a nasty feeling she'd said more than she'd meant to in the heat of her emotion. Maybe she should take some of it back. Quickly, she washed her hands and went out into the hall, almost colliding with the centre manager who was carrying a lunch tray. The stench of cauliflower was nauseating.

'Where is she? The journalist?'

'You've missed her. Said she'd got everything she needed and would let us know when we're on air. Exciting, isn't it? She spoke to nearly all of us including –' she lowered her voice '– Lisa, who insisted on butting in. Honestly, I sometimes think that girl's a bit simple.'

Susan made her way back to Joy, who was already sitting at the table for lunch. 'Did she interview you? After me?'

Joy's eyes glittered with disappointment and jealousy. 'No.'

'Bitch.'

'That's not like you.'

'This place makes me not like me.'

'I know what you mean.'

Susan took her plate next to Tabitha's wheelchair. Her daughter was scooping up carrots and thin slices of lamb in anaemic gravy, then shovelling the ghastly mix into her mouth. Cutlery skills were a barrier they still had to conquer.

'Moremoremore.'

Tabitha leaned over to her mother's plate and closed her fist over the cauliflower. Cheese sauce oozed through her fingers on to Susan's untouched lunch. Laughing, Tabitha took her fist back to her mouth, slopping some of the cauliflower in and allowing the rest to fall down her T-shirt, which had already been changed twice that morning.

'Whoopsadaisy,' said one of the helpers. 'Let's mop you up, shall we, Tabs, and get Mum another helping?'

Susan closed her eyes to hold back the tears. 'It's all right, thanks, Lisa. I'm not hungry.'

'Go on.' The girl was sponging Tabitha's T-shirt.

'No, honestly.' The sight of liquid cauliflower in Tabitha's fist had taken away her appetite. If only Josh had listened to Susan's gut instinct about those bloody jabs, Tabitha might have been a very different child.

7

Mums@Home
MESSAGE BOARD
From Scummy Mummy: The best way to discipline the kids is
to be consistent. If you say you're going to do it, DO IT!

Mark watched Ed sitting at the top of the tall, shiny blue
swimming-pool slide, fear and determination etched on his face.
He wanted to go down, needed to go down, to save face in front
of his sister.

'Get a move on, Ed!' he called, from the spectator gallery, cupping his hands round his mobile phone. There was so much
shouting and laughing it was difficult to make himself heard. He
raised his voice: 'Just do it. You'll be fine once you let go.'

He turned to speak into the phone to his client, a company
that made electronically coded building bricks. 'Sorry, there's a
lot of noise here. Right. I've got *Kiddy* magazine to agree to run
a piece in November.'

Go on, Ed. *Go on.*

A mother next to him, wearing a baby sling, tutted. 'Poor kid's
scared. That jumbo slide is really steep.'

Couldn't she see he was talking? OK, so a noisy indoor
swimming-pool in the summer holidays might not be the best
place to take part in a telephone conference but he'd had no choice.
His client had been insistent on this particular time, just as the
kids had been insistent about coming here. It was so hot and
steamy that he could feel sweat breaking out under his armpits.
'Well, I'll push for December, but it was November they were
talking about.'

The woman nudged him. 'Your son's in trouble up there. Aren't you going to do something about it?'

Mark wavered. Ed looked terrified. 'Hello, can you hear me? Sorry, I'm losing you. The reception's terrible. I'll ring back.'

Sometimes lying was the only option.

'Ed,' he called 'just let go and you'll be OK.' He glanced at the woman, whose lips were tight with disapproval. 'He's well within the age limit,' he said defensively. 'He's small for eleven but he can do things when he wants to.'

Like telling his dad to fuck off. What would the woman, who was dressed in neat pink jeans that co-ordinated with the sling, think of *that*? Maybe that was why he didn't feel much sympathy for Ed at the top of the slide. It was easier to be nice to kids when they were nice to you – he hadn't appreciated that when he was working in a proper office and only saw them in the evening.

'He's at Coneywood School, isn't he?'

'Sorry?'

It was so noisy, with the kids' voices bouncing off the walls, that he could hardly hear himself, let alone the woman.

'I said, "He's at Coneywood School, isn't he?"'

Mark nodded, bracing himself.

The woman shifted the sling and stroked the baby's cheek with one finger. 'Thought I recognised you.'

Her perfume, which was strong, reminded him of a heady, expensive fragrance Hilary had worn in the early days and which he'd never liked. The combination of that with the chlorine was potent. 'Really?' Be polite. Don't say anything that might lead to more conversation.

Florrie's voice floated down from the platform where her brother was sitting. 'Come on, Ed, just one little push.'

Visions of the labour ward flashed into his head. The word 'push' always did that to him. Hilary, eyes wide with panic. Hilary, out of her mind with pethidine, swearing at him, telling him how much she hated him for putting her through all this.

'Scaredy-cat, scaredy-cat,' chanted Florrie.

'Don't push me!'

There was a queue of impatient kids behind his son. Mark felt as though the walls were closing in on him – why the hell had he agreed to come here? 'Just turn back and come down,' he called.

'I can't. I'll fall.'

'No, you won't.'

Mark felt hotter. Every mother in the place was looking at them now: the over-ambitious father with the terrified child at the top of the slide.

'I'll get him,' yelled Florrie. 'This way, scaredy-cat!'

Mark watched his children disappear over the back of the slide and, hopefully, down the steps. 'I wouldn't let him do that again,' said the mother. Her baby whimpered and she put her finger into its mouth. 'There, there, Mummy's here.'

'Thanks for the advice,' said Mark, stonily. He stared hard at her, willing her to appreciate her rudeness. But the message in her eyes was all too clear. *Single dads can't cope. Children need their mother*.

And the worst thing was that Mrs Busybody, with her pristine pink jeans, matching sling and hair that was blonde all the way through, not dark at one end and light at the other like Hilary's, was right.

The walk home through Cornmarket and down past the old Jam Factory was a nightmare.

'Scaredy-cat, scaredy-cat. Couldn't jump from the mat,' chanted Florrie.

'Shut up, Florrie. You used to hate heights too.'

'Didn't.'

'Did.'

'How do you know? Mum was at home then.'

Mum, alias Hilary, who had been so like the other mothers they were threading past now – taut, intelligent, highly nervous, and usually graduates who had found themselves unable to leave the city of spires. Who had married and had children they were incapable of looking after. Who needed to get out to preserve their self-esteem.

Two months. That was how long she'd been gone. Another four to go.

'Dad, when's Mum coming back?'

'I told you,' said Mark, carefully. 'Just before Christmas.'

'I don't see why she had to go to America.'

'We've been through this before. It was a great opportunity and she couldn't turn it down.'

Ed kicked a Coke can along the pavement. Honestly, the rubbish problem in Oxford was getting worse, Mark thought. 'If Mum was here, she wouldn't have told me to go down that slide.'

'How do you know?' demanded Florrie.

Ed spun the can so it landed in the gutter. 'Just do.'

'Don't.'

'Do. Why can't we ring her when we get back?'

Ed was walking ahead. The back pocket of his shorts, Mark suddenly noticed, was ripped off, making him look uncared-for.

'Because it's difficult to get through. It's easier for her to ring us, you know that. And what happened to your back pocket?'

'He tore it off. It's cool.'

'Shut up, Florrie. Why can't we email Mum instead?'

'I told you that, too. She's still getting her email address sorted. They've had big problems with the server.'

'Anyway, you need to get on with your project,' said Florrie sharply. 'I'm doing mine. It's on foreign holidays.'

'I didn't know you had holiday homework, Ed,' said Mark, 'and you promised me you'd try really hard at school next term.'

'What's the point?' Ed scowled. 'One of the richest men in Britain left school early so why should I bother?'

Thanks a bunch, Richard Branson. 'He was unusual, Ed.'

'I want to be unusual too.'

Why couldn't Mark ever win? 'What's your project about, anyway?'

'Your anus.'

'*Ed!*'

'It is.' He grinned wickedly. 'It's the planets. Uranus, Mars, Venus, that kind of stuff. It's no big deal, Dad. I can download it from the Net.'

'But you don't take it in if you do it like that. In my day, we made notes from books and really understood it.'

'My very envious mum just stole Uncle Ned's underpants,' said Florrie.

'What?'

'It's how our teacher taught us to remember the position of the planets from the Sun. The first letter of each word stands for a planet. Mercury, Venus, Earth, Mars . . .'

'Shut up, Florrie. You're such a show-off. And it's all crap, anyway.'

'Ed! You're not to use words like that.'

'Why not?' Ed glared at him. 'What will you do?'

Refuse to take him on holiday, even though they couldn't afford one anyway? Threaten him with a lifetime's pocket-money deprivation? It was at times like this that you wanted to punish them, but you had to carry out your threats. That was what some woman had said on Mums@Home today, and she was right. And occasionally, as someone else had added on the Message Board, you had to ignore bad behaviour so they took notice of you when you *did* get mad.

Besides, all things must pass. That was true too. One day Hilary would be home. So why didn't that make him feel better?

He waited until after supper (Daphne's lasagne from the freezer), when Ed was doing his trumpet practice, to write to Hilary, saving the important bits for the end.

We had some problems at the swimming-pool today. Ed got stuck at the top of the slide and Florrie called him a scaredy-cat. He's still kicking other kids, by the way. How's it going at your end? Mark

He was the scaredy-cat for not having the balls to accept it was all over, even before she'd gone. But no, here he was, pretending as usual that everything was fine and telling her about Ed's problems as though she was capable of caring.

How did other single dads manage? More and more men were left to bring up their families. Daphne had cut out an article from the *Sunday Times*, which was meant, presumably, to make him feel better. He was, he thought wryly, as he made his way upstairs to the office in the top bedroom, almost as fashionable as his son's torn shorts.

He shut the door, turned on the computer (still so slow – he really ought to get it checked out) and stretched back in his ergonomically designed office chair, gazing at the book-lined wall in front of him. For the first time that day, he felt at ease. This was his only refuge. The only place in the house where he could pretend everything was normal.

Squawk, squawk.

What the hell . . . ? It sounded as though a parrot was loose. Bet Ed had gone and downloaded another of his screen-saver sounds. Yes. It was the Jungle Jingle, which made him feel as though he was in the Amazon instead of outer Oxford. Honestly, the things kids could do nowadays. Mark turned down the speaker volume and clicked on his inbox.

For once, it was relatively empty. Nothing that couldn't wait until tomorrow, apart from a very small parenting magazine that wanted a sample of a baby holdall that one of his clients had designed. 'Please let me know when you hope to run the review,' he emailed back. Probably never would. Most journalists asked for samples and it was only after persistent nagging that one or two might mention the product on their pages so that he earned his commission from the client.

Still, he was lucky, or so everyone kept pointing out, that he had the kind of job that lent itself to working from home. What they didn't realise was that there was no dividing line. He couldn't switch off when he left the office because the office was constantly there, in the spare room at the back of the house. And he had to get the kids to be quiet when important clients rang so that he didn't look like some unprofessional nerd as he had at the pool.

Mark took a sip of water. The email from Mums@Home was still in his inbox. His finger flirted with Outlook Express. Nicely designed home page. Easy to read. Log in. User name: *Mimi*. Message Board.

Hi, everyone. I'm new to this site. But I'd really appreciate your advice. I took my eleven-year-old son swimming today and he didn't want to go down the jumbo slide. I tried to get him to do it to get over his fears, but he freaked out and his big sister had to haul him off. Was I wrong? My son has also started kicking and pushing other kids at his new school, even though he should be too old for this kind of thing. PS My husband is scared of heights. Could it be hereditary? PPS My husband works away from home and the kids only see him every few months. I'm worried this might be affecting their development.

Send.

He hadn't meant to say so much but it had been scarily easy to bare his soul to a screen that didn't frown at his sex.

www.nortypics.com

Mark stared, shocked, as a picture of a semi-naked blonde flashed up on his screen. How had that happened? He hadn't touched anything.

To enter the site, key in your password now.

Had Ed been playing around on his computer? But even if he had, he couldn't have downloaded something like this. Not with the NannyOnline system.

'Dad! Dad!'

'What?'

Florrie burst into his study, sending a pile of files flying over the carpet, which badly needed vacuuming. 'It's Ed. He's trying on Mum's pink silk jumper – the one you gave her last year for her birthday.' She giggled. 'Come and look. It's really funny.'

8

Mums@Home
MESSAGE BOARD
From Lawyer Mum: I drew up a labour contract before I went into
hospital to prevent them giving me an epidural. A friend lent me
a TENS machine and it was brilliant at taking away the pain.

A TENS machine! She'd have to check it out on the Net but
not until she'd sorted this out first. Lisa could hardly believe it.
How could the bastards have taken her washing again? She
didn't mind too much about the tea-towels but she needed the
maternity pants. Two pairs was barely enough as it was.

They couldn't have blown off the balcony, she thought, leaning
over to check. She'd been ever so careful to tie them on to the
line with a double set of pegs after the last lot had gone. No. It
was definitely the kid next door. Had to be. There was just a low
wall between her and them, although *she* wouldn't jump over it
with the car park six floors below.

'Morning, Lees, how're you doing?'

Lisa stared at Kiki. She hated people who were nice as pie one
day and cows the next. 'Your Tommy's nicked my pants again.'

'How do you know it was him?'

Lisa coughed loudly, indicating her disapproval at Kiki's
cigarette fumes. So bad for the baby. There'd been a piece on
Mums@Home recently, relating cot death to smoking. 'I hung
them out last night and they've gone, just like last time. You ought
to watch that kid of yours. Saw him smoking the other day. It's
not right. Not at his age.'

She watched as Kiki flung her cigarette over the edge of the balcony. 'Don't you go telling me how to bring up my kids. You wait till it's your turn. Then you'll know what it's like.'

'But Tommy's only twelve. He shouldn't be smoking or stealing.'

Kiki screwed up her face. Without her makeup, thought Lisa, she looked even younger. She couldn't have been more than fifteen when she'd had Tommy.

'Like I said, you look out for your kid and I'll do the same for mine, Miss Busybody. If you're not careful, I'll get my Colin to come round and have a word with you.'

'Colin?' Lisa took a step backwards towards the safety of the flat. 'Thought it was Liam. Or was that last week?'

'You little c—'

Hastily, Lisa shut the door and leaned against it in case Kiki tried to ram it. The marks on the other doors in the block showed this wasn't uncommon. She'd have to go out now and get another pair of pants. Lucky it was Saturday and not a working day. It looked like being an August scorcher too, which would make a change after last week.

Lisa went into the kitchen to put the kettle on – sweet tea was *so* comforting – and sat down at the breakfast bar, which was getting even more wobbly. Those metal legs needed fixing. She'd already rung the council about it but a fat lot of good that had done. They still hadn't sorted the wet patch on the bedroom ceiling.

Lisa stroked her stomach lovingly. 'Better get that done, before you arrive, love.'

There was something else she needed to do before she went shopping. Now, what was it? The trouble with pregnancy was that it affected your memory. Everyone said so, and it was true. That's right! She was going to Google that TENS machine, wasn't she, to find out a bit more?

Sitting down at the computer, Lisa logged on. 'TENS', not 'ten'. Impatiently, Lisa tried again. Why did computers always think they were smarter than you? That's better. Lisa read the information in front of her. 'Look at that, Rose! Transcu – transcu-what-do-you-call-it electrical nerve stimulation. It takes away the pain by pressing pressure points in your body. Blimey, costs enough, doesn't it? Still, it'd be nice to try one out, wouldn't it?'

There had been a time when Lisa loved shopping, but now it took ages to get out of the flat: she had to check twice, just to make sure, that the cooker was off and the windows shut. Then some-times – well, quite often, to be honest – she had to go back and make sure she really had shut the front door and double-locked it.

You can't be too careful, she reassured herself. There had been another break-in last week, only a floor below. Not that there was much to take from her place, apart from the com-puter, but she still didn't fancy waking up to find some crazy teenager high on crack, desperate for the next fix and smashing her window.

Right. That's it. Push door to check it really is shut, then down the concrete steps that smell of piss. Past Tommy Ball and a group of his mates. Ignore them.

'Got your pants on, Lisa? Big ones, are they? We've got a pair just like them, haven't we, Alex?'

So he *had* nicked them. If he wasn't so much taller than her, she'd clobber him.

'Too posh to talk to us?'

He was walking behind her, so close she felt scared.

'My mum says it's no wonder you haven't got a bloke.'

Nearly at the bus stop. Lisa began to perspire with walking faster. Her body, especially from the waist down, felt as though it was dragging her towards the pavement and her breasts felt large and hot. Amazing to think that something so tiny could make her feel permanently exhausted.

It was an effort to climb up into the bus. Lisa placed her hands protectively over her stomach as she moved down the aisle. That story in the papers about the woman who'd miscarried because someone had collided with her in the street still haunted her. Come to think of it, she hadn't felt Rose move since breakfast – sweet Mary, don't let anything have happened.

Then she felt it. Relief flooded through her. And again. A definite kick. Not that strong but enough to tell her Rose was awake. Lisa beamed. As long as Rose was all right, she'd be all right too.

The shopping centre was packed. Lisa sat down for a few moments to catch her breath on the concrete wall that ran along the inside of the mall, lining the plant section down the middle. Her legs were swelling in the heat and she massaged her calves to ease them.

An older woman came towards her with a pushchair and Lisa moved up to give her room. The baby was smiling at her, and Lisa's heart lurched. 'What a lovely kid!'

The mother picked up the dummy that had fallen on the ground, sucked it and put it back into the baby's mouth – Lisa winced. 'She's all right.'

All right? She was gorgeous. Lisa leaned forward: she wanted to touch the baby's soft skin. 'Smiling at me, are you, love?'

The mother snorted. 'Does it to everyone.'

Lisa felt a twinge of envy. Her own mother had constantly scowled, which made her all the more determined to smile a lot after her baby was born. 'Did you talk to your baby when you was expecting?'

The woman was giving her an odd look. 'Not that I can say.'

'Only I was watching something about it on the telly. How you should talk to babies in the womb. Apparently they can hear everything.'

'Blimey. I hope not.'

The woman was getting up now.

''Bye,' said Lisa, waving to the baby. 'How cute is that! She's waving back!'

'Yeah, she's just learned. 'Bye, then.'

And the woman was gone, swallowed into the Saturday crowds. Carefully, Lisa got to her feet. 'Can't sit here all day, can we, Rose?' She headed towards a large baby chain store. It was busy this morning. But not one assistant on the floor. Never was. They were all behind the counter.

'Got any TENS machines, like?'

The woman at the front of the queue frowned at Lisa for interrupting, but she didn't care.

'Sorry,' said the assistant. 'We're out of stock. You might be able to get one online.'

She could if her credit card had enough money on it. Sighing, Lisa moved on to the underwear section. Looked like they were out of maternity pants too. Still, she could have a flick through sleepsuits. Such lovely colours. Lemon, green, blue and, *yes*, rose . . .

'Lisa! It *is* Lisa, isn't it?'

Reluctantly, she looked up. It was one of the mums from the centre, the plump one with the kind face and the daughter who did jigsaws all day.

'Yeah.'

'Busy today, isn't it? I'm trying to get a present for a niece – should have known better than to come on a Saturday.'

Lisa felt irritated at having to make small-talk. She'd wanted to feel the clothes in peace, run her finger along the seams, imagine what it would be like to hold her new baby.

'Stocking up, are you? How exciting!'

A wonderful thrill pulsated through Lisa. She was expecting a baby! Sometimes it didn't seem real. It wouldn't make up for what had happened, of course, and she couldn't stop being frightened in case something went wrong again. But it was better, so much better, than not being pregnant.

'When are you due?'

'I'm not sure. My dates are a bit uncertain.'

'I had the same problem with my daughter. In fact, I sometimes wonder if that's why—' She stopped suddenly. 'But you'll be working at the centre for a bit longer, won't you?'

Lisa nodded.

'Good. Tabitha really likes you.' The woman smiled shyly.

'She's got a thing about your hair. You've probably noticed from the way she tries to stroke it.'

All these questions were making her nervous. 'Sorry, I've got to go now. My partner's waiting.' Lisa jerked her head at a man by the door. He was short, fat and bald but he was on his own. He'd do.

'That's nice. You wouldn't get many men shopping here on a Saturday. My ex hated it.'

Suddenly Lisa felt as though the shop was closing in on her. She couldn't breathe. If she didn't get out, she'd go mad.

'Lisa?'

What did she want, touching Lisa's arm like that?

'You've still got something in your hands. Don't forget to pay. I did that once and it was really embarrassing.'

'Thanks,' she mumbled.

A child yelled and they looked at the door from where the noise was coming. The short, fat, bald man was kneeling down, trying to pacify it. A woman with a six-month bump was next to them. They were clearly a family.

Tabitha's mum smiled sadly, and Lisa knew she'd seen through her lie. 'Well, I'd better be off and post this, then.' The woman glanced down at the carrier-bag she was holding. 'My dad's looking after Tabitha and I can't be long. See you next week.'

Lisa made her way to the till with the sleepsuit, looking back over her shoulder as the woman disappeared into the crowd. The kid was still yelling but the father was still patiently kneeling next to it, wiping its face with a tissue, trying to make it feel better.

It wasn't fair. It wasn't fucking fair.

Sorry, everyone, but my daughter Florrie has got to do some market research for her school holiday project. All you have to do is say where you're going on your summer holiday and then send it back to us. Please don't delete.

Smile, Mum. You're on my web camera! Isn't it brilliant? Ben set it up for me.

Dear Mrs Thomas, Thank you for subscribing to our free horo-scope service. This month will be a turning point for you. But you'll need to be open-minded if you are to use these oppor-tunities wisely.

Maternity Bras just for you! Made to measure online. Postage and packaging free.

Mums@Home.co.uk

JOIN OUR ONLINE DISCUSSIONS ON

How to survive the summer holidays.

Rowing in front of the children: can it be healthy?

How not to be a wicked step-mother.

TIP FROM CELLULITE MUM OF LITTLEHAMPTON

Stick a picture of yourself from your thin days on top of the biscuit tin.

CHUCKLE CORNER FROM GOING GREY OF MANCHESTER

Men are just like kitchen tiles. Lay them the right way and you can walk on them for ever.

THOUGHT TO KEEP YOU SANE FROM EARTH MOTHER

One day, they won't need their nappies changing. They'll be changing your incontinence pads instead.

9

The traffic was horrendous but the hold-up had given Caroline time to check her emails on the laptop in the back of the taxi. Now, still stuck and bored, she logged on to Mums@Home.

Strange, really. Even though her interest had initially been professional – it had given her some good ideas for the magazine – many of the subjects were also personally relevant. Like 'How not to be a wicked stepmother'.

Caroline gazed unseeingly out of the window as they passed Madame Tussaud's on the left. If Roger had left her, that woman might have become the children's stepmother, and she'd have had them every other weekend. The magazine had done features on mothers who, through no fault of their own, had to allow the other woman to be with their children as part of the access agreement. Just thinking about it made her feel sick.

She still felt a bit wobbly when the taxi driver stopped. The traffic had made her seriously late, and even though Jeff would wait, they would have less time to talk. In her haste, Caroline tipped the driver more than necessary and flew up the stairs to the club. Its situation, overlooking Marble Arch, suggested a smart establishment for well-heeled professionals. In fact it was a comfortable four-storey Georgian building with sofas, deep chairs and pots of coffee or tea. Upstairs, there was a dining room, of the steak-and-kidney-pudding variety, and a ladies' with proper cotton hand towels instead of hand-dryers where, more than once, she had cried her eyes out after one of their heart-to-hearts.

Although he was officially Roger's friend, from their university days, Jeff had become hers too over the years. He'd been at christenings, confirmations, Annabel's A-level celebration and even her mother's funeral. He had never married, despite Caroline's attempts to match-make him with various friends and even her sister, and she had the feeling that he enjoyed being part of their family. They needed him too, especially in the fallout after Roger's affair.

'Caroline!' Jeff sprang up from a sofa to plant a kiss on both her cheeks. A woman standing by the coffee gave them an inquisitive glance.

Although she felt wretched, Caroline was mildly amused and flattered. He was, she reminded herself, an extremely attractive man, not just in looks but in the way he listened to everyone and made them laugh. 'So sorry I'm late,' she said.

'Not at all. You look amazing.'

She bit back the automatic comment: if that was true, Roger wouldn't have strayed.

'I thought we'd have a spot of lunch upstairs. Is that all right with you?'

'Lovely. I don't want to take up too much of your time.'

He consulted his watch. 'I've got just over an hour before my next client. Wish I had longer but . . .'

'It's all right. Sure I'm not a nuisance?'

His eyes smiled at her. 'Caroline, you could never be that. Would you like the cloakroom first?'

'I'm fine, thanks.'

'Marvellous. I've booked a table. Let's go, shall we?'

Caroline allowed Jeff to tuck into his steak-and-kidney before she let him steer her into serious conversation.

'OK, so you've brought me up to date with Annabel and that lazy godson of mine. Post A-level stress is a great idea and I wish I'd thought of it. But what about you, Caro? You sounded so upset on the phone last week. Something hasn't happened, has it?'

'He hasn't gone back to seeing her, if that's what you mean. At least, I don't think so.'

She toyed with her salad Niçoise. Wordlessly, Jeff topped up her sparkling water.

'Thanks. Sorry. That's better. No, it's almost silly, really.' Succinctly, she filled him in on her editor's brief. 'Interviewing women who have "got over it" will make it all come back. For two years now I've tried to block it out, or I couldn't cope. I'm also worried that *she* is going to read it – we're one of the top women's monthlies, you know – and then she might get in touch with him, if she hasn't already and . . . oh, God, Jeff, I don't know what to do.'

Jeff dabbed his mouth with the dark blue linen napkin. 'You might find that interviewing women in your situation is cathartic.'

'If they exist,' said Caroline, grimly. 'One of the girls in the office said that no self-respecting woman would take her husband back. So I must be incredibly weak.'

Jeff reached for her hand and squeezed it. 'No,' he said. 'You're incredibly strong. You held the family together at a time when it had to be held together. Annabel was mid A level, Ben was doing GCSEs and Georgie was too young to have an absent father.'

Caroline felt tears welling again. 'I know, but I hate saying I can't do something. I remember at school when they said how difficult it was to be a journalist and in many ways that was what drove me to do it. Now I can't help feeling I've bitten off more than I can chew. I'm not sure it's possible for a marriage to survive after this kind of thing.'

'People of our parents' generation did it all the time,' he said reflectively. 'My aunt had several affairs. She used to boast it kept her marriage going.'

'But our generation's different. Sometimes I think we're more moral because we won't tolerate affairs like our parents did.'

Jeff nodded. 'I have to say that I'd find it hard. But so does Roger.'

'Do you talk about it?'

He hesitated. 'Occasionally. The other month, he said it was

61

as though he was carrying a cross every day of his life because he hated himself so much for having hurt you.'

She hadn't known that. 'Then why doesn't he tell me? He's so polite all the time and when we . . . when we make love, it's so stilted.'

He stared at his plate, plainly embarrassed. 'But you've got to forgive him. Think of the children.'

Panic rose inside Caroline. 'It's not as simple as forgiveness. It's trying to get back to what we had before that's difficult. It's like carrying an invisible scar.'

He glanced at his watch again. 'I know women are meant to feel these things more keenly but can't you try a bit longer? Look, I'm sorry but I've got to go.'

She'd made him uncomfortable, saying so much. 'Me too.' She tried to sound light. 'Otherwise I'll have to stay late in the office and won't be back for Georgie.'

He grinned, clearly glad to be back on safe ground. 'And even though she's got a key of her own, she'll either have lost it or go straight in to watch television instead of doing her homework.'

Caroline smiled. 'You know my lot too well.'

'I hope I've helped,' he said, hesitantly.

'Yes, you have,' she lied. 'Thanks.'

They brushed cheeks; his was stubbly against hers.

'I just want the old Roger back.' She looked up at him pleadingly. 'Is that really so impossible?'

He stared down at her, eyes locking with hers. 'I don't know, Caro. All you can do is carry on trying.'

'Where've you been?' demanded Zelda, tersely, as she wove her way through the Features department towards her desk. 'Karen's been looking for you. She's changed the flatplan for the twenty-third and wants to bring forward the infidelity feature by a week.'

Caroline checked her diary on-screen. 'That means I've only got until next Friday.'

'You could try Good Publicity.'

'I have. And I've got some other leads too.'

For the next hour, she sifted through self-help groups and marital organisations, mainly through Google.

Respected women's magazine needs to interview a woman who has fought to save her marriage after her husband's affair. Can pay an interview fee.

Jeff had hit home when he'd suggested it might be cathartic for her to hear other women's stories and possibly share her own. Heaven knows, she needed to talk to *someone*. Jeff hadn't proved the sounding-board she'd hoped for and Janie, her sister, was too far away. Other women had best friends but the pressure of working and bringing up a family had meant she'd lost touch with her old university friends. Besides, maybe a stranger would offer more objective advice.

Caroline glanced at Zelda, who was doing a telephone interview with a psychologist to get what they called a 'psychobabble' quote for their feature on 'Kids' Nasty Habits'. She put her handbag on the desk in such a way that Zelda couldn't see the screen, then logged on to Mums@Home. User name: *Part Time Mum* – because that was what her job had made her. Message Board.

Hi. I want to know if anyone out there can tell me if it's possible to go on after your husband has had an affair. Two years ago, I had an anonymous phone call from a 'stranger'.

Caroline's fingers shook as she felt the familiar gut-wrenching sickness wash over her yet again. Georgie had been ten when it had happened. She'd been nagging her to get into the bath before Roger got home so that some semblance of peace and order would greet him when he came in. Then the phone had rung.

Georgie, always fast, had got there first. 'It's for you, Mum.'

Inwardly groaning, she had taken the receiver, wondering who would ring at peak bedtime.

'Caroline?' A woman's voice. Slightly harsh.

'Yes?'

'You don't know me. I'm a friend of Elaine.'

'Elaine?'

She sounded impatient. 'You know: one of your husband's major clients.'

Visions of some office accident – a road crash? – flashed through her head. 'Is he all right?'

'Don't play games, Caroline.'

'What do you mean?'

'What are you going to do about it?'

This was crazy. 'About what?'

'They're in love, Caroline. You know that. What are you going to do about it?'

'In love?' Her voice came out as a pale whisper.

'Who's in love, Mum?' Georgie had said, tugging at her jumper.

She'd gripped the receiver. 'Who are you?'

There was a click. 1471. Caller withheld their number.

'Who's in love, Mum? *Tell* me!' Georgie was dancing round her.

'No one.' Caroline had stared at the phone as though it might reveal the answer. 'No one.'

In shock, she had immediately called Roger on the mobile. He'd been defensive but firm. Elaine was his client. Yes, they got on well but that was all there was to it.

She stopped typing and dropped her face into her hands. She and Roger had had a terrible argument while Georgie was, thankfully, in front of the television. But the older ones had heard it. She still couldn't bear to think of the damage it had done to them. Roger's eyes had been hard in a way she'd never seen them before. No, he had insisted. He hadn't had an affair, but if he had it was her fault for not showing him affection any more. For always putting her work and the children first.

Caroline's fingers raced across the keyboard again. Now she'd started, the words were tumbling out:

I'd met her a few months earlier at an office do. A bit older than me but very pretty, blonde and bubbly. Bright with a First in Maths from Oxford. She had a partner but no children. Yet I'd never seen her as a threat because my husband wasn't that kind of man. Ironic, isn't it? Then, the following night, she rang me herself. She said my husband loved her. She said all kinds of other stuff too but I can't recall the exact words. My mind has put up a kind of barrier, and I know that if I let it come down, I might be washed away completely. My husband then admitted he *had* had an affair, and for an agonising two weeks, he didn't know whether to stay with us or go to her. I begged him not to leave. I made him look at the magazine . . .

She stopped. The magazine was in her office drawer for safety. For some inexplicable reason, she felt a burning need to see it again.

Page nine. She knew it by heart. There they were. The two of them, pictured in one of Roger's professional magazines at a work conference in Switzerland. The woman had her hand on his arm and was looking up at him admiringly. By some appalling coincidence, the magazine had arrived the week before the anonymous phone call. If it hadn't been for the latter, she might have accepted Roger's lame excuse that it was just a 'social occasion'. Now the computer seemed to draw her in. It was like speaking to a priest in a confessional box.

You're probably wondering why I still wanted him. I think it was because I couldn't really believe this was my husband, despite the picture and phone call. It had been a mistake. He had done something stupid. And the children and I needed him. I couldn't imagine life without him; I'd always thought we'd grow old together.

Roger finally agreed to stay. He handed Elaine's file to someone else in the firm, saying he had too much on. I tried to start again but, two years later, it's still difficult. He says he loves me again but now I can't help thinking he only stayed out of guilt and for the sake of the children. I still can't believe he did it. It's as though I never really knew him.

There was more, much more, but she'd said enough. It would be easy to delete it but her finger was already hovering over Send. Could a marriage survive an affair? Forget the feature. She needed to know from someone who had been through it. Only then could she decide whether to carry on.

10

TIP FROM CELLULITE MUM OF LITTLEHAMPTON
Stick a picture of yourself from your thin days on top of the
biscuit tin.

Susan knew which one she'd use. She'd been standing with her
dad in his garden just after his fiftieth birthday, which meant she
hadn't met Josh. She hadn't realised how pretty she was. No one
had told her then, and now it was too late.

Susan stared down with loathing at her stomach, which was
bulging over her pyjama bottoms, then stuck the picture on to
the lid of the biscuit tin. If she *really* had willpower, she'd just
throw out the tin. Her old slim self smiled shyly up at her. Who
are you kidding?

There was a sound from Tabitha's room. Stealthily she peeped
in. Tabitha was lying with her back to her. Susan tiptoed over to
reassure herself that her daughter was still breathing, a habit she
seemed incapable of breaking.

It had taken her years to put Tabitha in her own room. The
doctor had suggested it might help them both to have a little in-
dependence. But it was so hard, thought Susan, as she watched
Tabitha's chest rise and fall in sleep. She craved freedom, but she
had to watch her daughter constantly in case something else,
something more terrible, happened to her.

She closed Tabitha's door quietly, then padded down the corridor in her slippers, pulled up a chair and opened Outlook
Express. She kept the computer on the kitchen table because she
seemed to spend more time there than anywhere else. Waiting for
it to boot up (so slow!), she listened to the birds outside the

kitchen window. For a minute, she could almost pretend she was the old Susan. Perfect peace and quiet.

> Mums@Home. Welcome! We're a friendly site for you to meet other mums and get practical and emotional advice. Click here for the chat link.
>   User name: *Rainbow.*

Amazing! There was a list of names who had logged in over the last few days, each with messages next to them. Some long, some short. Something from Earth Mother, who wanted to tell everyone about a fantastic non-biological nappy-cleaner she had discovered. A plea for help from a mum called Mimi, whose son pushed and kicked other kids in class – she knew about *that*, all right. Tabitha had had to be moved within the centre last year to stop her doing it.

Her eye ran down the list. Something from 'Expectent' Mum, who clearly couldn't spell. Susan felt a stab of jealousy. She'd give anything to be pregnant: she'd felt so envious of Lisa, browsing in the baby shop. If only she could have had Tabitha all over again, she'd do it so differently . . .

Pg Dn.

This could get addictive. Someone else was recommending a children's TV programme. Another was selling a brand-new pram (why?). And someone called Part Time Mum (how could motherhood ever be part-time?) needed marital help: 'Is it possible to rebuild your marriage after your husband has had an affair?'

Was it a serious question? Susan scanned the message. Poor woman! And they'd been married for how many years? At least nineteen, if the eldest was that old, providing it was the same marriage.

Reply. This mouse was in a bad mood today.

> From Rainbow to Part Time Mum: Sometimes things happen that you don't expect. And you do things that you don't expect

yourself to do, if that makes sense. When my husband left me, I didn't know how to go on, but I did. I personally don't think you can forget something like infidelity or men who don't take their family responsibilities seriously.

Send.

Susan watched the little arrow from her Send box flying across cyberspace to her new 'friend'. Had she been a bit strong there? It had seemed so easy to give advice while her fingers were fumbling across the keyboard. But it had been Josh and his irresponsible attitude she'd been thinking about, which had made her angry with Part Time Mum's errant husband.

At least she knew where she was with Tabs. Life was a lot less complex without a man. Besides, who would want the two of them as a package?

They spent the rest of the day in the sitting room. What had promised to be a bright summer day had turned grey and forbidding. No biscuits to relieve the boredom. Not with that picture on the tin. And no day centre. Not on a Friday since last year's cuts.

Thank God for jigsaws. One of the inexplicable things about Tabitha's condition was that her brain was as sharp, if not sharper, than Susan's own. Somehow, through sheer perseverance, her daughter always managed to piece a jigsaw together. It was the same with the computer. The centre had been given some rather nice ones by a local firm and had taught her to type, in her own clumsy way. As one of the helpers had pointed out, computers had revolutionised the lives of people stuck in wheelchairs.

'Finfin, finfin!' Tabitha looked up from the jigsaw on her tray, grinning.

'Fantastic!' Susan bent over to examine the scene of roses round a cottage door and children running down the lane in Victorian petticoats. 'I don't know how you do it, Tabs, I really don't.'

Her daughter's smile widened. Positive praise always worked

for her daughter. Susan handed Tabitha a plastic mug of unsweetened juice. 'Clever girl!' Until last year, she'd had to use a trainer cup but months of unstinting practice meant she could now drink through a straw. 'Shall we do our flash cards?'

Tabitha's face screwed up in anticipated concentration as Susan got out the packet of brightly coloured cards with groups of letters below. Between them, they had worked out their own code over the years. 'Fin' was Tabitha's way of saying 'finished'. 'Mummum' had been a fantastic breakthrough when she was six. Now they were working on 'mug'. Susan showed her the picture of a big blue mug. 'Look, just like yours! Watch my lips, Tabs. Mug, mug, mug.'

More frowns of concentration. 'Ug, ug.'

'Almost, Tabs. But you need the *m* sound in front, like Mum.'

Tabitha smiled. 'Mum, Mum.'

'Yes, but now make it into m-u-g. You can do it. Come on.'

Too late, she recognised the note of irritation that had crept into her voice. Tabitha's face crumpled. She flung herself hard against the back of the chair, knocking her head, which already bore a lump from when she'd done the same thing last week. Limbs flailing, she lashed out.

'Mind your jigsaw! Oh, no – *no*.'

Susan dived to save the tray but it was already falling, hitting the ground and scattering five thousand pieces of Victorian cottage and happy children. 'Oh, Tabitha, I'm so sorry.' She sat on her haunches crying softly, gathering up the bits. Tabitha, seemingly unmoved by the destruction of a project that had taken her hours of painstaking toil, had stopped flailing and yelling. Instead, she stared into the distance, eyes vacant. Susan preferred it when she was crying. What was she thinking of? Was she wondering, as Susan so often did, where the justice was in a life like this?

'Phone. Don't worry, I'll get it!' At bad times, like this, she couldn't help making jokes. 'Joy? . . . Hi. No, it's an OK time . . . What? Are you kidding? . . . But they can't. They just can't. What are we going to do?'

Eventually, after she had asked several more questions, to which Joy had given unsatisfactory answers, she put down the phone and returned to the lounge. Tabitha was still staring out at the garden. 'They're going to close the centre, Tabs,' she said, crouching beside the chair so that their faces were level. 'It's going to be merged with the big one on the other side of town. That's why the radio journalist was there the other day. They knew about it but didn't tell us until it was official.'

Tabitha's face didn't alter. Could she hear?

'What are we going to do, Tabs? You won't like the big classes. It's a longer journey. And the new centre isn't open in the holidays.'

She shouldn't share her burdens with her child.

'We won't take it, will we?' She stood up, fired with energy. 'We'll fight. Start a campaign. Put up notices.'

Of course!

'And maybe we could go on the Net. Someone might be able to help us. Don't you think, Tabs?'

She was still staring. What was there to see, for pity's sake? The farmer had finished cutting the field outside and there wasn't anything to look at except . . .

Susan froze. Too late, she had finally seen what Tabitha had been staring at. Could she hide behind the curtains? No. She'd been spotted. Automatically she ran her fingers through her hair, wishing she'd bothered with lipstick or even a dab of mascara that morning. Slowly she walked towards the door as the bell rang.

She opened it.

'Hello, Susan.'

She swallowed hard. 'Hello, Josh.'

11

Susan leaned against the front door for support, legs shaking. Josh! He seemed thinner and somehow taller than last time, with a moustache that suited him.

'Aren't you going to ask me in?'

She clung to the door for support, still keeping it half shut. 'You're in France.'

'Clearly not. Come on, Susan, stop playing games. I just want to see my daughter.'

'Well, she doesn't want to see you.'

'Really?'

Josh looked behind her. 'Hello, darling. How's Daddy's little girl?'

Tabitha had wheeled herself into the hall and was grinning, waving her arms like flags. Her delight at seeing her father was unmistakable.

'Daddy's little girl,' spat Susan. 'Some dad, who doesn't bother seeing her for more than a year.'

Josh glared. 'Don't start that again. You knew I was working in France. And it's not as though you made it easy for me to see her when I was in this country.'

She eyed him distrustfully. 'That's because I never knew what you were on.'

'For God's sake, Susan, you make me sound like some kind of junkie.' He held out his hands as though to show there was nothing in them. 'That stuff doesn't count.'

'Daddaddaddad.'

Susan wheeled round, horrified. She hadn't even known Tabitha could say 'Dad'. What else had she heard? Tabitha took in so much more than people realised.

Josh was crouching on the ground, holding Tabitha's thin hands and smiling up at her. 'How's my princess, then? Aren't you going to give your old dad a cuddle? That's right.'

Susan couldn't bear to see her daughter draping her long, thin arms round Josh's neck, ecstatic, when it was she, Susan, who was surely, after all her hard work, the only one entitled to such a rapturous reception.

'I've brought you a present, Tabs.' He held up an expensive carrier-bag with a French name on it. That's right, bribe her, thought Susan, bitterly. Just like you did me at the beginning, promising me everything, telling me we'd be happy for the rest of our lives.

'Shall I open it for you?'

'Well, she can't do it on her own,' snapped Susan. 'She can't do anything. I have to do it all for her.'

Tabitha looked up at her mother soulfully. I shouldn't have said that, thought Susan. In one brief second, she'd taken away all the confidence she'd worked so hard to create. Damn Josh. *Damn him.*

'It's a jigsaw, pet. Look! With a really pretty picture of Paris on the front. That's the Eiffel Tower – I'll take you up it one day – and that's Montmartre where artists draw and paint.'

Tabitha gazed at the picture, tracing the outlines with her finger as though to make them come to life. 'You still like jigsaws, don't you, Tabs?'

She nodded.

Josh stepped back. 'God, what's that smell?'

'Her nappy needs changing,' said Susan.

Josh twisted his hands awkwardly. 'Do you want me to help?'

She laughed hoarsely. 'A bit late for that, isn't it? Ten years too late.' She jerked her head towards the lounge. 'You can wait in there, if you like. We'll be a while.'

Josh looked awkward. 'Actually, I might go back to the car for a bit. There's someone I'd like you to meet.'

'Who?'

'Her name's Stephanie.'

'And who exactly is Stephanie?'

He addressed the wall behind her, just as he had in the old days when he had done something he knew she wouldn't like. 'Well, she's a nurse . . . but she's also my wife.'

'Wife?'

He nodded to the skirting-board. 'We got married last month. And she'd like to meet her new stepdaughter.'

'Hi, everyone! Do I hear a little bird talking about me?'

Flipping heck! Had she left the front door open?

'You must be Susan. I'm really glad to meet you at last. And Tabitha! Hello. I'm Steff – that's two *f*s not a *ph* – and your dad's told me all about you. He's *so* proud of you. Gosh, don't you look like him? Exactly the same smile!' A tall, slim woman with a short blonde bob bounced into the room as though she owned the house.

'We were just going to change Tabitha's nappy,' said Susan, pointedly.

'You must let me help you.' Steff was bobbing up and down with enthusiasm. 'Did Josh tell you I'm a nurse?'

This was unbelievable!

'Yes to the last bit, and no thanks to the first.'

'I think Tabitha feels differently,' said Josh, quietly.

Tabitha, gazing up at the intruder, was nodding furiously, her eyes glued on Steff's hair, swept fashionably across her forehead. Her impressionable daughter was already infatuated by this tarty stranger who belonged more to a soap opera than Pheasants Way, thought Susan, despairingly.

'We can manage quite well on our own,' she said firmly. 'Now, if you don't mind, perhaps you two could wait for us in the lounge and then I'll make a cup of tea.'

'Oh, we don't want to be any bother.' Steff's eyes, a brilliant blue, darted to the room on the left as though she knew instinctively that it was the kitchen. 'I'll put the kettle on, shall I?'

An hour later Susan had to admit that, infuriating as Steff was, she knew her stuff. When Tabitha wanted to get out of her chair to show her father how, on a good day, she could walk as far as the handrail in the hall, Steff helped her back into the chair, using precisely the right techniques: 'That's it, Tabs. Brilliant.'

How dare she call her 'Tabs' when she'd barely been introduced? But her daughter was grinning broadly, first at her father, then at Steff and then at her father again. 'Pritpritpritprit.'

'What's she saying?' asked Josh.

Susan would rather have died than explain that this was Tabitha's word for 'pretty'.

'Of course, when I worked in Stoke we did this sort of thing all the time,' said Steff, stroking Tabitha's hair.

Susan gritted her teeth. 'She doesn't like being touched.'

'Doesn't seem too bothered to me,' pointed out Josh.

'No, Susan's right. I'm sorry. I shouldn't be so familiar but that's my way, isn't it, Josh? And you've got such pretty hair, Tabitha! Exactly the same colour as your mum's.'

'So you used to live in Stoke-on-Trent?' said Susan, forcing herself to make polite conversation.

'Stoke-on-Trent?' Steff frowned. 'No. Oh, I see. Stoke. I was at Stoke Mandeville – it specialises in spinal injuries. It's near Aylesbury.' Tabitha made a grunting sound. 'Want your drink, do you, pet? Here it is. Fantastic! You can use a straw. Lots of my patients spend years trying to do that.'

Any minute now and she'd throw the second cup of tea, which Steff had insisted on making for everyone ('Sit down, Sue, let me do it'), in her face.

'What are the facilities like round here, Tabs?'

Tabitha frowned worriedly.

It was all very well trying to involve her, thought Susan, but couldn't the woman see that her poor daughter couldn't reply? 'Not good,' she said. 'The hospital's all right but we only get to see the consultant every six months. She goes to a centre where there are computers for the ones who can use their fingers, and other activities.'

'Jigjigjig,' interrupted Tabitha urgently.

'That's right, love. That's where you do your jigsaws.'

'Jigsaws?' Steff's admiration was sickening. 'That's fantastic. Let me look at your hands. Yes, I can see. Those fingers move nicely, don't they? And it's great that you've got computers at your school. It's amazing, you know, Susan, how many special-needs patients can work a keyboard – less pressure on the hands than many other manual skills. But how do you stimulate her during the school holidays?'

Susan felt as if she was being interviewed by Social Services. 'Well, the centre's open in the holidays at the moment, although it's going to close and merge with—'

There was a crash as Tabitha dropped her cup. 'Nnnnn.'

'But we're going to fight for it, aren't we, Tabs? Oh dear, has the juice gone over your lovely skirt, Steff?'

Josh was already on his way to the kitchen for a cloth. He came back with a grubby tea-towel. 'That was going into the wash,' said Susan. 'There are some clean ones in the top drawer. I'll get one.'

'No, please, don't bother. This will do fine.' Indeed, Steff didn't seem put out by the spreading stain on her skirt. Instead, she glanced up at Josh adoringly. 'Actually, Sue, we've got a huge favour to ask, haven't we, darling?'

Josh was crouching by Tabitha's chair, holding her hand. He looked up expectently like a small boy. 'Would it be all right if we took her out for a walk? I'd love some time with her. And we'll be careful, honestly.'

'No. I'm sorry. There's more traffic since you were here last. And there aren't enough ramps. You won't know the way to the park any more and—'

Susan stopped. The tears were coming as fast as she was running out of excuses.

'Sue?' Steff touched her arm gently. 'Sue, I understand. But do you mind if we have a little word on our own? In the kitchen?'

Too scared to speak in case she blubbed out loud, Susan allowed herself to be steered out of the room.

Steff sat down at the table. She nodded at the seat opposite. 'Please.'

Reluctantly, Susan obeyed, hoping the other woman wouldn't notice the marmalade smears that were still there from breakfast. Steff leaned across the table and took Susan's hand briefly. Her hands were soft and her nails immaculate. 'Sue, this is so important to Josh. He's told me all about it. Everything. He feels terribly guilty and he knows he shouldn't have walked out on you.'

'Too bloody true,' said Susan.

'But he's older now. He's learned his lesson, just like we all do.' Steff squeezed her hand but Susan pulled it away. Steff's eyes watered as though she was the one who was entitled to be hurt. 'He's clean too. Honestly. I know about his history and I also know he doesn't take anything any more. All he wants is a more active role in caring for Tabitha. We're not going to try to take over, but when we move to Bedford we'll be that much nearer.'

She was horrified. 'You're moving to Bedford?' It was only ten miles away! They'd be here all the time.

'But we won't get in the way. Promise. We'll only come when you say. Just give Josh a chance. That's all I ask. And let us start by taking Tabitha for a little walk now so she can have some time with her father. Every daughter ought to have that.'

Susan wanted to refuse, but her body felt as though it belonged to someone else. Everything that Steff had said made sense. If she was honest, she'd made life so unbearable for Josh, after that MMR decision, that she wasn't surprised he'd walked. Yes, of course he should have seen more of them afterwards, but she couldn't shut out that picture of the joy in Tabitha's face at seeing her dad. What right did she have to deprive her poor daughter of that? She'd often seen Tabitha's jealous looks when other dads arrived at the centre. 'You'll be careful with her?' she said at last.

'As careful as we would with a newborn baby.'

Susan shuddered, remembering what a perfect baby Tabitha had seemed. 'He told you everything?'

Steff squeezed her hand. 'There's no proof, you know. All the evidence shows that the MMR—'

'Don't talk about it,' said Susan, fiercely, tears swimming into her eyes. Furiously, she willed herself to get rid of them. Look out of the window. Her neighbour's washing was flapping on the line. Clean, crisp washing. Nice and normal. 'All right. Just a short walk. I'll tell you where to go. And, please, Steff, look after her.' This time she couldn't stop the tears. 'She's all I've got left.'

Steff grabbed her hand again. 'I promise. I know this is difficult for you, but I'm not a wicked stepmother. I just want Josh to be happy. And Tabitha needs two parents. Every kid does.'

Susan stood at the window, watching them push Tabitha down the street. Her daughter had crammed a fist into her mouth, the way she did when she was very excited. No loyalty. No looking back for her mother. Almost out of sight now. Gone.

An hour, Steff had said. How was she going to pass a whole hour on her own? Crazy. For years she had craved more time to herself and now she didn't know what to do. Read? She wouldn't be able to concentrate. Watch television? A waste of a beautiful day. Garden? She could make a start on those weeds. But she really wanted to talk to a friend. Joy? No. She'd tell someone else about Josh and then everyone at the centre would gossip.

From Rainbow to Mums@Home: My ex-husband, who hasn't been near us for more than a year, has just turned up out of the blue. He's got married again and his wife wants to be my new best friend. My ex wants to see more of our twelve-year-old daughter even though he left when she was a baby. He's taken her out now and I feel so alone. She didn't even wave goodbye. I'm also scared in case he doesn't look after her properly. How do mothers cope when their kids go to the other parent at weekends?

Briefly, Susan reread her message. She'd deliberately failed to mention that Tabitha was disabled because it would have defeated the object of joining a group in which she wanted to be normal. On the other hand, if she didn't describe Tabitha's circumstances, it would be difficult to explain why she felt so worried and betrayed. Send.

Just pressing the button made her feel better. And no one would tell. That was the beauty of being Rainbow. Now for those weeds.

She'd just found the trowel under the sink when the phone rang. She knew it! Something had happened. The wheelchair had tipped over. Tabitha was hurt. How could she have let them go?

'Mrs Thomas?'

'Yes.' She could barely get the word out.

'This is Bekki Adams from the *Gazette*. We're doing a story on the centre closing and I was given your name. I wonder if you could spare the time to give us a quote on what this means to you.'

The relief that Tabitha was all right made her babble: 'Yes, I can. But you're wrong about something. The centre isn't necessarily going to close. We're starting a campaign to save it.'

'You are? Fantastic. I didn't know.'

Her enthusiasm gave Susan hope.

'Can you help us, er . . . Bekki? Could you run a piece encouraging readers to support us?'

'I'll need to check with my editor first,' the girl sounded excited, 'but it sounds a great idea to me.'

12

Mark stared at the screen, wondering where he had gone wrong. Why weren't his own kids into innocent pursuits like collecting leaves or postcards instead of being glued to MSN, computer games where everyone got shot or that awful music channel on Sky?

Briefly, he wondered if Julie of Eastbourne could be persuaded to swap kids for a week. Any child who was prepared to keep a nature diary would be a doddle to look after. It was all he could do to get his lot seated at the table for breakfast. 'Ed, can you hurry up?'

'I can but I won't.'

'Stop being so difficult. And eat up.'

'I *hate* brown bread, Dad. Why can't we have white bread like Mum used to give us?'

Mark wiped fingers, stained with blackberry jelly, on the DAD apron that the kids had given him, via Daphne, last Christmas and hoped he'd been right to play down that awful cross-dressing scene the other day. Somehow it didn't seem right for a boy to fuss about the kind of bread he got for breakfast, just as it wasn't right for him to wear his mother's pink silk evening top. It might be her bra next, if this went on. 'Because white isn't healthy for you.'

'It is, if it's got those wholemeal bits in it like that stuff on television,' piped up Florrie.

Ed studied his plate unenthusiastically. 'And why have you given me an E?'

Mark nearly dropped the margarine tub. 'A *what*?'

'An E!' Ed waved a large white tablet in the air. 'Our biology teacher says we should never have anything that's got a circle on it. It could be Ecstasy.'

'For pity's sake, Ed, it's a bloody vitamin pill. Look!'

Mark waved the bottle in front of him. It had a large jolly smiley face on it, promising a lifetime of vitality.

'Well, it shouldn't have a circle.'

'Write and tell the manufacturers.'

'I will.'

He probably would too, thought Mark, trying to sponge blackberry jelly off his poorly ironed blue and white striped shirt. When Ed wasn't behaving like an uncontrollable toddler, he was coming out with observations that showed a fine line in lateral thinking. That child would go far, but it was anyone's guess whether it would be up or down. He was still worried about those nubile pictures on the computer. 'Are you sure you didn't download that teen site?' He couldn't bring himself to dignify it with its full name.

'I *swear*. I told you, these things just pop up sometimes.'

Ed's eyes shone with such righteous indignation that Mark knew he was telling the truth.

'And what about Mum's jumper?' said Florrie, mischievously.

'Shurrup. I told you. I *wasn't* wearing it. I was just smelling it.' He flushed. 'It reminded me of her.'

Florrie slid off the kitchen stool. 'How sad can you get?'

Mark patted Ed briefly on the shoulder to show he understood. 'Come on, you two, or I'm going to be late.'

The meeting, thank goodness, was on the Paddington side of London. Providing they got out now *and* there was a space in the station car park, he might just make it after he'd dropped the kids off at the holiday club.

'Ouch, Florrie – fuck off.'

'Ed, don't use that word!'

'It's not a word.'

Mark ran his fingers through his hair. 'Then what the hell is it?'

Ed grinned. 'Two words.'

His son was going to be the death of him. 'If I'd wanted to work in the mental-health industry, I'd have done so. Now, get your butt upstairs and brush your hair.'

'No.' Ed gave him two fingers from the staircase. 'It's *my* hair.'

'Well, I sired it.'

'What does "sire" mean?'

'Provided the sperm,' replied Florrie, promptly. 'He provided sperm during sexual intercourse with Mum to make you and your hair.'

'*Don't talk like that.*'

'I just have.'

'Well, stop it.'

'Make me.'

She was upset. It was as hard for her as it was for him. 'Florrie.' Mark tried to put his arms round her but she pushed him away. 'In the car, both of you,' he said, more softly. 'But clean your teeth first.'

There was a soft thud as the post fluttered through the door. For the past month, Ed had been on tenterhooks to see if he'd won a competition for Wattevers tickets that he'd entered through the *Funday Times*. Mark didn't have the heart to tell him that he'd have heard by now.

'There's a postcard from Mum!' yelled Ed.

Florrie, toothbrush in hand, flew back down the stairs. 'Where?'

'Shut up, I'm reading it.'

'Share,' commanded Mark, looking over Ed's shoulder.

The sight of the large loopy writing, almost unreadable, like many bright people's script, made his armpits sweat.

'She's been roller-skating,' said Ed, disbelievingly. 'In Central Park. Look. There's a picture. I want to go roller-skating. I keep telling you.'

'We'll go next weekend.'

'But I want to go roller-skating in Central Park, not boring old Oxford.'

Florrie nodded. It wasn't often they were in agreement. 'She doesn't say when she's coming back. And why isn't there a post-mark?'

'I don't know. But it's a pretty stamp, isn't it? I could get you an album if you like and we could start collecting them.'

'For God's sake, Dad, that's so *sad*.'

'Well, what about a holiday diary, then? I'll give you a tenner if you write something.'

Florrie looked mildly interested. 'Every day?'

'No. You get one tenner in total.'

'In your dreams, Dad.'

He sighed. 'Look, we'll definitely go roller-skating. That's a promise.'

'Tonight?' asked Ed, picking his nose.

Mark ran his hands through his hair in frustration. It was so hard getting everything right. There was so much to remember and do that he needed a spreadsheet to record all their activities and his jobs. 'Not tonight. At the weekend. Now, in the car – fast. And don't flick that. Here's some loo paper.'

Why, he asked himself, gazing out of the window at the Oxfordshire countryside as the train sped towards London, couldn't Hilary have been a normal mother like her own? Daphne had been a traditional intelligent, stay-at-home mum who had given birth to one very bright daughter. Keen to give her the opportunities she had never had, she'd encouraged her to go to Oxford, after which Hilary had got a place on a banking course for graduates. Then she'd got married, had the kids and con-tinued working.

'Aren't you happy?' he had asked her, when she'd been offered the New York job that he hadn't even known she'd applied for.

She'd looked at him with those serious eyes and the classic English-rose face that had first attracted him to her. 'Define happiness, Mark. Is it putting up with kids who answer you back so you can't think clearly any more? Or suddenly realising that society expects you to put someone else – two other people, or three if you include you – before yourself for the rest of your life? If I'm going to make something of myself, it means being selfish. If I put the kids first, they'll have exactly the same identity struggle in twenty years' time. At least, Florrie will. It's worse for girls. I've been brought up to go places, Mark. I can't do that here any more.'

He should have told her that, yes, she was being a selfish cow and that plenty of other mothers and fathers were making sacrifices, if that was what you called it. But he'd been too scared of losing her. They had continued to make love, always at his instigation, until the day she went.

The train stopped at Reading station. Already? He still had some fine-tuning to do on the press release for Educational Fun Toys, the new client he was meeting. Mark opened his laptop. Better check his emails in case the EFT people had changed the arrangements. Good. Nothing in his inbox that couldn't wait until later. His index finger hovered over the integral mouse. He'd like to see if anyone had replied on the kicking issue but there was only another thirty minutes until the train got into Paddington. That press release should come first but . . .

Mums@Home. Message Board. Mark's chest lurched slightly. He hadn't really expected anyone to bother but there were two replies for Mimi. Grateful that both seats next to him were empty, he skimmed the messages. One, from someone called Rainbow, was very New Age, and the second had come from 'Expectent' Mum.

From Rainbow to Mimi: My daughter used to lash out at other kids and the teacher had to move her in class. That didn't work but then another mum said it was because of frustration and I needed to find her another outlet. So every time she did it, I got her to clap her hands really loudly. I'd clap mine too and it became a game. Now she's stopped.

A *clapping* game? As if that would work on Ed!

From Expectent Mum to Mimi: If your kid is so orful, you must be a pretty lousie mum. If it were my kid, Id give it a smack. Thats what my mum wuld have done.

Mark shifted uncomfortably on the seat. It served him right for asking advice from strangers who couldn't even spell. Maybe he was a hopeless mum but was that because he was actually a dad or because he couldn't do it right?

Scanning the messages for any more hatemail, he stopped in his tracks.

I want to know if anyone out there can tell me if it's possible to go on after your husband has had an affair.

Mark went cold. There had definitely been times, before Hilary went, when her behaviour had been so erratic that he had wondered if she'd been cheating on him.

Looking back at what happened, I feel really stupid because I didn't guess the truth. But I honestly didn't think my husband would do that kind of thing.

He could understand that, all right.

From Mimi to Part Time Mum: You're not stupid. You trusted in someone and they let you down. But trust is an intrinsic part of love. Neither can flourish without the other. My husband is working abroad temporarily but I'm pretty certain he doesn't play around. I'm not sure, to be honest, if a marriage can

SOPHIE KING

really survive an affair. There are people who say they've done
it but I can't help wondering if they really loved each other in
the first place.

Send. For what it was worth. Hopefully, 'Expectent' Mum would
read it and learn how to spell words like 'intrinsic'. And now he
really did have to deal with that press release. Mums@Home was
getting too much in the way of real work.

The meeting went well, although the client, a sharp-brained, lean
young man in his late twenties with a degree in child psychology,
kept giving him odd, furtive looks. Was it him or his presentation?

'That's great, Mark. I like it. And the list of possible contacts.
Go ahead and send out the release.'

Mark sighed inwardly with relief. This client could be big. Very
big. Just like private-school fees.

Clive Hastings ('Call me Clive') touched his arm lightly. 'There's
only one thing.'

Mark's heart sank. He hadn't got the contract after all.

'You might like to check out your hair in the bathroom. Looks
as though something nasty's landed on it.'

Automatically, Mark patted the top of his head. Feeling something sticky, he brought down a sample in his fingers. 'Blackberry
jelly!' He stared at it, aghast. 'Don't say I've been walking around
with this on my head since breakfast.'

Clive's eyebrows nearly hit his bald patch. 'Blackberry jelly?'

'Yes.' Mark laughed awkwardly. 'I must have smeared it on
myself when I was spreading my son's toast for breakfast.'

Clive slammed his hand on the edge of the desk. 'A working
man who makes his son's breakfast! That's what I like to hear. I
can tell, Mark, that you're exactly the right man for this job.
Educational Fun Toys needs representatives who are fully inte-
grated into parenthood.' His eyes flickered. 'Is that part of your
culture, by any chance?'

Mark bristled inwardly but forced himself to sound polite, which years of practice at public school had instilled in him: 'I wouldn't say so.'

'I see. But you obviously believe in joint parenting?'

In a blinding flash, Mark felt exactly like Ed when he was about to tell a whopper: 'Absolutely. Hilary's always saying that if anything happened to her, I could run the house.'

'Be a bit difficult to run a business like yours at the same time, wouldn't it?'

'If you ask me,' said Mark, solemnly, 'it would be virtually impossible.'

The meeting overran just long enough for him to miss the train home by three minutes. The holiday club closed at five, which was crazy if you were a working parent, and he wouldn't get there until half past. He'd have to ring the emergency number and explain.

'I see,' said one of the helpers, who clearly didn't. 'Are you sure you can't get back any earlier?'

Hadn't he made his situation clear? 'Not unless the train turns into a plane.'

'Well, I suppose someone will have to wait, won't they? But we won't be able to do it again.'

Frosty. He shouldn't have mentioned planes. But it was so frustrating sitting here at this rickety metal station table with an insipid cup of expensive coffee when he needed to be at home with the kids. It reminded him of an evening last year when Hilary had got back late from a conference in Leeds. She had missed a train too but he had been unreasonably cross at having to babysit instead of playing squash. Now he felt guilty.

By the time he reached the holiday club, both kids were sitting outside on the steps, plastic lunchboxes at their sides. It was beginning to rain and Florrie's hair was damp. If they got a cold, it would be his fault.

'Where've you been, Dad? You're really late.'

'Where's your supervisor?'

'Gone. She had a date. I said I'd look after Ed.'

Ed stood up indignantly. 'I don't need looking after. When that tramp asked for money, I gave him a quid so he wouldn't hurt us.'

Mark felt his armpits sweat. Oxford was full of down-and-outs, many high on heroin. 'And he went away?'

'Yeah.' Ed's voice had the confidence of youth.

Cross with himself, Mark shepherded them into the car. 'I'm going to complain. She promised to wait,' he said.

'Don't!' Florrie was horrified. 'She'll take it out on us. Anyway, it's your fault for being late. Smell this, Ed.'

'Ugh! Dad, she's just rubbed her hand under her armpit and held it in my face.'

'No. *Stop!* Dad, he's just rubbed his hand in his pants and he's suffocating me with his stinking—'

'THAT'S ENOUGH!' Mark yanked the key out of the ignition. 'See this? If you two don't stop it immediately, I'm going to throw it as far as I can out of the window. Then we'll have to walk. Get it?'

'Someone's had a bad day,' muttered Florrie.

'Yes, I have. And I don't want another word until we get home.'

It worked for a few minutes, and Mark drove slowly down the Woodstock Road towards Summertown, past the speed cameras to trap tense parents. What had got into him? Why couldn't he have been more rational?

'Dad?'

'Yes?'

'Why has Florrie got jam on her face?'

'I don't know. Why have you got jam on your face, Florrie?'

'Bugger off, Ed.'

'*Florrie!*' Mark swerved to avoid a red van racing him round the busy Headington roundabout.

'He's teasing me about my spots again, Dad.'

Spots? Jam. Little sod.

'Ed, you've just lost your pocket money.'

'Aren't you going to punish Florrie too?'

'She hasn't done anything.'

'She's lost her trainers.'

Safely on the other side of the roundabout, Mark glanced round. Florrie was barefoot. Why hadn't he noticed? 'What happened?' he said, forcing himself to speak quietly.

'I mislaid them.' God, she sounded so like Hilary as well as looking like her. For some weird reason, she was much paler-skinned than Ed, who was getting more and more like him. Sometimes they seemed nothing like brother and sister and he knew people wondered occasionally if Florrie was really his. But that was genes for you: his father had been light-skinned too.

'I lost my shoes when we were waiting for you. We were playing catch and they fell into the river.'

Mark's mouth was dry. 'But you were nowhere near the river.'

'We went for a walk. You were so late and we were bored.'

For a brief horrible second, he had a vision of making an emergency call to Hilary to say there'd been a terrible accident . . .

'I'm sorry, kids.' He glanced in the rear mirror, palms sweating on to the steering wheel. They were both sitting still, waiting for him to go mental again. 'It was my fault for missing the train.'

Florrie's voice was almost inaudible. 'You won't tell Mum about it, will you?'

'No,' said Mark, quietly. 'I won't.'

13

Rowing in front of the children: can it be healthy?

Lisa felt so cross when she saw stuff like this. It almost put her off Mums@Home. In fact, it got her so mad that she just had to send off a reply even though it would make her late for work: 'Rowing is reely bad for kids. Even babies can hear things before their born.'

Sometimes she wondered if that was why she'd lost Hayley. Kevin hadn't actually hit her, not that time, but he had scared her witless, the way his eyes had flashed and gone red and glittery. She'd locked herself in the toilet and sat, shaking with fear, not daring to come out until she heard the door slam. The next day the bleeding had started.

The doctor had said it would be better if she could cry. But the tears wouldn't come. Then the doctor had said something about people being so upset that they bottled up the grief inside them, which wasn't very good for them. Even going to mass, which she'd always done as a child with her mum, hadn't helped much.

DO YOU WANT TO TURN OFF THE COMPUTER?

YES.

Lisa shut it down, touching the crucifix round her neck for luck. Sometimes she'd like to turn off her mind too. But she needed to get to work now or she wouldn't get paid at the end of the week. She was doing extra shifts at lunchtime in that special-needs place next door because she needed the cash. Babies were expensive.

The nursery was already busy when she got there, and Mrs Perkins, the manager, had been sharp. As punishment, she'd been told to take Aaron to the toilet. Everyone hated that job. Aaron was meant to be potty-trained but he was always having accidents.

'Miss Smith, I've got the floor wet.'

Lisa recoiled. How was Aaron going to cope when he went to big school in January if he couldn't aim into the toilet? And now she was getting bigger it was difficult for her to kneel on the floor and mop up the mess. When she'd got the job of 'auxiliary helper', they hadn't told her it involved that kind of thing. Nor had they told her it sometimes meant helping out at the special-needs centre next door, although she didn't mind that. Poor kids. She felt sorry for them and their parents. When she thought of them, she always had to touch her crucifix to make sure nothing would be wrong with Rose when she was born.

Still, at least working at the centre meant she could pick up a baby. Lisa loved the smell of their soft skin. And the way they looked at her, as if they knew what she was thinking, melted her insides.

'Come on, Aaron, wash your hands . . . That's right.'

On the whole, the kids were sweet, like Daisy and Annie. But there were a couple of boys like Aaron who were what her mother would have called real little buggers. There were times when she felt like giving him a good hard smack. But you couldn't. The rules were so strict nowadays. You weren't even meant to give them a cuddle if they fell over, although Lisa had broken that rule a few times with Daisy and her other favourites.

'Come on,' said Lisa, sharply, and took Aaron back into the play area. Bloody hell, he stank of pee and she bet his mother hadn't put a spare pair of pants in his bag. 'Let's do some reading, shall we?'

She'd spent last week helping them put up new posters on the walls with big bright letters to help the rising-fours learn to read. There was also a small slide, a sandpit, a Wendy house and several tables with crayons.

'Mrs Smith, I can't do up my laces!'

Lisa abandoned Aaron and knelt down beside Daisy to help. She loved it when the kids called her 'Mrs'. She might have been a Mrs by now if Kevin had stayed. Then they would have been a proper family. She could see it now. Sometimes it seemed more real than the life she was leading. Her mother had always said she lived in Cloud Cuckoo Land, but what was wrong with that if it made you feel better? 'I'll show you again, Daisy. You always start with the right shoe, like, because it's lucky. Then you cross this lace over the other and under the bridge.'

'Thank you.'

She was wearing a cream and pink dress that Lisa had seen in the baby shop. Lisa smiled as Daisy's warm little hand reached out to pat her stomach. 'When's your baby coming, Mrs Smith?'

'Not yet, Daisy.'

'But when?'

'Daisy, over there now, please. To the counting table,' said another voice.

Lisa hadn't realised that Mrs Perkins was so close.

'Lisa, can I have a word? Over here, in the corner . . . Thank you. I heard what Daisy said and I must say I've been wondering myself. Are you expecting by any chance?'

She nodded, beaming. It was so *good* when people said that.

But Mrs Perkins didn't look thrilled. 'And can I ask when you're due?'

'I'm not sure. My dates are a bit confused. I'm waiting for another scan.'

Mrs Perkins pursed her lips. 'I see. Well, I'd appreciate it if you can let me know as soon as possible.'

Lisa straightened the puzzle on the desk. 'It won't be for a while.'

'Right.' Mrs Perkins looked relieved. 'You're very popular with the children, especially the girls. And you've got a knack with them, more so than many other assistants we've had.'

'Ta.'

Mrs Perkins sniffed. 'So don't let me down. Will you?'

*

'Hiya, Tabs, how you doing?' said Lisa, cheerfully, as she put the plate on the table. 'Look! Your favourite. Pasta with cheese sauce. Hang on a minute, Danny, I'm just coming. Hungry, are you?'

'Did you get what you wanted the other day?'

'What?' Lisa hadn't realised Tabitha's mother was at the table too. 'Oh, yes. Sort of.'

She turned away, embarrassed. She'd remembered how the woman had seen through her fib about the man in the shop.

'You know, I've brought Tabitha up on my own – it's all right, no one else can hear us. I just thought it might help. My name's Susan, by the way.'

Lisa was tempted to tell her that it wasn't any of her business. But the woman's kind face softened something inside her. 'It's not what you think,' she found herself saying. 'I'm not really on my own.'

'That's good.' Susan clearly didn't believe her. She patted Lisa's arm briefly. 'Have you got friends and family to help you?'

'Loads.' Lisa beamed. 'I'm really lucky.'

'Good.' Susan seemed relieved. 'I've got my dad. He's been great but it's not quite the same.' She sighed and her eyes took on a faraway look. 'Oh, well, I'd better get on with helping Tabs eat her lunch. Whoops. Too late. I'll get a cloth.'

It had been a long day. Lisa hadn't fancied supper earlier but now her stomach was making weird noises. In one way, she felt hungry but she also knew she could force anything down. Not with tomorrow nearly here.

August 15. Hayley's birthday. She counted on her fingers. September, October, November, December. Just four months to go until her Mums@Home little bear's wish came true.

Sky's birthday was 9 January and she would be eighteen months now, although if Hayley hadn't existed, Sky wouldn't have happened. Lisa knew the dates off pat and could work out exactly how old they would be now. A woman in a flat below her had had a baby when she should have had Hayley. The kid was nearly three now, and every time Lisa saw it, she felt resentful.

Keep their memories alive, like the voices in her head told her to do. It couldn't do any harm, she reasoned. A bit like touching wood and walking round cracks in the road. And it had all worked because now she had Rose to look forward to. Rose who would love her in a way that no one had ever loved her before.

Lisa sighed with satisfaction as she thought of everything waiting in the spare room. The lovely white frilly cot in the corner with the pink and white sheep mobile that played 'Brahms' Lullaby'. Music was so important for a baby's development. She knew that already, even though Julie of Eastbourne had been banging on about it on Mums@Home. She'd also found a nice bouncing cradle too from a car-boot sale last month; the movement made babies go to sleep, again according to Julie, who sounded like a right know-all. And she'd got stacks of nappies from the chemist, who was selling stuff off cheap before he closed down, and a plastic changing mat with more pink sheep.

She was going to be the perfect mother.

Lisa thought of everything she had learned from her online babycraft classes. They were really good even though nappies were called 'diapers'.

'SHUT UP!'

'NO, YOU SHUT UP.'

Lisa thumped the lounge wall angrily. Kiki was so noisy. How would Rose sleep if Kiki was going to go on like that? Someone on the other side thumped back and flakes of plaster floated down. She'd definitely have to ring the council tomorrow in her lunch break. In fact, after Rose was born, maybe she should get out of here. They could live somewhere nice, like Oxford. She had been there once on a school trip – lots of shops, a nice river and stuff.

Thank heaven, the shouting had stopped. It was getting darker, too, so she must have dozed off. The computer clock said it was six minutes to twelve but it was five minutes slow.

60, 59, 58, 57 . . .

Midnight.

Outside, someone started yelling again and glass shattered. Lisa stood up stiffly, and took the little pink and white cake out of its packet. Three candles. Carefully, she lit each one.

'Spontaneous abortion,' the ginger-haired doctor had called it. Lisa had told him what she thought of that. An abortion was something you *chose* to do, not something that hit you smack in the face and ruined your life. And when she looked up 'spontaneous' on the computer dictionary, it turned out to be something nice that you did on the spur of the moment. Didn't these people have *any* feelings?

'Happy birthday, Hayley.' She blew out the candles with gentle puffs. One, two, three. 'Happy birthday, my lovely daughter.'

Reverently, she got out the rosary beads she'd had since she was a child. A special kind of peace flooded through her as though they were restoring order to her life. 'Hail, Mary, full of grace . . .'

Lisa smiled to herself when she'd finished. It would be all right now.

Hi, Annabel. Hope this reaches you in some cyber café wherever you are. Miss you loads. Ben's OK but Mum and Dad still arguing. Got five goals in the match last week and met this cool boy on the train. Don't tell Mum.

For the urgent attention of Mrs L. Smith. Congratulations! You have won first prize in the lottery sweepstakes. All you have to do is fill in your bank details below . . .

Dear Mr E. Summers,
Thank you for your recent email. We can assure you that we did not intend to confuse customers by placing a 'smiley face' on our vitamin tablets. I am also afraid that our company does not make 'miracle spot cures' for your sister.

www.losethreestones.com. Recipe for cabbage soup. Boil one
large cabbage, finely sliced . . .

Mums@Home.co.uk
JOIN OUR ONLINE DISCUSSIONS ON
Can a marriage survive an affair?
Disposable nappies or terries? The debate continues.
TIP FROM FRAN 3
Can't get hold of your kid on his mobile phone? Make sure
you've got a list of his friends' numbers so you can ring them
to find out where he is.
CHUCKLE CORNER FROM MAD MUM
FIVE THINGS A MAN KNOWS ABOUT A WOMAN
1
2
3
4
5
THOUGHT TO KEEP YOU SANE FROM BIG MUM
This time next week, today won't seem so bad.

14

Caroline paused outside her son's bedroom, wincing at the computer printout he'd stuck to the door.

> www.getevenbigger.com. Extend your penis now! Safe, simple
> and effective. Ten minutes and you've got yourself an enormous
> tool. Results are permanent and no surgery is needed.

The rest of the door was festooned with posters of naked women in provocative positions and a KEEP OUT notice. In her day, they'd decorated the inside of their school desks; hers, she recalled, had had postcards of ponies. Maybe that was where she'd gone wrong in life.

She knocked loudly. No answer. Teenagers were entitled to their privacy: she'd written something about it only the other month. Well, blow that. 'Ben, come on. It's nearly lunchtime! Are you going to lie there all day?'

There was a muffled grunt from the bed as Caroline picked her way through piles of jeans, sweaters and *GQ* magazines strewn on the floor, holding her breath against BO, stale air and a cheesy smell that might or might not have been feet.

She slipped on one of the magazines, then bent down to pick it up, automatically scanning the coverlines.

FIFTY WAYS TO HAVE GREAT SEX!

Fifty?

'Close the bloody curtains!'

Shaken by the roar, which proved her son wasn't as fast asleep as he had looked, she stumbled over a pile of CDs. There was a sharp crack.

'What have you broken now, you stupid woman?'

'Don't talk to me like that.' Caroline pulled back the duvet to jolly him along. Good God, he was naked! It had been a long time since she had seen her middle child without any clothes on. His legs were startlingly hairy, more so than Roger's, and there were angry yellow pustules on his back, matching the ones on his face.

'That's Newfound Glory you've gone and smashed.' Ben was out of bed now, wrapping his duvet round himself indignantly. 'Do you know how much it cost?'

Well, at least he was talking.

'Yes, as I probably paid for it,' said Caroline, drily, wading back to the door. 'Stop being so rude. And if you don't get up now, it'll be bedtime. You promised Dad you'd find a job this week.'

Ben retreated to the safety of his bed and buried his head under the pillow. 'I've tried. There aren't any.'

'What about the pub? Or Tesco?'

'Full up.'

'Then why were they still giving out application forms when I asked for one yesterday?'

'Chill out, Mum. I need to rest. I worked bloody hard for those exams.'

That one again. 'Ben, we all work hard, but you finished nearly six weeks ago. Dad's right. It's time to face the real world. And another thing. Will you please remember to take your antibiotics or your skin will never get better?'

She hadn't meant to be so hard. She softened her voice, trying to sound jokey. 'It's a good thing you don't have to remember to take the pill or you'd be pregnant by now.'

'Go away, Mum. You're boring.'

'Thanks very much.'

Pity it wasn't a working day. Then she could have gone into the office to write about parenting instead of doing the practical bit.

She still had the magazine under her arm. Boring? Illogically, that stung more than anything else. She locked herself into the bathroom, sat on the loo lid and flicked to page fifty-nine. Surprisingly, the text was less rude than practical. In the early days, she and Roger had had what she'd thought was a good sex life but it had dwindled with the exhaustion of work and children. Now, with supreme irony, her older two children were probably having more sex than she was.

Caroline reread tip number five. She'd never thought of that one and, for the first time in goodness knows how many years, her pelvis had begun to throb. She slid her hand down the front of her pants and followed the instructions. Oh, my God. OH, MY GOD.

Sometime later, she came downstairs, cheeks flushed. The dishes were still in the sink, waiting to be put into the dishwasher as soon as she'd unloaded it. After that, she'd clean behind the sofas where, as Roger had acidly pointed out last night, Mrs B rarely ventured ('Is it worth paying that woman money, Caro?'), then drive to the sports club to see Georgie in her match. That was what a mother should be doing. Not locking herself into the bathroom with her teenage son's sex magazine.

Good! The post! Caroline flew to the door as a long envelope, addressed to Roger, fluttered to the carpet. Before leaving, Annabel had promised to send regular postcards and emails. In her last phone call she'd said it was hard to find postboxes or Internet cafés, let alone pay-phones. And her mobile didn't work in remote places.

This time last year, Caroline had had all three children at home. Now there were two. Next year, it would be one, and at some point in the future, none. Just her and Roger. What would they do? Nothing, since Roger's affair, brought her pleasure any more. She'd even lost heart for shopping.

Maybe she should pop back upstairs to check her inbox before she went out in case there was anything from Zelda or Annabel. The computer was kept in her elder daughter's room so that she and Roger could, in theory, monitor the children's Net activities, but after all these months, the reminders of her absent daughter punched her in the stomach: posters of unsavoury young men with earrings in unspeakable crevices, makeup on her dressing-table, a prospectus from the university she was going to when she returned from her gap year. Tidy. Too tidy. Clothes hanging in the wardrobe. Nothing on the carpet. At night, Caroline even turned on the light; it made her feel that Annabel was a bit closer.

Caroline keyed in her password and opened her inbox. Speed-reading, she checked the senders to sift out the urgent ones. There were various press releases from PRs for the Parenting page, sent on by the features secretary, and something from Zelda, marked urgent, about a feature on educational toys that needed to be in shortly. A short email from Jeff, hoping 'all is well'. And nothing from Annabel, naughty girl.

Distraction. That was what she needed. Mums@Home. Log in. Message Board. She froze. Four people – four! – had replied to her question about Roger.

> From Earth Mother to Part Time Mum: Give him another chance. You owe it to the kids. Yes, he was wrong but it's our job to pick up the pieces. Have you considered stopping work to give your husband more time? And take care over your own appearance so he wants you again.

Such old-fashioned advice! But what did she expect from a group of parents who lived their lives online? Yet the pathetic thing was that after it had happened she *had* paid particular care to her own appearance so Roger desired her again.

> From Expectent Mum to Part Time Mum: Chuck the barstard out. Hes not worth it.

Dodgy spelling but truthful. The writer seemed angry. So why wasn't *she*? Anger would be so much more helpful than the hideous hurt that wouldn't go away.

From Pushy Princess to Part Time Mum: Make him feel really guilty so he showers you with 'sorry' presents. When the kids are older, you could bugger off.

Is that what some women really did?

From Mimi to Part Time Mum: It's very difficult to trust someone again when that trust has been eroded.

Yes. *Yes.*

Curiously, she scanned the rest of the chat messages. 'Expectent' Mum had been unbelievably cruel about kicking to poor old Mimi. Suppose she took it to heart?

From Part Time Mum to Mums@Home: I totally disagree with Expectent Mum. We all had ideas about bringing up kids before we had them ourselves. Eleven *is* much older than the usual age for kicking, but children who are troubled about things often resort to regressive behaviour. My youngest, Georgie, was quite difficult until she was eight or nine. Now my kids are reasonably well balanced, apart from my eighteen-year-old who spends all day in bed after A levels. My advice, for what it's worth, is to tell him off firmly and then don't refer to it until it happens again. If you make a big deal, he'll keep going. And, Mimi, thanks for your advice to me.

Send.

Too late, she wished she hadn't. Who was she to offer help to others? She couldn't even cope with her own problems: work, Roger, Annabel . . . Sometimes it was all too much. Caroline sighed as Ben's music, which sounded quite pleasant for a change, drifted along the corridor. Impulsively, she hugged herself. How would it feel to be loved again? Really loved? Slowly she began to dance, yet in her head it wasn't Roger holding her, or even George Clooney. It was a faceless stranger, staring down at her with such intensity that her entire body vibrated with longing.

'Mum, what are you doing?'

Ben was standing at the door in his checked boxer shorts and T-shirt with the slogan 'I ROCK CATHOLIC CHICKS'. Roger, who'd had a Catholic upbringing, had nearly had apoplexy when his son had come home with it from Camden Market the other month.

'Nothing.' Caroline covered her confusion by pretending to tidy her desk. 'Nothing at all.'

15

'Edgetoffthecomputer*now*.Ineeditforwork.Anywayyou'remeantto bedoingyourholidayworknotgoingonMSN.YesyouwereIsawyou. You'vejustminimisedit – thereitisonthebaratthebottom.'

Eventually, Mark got Ed off the computer so he could check his emails and brief Clive on his campaign to get the maximum amount of press coverage for EFT. 'I've already got two magazines interested and I think I may have a third,' said Mark, scrolling down his inbox in the hope that another journalist had been hooked since he last looked a few minutes ago.

'Sounds good.' Clive was guardedly pleased. 'So, when do you think we'll see something in print?'

'Two of the magazines are weeklies so, with any luck, maybe late September.'

'Why not sooner?' His client sounded distinctly disgruntled.

'Because they have six-week leadtimes. They couldn't—'

'*Dad! Dad! He's hurting me again.*'

Mark leaped up to shut his office door. 'Sorry. They couldn't do it any faster. It's not bad timing in view of the toy fair in—'

The door flew open to reveal a distraught Florrie, tears streaming down her face. 'Look! He's left marks all over my legs.'

Holding his finger to his lips to warn his daughter to be quiet, Mark flew past into the bathroom, the only room in the house which had a door that actually locked.

'What's going on, Mark?'

Think. *Fast*. 'We've got some building work going on outside. Now, the third magazine, is talking about doing a double-page spread and—'

BANG, BANG, BANG. Christ, the door was going to break down

if they didn't stop. And now Ed was playing his trumpet, although 'playing' was the wrong word: he had to be making that dreadful din on purpose.

'Jeez, Mark, your builders are noisy. They sound as though they're in the same room.'

'It is a bit difficult, isn't it? Look, can I ring you back?'

'Not really. I've got another meeting. Pity – I wanted to give the board an update.'

'Well, to be honest, there's not much more news than—'

'Dad, he's hitting me with the trumpet!'

'Sounds like your children need you.' His client's voice was acrid with disapproval. 'Call me on Saturday, can you?'

Mark leaned out of the window, so he could hear better above Florrie's yells. 'Any particular time?'

'Seven fifteen. Before I go into my breakfast meeting.'

He was gone. Seven fifteen, a.m. not p.m. On *Saturday*!

'What the hell do you think you're doing?' He flung open the door, grabbed Ed by the shoulders and the trumpet fell on the floor. He could have shaken him, he really could. 'You *know* I work from home. You *know* I have to give some kind of professional image. That was a new client. You know what a client is, don't you?'

'Someone who pays our school fees,' said Ed, sulkily.

'Exactly.' Mark paused, remembering how Hilary had joked that Ed's first word was 'client' because that was all Mark talked about. There had been a nugget of truth in it, which still made him feel guilty. 'And if my client hears you two screaming, he'll think I'm not capable of doing my job.'

'You're hurting me, Dad. Leggo.' Ed squirmed out of his grip.

'Then next time be quiet when I'm on the office line. And for God's sake, stop fighting her. Florrie, are you all right? My God, those bruises are *awful*.'

'They're the ones he did last week.' Florrie sniffed. 'These red ones are what he's done now.' She threw a furious look at her brother. 'I'm going to tell Dad now, cos of this.'

'*No!*'

Ed flung himself across the room at her.

'Get off her, Ed.' Mark pulled him away from his sister. 'Tell me what?'

'*If you tell him, I will never forgive you.*'

Florrie smirked. 'Ed's disabled the NannyOnline system. That's why that dodgy site came up and loads of other stuff as well.'

'You what? But how? You can't have.'

'Someone taught me at school,' mumbled Ed. 'Wasn't my fault.'

'Hang on, let me get this right. You can disable a filter?'

'Only if you know the password,' piped up Florrie. 'It's on your noticeboard along with all that other stuff, like your pin numbers.'

What would Hilary do in a situation like this? What should *any* parent do? He felt so bloody powerless. Mums@Home was right. He knew nothing about women and nothing about kids. 'Ed. Go to your room. No television or MSN for a week – no, a month.'

'Make me.' Ed glued his feet to the floor as Mark tried to frog-march him down the corridor.

'I bloody will if I have to.' Mark tried to lift his son up but Ed's feet were flailing against his body. 'Stop it, you're hurting me – Ed, I said *stop it*.'

'*Cooeee*, everyone. Only *meeee*!'

'Not now.' Mark gritted his teeth, opened Ed's bedroom door with his knee and threw his son on to the floor. 'That's it, Ed. You're in serious trouble now.'

'You've hurt me.'

'*Cooeee!*'

'Granny!'

Florrie was already downstairs.

'I want to see her.' Ed pushed past him roughly. 'Wait till I tell her what you've been doing.'

Slowly, Mark followed him down the stairs.

'Hi, Daphne. How was your trip?'

His mother-in-law held out her arms and Mark braced himself for the inevitable clasp to her bosom. She released him with an enormous beam, having grazed his cheek on her large onyx earrings. 'Fantastic, Mark. Absolutely fantastic. You really *must* go to the Galapagos Islands some time. It's amazing. You haven't lived until you've been.'

Daphne always said the same about whichever exotic place she'd visited. Mark still couldn't work out how she afforded the trips. She'd been left in a reasonably comfortable position when Hilary's father had died, but not that comfortable. Still, she certainly saved money in other ways, usually by eating with them. No, that wasn't fair. She'd been very helpful since Hilary had left and he'd had to persuade her to take the Galapagos trip, which had been booked months before. He just wished she didn't talk so much or come in and out of his house when she felt like it.

'Now, I've brought you some little things.'

'Oooh!' Florrie fell on the pair of cheap star-shaped clip-on earrings. 'Thanks, Gran. But maybe I ought to give them to Ed.'

'What do you mean, dear?'

Ed kicked her. 'Shut up, Florrie.'

'Ow. Now I *will* tell her. I caught Ed wearing one of Mum's jumpers.'

'Oh dear.' Daphne shot Mark a worried look. 'Now, Ed, what did you want to do a silly thing like that for?'

'Piss off.' Ed flew upstairs, slamming the door behind him.

'I'll explain later.' Mark put the kettle on. 'Sit down and I'll make a cup of tea.'

'Have you got any herbal? No? Just hot water, then. I met this wonderful couple on the plane who make their own herbal drinks and you wouldn't believe the benefits. It can *revolutionise* your colon. But tell me.' She dropped her voice. 'How's Hilary?'

He shut the door. 'The same.'

Daphne sighed. 'I knew I shouldn't have left you.'

'It wouldn't have made any difference.'

She kicked off her shoes and put her feet on a chair. 'Sorry, darling, but you need to let the air circulate. Did I mention that this couple were qualified podiatrists as well? Absolutely *fascinating*! I'm going to see if there's a course on it.'

'Really?' Mark tried to express polite interest. Daphne was always finding something *absolutely fascinating* and then, within a few months, finding something else equally fascinating instead. Before she went away, she had been advocating a painting-for-beginners class.

'Now, what's this about Ed wearing Hilary's clothes?'

Mark groaned. 'It was a jumper and he was smelling it because it reminded him of her.'

Daphne's eyes filled with tears. 'Oh dear. Poor child.'

Mark patted her shoulder. 'I know. The kids miss her and, to be honest, Daphne, I think we should tell them the truth.'

'No, absolutely no. We promised, remember?'

'Promised what, Gran?'

Mark stiffened. How long had Florrie been standing outside the door before she'd flung it open?

'Hello, darling.' Daphne beamed. 'Oh dear, I've knocked over my hot water. Sweetie, would you get me a cloth?'

'Promised what?' repeated Florrie, sullenly. She fetched the J-cloth from the sink and carried it, dripping, to her grandmother. She began to sob. 'You were talking about Mum, weren't you? She's left home, hasn't she? That's what happened to a girl at school. Her dad went and they told her he was working in Dubai.'

'No, darling, no.' Daphne gathered Florrie to her. She sat like an overgrown doll on her grandmother's lap, her head resting against the older woman's crinkled cheeks, tanned from the sun. 'I promise you on my absolute honour that Mummy would never leave you. Would she, Mark?'

'Of course she wouldn't, poppet.' Clumsily, he put his hand on hers. But she pulled away. Hurt, Mark recalled how when she was little he could always pull her on to his knee and make it better.

'We must be proud of her,' Daphne added. 'She's a very clever woman, your mum. And she'll be home by Christmas. I promise. Isn't that right, Mark?'

He nodded. 'Look, I need to check my emails. There's a bit of a work crisis on.'

'That's all right. We girls need a bit of time together, don't we, darling?'

Florrie, head still buried on Daphne's shoulder, nodded.

It was such a relief to escape to his study, away from all the lies and tension. 'It's so difficult being an intelligent parent.' That was what Hilary used to say after one of Ed's tantrums or Florrie's rudeness. He hadn't understood: he'd been confused by the edgy woman who burst into tears at the slightest provocation and was so different from the Hilary he had married. It had got worse when she'd been promoted and began working even longer hours, relying on a string of first nannies and then au pairs to hold the fort.

YOUR INBOX IS FULL.

Mark groaned. Now, on top of everything else, he needed to delete some messages for new ones to come through.

Here they came, tumbling on to his screen; a mass of tirades from clients, possible editorial from a couple of journalists and a load of other stuff that was as important to him as those pamphlets that came with the Sunday papers.

It was also the ultimate excuse to put off proper work, thought Mark as his fingers began to fly across the keyboard.

From Mimi to Part Time Mum: Thanks for the kicking advice. Ed's still doing it and Florrie – my daughter – now has bruises on both legs. I'll have to tell their holiday club or else I'll be had up by Social Services. I'd like to tell their dad but he's still away. I'm not sure I'm really cut out for this working-from-home business. I used to work in Central London, but since my husband started working away I set up on my own at home so, in theory, I could look after the kids. My mother-in-law helps but she makes me feel inadequate because she's always giving me advice and barging in without knocking. Don't know how you manage to get to an office *and* have three kids. Am enjoying Mums@Home – it's a break from all my work emails.

From Part Time Mum to Mimi: Didn't realise you work from home. So you're really part-time like me. The office is bliss, actually. Sometimes it's a huge relief to get away from them. Sympathise about the mother-in-law. Mine is safely tucked away in Scotland. My husband doesn't work abroad but he might as well. He's got the kind of job that means he's not usually home until really late. I joke that during the week I'm a single mother.

That was quick. For a minute, he felt tempted to reply again – even tell her about Hilary. No, she'd think he was a nutter to pretend he was a woman. And there were already a few weirdos in their group, including that outspoken 'Expectent' Mum. But what Part Time Mum had said about getting out of the house made sense. It did help. And, frankly, he was looking forward to that meeting with Zelda someone from *Beautiful You* magazine next week, which would hopefully result in some editorial. Maybe that would appease EFT – a client he couldn't afford to lose.

'Dad, there's nothing to do.'

Oh, for God's sake. In his day, kids had amused themselves. 'Well, can't you read or play a game?'

Florrie eyed the computer. 'We want to go online.'

This was his fault for not doing enough with them. He had failed to stimulate their imagination. 'Why don't we do a museum?' he suggested. 'Or even go camping for the weekend?'

Both children looked horrified. 'Get a life, Dad,' said Florrie. 'That's really sad.'

Was it?

'When I was your age, I used to write stories,' he said, remembering.

'I'll write to Mum,' said Ed, suddenly.

Florrie shrugged. 'OK. So will I. Although I think it's weird she hasn't got an email address yet.'

'I told you. They're still sorting one out.' He handed them some writing-paper. 'When you've finished, I'll post them for you.'

There was only one problem, he reminded himself, as he left them to it.

Hilary never wrote back.

16

Five minutes until they were due back, thought Susan, nervously, checking the lounge clock with her watch to make sure she was right. Last weekend when Josh and Steff had taken Tabitha for that first walk they'd returned exactly when they'd promised. It had surprised her because Josh had never been punctual in the past and she would have bet he'd be late this time.

But there they were, rounding the corner, Josh pushing and Steff walking alongside, laughing. They looked, thought Susan, with a blinding stab of pain, like a normal happy family on a Sunday-evening walk, despite the wheelchair. It was all she could do not to bound up, like some pathetic puppy, to meet them.

'Was she all right?'

Steff beamed, holding Josh's hand. 'We had a great time, didn't we, Tabs?'

Suddenly Susan realised she'd done something that she'd always hated other people doing: she'd asked someone else about her daughter, not Tabitha. Furious with herself, Susan crouched so she could look into her daughter's eyes. 'Did you enjoy it, love?'

Josh bent down and gently smoothed back his daughter's hair. 'She can say quite a bit, now, can't you, Tabs? You've really come on.'

'Yes, well, it's been a while,' said Susan, drily. 'Don't assume you can catch up that fast in two visits.'

Josh looked uncomfortable. 'I know, but that's going to change now we'll be living nearer.'

She didn't need reminding. 'Come on, Tabs, let get you in.'

Steff opened the front door wider. 'I'll help you.'

'No, thank you. We can manage fine on our own.'

That was better. Firm voice. Look her in the eyes. Show her who was mother. If she thought she could come running in to play happy families, she was sadly mistaken.

Steff and Josh made themselves comfortable on the sofa. She felt like a teenage gooseberry. Steff flushed. 'I'd offer to make a cup of tea but I don't want to interfere.'

Nice to see she was getting the message.

'You've done a great job with Tabitha, Susan,' said Josh. 'Really. Steff's awfully impressed.'

'Glad to hear it.'

'No, don't take it the wrong way.' Steff stood up and, for a ghastly minute, Susan thought she was going to take her hand. 'I know how difficult it is. I've worked on wards with people in Tabitha's situation.'

'Wards?' Susan laughed hoarsely. 'Not quite the same as living the life, is it?' She looked down at Tabitha, who was already engrossed in the new jigsaw Josh had brought, reminding herself silently to be careful about what she said.

'No,' said Steff, slowly. 'But I still learned a lot. Hope you don't mind me asking, but how much physio does Tabs get a week?'

'A week? I don't know what it's like at Stoke Mandeville, or wherever it was you were, but round here we're lucky to get one session a month. And I told you the centre's closing because of cuts. Now, if you don't mind, I'm going to put the kettle on.'

'One physio session a month?' Steff had trailed behind her, out to the kitchen. 'That's awful. No wonder . . . I mean, Tabs can walk a bit, can't she?'

'Yes. As long as someone's there to catch her and there's a handrail.'

'And she's great at using her hands to do jigsaws.'

'It helps make them stronger.'

'Exactly.' Steff's blonde fringe was bobbing up and down. 'So if she had more physio, she could make even more progress.'

Susan slammed down the teapot. 'Look, Steff, I appreciate your concern. And I can also understand that because you're with Josh now, you want to do everything you can for his daughter. But, believe me, I've argued my head off for more physio and they won't bloody give it to me. I've learned the exercises myself and I do some of them with her as well as I can but I'm not a nurse and—'

'Precisely,' said Steff, quietly. 'But I am.'

She'd walked into that one, Susan thought.

'And I could give her physio. I could treat her right here, if you like. Or at Josh's place if she came to stay with us for a weekend.'

'Oh, no. Oh, no. Don't start thinking you're taking her away from me.' Susan was shaking. 'You can't do that.' She sank down on to the kitchen stool. 'You can't.'

'Steff!' Josh was standing in the doorway, frowning. 'I asked you not to mention that to Susan yet.'

'Why not? She's her mother. She's entitled to know what we hope for. And I want us to be friends. I really do, Sue. I want us to be good friends.'

Susan couldn't stop the tears. 'You can't have Tabitha. I'll take legal proceedings.'

Josh laughed. 'Go ahead. We've been through that one before and you know perfectly well what happened. You got custody but I had full visiting rights.'

Susan raised her swollen face. 'Which you failed to take up.'

'A mistake I'm rectifying now.'

'Stop, please!' Steff put her arm round Susan. 'Josh, you can see she's upset, and it's understandable. Sue, I just want you to think about it. Every now and then – say, once a month – we'd love to have Tabitha for a day or, even better, a weekend. It would also give you a break.'

'I don't need a break,' said Susan, sullenly.

'Don't you, love?' Steff's eyes moistened understandingly. 'I think that if I were you, I'd need one. Especially if you don't succeed in saving the centre. Just give it some thought, will you, Sue? That's all we're asking.'

17

TIP FROM FRAN 3
If your kid throws a wobbly in the supermarket, say in a loud voice, 'Stop or I'll tell your mother when we get home.' Then no one will blame you for the brat.

How bad was that? Lisa was so cross she couldn't get it out of her head even though she'd already posted a disapproving message.

If a kid has a tantrum in the supermarket, it's the parents fault for not bringing them up rite. Its evil to say they belong to someone else.

Fran 3 would know that if she was standing in the maternity wing, like Lisa was right now, on a sunny Monday morning. Careful. Wait for the automatic doors to open and close three times for luck, then go in.

Past the League of Friends shop. First right. Second left. She was getting to know the layout now. The blue footprints on the lino to the right went to A and E, the red footprints up the stairs to Gynaecology, and the yellow footprints to the left to Maternity.

If she placed her feet very carefully on the yellow footprints, she'd be safe, like you were if you didn't tread on the cracks in the pavement.

'Excuse me.'

Lisa found herself almost chest to chest with a short, ginger-haired man in a white coat. The shock of recognition was so acute that it almost knocked her over.

'I'm so sorry,' he said, sidestepping round her.

All the words, all the things she had told herself she would tell him if she saw him again, flew out of her head. Instead she walked on as fast as she could, forgetting for once to mould her feet to the yellow footprints. Rounding the corner, she couldn't stop herself looking back. At the same split second, the ginger doctor did the same and Lisa's heart pounded. Did he remember her? Fat chance. He must have seen thousands of women since then.

'Nature's way,' he had said, after the miscarriage. 'Miscarriage is often nature's way when something isn't quite right.' But how did he know? And, anyway, she wouldn't care if there *was* something wrong with her baby. She just wanted someone to love, someone who would love her back.

The antenatal clinic was packed. Lisa shifted awkwardly on the plastic seat, which was making her bum ache.

'Makes you feel like a stuffed marrow, doesn't it, in this heat?' said the woman next to her. She had a toddler on her knee, sucking purple juice from a bottle.

Lisa eyed the drink suspiciously. 'Is that sugar-free?'

The woman's face hardened. 'Why?'

'There's been a big scare about it. Didn't you know? All over the Internet, it is. About toddlers ruining their teeth on juice. Bottles are the worst. Isn't she big enough for a trainer mug yet?'

'It's none of your bleeding business. What are you – a social worker? I don't hold with them, I tell you.'

'I'm just saying you ought to be careful with bottles and juice that's not sugar-free.'

'Julie Evans!' A midwife came out to the front of the clinic, clipboard in hand. The woman flashed Lisa a dirty look, hoisted her toddler on to her hip and waddled off, muttering about busybodies. Lisa helped herself to *Baby Beautiful* magazine and a white plastic cone of water from the machine. Water was so good for you. Earth Mother had been telling her that. Her baby would never drink sugary muck like that other poor kid.

Lisa read for nearly half an hour while the room thinned out. Everyone else seemed to have been seen except her and another girl who took Bottle Woman's place. This girl wasn't reading. Lisa could tell she was ready to chat, which suited her. She'd finished the magazine and didn't fancy anything else in the pile.

'How long have you got?' asked the girl.

She had a small but unmistakable bump under some rather nice maternity jeans. Lisa eyed them enviously, recognising them from a well-known chain store. 'Not sure, really. My dates are a bit weird.'

'Going to give you another scan, are they? They had to do that to me and all.' She leaned towards her and Lisa recoiled. The girl reeked of cigarette smoke. 'I hate hospitals, tell you the truth.'

'Me too.' Lisa moved away a bit in case the smell of the fags on the girl's clothes went down her lungs and into Rose. 'But this one's better than the old one.'

'Thought they'd pulled it down years ago.'

'They did. I was there when I was a kid.'

'Why?'

'I had a burst appendix. Really ill, I was.'

The girl frowned. 'That's nasty.'

'Yeah. And the scarring blocked one of my tubes.'

'Blimey. That happened to a friend of mine. You're lucky to get pregnant, then. She's having IVF.'

'She must be loaded.'

'Excuse me, dear.'

Lisa looked up at the midwife who was hovering with her clipboard.

'You've been here for a while. Did you give your name at the desk?'

'Yes.'

'Mind giving it me again, duck?'

'Lisa. Lisa Smith.'

'Lisa . . . Lisa. We don't appear to have you down, dear. Are you sure you've got the right day?'

Lisa delved into her carrier-bag and brought out a scrap of paper. 'I wrote it on this cos I left my hospital card somewhere. Oh, bugger. It's for next week. Sorry.'

The midwife patted her shoulder sympathetically. 'Poor you. And you've had such a long wait, haven't you?'

'That's what pregnancy does to you,' said the girl. 'Forget things all the time, I do.'

'I could ask Doctor if she'd see you, if you like,' said the midwife. 'Just let me check your details on the screen.'

'Don't bother.' Lisa heaved herself up. 'I need to get back so I'll ring when I'm home.'

'Sure? I'm sorry you've wasted your time, dear.'

Lisa shrugged. 'It's my day off. Didn't have much to do anyway.'

Follow the yellow footprints back out of the clinic. Right foot on the right print, left on the left. Then everything will be all right. Straight ahead.

'Can I help you?'

When she stood at the desk like this, she had a really good view down the corridor. Some curtains were open and she could see mothers sitting up in bed in large nighties. Some were reading magazines but others had their babies on their laps or were feeding them.

All the parenting sites said it was best to breastfeed. But if she couldn't, she had enough bottles ready.

'I'm here to see a friend. Lisa Smith.'

A woman trundled past in slippers and a dressing-gown, holding a tiny scrap in pink. Lisa's eyes went with them. She could smell its face, nuzzle its tiny neck, pretend she was buttoning up its tiny sleepsuit.

'Lisa Smith?'

The nurse frowned as though she'd already detected the false name. She was young. Hard-looking. 'We don't have anyone of that name here, but I only came on this morning. I could ask someone else if she'd been discharged.'

'No.' The baby and her mother had gone behind a curtain now. She'd seemed like a good mother. Not like Lisa's mum. If she'd listened to Lisa when she'd complained about her stomach hurting her appendix might not have burst. And she'd have had two tubes to get pregnant with, instead of one. Still, like it said on that American spirit-and-destiny site, if you didn't forgive, it could be really bad for your health and, if you were pregnant, you could pass on bad vibes to the baby. That was why she still emailed her mum.

'No, it's all right, thanks. I'll ring her.'

Back. Quickly. Down the steps and out before she was stopped. No time to check the footprints.

'Lisa!'

A tall stringy youth with a fag in his fingers was squinting at her. 'Fancy seeing you!'

There was a girl next to him. A very young girl in a short skirt and a T-shirt. A terrible cold realisation swept over her.

'Kelly, what the fuck are you doing here?'

Kelly smiled nastily, tucking her hand into Kevin's. 'We've just been for our six-week check-up, haven't we, Kev?'

Lisa could feel her throat tightening with panic. 'That's yours?' She jerked her head at the sling round Kevin's neck. It was exactly the kind she'd ordered on the Net last week. Inside, she could just about make out a tiny puckered face, screwed up in sleep.

Kevin nodded.

'What's that to you?' demanded Kelly.

Lisa stared at Kevin. 'But you didn't want kids. You said. And you, Kelly, how could you? He was mine!'

'Hey, girls!'

'Maybe he wanted my kid, not yours,' said Kelly, taking Kevin's arm.

He laughed, revealing stained teeth. 'Yeah, maybe I did.'

Lisa pushed past them, unable to breathe.

'Oy! Be careful. We've got a baby here, you know.'

Run. Run across the car park to the bus stop. Gasp for breath. Choke back the tears.

When she'd lost Hayley, Kevin had been so cruel. 'Didn't want it anyway,' he'd said. But in a funny way it had helped at the time. She'd told herself that if Kevin hadn't wanted kids, that child wouldn't have had a proper father. But now he'd changed his mind and that bitch in the short skirt had succeeded where she hadn't.

Lisa sank on to the broken blue plastic seat at the bus stop and leaned forward, arms round her neck to shut out the world.

'You all right, love?' asked someone walking by.

She shook her head as the sobs poured out of her. Her entire body shook. God knows what this was doing to Rose inside. The voice had sounded kind. Soft. Motherly. She willed it to speak again. But when she lifted her head, whoever it was had gone. Even worse, the bus, which she'd dimly heard arriving through her sobs, was disappearing round the corner.

SEPTEMBER

JUST THREE MONTHS, EVERYONE, UNTIL THAT WISH COMES TRUE!

Hi mum. Do u get my emails? I think you must becuase they dont come back. There's sumthing I want to no. You used to say I was a dificult kid. Did you ever pretend I wosnt yours?

Hi, scumface. I'm going to tell everyone at the holiday club that it was you who ripped the snooker-table cover unless you give me five quid. And don't think of showing this to your dad cos if you do, a lot worse will happen to you.

www.yummydiets.co.uk. Try our delicious low-fat lasagne without pasta.

Dear Annabel,
We haven't heard from you for ages and we're getting worried. I'm hoping you'll pick this up next time you check your emails. Please ring URGENTLY.
Love Mum

Mums@Home.co.uk
JOIN OUR ONLINE DISCUSSIONS ON
How to get a girl – or boy!
Husbands v. children. Is it wrong to put the kids first?
Are your kids addicted to the computer? A new report says parents are being driven to distraction by computer-obsessed kids.
TIP FROM FRAZZLED MUM
Set the kitchen clock five minutes fast. Stops you being so late.
CHUCKLE CORNER FROM BIG MUM
Why do men become smarter during sex? Because they're plugged into a genius!
THOUGHT TO KEEP YOU SANE FROM PUSHY PRINCESS
Behind every successful woman is herself.

18

If she didn't find a case history for the affair piece soon, she'd have to tell Karen, who'd already extended the deadline reluctantly to the following month's issue. It wasn't good, bearing in mind the staff cuts that had been sweeping the company during the last year.

'Caroline Crawford speaking.'

'Hello, darling.'

It was so confusing, the way Roger oscillated between cool and effusive. Was that because he didn't know how he felt?

'Hi.'

'Any news from Annabel?'

'No.'

'Don't worry. She's too busy to call, that's all. Listen, David rang to see if we're going on Friday. What do you want to do?'

Across the office, Caroline could see Karen coming towards her desk. 'I thought we weren't going.'

He sounded petulant. 'It would give us some time together.'

Automatically, she thought of the current heated discussion on Mums@Home: 'Husbands v. children. Is it wrong to put the kids first?'

Karen was getting nearer and Caroline tried to think fast. David had been a mutual university friend and it was his forty-fifth. They ought to go, but nowadays anything that meant putting on a We're-a-couple face seemed so false.

'I've found a room.' He named a nice hotel they had stayed at once before. 'And Ben's old enough to look after Georgie.'

'OK.'

'You don't sound very enthusiastic.'

'I'm busy. That's all. Must go.'

'Caroline.' Karen was standing over her, disapproval radiating from her immaculately made-up eyes. Personal phone calls were only allowed when there wasn't an office crisis. 'What's the latest on the affair piece?'

Caroline glanced at her notepad as though it might provide sudden inspiration. 'Not good, I'm afraid. I've contacted all my leads and I can't find anyone who'll talk, even anonymously. I was just going to email you about it.'

Karen's eyes narrowed. 'Pity. Maybe I'd better put a couple of freelancers on to it to see if they can help.'

Caroline felt raw. The magazine relied on a regular core of freelancers, mainly to write their own features. If they were asked to help find case histories for someone else's, it was an admission of defeat on the original writer's part. 'I'll keep trying too.'

Karen was frowning. 'If nothing comes up by Tuesday, we'll have to reschedule. Maybe bring that educational-toys piece forward. How's that going?'

'Really well.' When had she learned to lie so convincingly? Before or after Roger?

'Good.' Karen nodded, unsmiling. 'Email me at the end of the day to let me know how you're getting on.'

Caroline watched Karen's elegant back (definitely Louis Feraud today) weave away from her. Surely someone somewhere could help.

Mums@Home. Her fingers seemed to home in automatically. In the last few weeks it had almost become a habit. A relaxation where she could be herself and not a journalist. Caroline scanned the Message Board. So 'Expectent' Mum had lost a baby. Maybe that explained her terse attitude to poor old Mimi about kicking. Caroline had never had a miscarriage but her sister had, in Australia, and she'd interviewed countless women for infertility pieces over the years. What else had happened? Caroline felt cold as she read Rainbow's post. That was exactly as she'd feared:

losing the children at weekends to the ex and his wife was precisely why she had fought for her marriage.

Is it wrong to put the kids first?

No. It was natural. From the minute you held your first baby
in your arms, you realised you could never again put yourself or
anyone else first.

Caroline logged off. A night at a hotel? Yes. And this time she'd
try really hard to forget. She had to.

'Why isn't Georgie in bed?'

'Chill out, Mum, she's fine. We're watching a film. It's Friday
night, for God's sake.'

Caroline cradled the phone between ear and shoulder while she
applied brown kohl pencil to her inner eyelids in the hotel mirror.
'What kind of film?'

'*Mum*, you're pissing me off. Go and have a good time with
Dad. Speak in the morning.'

Ben had gone. Whatever happened to respect? If she'd talked
to her parents like that, she'd have lost her pocket money or been
grounded.

'I've said it before and I'll say it again. You're too soft on him.'
Roger was fiddling with his bow-tie in front of the hotel mirror.

Caroline turned her back. It was easier to argue her case to a
wall than to her husband's face. 'He won't listen to me.'

It was an all too familiar patter, which she had promised herself to avoid. It had been so much effort to get away – sorting
out meals *and* impressing on Ben the importance of locking up
at night – that it was a waste to spoil the weekend with yet another
argument.

'Can you zip up my dress?'

She felt his fingers on her skin. Cold. Disinterested. Yet the
weekend had been *his* idea.

'That's pretty. Is it new?'

'No. I bought it ages ago.'

Three years ago. A whole year before she'd found out. She

measured everything that way. The family photograph that she had naïvely persuaded everyone to sit for when, with hindsight, Roger had been seeing that woman for at least three months. The sofa they had chosen together when, according to her calculations, he must have been seeing *her* for six months.

'We're going to be late.' Roger glanced at her. 'You look nice.'

Smile. Children need parents. She needed her husband. 'Thanks. So do you.'

The band was amazing. All those songs from the seventies and eighties she'd thought she'd forgotten but to which her feet were urgently tapping in hungry nostalgia. All around her were friends she hadn't seen for years, some with their original partners, some not. She'd hugged and kissed so many that it was almost as though she was back at Oxford. Only one thing was wrong.

Roger.

Somehow all this seemed such a sham and she hoped he wouldn't suggest dancing: such close contact seemed even more of a pretence.

'Hi, you made it!' Their host, beaming with excitement, came up to them at the bar. 'Sorry, so many people here that I must have missed you arriving. Caro, you look gorgeous. Roger, you're a lucky bugger. How long have you guys been married now? Twenty years?'

'Twenty-two,' said Caroline, evenly.

'Not long till your silver. God, some people have all the luck.'

'How's Marie?'

'You mean Tanya,' said Roger, quickly.

Caroline flushed. 'Sorry, Roger didn't tell me.'

'I did, actually.'

David drained his glass. 'Tanya's great. Come over here and meet her. Another drink first? No? Great, Roger. That's the spirit!'

David's new girlfriend was incredibly tall, confident and curvy without being plump. 'I wish you'd told me about Marie,' Caroline hissed into her husband's ear, when Tanya was busily engaged in nuzzling David's.

'I did.'

'You didn't. What happened? I liked her.'

'Come on, you guys!' David broke away from Tanya. 'Let's dance!'

'What?' Roger cupped his hand to his ear. 'I can't hear you.'

Of course he could, thought Caroline. The music was loud but she could hear him.

'I said, let's dance!' David yelled.

Had Roger ever danced with *her*? wondered Caroline as, reluctantly, she allowed herself to be led out on to the dance floor. Almost as soon as they got there, the music quietened. A quiet one. Everyone else was drawing towards each other. Roger took a hesitant step in her direction, placing his hands on her bare shoulders.

'Do you mind if we sit down instead?' she said quickly. 'My headache's come back.'

'Fine.'

She shuddered at the coldness in his voice and his failure to express sympathy about her headache, even though he probably guessed it was non-existent. Wordlessly, she followed him across the floor to some chairs outside the marquee. Across the lawn, she could just make out the outline of Magdalen College where once, in another life, she and Roger had smooched at a memorable summer ball with their lives stretched out before them.

'Feel better now?'

'Sort of.'

Roger yawned. 'I don't want to stay late. Do you?'

'No.'

'There you are! I've been looking for you two everywhere.'

Jeff was beaming down at them with a pretty, petite blonde on his arm. 'This is Serena. Serena, Roger and Caroline.'

'Hi.' The girl, who couldn't have been more than twenty-five, simpered at them. 'We got here late because we stopped off for a rest.' She giggled and Jeff looked away, embarrassed.

'We were just going, actually. Caroline's got a headache.'

'Poor you.' Jeff fumbled in his jacket pocket. 'Want something for it? I never go anywhere without these.'

'Thanks.'

'Hang on and I'll get you some water to have with them.'

'I'll come too.' Caroline followed Jeff to the bar, leaving Roger with the blonde.

'How's it going?' he asked, putting his arm round her lightly as he shepherded her through the crowd.

'Not great.'

'You look gorgeous.'

'Thanks.' She looked over her shoulder meaningfully at his date. 'So does she.'

Jeff shrugged. 'Sometimes I wonder if I'll ever find the right person or if I really know who I'm searching for.'

'You will when you see her,' said Caroline, reassuringly.

'You're probably right.' He handed her the water. 'Have a nice evening, Caro. And good luck. A weekend away might be just what you two need.'

There was no getting out of it. A vast double bed in a gorgeous bedroom with mahogany headboard and crisp cotton sheets. A weekend away without the children. It had been nearly two months since the last time they'd been intimate. If they didn't do it tonight, it was a clear admission he didn't want her. Or she him.

He was already in bed when she slid in after the bath. 'Do you feel too tired?'

Yes.

'No.'

He moved towards her and she wriggled out of her nightdress.

'You're tight,' he mumbled.

Always her fault. *Think*. Harrison Ford. That actor on television. Harrison *and* that actor on television. That was better. She gasped, her breath quickening. Almost immediately, it was over, like a little wave, now out of sight. Always the same, even when she and Roger had first got together. Never the huge ocean you read about. Was it her? Or them?

He was pumping now. If he couldn't come, it meant she didn't turn him on. The corner of his mouth was turned up with concentration, the way it always was when they made love. What could she do to hurry him on? What had the other woman done?

Roger gasped. He was there. Thank God for that. A few minutes later she washed him away angrily in the cream en-suite. 'Think of the kids,' Jeff had said. And he was right. They had to come first even if that meant keeping up this sham of a marriage.

She heard the ring when she was in the deepest part of her sleep. Fumbling in the dark for her usual lamp at home, she remembered she wasn't in her own bed. Georgie. Something had happened. Or Ben. Or both.

'Roger! Phone!'

He was never good at getting up in the night.

Her fingers finally closed round her mobile next to the bed.

'Hello?'

'Mum?'

Annabel's voice was thin and distant.

'*Annabel!* Are you all right?'

Roger turned over, groaning. 'What a time to ring!'

'Shush. Where are you, darling?'

'Still in Thailand. It's so brill that we stayed on a bit longer. We're flying out to Darwin next week.'

Relief gave way to irritation.

'Why didn't you ring earlier? We were so worried. And it's the middle of the night here.'

'Is it? Sorry, I should have worked that out. Still, at least I've got you. I've lost my phone and I had to queue for *hours* for a pay-phone. Then I rang home and Ben said you were on the mobile. Anyway, I'm having a fantastic time and we've teamed up with some friends we met on the plane. Look, I've got to go because there's this huge queue outside. I'll email you from Australia. Give my love to Dad.'

'Hang on and I'll pass you over. Roger, wake *up*.'

'She's gone,' he said accusingly.

Caroline sank back against the pillows, weak with relief and disappointment that her daughter had hung up so soon. 'There was a queue for the phone. She's lost her mobile.'

'Not again. We'll have to cancel the contract or someone could be running up a huge bill somewhere. Well, at least she's rung. See? I told you she'd be OK.'

'Yes.' Caroline turned over, feeling like a criticised child. 'You did.'

Annabel was safe. Now all Caroline had to do was ensure she had a family to come back to when she finally returned.

19

It was Saturday. In a way Mark was relieved that the kids hadn't shown an interest in camping (wet canvas wasn't his thing either), but he was also concerned. Didn't kids want to *do* anything any more? 'Don't think I'm going to let you two sit here all weekend, slobbing out.'

Ed stretched on the floor, burying his head under a cushion the way he always did when they had this kind of argument. 'What else is there to do?'

'Lots of things.' Mark thought frantically. 'There's a dinosaur exhibition at the fire station or that kite-flying competition in the park.'

'Thrills and spills,' said Florrie, scathingly. 'It's boring here, Dad. I wish we were back in London.'

'Well, we're not.'

He hadn't meant to be harsh. Maybe it was because he felt the same. If it wasn't for Hilary, they could be living a normal life like any other family . . .

'Come on.' He switched off the television and slipped the remote into his pocket.

Ed lunged at him. 'Give it back.'

'No way. We're going shopping. And do you know what's top of my list?'

'What?' asked Florrie, sullenly.

'A new filter for the computer,' said Mark. 'One that neither of you can disable.'

After shopping, he suggested McDonald's. 'Great,' said Florrie, happily. 'Mum never lets us have fizzy drinks.'

'She doesn't?' He hadn't known. Well, too bad. The noise inside and the smell of chips were comforting. The kids seemed happy stuffing themselves and it gave him a bit of peace and quiet. No wonder these places were crammed with parents.

He had time to reflect, too. There was still so much to do. He hadn't done the weekly wash – Ed had worn the same boxers two days running – and he needed to do a supermarket shop. Then there was that stuff for Clive . . .

SHIT.

'What's wrong, Dad?'

He should have rung Clive at seven fifteen on Saturday morning.

He fished in his pocket for his mobile. Bloody hell, *no*. It was flashing 'Battery Low'. He dialled Clive's number. Just as it picked up, the phone went dead. 'We've got to get back.'

'Why?'

'I've forgotten to call someone.'

'Ring them from your mobile.'

'The battery's gone. Here, let me use yours.'

Ed looked shifty. 'I've left it at home.'

'Florrie?'

She glanced at Ed. 'Me too.'

'Right.' Mark leaped to his feet. 'I'll find a pay-phone.'

Didn't anyone use pay-phones any more? When he'd located one, it only took phone cards, not coins. Cursing, Mark decided it would be easier to go home and make the call.

The traffic, of course, was horrendous and it didn't help that it had started to drizzle, which made everything even slower. His tension was rubbing off on the children too. 'Ed, if you upset Florrie one more time, I'll write to the head.' He screeched into the driveway, just missing the wooden post on the left.

'I'm starving, Dad. I want some toast.'

'But we've just eaten! And I haven't got any bread in the freezer.' Mark leaped out of the car. 'I'll go shopping in a minute. Just let me check my emails and make that call.'

He ran upstairs. There it was. Just as he'd feared. A demand in his inbox from Clive for an update. Hastily, he typed an excuse, claiming problems with his server, and promising to ring on Monday.

The phone. *The phone!* Maybe it was Clive, ringing back.

'I'll get it, Florrie.'

Too late.

'*Mum!*' Florrie's face broke into a broad grin and Mark's chest tightened.

Hilary? *Hilary?*

'I want to speak to her.' Ed yanked the phone away.

'Give it back. Ow!'

'Ed, stop *kicking* her. Hilary, are you still there? Hi, how are you?'

'How do you think I am?'

He could barely hear her or concentrate, with Florrie tugging at his sleeve. 'I want to speak to Mum. Give her to me.'

'Mum? . . . Yeah, we're OK. Have you been up the Empire State Building yet? . . . Why not? It's meant to be really cool . . . Yeah, I will.'

Florrie put the phone down. 'She had to go. What's the point of being in New York if you don't see the Empire State Building?'

'She sounded very quiet,' said Ed. 'Like she didn't want to talk to us.'

'Of course she did.' Mark floundered for something to say. 'She was probably tired.'

'She was tired before she went,' said Ed, slowly. 'She said she was tired of us too.'

'She didn't mean it. Parents often say things they don't mean. She loves both of you, you know that. Now, what's this? Great!'

Triumphantly Mark held up a packet of frozen bread that had worked its way to the back of the freezer. 'We can have that toast after all.'

'I'm not hungry now,' said Florrie, going out of the kitchen.

'Nor me.'

Mark listened to them trundling up the stairs. For God's sake, Hilary, if you can't be bothered to talk when you ring, don't ring at all.

20

It was the same now every day, thanks to Josh's re-entry into their lives, with the glamorous and impossibly slim Steff. As soon as she was dressed and sitting in the lounge, Tabitha would stare wistfully out of the window.

'Daddad, Daddad.'

'He's not coming today, love. He's at work. Now, let's get on with that nice jigsaw, shall we?'

But when Tabitha had finished the one her father had given her, she wasn't interested in doing another. When she wasn't looking out of the window, she wheeled herself over to the table where Susan had taped the pieces together to stop them breaking up and stared at the picture. The message was clear. If she couldn't have her father, she would love his present instead.

Even going to the centre didn't help. 'What's up with you, Tabs?' asked Lisa, as she laid the tables for lunch with cutlery that half of them wouldn't use. 'You're not joining in like you usually do.'

'Joining in' was a bright and breezy term for – depending on individual limitations – playing on the computer, staring into space and mouthing group songs.

Susan bit into another stale Bourbon even though she knew she shouldn't. What was the point of the picture on the biscuit tin? Oh, what the hell. 'Her father's made contact again. With the new girlfriend.'

'That's good for her, innit?'

'Depends if he goes off again, which would break her heart,' Susan said thoughtfully. 'He seems to have got more reliable but you don't really know, do you? Now they want to take her out at weekends. Maybe have her to stay.'

'Give you a break, wouldn't it?' Lisa scuffed at the floor with her toe. 'When I was Tabitha's age, my mum wouldn't let me see my dad and we lost touch. I see why she did it, like, but part of me feels resentful, if you know what I mean.'

The biscuit stuck in Susan's throat. 'I do but—'

'Look!' Joy came rushing up. 'Here's the photographer.'

'Photographer?'

'From the local paper. They're doing a piece on us. Didn't they ring you? They got in touch with me and asked if I'd give them an interview.'

Local paper. Of course! She'd forgotten, with all this stuff about Josh.

'Mrs Thomas?'

Susan nodded.

'I'm Bekki Adams from the *Gazette*. We spoke on the phone, didn't we? I wondered how you were getting on with your campaign to save the centre?'

'Campaign?' Joy's mouth fell open.

Hastily Susan swallowed her mouthful of biscuit, which scratched her throat in her effort to get it down unnoticed. 'Well, we've only just started. This is my friend Joy. She's going to help me. We're just beginning to make plans and, of course, we need to run them past the manager.'

Bekki's pencil was poised on her pad. 'Have you got any ideas on how you're going to start? My editor was very keen on running a piece about it.'

'We're going to have a march,' said Joy. 'A wheelchair march. Through the town on Saturday week.'

'Er, that's right. And we're getting flyers printed to put through people's doors,' added Susan.

'We're hoping to see the local MP too.' Joy's earrings trembled with enthusiasm.

Bekki's pencil flew. 'Chas Craven? You've got an appointment with him?'

'Not exactly, but Joy's ringing his office to find out if he'll see us.'

'Great!'

'And we're going to be on the radio too.'

'Right.' Bekki looked around. 'I wonder if I could interview your daughter?'

'Tabitha doesn't talk much,' said Susan. 'That's why she needs help.'

'But she can say a few words,' added Joy. 'Look, here she is, coming up in her chair.'

'Careful. I haven't said too much to her about the centre closing. I don't want to upset her.' Susan knelt in front of her daughter. 'Tabs, this lady wants to talk to you about coming here. She wants to know if you like it.'

Tabitha stared at her stonily.

'Go on,' said Susan, heavily. 'Say something, Tabs. Anything.'

'Daddad, Daddad. Daddad, Daddad.'

'Sounds like "Dad",' said Bekki, brightly. 'Are you a bit of a daddy's girl, then?'

Susan didn't trust herself to speak.

'He doesn't live with them any more,' said Joy, in a loud whisper. 'A lot of families break up with this sort of thing.'

'I'm sorry. Well, I think I've got what I need. Thanks very much. Ah, there's the manager now. I'll just nip over and have a word. Can I check I've got your names spelt correctly? Yes? Good. Oh, and I need to give your ages too if you don't mind and where you live.'

'Thirty-six,' said Susan, quietly. 'Pheasants Way, Grendon Parslow.'

'I'm thirty-two,' said Joy, brightly. 'And I live in the next village, Whitley.'

They watched the girl head off. 'Liar,' said Susan, nudging her friend.

Joy sniffed. 'I could be thirty-two. Everyone says I don't look my age. Anyway, what's this about a campaign?'

'It's something that came to me. Why should we take this lying down?'

'Quite right. Gosh, when you talk like that, Susan, you look all

137

different – kind of lively and sparkly. A march is a really good idea but if we're going to make it work we'd better get everyone together.'

'Come on, then,' said Susan. 'Let's get started.'

By the time they got home Tabitha was exhausted. Susan made her favourite supper of scrambled egg and she had it on her tray in front of *EastEnders*, which she adored.

She might as well sit down and read the local paper, Susan thought; the problem with the computer was that it stopped you reading. Briefly, she scanned the local news. Someone had been mugged. A house had been set on fire, although the occupants had been rescued, thankfully. An unemployed dad had been done for shoplifting. A whole page about kids at the local comp who were going on to uni – in her day it had been 'university' or 'college' – after passing their A levels and other exams that Tabitha would never take.

Susan sighed, running her fingers through her hair and turning to the Sits Vac. Although she'd rather die than admit it, this was one of her favourite sections of the local paper. She could flick through and circle the jobs she fancied, pretending she was a normal mum who was thinking about returning to work.

ESTATE AGENT NEEDS WELL-PRESENTED MATURE WOMAN, TO SHOW CLIENTS ROUND NEW ESTATE HOUSES. OCCASIONAL WEEK-ENDS ONLY.

Susan paused, pen hovering. Occasional weekends? Well-presented? She glanced down at the ladder in her tights. Well, she could be. Josh and Steff's suggestion about having Tabitha had hit a nerve and, yes, it would be awful to let Tabitha go, but might this be her chance to *do* something? On the other hand, was she up to it, after being out of the real world for so long?

Carefully, Susan tore out the advert and put it under the teapot. She might not ring. She probably wouldn't. But she'd keep it. Just in case.

21

From Expectent Mum to Mums@Home: I've heard that the
best way to have a girl is to have sex at least four days before
you ovulate. Thats what I did and Im sure that both the babies
I lost were girls.

Lisa sent the message; it gave her a nice warm feeling to think
she might be helping. It had also helped pass the time. The clock
on the monitor said it was 3.05 a.m. but the noise next door still
hadn't died down. Maybe if she went back to bed she could block
her ears with the pillow.

'Oh! *Oh!* OH!'

Kiki's screams of excitement were so clear she might as well
be on this side of the wall, Lisa thought. She banged on it in
protest, bruising her knuckles, then turned over, pulling the duvet
over her head.

'Oh! *Oh! Oh!*'

Maybe Kiki was making a girl right now. Lisa stroked her tummy
gently to shield it from the noise.

The ohing had stopped now. Instead, Kiki was giggling and
Lisa could hear a deeper voice too. Then the gasps again. What
did they want? An audience?

Irritably, Lisa sat up in bed, clasping her arms round her knees.
She was so awake now that even if the row next door stopped
she knew she wouldn't get to sleep. The neon light on her alarm
radio showed it was now 3.16 a.m. Kevin used to wake up in the
middle of the night for nookie, she recalled wretchedly. And to
think he was a dad now. With Kelly! What a bitch.

Stop, she told herself. Earth Mother had sent her a long message recently, pointing out how bad it was for the baby if you had negative thoughts. Lisa forced herself to think of roses, big, blowsy, pink ones, like she'd seen in the market the other day. Earth Mother said that Barbara Cartland, who wrote romantic novels apparently, had thought beautiful thoughts when she was pregnant. It was lucky, and Lisa was all for that.

Luck was so important in life. That was why you had to do everything the right way – even getting out of bed. She swung her legs over the side. Right slipper first, then the left. Switch on light *after* she'd put on her slippers.

Lisa parted the curtains to look outside. Even though it was so late, there were loads of lights on. Down below, she could see a group of kids walking across the concrete yard and up the stairs leading to her block. They were singing and pushing each other. Lisa braced herself for the thumps on her door.

'Wake up, Lees. We know you want it!'

Don't move. Don't say anything.

'Come on, let us in, love.'

One laughed coarsely. 'Yeah, let us in. We bet you're warm inside!'

More laughter. Lisa sat on the edge of the sofa, not daring to move in case she made a noise. She could hear them moving on now but still her heart was pounding. They didn't mean any harm, she told herself. Some of them were hardly older than her kid brother. Just bored, they were, and who wouldn't be in a place like this?

Lisa stroked her stomach again. When she had her daughter, she would never be bored or lonely. But right now it was only 3.42 a.m. and she had the rest of the night to kill. It didn't help that the computer took so long to start up again.

From Earth Mother to Mums@Home: Thought I'd add my bit about the sadness of miscarriages. I've had four myself but it's usually nature's way.

Not that again. She'd thought more of Earth Mother. She scrolled down the Message Board. Here was a new person called Flipper who hadn't had any miscarriages but was still trying to get pregnant. And Rainbow who – blimey – had had a miscarriage before her daughter: 'You never forget, but a new baby helps to heal the pain.'

That was more like it. But if she didn't have this baby soon, the pain would kill her.

When Lisa woke, the sun was pouring through the window even though the council hadn't cleaned it since last Christmas. Her heart sank at the thought of work. Maybe she could call in sick. Besides, she had so much to do that there really wasn't time to go to the centre today. She needed at least three more sleepsuits, according to the list Earth Mother had sent, and another cot mobile. She fancied a Moses basket too, but it would be difficult to get one out of the shop without being spotted. The last time she'd looked, they'd had security tags on them.

She got dressed, had a slice of toast and headed for the bus stop. For once the bus was on time and an older woman even gave up her seat. 'You need it more than me, love,' she'd said, eyeing Lisa's bump. And Lisa had felt a thrill shoot through her.

It lasted all the way to town and she didn't even mind that the shops were packed. Mind you, it would be just her luck if someone from the centre saw her. Still, she could always say she'd felt better and had to go out to get some shopping.

'This one's pretty!' An oldish woman was holding up a dress for her husband's inspection.

He frowned. 'Too frilly. What about this?'

'I fancy this one,' Lisa couldn't help saying. 'I bought it for my daughter, Hayley, last week and she looks lovely in it, like.'

The woman nodded. 'It is nice.' Her eyes travelled to Lisa's loose dress.

Lisa loved it when strangers did that. 'I haven't got long to go now with the next.'

'Take it easy,' said the man.

Lisa felt a stab of gratitude. 'I will.'

She took the sleepsuits towards the window to check the colour against the light. For a minute there, she'd really believed she'd bought that dress for Hayley and that Hayley was alive and well to wear it. If Kevin hadn't bunked off, it might have been true.

Then she stopped, unable to breathe. Just inside the shop, near the reduced rail, was the most beautiful baby she had ever seen. Its tiny face was soft in sleep, its rosebud mouth slightly twitching. She – it had to be a she – had a pink blanket lightly draped over her.

And she was totally, utterly alone.

Lisa found herself walking up. 'Hello, darling. Aren't you lovely?'

She stroked the baby's cheek. It was softer than anything she had ever felt. It would be so easy to take hold of the pram and . . .

'Sweet, isn't she?'

Lisa swivelled round. It was the woman she'd been talking to a minute ago. 'I couldn't help looking,' she said shakily.

The man nodded, grinning. His fingers, she noticed, were stained with nicotine, like her ex's, but he seemed so much nicer than Kevin. 'We're always being stopped by strangers who say exactly the same.'

Lisa's voice came out low and wobbly: 'Better keep your eyes on her, then. You can't be too careful nowadays.'

'I put her there because it's a bit quieter,' said the woman, confidentially. 'She's such a light sleeper. Is yours?'

'What?'

'Your daughter. Is she a light sleeper?'

'Yes. Very.'

Suddenly she hated these people. Really hated them for having something she wanted so badly that it hurt like a heavy stone in her chest. 'Better go now. I've left Hayley with my mum and she'll be expecting me.'

She'd got as far as Pilot, just three shops down, when she felt the hand on her arm. 'Excuse me, madam, but I'm afraid I have to ask you to come with me.'

Lisa shoved away the short, squat, burly man in security uniform. 'I didn't take it. I didn't! I was just looking.'

'Well, what are you holding, then, madam?' he asked scornfully.

Lisa looked down. In her hands was a pink sleepsuit. Clear as daylight. Why hadn't it had a security tag? People were turning to stare at her. Her fingers and armpits began to sweat. 'It's a mistake. I saw someone I knew outside the shop and I started talking to them. I forgot I was still holding it.'

'This way, please, back to the shop.'

She tried to shake off his hand but he had a really firm grip. 'Leave me alone. I've told you, I wasn't nicking anything, like. It's a mistake.'

'You can explain to the manager. Can't you?'

The security man had his hand firmly on her arm. Lisa's skin crawled with embarrassment as he marched her past the sleepsuit rails and the till, where that couple with the baby were waiting, the pram safely with them now.

'Everything all right, love?' asked the man, frowning.

Lisa couldn't bring herself to look at him.

'She's crying,' says his wife. 'Do you feel poorly, love?'

Lisa choked back a sob. 'They think I nicked this,' she whispered hoarsely. 'But I didn't. I just forgot I had it.'

'This way, miss, please,' the security man said impatiently.

'Hang on a minute.' The man, who was even bigger than the security bloke, stepped up close. 'There's been some mistake. This young lady was talking to us just now by the door. You can see how upset she is. She can hardly talk. Like she said, she forgot she was carrying something.'

The security man hesitated. At the same time the manager came up. Lisa breathed a sigh of relief. She was a different one from last month when she'd almost been caught then.

'What's going on?'

Lisa didn't have to explain. The couple started doing it for her.

'You've treated her disgracefully. Everyone knows how forgetful you get when you're expecting. I'm always forgetting stuff. And you said you were in a rush to get back to your mum, didn't you, love? Isn't she looking after your other kid?'

Lisa nodded tearfully. The story seemed so real that she almost believed it herself. The manager glanced at the other customers, who were all agog. Clearly she didn't want an audience any more than Lisa did. 'I'm sorry. There appears to have been a mistake. Perhaps I can make it up to you with a voucher.'

'You need more than a voucher,' said the mother, sharply. 'She's only a girl. Look at the state you've got her in.'

'It's all right.' Lisa sniffed convincingly. 'A voucher would be fine.'

The beautiful baby with the rosebud mouth began to cry and her mother rocked the pram. 'Sure you're all right, love?'

Lisa nodded. 'Thanks for everything.'

'Any time.' The man gave the manager and the security guard a nasty look. 'Lucky we were here.'

CV – DRAFT ONLY
Susan Thomas, 36 [No, she'd make that 34.]
Past experience: sales executive on local newspaper.
Recent experience: none. Career break as mum.

CAMPAIGN POSTER –
ROUGH COPY TO BE APPROVED BY JOY

Keep our centre open! Greenfields Centre is for
children who need extra help. The council
intends closing it to merge with a bigger centre
with less one-to-one attention. We're planning a
protest walk on Saturday 22 September and we
need your support.

Dear Mum, Hope this postcard reaches you safely in America. It's SO boring in Oxford. There's nothing to do. Can we come and see you? Love Ed

Hi Annabel,

This is the THIRD email I've sent and you still haven't replied. Ben still hasn't got a job and Dad's cross about it – but don't die – Ben's going out with the girl from the supermarket's cheese counter because he says she gives him titbits. Heard Mum crying in the bathroom yesterday but she said she had something in her eye. School starts soon, worse luck. Please come home soon. Love Georgie

Mums@Home.co.uk

KEEP SENDING IN YOUR NEWS AND VIEWS! JOIN OUR ONLINE DISCUSSIONS ON

More advice on how to conceive a girl.

Can you trust your ex to look after the kids safely during access weekends?

How often do you 'do it'? Go on, girls – come clean!

TIP FROM BAD MUM

When the kids shout at you, whisper back. They'll stop yelling eventually, so they can hear you.

CHUCKLE CORNER FROM PUSHY PRINCESS

If he wants breakfast in bed, get him to sleep in the kitchen.

THOUGHT TO KEEP YOU SANE FROM CAMPER MUM

If all is not lost, where is it?

22

Caroline just managed to squeeze on to the tube before the doors shut. Losing so much weight after she'd found out about Roger – perhaps she should call it the 'affair diet' – had its compensations. Breathing through her mouth – the stale air reeked of sweat – she wedged herself between a man with a large holdall, which pressed against her knees, and a woman in a navy suit with a pushchair, briefcase propped behind it.

Caroline decided that the woman was dropping off her child at some smart office crèche – so many firms had them nowadays – before a gruelling day after which she would drag the poor kid home again. At least job-sharing meant she could have some time at home, except on days like today. Zelda had rung last night in a panic because Aurora's earache was worse. Could Caroline swap days and go in tomorrow? She'd make it up either later in the week or early next.

It was a relief to have an excuse to get out of the house, even though Georgie's sports club wasn't on this week, which meant Ben was nominally in charge of her. In practice, this meant he still wouldn't get up until midday so Georgie would be left to her own devices. Twelve, nearly thirteen, was a difficult age. Too old for a childminder. Too young to be left alone.

'Let the passengers off the train first,' the loudspeaker reminded them.

The holdall man exited, as did the mum with the pushchair. Miraculously, there was a seat on the right. Caroline headed for it, only to be beaten unapologetically by a man with almond-shaped sunglasses, who kept looking at the girl in boots beside her.

How often do you 'do it'? Go on, girls – come clean!

Very crude – was it her imagination or was Mums@Home getting that way? – but she would read the responses. Meanwhile, possibly fired by the almost tangible heat between the chap in sunglasses and the girl in boots, Caroline spent the rest of the journey hanging on to the rail above her and wondering what else she had missed out on in life.

'Morning, Caroline.'

'Hi, Pat. How are you doing?'

Pat was the features secretary. Always on time. Always reliable. A single mother who didn't moan. Occasionally she asked Caroline's advice on issues like how she could get her three-year-old daughter to stop coming into her bed. Otherwise she seemed wonderfully in control. Caroline often thought this was ironic, considering that, unlike the secretary, she was features editor of a Parenting page, yet was struggling to be an all-round mum.

'Thought it was Zelda today.'

Caroline dumped her bag next to her desk and poured herself a cup of water from the machine. 'Aurora's ill again. We've swapped.'

'Her appointment's here already.' Pat gestured towards the meeting room. 'Got here early so don't rush.'

'Appointment?' Caroline flipped open the diary that she and Zelda shared. There it was. Ten a.m., PR for EFT. 'She didn't tell me. What's EFT?'

Pat waved a brochure. 'He gave me one of these.'

Zelda could have mentioned it. Then again, she'd sounded distraught over Aurora. Bother. Caroline had hoped to spend the morning making one last attempt to find an affair case history, not do the toys piece.

'Be an angel and bring us in some coffee. And I know this is naughty but can you come in after twenty minutes and say Karen needs me urgently? I really haven't much time for this.'

Pat nodded understandingly. 'The toys look good, actually, and he seems a nice bloke. Not pushy.'

Caroline drained her water and walked reluctantly towards the meeting room. Zelda had done this to her before. If they were going to job-share, she really had to be more organised.

'Zelda?'

'Actually, I'm Caroline. Zelda's not in, I'm afraid.'

A very tall man stood up from the chair by the desk, holding out his hand. 'Hello. Nice to meet you, Caroline.' His gaze held hers. Nice eyes. Warm smile but not over-effusive like so many PRs. Olive skin – Sri Lankan? Public-school accent. Professional manner. Good-looking. Navy jacket with slightly worn lapels and grey trousers. Firm handshake. Which made the pit of her stomach wobble and an inexplicable apprehension swim up to her chest and diffuse throughout her body.

Fifteen minutes later, Mark had almost finished outlining the virtues of EFT – promoted hand co-ordination in toddlers; firm evidence that the toys encouraged mental stimulation.

'The range sounds really interesting,' said Caroline, wishing they'd had toys like this when her lot had been younger. 'We might include them in the Tried and Tested feature we're working on.'

'Fantastic.' He leaned towards her, pointing out another product. His sleeve had a button missing and she could see the dark hairs on his arm as it rode up. 'You're welcome to borrow some if you'd like to try them out on friends.' His eyes travelled to the ring on her left hand. 'Or your own children, if you have them.'

Caroline shook her head. 'Mine are too big for this.'

'Mine too. How many have you got?'

Why was he looking at her like that? 'Three.'

A flicker of something (sadness?) passed over his face. 'We've got Florrie who's twelve, nearly thirteen, and Ed, who's eleven.'

Florrie and Ed? *Florrie and Ed?*

'Do they get on well?' she asked carefully.

Mark laughed. 'I wish. Florrie's very self-opinionated and Ed's going through a really difficult stage at the moment. He's into kicking and other bad behaviour and it's driving me mad.'

Kicking? Ed? Was this possible?

She doodled nervously on her notepad. 'That must be hard for your wife.'

The shadow flitted across his face again. 'Actually, she's working abroad so I'm in charge. A sort of part-time dad. They're at a holiday club at the moment but school starts soon.' He folded up his papers. 'Sorry. You don't want to hear all this.'

Oh, yes, she did. 'No. I mean, yes. I know what it's like, juggling kids and a job. Zelda and I job-share, as I explained, which is why you've got me today.'

'I'm glad I did. I mean, you seem to understand.'

'Most parents would.' She hesitated, needing to know if this was coincidence or not. The only way to find out was to drop him a clue. 'My eldest daughter, Annabel, is having her gap year, which is freaking me out. It's awful not knowing where she is. Then I've got Ben, who's just done his A levels.' She took care to say his name clearly. 'And Georgie, who's nearly thirteen and sports mad, not to mention being addicted to the computer.'

Just one look at Mark's face was enough to prove her 'test' correct.

'Ben?' Something flickered in his eyes. 'Is he a little job-shy, by any chance?'

She nodded, incredulous.

'And Georgie plays rugby?'

Another nod.

'They say it's a small world,' he said softly.

Caroline's mouth dried up. This man – this *stranger* – knew about Roger's affair! He'd seen her pathetic email all about that woman's phone calls and the pictures. How awful . . . She could feel her neck breaking out in red blotches, the way it always did when she was embarrassed. 'This is weird,' she said, her voice cracking. 'Really weird. And why did you call yourself Mimi?'

He looked worried. 'Honestly, I'm not one of those cyberspace oddballs you read about. But I thought if I registered as a dad, no one would take me seriously – plus the fact it's called Mums@Home. I get so many funny looks at school . . . And I wanted to get some honest advice from people who wouldn't judge me.'

'I think I see.' She felt her palms sweating. 'But that stuff about my husband I sent out . . . Do you mind if we forget it? It doesn't seem professional and I wish I'd kept quiet now.'

'I don't. I think it makes both of us more human.' His eyes twinkled. 'It's nice to know you journalists have the same feelings as the rest of us. You're meant to be tough nuts.'

'I hate it when people assume that,' said Caroline. 'I'm not a newspaper hack, you know. My pages are very different. Anyway, PRs are meant to be pushy and can't write grammatical press releases.'

He raised his eyebrows. 'Does that include mine?'

She considered. 'Yours are OK, actually.'

He had a nice smile. 'I reckon we're even with our confessions. And maybe that email isn't such a coincidence, after all. We work in similar fields. I heard about Mums@Home through Good Publicity and I wouldn't mind betting you did too.'

She nodded. 'They say we're only six handshakes away from everyone else in the world. Cyberspace must bring us a lot closer.'

'Exactly.'

What was wrong with her? She couldn't take her eyes off his face and her knees were weak, like a teenager's. 'I can't help wondering, though . . . Why is your wife working abroad? I don't mean to sound personal but it's quite unusual, isn't it?'

Mark looked away. 'She's an unusual woman.'

Caroline's instincts told her to wait.

'Hilary is . . .'

'Caroline.' Pat was at the door. 'Sorry to interrupt but Karen needs you.'

Mark was up in an instant. 'I won't take any more of your time. Thanks very much.'

Caroline gathered up her papers and pad. Her hands didn't seem to belong to her. 'I enjoyed meeting you. Send me some of the products and I'll let you know if we use them.'

'Thanks.' He glanced at the door. Pat had gone.

'Nice to meet you, Mimi.'

His hand was warm. 'You too, Part Time Mum.'

She wandered back to her desk in a daze.

'What did you think?' asked Pat.

'Er, about what?'

'Nice toys, weren't they? He left me one for my daughter to try out.'

Clever. Or generous?

'Good-looking too. Like that gorgeous actor in *Holby City*.'

'Was he?'

'Well, he certainly thought you were fit. You should have seen the way he was looking at you.'

'*Pat!*'

She giggled. 'Oh, nearly forgot. I took a message from someone at an organisation for Singles. Here's the number. Said she might have someone who could help you.'

Sometimes seemingly impossible features managed to come together. A social group for the over-thirties had sent out an email to members, asking if anyone would talk about how they had repaired their marriage after an affair. Someone called Carmen had agreed to be interviewed on the phone later that afternoon, after she'd got back from work. Jubilantly, Caroline emailed Karen accordingly. Her reply was swift.

We need two more cases. Put a freelance on to it.

Not 'well done', just two more at the double. Karen had been a writer once. Had the demands of editing instead of writing made her forget how hard it was to find people who were prepared to bare their soul in print for very little money? Reluctantly,

Caroline called two of their regular freelancers, stressing the urgency of the piece. Then she rang Ben on his mobile.

'Leave a message.'

Curt. And said so fast that it was hardly intelligible. Please, Georgie, pick up the house phone.

'Yeah – what now?'

'Georgie!' She was shocked. 'That's a really rude way to answer the phone.'

'Sorry, Mum. I thought you were one of my friends. Anyway, according to the *Funday Times*, you shouldn't give your name or anything like that cos child molesters can track you down. And you wouldn't want that, would you?'

The child was too smart for her own good. 'Have you had breakfast?'

'Yes. Toast. Stop fussing. I asked Beth round. Is that all right?'

'As long as Beth's mum knows. And don't cook anything. I've left you a salad in the fridge. Ben still asleep?'

'What do you think, Mum?'

'Georgie, a bit more respect, *please*. OK, I'll ring later in the afternoon. And if you go out, mind how you cross the road.'

'Mum, I'm not a baby.'

More's the pity, thought Caroline, putting down the phone. Whatever she'd thought at the time, babyhood was easier to deal with. At least you knew where they were.

Caroline would have preferred to interview Carmen, who lived in York, face to face but there wasn't time. Anyway, interviews like this were often done on the phone and sometimes people revealed more that way than if you were with them. Luckily, Carmen seemed quite happy to chat away, maybe because she was a tele-sales operator. 'I took my husband back because he was sorry, and I felt the kids needed a dad.'

'I can understand that.' Caroline's pencil flew across the page. Over the years, her shorthand had got rusty so now it was combined with longhand, and only she could understand the result.

'But how did you cope at the beginning, in bed? How did you stop yourself thinking about him doing it with the other woman?' She hated asking questions like that. So sordid. But readers would want to know – *she* needed to know.

'If you started thinking that way, you'd crack up.' Carmen's matter-of-fact Yorkshire sense seemed at odds with her Spanish-sounding name. 'I said we'd start again and we have.'

More emotion. Karen would want more feeling. 'But it's not that easy, is it, Carmen?'

'Why not? We all make mistakes.' Carmen lowered her voice. 'To be honest, I had an affair before he did and he forgave me. So I felt I had to do the same.'

'Do you think he had his to get even?'

'No.' Carmen gave a throaty laugh. 'We were just pissed off with each other. The kids were getting us down. So were our jobs. But it made us realise how much we loved each other. Neither of us could imagine living with anyone else. Not after all these years. And that's all there is to it, really. Loads of people have affairs but it doesn't have to be the end of a marriage. That's why I volunteered for the helpline.'

Caroline asked a few more questions. Incredibly, Carmen didn't mind being photographed. Yes, she'd ask her husband too, but she didn't think he'd agree. It didn't matter. As long as they had one case history who'd be identified and photographed, it was all right.

Caroline had just finished writing up the feature when the phone rang. It was one of the freelancers she'd called that morning. Somehow the girl had found two more case histories and was filing by tonight. How had she done it? Still, at least it meant the feature was in the bag. And, strangely, it hadn't been as painful as she'd feared.

The only thing was that she couldn't work out if Carmen was downright stupid or incredibly courageous.

After lunch she phoned home again.

'Yes?'

She could hear loud music in the background, and giggling. 'How many friends have you got round, Georgie?'

'Just a couple. Do you want to speak to Ben?'

'Nice to know he's up.'

'He's on the computer. Hang on.'

Ben's yawn hurt her ear.

'Have you had breakfast?'

'Not yet.'

'Well, please make sure the girls have something to eat. And can you put the washing on the line?'

'Where is it?'

Caroline bit her lip. 'In the machine . . . Ben, you will look after them, won't you? I don't want them going into town again like they did last week.'

'Chill, Mum. Got to go. 'Bye.'

What was she doing here, writing a Parenting page, when her kids were home alone?

'Parcel for you, Caroline.' Pat heaved a box over to her desk. 'Looks like that EFT stuff. Quick, wasn't he?'

'Obviously desperate for the publicity.' Caroline ripped off the brown tape. There was a letter at the top. An Oxford address. Summertown. Near where the party had been held the other weekend. How odd.

Feel free to keep the contents. I promised your friendly sec-retary a couple of games for her daughter. Very nice to meet you today. I don't suppose you're free for lunch on Friday?

Caroline screwed up the note and tossed it into the bin. 'Pat, any chance you could do a Tried and Tested for us? You can keep the stuff afterwards.'

'That would be great. Thanks, Caroline.'

Lunch on Friday? They'd covered everything, work-wise. Which meant he wanted to see her, or maybe curry favour. She desperately hoped it wasn't the latter. Against her better instincts, she wanted to see him again. Talk to him. Laugh with him the way they had done so easily in the office.

From CarolineCrawford@beatifulyou.com to mark@marksummerspr.com: Friday would be good. Preferably near the office as it's a working day.

Almost immediately, the reply came back.

Fantastic. See you at one. Any more advice on grievous bodily harm/long-distance marriages gratefully received. Regards, Mimi

23

How often do you 'do it'?

That Mums@Home question wouldn't go out of his head. Quite a lot, at the beginning of our marriage, he felt tempted to write, and then, not at all. Nothing now for months. He'd almost got used to it but not quite. Part Time Mum had unsettled him – and not just because of her looks. It had been a long time since he'd been able to talk to someone so easily, but right now there were more pressing matters to worry about.

Like Viyella blouses and grey trousers.

Term started next week and he still hadn't sorted out their school uniform. 'All the organised mothers will have snapped up the sizes you want,' Daphne had warned. Ed had grown so much that last term's trousers definitely wouldn't do. And Florrie's ever-expanding chest was clearly beyond the strength of her blouse.

Daphne had promised to help but she'd enrolled on another course and, besides, he wanted to prove he could do it alone. So far, though, he'd been too busy with work, not to mention ferrying them to holiday club, doing all the meals, laundry and weekend activities, and there simply hadn't been time. Guiltily he thought of the numerous occasions on which he had come home late from work to find Hilary tearing her hair out – over-dramatically, he had thought at the time.

Mark bent down to pick up a wet towel that Ed had left on his bed. Didn't they ever *think*? What would his son be like as a teenager?

The phone rang. The *office* phone. Forget damp towels. Grab mugs still by their beds from the last week to take downstairs after call. Put on professional voice. 'Mark Summers PR.'

'Mark? It's Caroline. From *Beautiful You*.'

His pulse raced. 'Hi. How are you doing?'

'Very well, thank you. I just needed to check a couple of prices for some of the toys.'

Damn. He'd slopped some juice on the carpet. 'Can you hang on a second?' he asked, rubbing the stain with his foot. Putting the clutch of mugs down on his desk, he reached for his price list and knocked over a mug of cold tea. 'Blast.'

'What's wrong?'

Mark sank on to his office chair. 'I was just tidying the kids' rooms when you rang. I know it's crazy but I can never get down to work unless the house is in some kind of order.'

She laughed. 'I'm the same when I work from home.'

'You are? Well, I've just found about fifteen mugs in their rooms . . .'

'They never bring them down, do they?'

'Exactly. And now I've gone and spilt tea over the carpet.'

'Put kitchen roll on it. It absorbs it.'

'Really? I'll try it. Sorry, I must sound so disorganised.'

'No. You sound normal and, believe me, that's refreshing in a PR.'

'Thanks very much.'

'What I really meant was that lots of PRs I come across are very glamorous. They're either childless or have live-in nannies.'

He'd heard the embarrassment in her voice. 'I always loathed the idea of someone else bringing up my kids, but at the moment I'd give anything for Mary Poppins to waltz in and take over.'

'Me too. Listen, Mark, sorry to rush you but I really do need those prices by lunch. Can you email them to me?'

He didn't want to let her go. 'Sure. Oh, and, Caroline?'

'Yes?'

'I'm really sorry but I can't make Friday now. One of my clients needs to see me.'

'It doesn't matter.'

Yes, yes, Caroline, it does. 'Can you make the following week? Friday again?'

There was a brief pause. 'I think so.'

'Great. About one? Do you know Bea's Beautiful Bistro? It's near Marylebone station.'

'I'll find it.'

'Great.' He was horribly conscious of repeating himself. 'I'll book a table.'

Now why, he asked himself, as he put 'kitchen roll' on his shopping list, had he done that? The guilt he had felt ever since he'd sent that email had made him cancel the lunch. But the disappointment in her voice had mirrored the feeling in his heart.

From the minute he had seen Caroline – no, *talked* to her on Mums@Home – it was as though a light had switched itself on in his head. But she was married. And so was he.

Mark thumped up the stairs to his office. Just as well he had work to take his mind off things.

It was, thought Mark, as yet another mother pushed past him, a miracle that any child ever got to school on the first day of term fully clad in regulation uniform, each item marked with a proper nametape rather than scrawled in Biro on the collar. And it would also help if the shops had the right clothes in stock.

'Are you sure you don't have a thirty-two-inch jumper?' he asked the assistant, who looked as though she should be in year nine.

She gave him a withering stare – the sort he had got used to in dorm during the seventies, when it was still acceptable to vilify someone for being 'black'.

'Not if it isn't on the rails.'

How many times had he heard that one this afternoon? 'My hands are rather full at the moment,' he said drily, gesturing with the collection of uniform he had managed to acquire. 'Perhaps you'd look for me.'

She gave a nominal flick through the rail. 'No. Sorry.'

'How long will it take to order?'

'Four weeks, minimum.'

'But it'll be nearly half-term by then.'

'We sold out last week.' Not a hint of apology in the girl's voice. 'Most people have already got their uniforms.'

'Dad. *Dad!*' Florrie, in the changing room trying on hockey skirts, stuck her head out through the curtains. 'Come here!'

'Coming.' God knew where Ed was. He turned back to the child assistant. 'Well, could you see if you've got a pair of twenty-six-inch-waist long grey trousers with turn-ups, please?'

'*Dad!*'

Where was Ed?

'Yes? What is it?'

'No, don't come in.'

'Sorry.' A woman coming out of the next cubicle with her daughter glared at him and he felt terribly embarrassed, the only dad on a floor full of women. 'What's wrong?'

Florrie's face was creased with distress. 'I've started.'

'Started what?'

'Ssssh.'

Florrie, her head still stuck through the curtains, checked that no one was nearby. 'My periods,' she hissed.

Oh, Christ.

'You've got to get me something.'

'What?'

Florrie's face was getting redder.

'You know. Some STs.'

'STs?'

'Ssssh.' Florrie's eyes were full of tears now. 'Sanitary towels. Go to Boots next door. And hurry. Please.'

Mark turned and almost collided with the assistant. 'I've got the trousers.'

'Fine. Can you hang on to them for me? I've got to get something.'

The girl looked at Florrie's cubicle. 'Has your daughter finished? We're very busy.'

'She'll be out soon. When I'm back.'

As Mark jostled his way out of the shop, all kinds of thoughts were whirling round his head. Periods? Started? But she was only twelve. Was that old enough? And why hadn't Hilary warned him? Or Daphne?

Boots was packed. It was difficult to see what was where and he didn't want to ask someone. Hair care. Deodorants. Plasters. Maybe they'd be in that section. No. Damn. *Damn*. And even if he did summon up enough courage to ask, there wasn't anyone *to* ask. In his day they'd had assistants on the shop floor, not behind tills. He'd just have to queue. Pharmacy would be best.

It took a good ten minutes to get to the desk by which time he had probably caught a cold from the man in front who was sneezing all over the place. Another child assistant. Where did they get them from? 'Excuse me, can you tell me where sanitary towels are?'

'Feminine Hygiene. Behind you on the right.'

Did she have to speak so loudly? And – bloody hell – how many kinds were there? Light flow. Heavy. Slimline. Winged? No, not the mobile. Not now.

'Mark Summers PR.'

'Mark? It's Caroline again. Sorry. That price for the toddler activity set seems to be different from what it says on the website. Is it fourteen ninety-nine or thirteen ninety-nine?'

He hesitated. 'I think it's fourteen ninety-nine, but I'll need to check when I get back to the office.'

'OK.' She seemed rushed.

'Sorry.'

'That's all right.'

For one crazy moment, he felt like confiding in her. Light flow or winged for a daughter who had just started her periods and was waiting for him in the school-uniform shop's changing room? 'See you on Friday, then,' he said.

'Actually, that was the other thing. I'm afraid I can't make it.'

His body jolted with disappointment. 'Oh. Right.'

'But I could do the one after that, if that's all right.'

He'd make sure it was. 'I can hear you're busy.'

'Yes, I'm, er, in a meeting.'

'See you, then.'

'Yes. 'Bye.'

Light flow. Heavy flow. Winged. Wingless. He'd take the bloody lot.

Ed still hadn't turned up even after Mark had delivered the bag to Florrie through the curtains. It wasn't fair that the child had to do this on her own without a mother. And it wasn't fair that Ed should wander off. Still, at least Mark had school trousers for when he finally came back.

'He's probably in HMV,' said Florrie. She was walking beside him awkwardly.

'Probably.' He looked down at his daughter who, until an hour ago, had been a child. 'Are you all right?'

She flushed. 'Fine.'

'Granny's coming over for tea tonight.'

'I know.'

At least she could talk to her.

Ed wasn't in HMV. Nor was he in Virgin. Mark began to feel sick.

'You'll have to put out a notice,' said Florrie, importantly.

Exactly what he'd been thinking. But where? And Ed might not be in the Clarendon Centre but in one of the many shops up and down the high street. 'Maybe he's getting rugby boots,' said Florrie, suddenly. 'He said he needed them.'

It was an inspired guess. Ed was sitting down in FootLocker, surrounded by an array of boots. 'Hi, Dad.'

'Where the hell have you been?'

'I told you I was going to look for rugby boots.'

'No, you didn't.'

'Did.'

'You didn't and we're going.' Mark grabbed his arm.

161

'Get off. I've found a pair.'

Just in time common sense reminded Mark that rugby boots were one of the few remaining items he needed to get. 'Do they fit?'

'The man said so.'

Mark eyed the spotty youth hovering by the footstool. 'Are you trained to fit children's shoes?'

'*Dad!*'

'Well, are you?'

'Nah. But these aren't kids' shoes. They're size six.'

When had Ed grown to a six? Mark got down and prodded his son's foot. His toe seemed reasonably near the end but not touching, and the width felt all right. 'Run round the shop.'

Ed was puce with embarrassment. 'I can't.'

'Run round or I go.'

'What? I can't hear you. Stop whispering.'

'I said, run round or I go.'

'OK, there's no need to shout.' Reluctantly, Ed walked round a stand of shoes.

'Do they slip?'

'No.'

'How much are they?'

'Eighty-nine pounds,' said the boy.

'*Eighty-nine pounds?* That's ridiculous.'

Ed pouted. 'Nothing else fits.'

There was only a week before school started. It was blackmail.

'OK.' Mark fished out his credit card. He'd have to pay next month. 'But don't run off like that again. I didn't know where you were. Do you need football boots too?'

'No. That's the spring term.'

Thank God for that. Just rugby. And non-contact rugby too, this year. Like non-contact marriage, really. No touching. Just chasing. Well, he'd made more than enough allowances for Hilary. But Florrie's period was the last straw.

Time to blow the whistle.

*

'Cooee, only me!'

For once, he was glad to see his mother-in-law. 'Florrie's started her periods,' he mumbled, racing to the front door to get to her before the kids did.

'That's early.' Daphne raised her eyebrows. 'Hilary was the same.'

'Can you talk to her, check she's got everything she needs? I bought some stuff but I'm not sure if it's right.'

'Of course, dear.'

'Thanks. How was your course?'

'Not as inspirational as I'd hoped, actually, Mark. I'm not sure that beginners' Croatian is really for me. Now, I'll just put this shepherd's pie into the oven to warm through, shall I?'

Clearly she was more comfortable with cooking than she was with periods. Perhaps, thought Mark, as he opened the post while Daphne busied herself with the oven, it was her generation.

'I like to open my post in the morning in case something needs sorting out,' she said. 'Is there any cheese I can grate over this?'

Mark ripped open an envelope. 'I didn't have time earlier. And, no, there isn't any cheese.'

She put the kettle on and wiped toast crumbs off the side. 'Are they looking forward to school? Hopefully they'll settle down better than last term.'

'I hope so, too. But they still keep saying they preferred their old school.' He stared at his Visa statement. 'Bloody hell! There's a bill here for over two hundred quid from some mobile-phone company. And it's not mine.'

'Are you sure?'

'Look!'

Daphne scrabbled for her glasses, which hung from a chain round her neck, and peered at the statement. 'Someone's taken your number. You need to report it. That happened to a woman in my crystal-healing class last year.'

'It was Florrie.'

'What?'

Ed had wandered in, munching a packet of Hobnobs. 'Florrie. She used your card to top up her phone.'

'Don't eat those biscuits, dear. They'll spoil your appetite. I've just put your dinner into the oven, although it would be a bit nicer if your father had some cheese to grate over it.'

'*Florrie!*' Mark stood at the bottom of the stairs. 'Come down here.'

He waved the statement at her. 'Ed says you used my card to top up your mobile phone. Is that right?'

'Yes.' Florrie leaned sullenly against the banisters. 'I did it online so I could ring Mum in America.'

Mark's head spun with disbelief and apprehension. Online? She must have keyed in the security number on the back of the card. Although the fraud was irrelevant in view of why she had done it.

Florrie glared at him accusingly. 'I've been ringing round to find which branch of the bank she's working for in New York. There's about six out there but no one had heard of her. I've just tried again and this time I got through to some woman in something called Human Resources. She didn't want to tell me anything at first but then I explained I had to get hold of my mum urgently. So she checked and told me they didn't have anyone called Hilary Summers. There was one in London but she's left.'

She grabbed his wrists and tugged at them angrily. 'That was Mum – so if she's not in New York, like you said, and she's not in London, where *is* she?'

24

Can you trust your ex to look after the kids safely during access weekends?

Not according to Singleandlovingit Mum whose ex-partner had let their son walk along the top of a park wall – and break his arm when he fell off. Suppose Josh let Tabitha slip when she was getting out of the wheelchair or the bath?

You needed lots of common sense and patience to bring up kids, which Josh had never had when he was at home. But Susan was used to it – used to the week dragging so that each minute on the clock seemed like five. She'd often heard 'normal mothers' moaning about how boring it was trying to amuse small children, but they ought to have a go with Tabitha. It wasn't just the boredom; it was the mental and physical exhaustion involved in getting her to do the smallest tasks.

This week, however, had been wonderfully different. She and Joy had spent ages working out what to say on their flyers, then printing them. The other mums had helped too, and some of the staff, including Lisa, bless her, had heard about the campaign and offered to put posters up. 'Anything I can do to help?' she had said, smoothing the bump under her dress. 'You're doing a great job. Sometimes I get really scared in case there's something wrong with my baby.'

'I'm sure you'll be fine,' said Susan, trying to sound reassuring. No point in saying what others had said to her, that somehow she'd find the strength to cope. Meanwhile the campaign was providing much-needed shape to her life, and even Tabitha was getting excited.

She had no idea if Tabitha knew what 'campaign' meant, but

she'd always made it a rule to talk to her daughter as though she understood. 'Do you want to help?'

Tabitha nodded energetically.

'Great. You can come on the march with us next Saturday.'

Tabitha's face fell. 'Daddaddad.'

No one could ever accuse this child of being thick. She knew Josh collected her on Saturdays. 'Don't worry. You'll still see Dad.'

The centre manager had notified the council and the police. They were going to walk down the pedestrianised part of town, carrying their banners and handing out yet more leaflets.

Susan's father had promised to come with them, even though it was a sixty-mile drive from his home. 'Good idea,' he said, on the phone. 'I can't believe the cuts this government's making. It's a scandal, an absolute scandal. You get little enough help as it is. I wish I lived nearer, love.'

Susan sighed. They'd been through this so many times that it was becoming like one of her depressing rituals with Tabitha. Her father had remarried, some ten years ago, not long after her mother had died. June, his new wife – it seemed inappropriate at Susan's age to call her a 'stepmother' – didn't want to leave the town she'd been born and brought up in. And although Susan got on well with her father, and nominally so with June, she couldn't help feeling that the benefit of an extra pair of hands would be outweighed by the invasion of her privacy. June was one of those people who always knew best. A bit like Steff.

'June says you must make sure Tabitha's well wrapped up. It's going to be pretty chilly on Saturday.'

Susan's lips tightened. 'I know.'

'She's bought us new Thermoses and says don't worry about the sandwiches, she'll organise some.'

'I don't want to bother her. Wouldn't she be best at home, especially if her back's playing up?'

'Nonsense. The more support the better.'

Susan braced herself. She had to tell him now or he'd only find out for himself. 'Josh turned up a few weeks ago.'

'He *what*? Some cheek! I hope you showed him the door.'

'He wanted to see Tabitha.'

'Bit late for that, isn't it?'

'Hang on, Dad. That's what I thought. But she was so pleased to see him that I let him in. He's got married again. To a nurse.'

Susan's father grunted. 'Let's hope she knows what she's let herself in for.'

Susan took a deep breath. 'She's not too bad, actually. And they'll be on the march. Tabitha wants them to come.'

'Well, they'd better not walk anywhere near me or I'll give him a piece of my mind.'

'I feel the same way as you but there's this group I belong to, a kind of online chat group, and we've been talking about it. Some of the other mums said that even though it's painful when the kids see or stay with their exes, they've got to do it for the kids' sake. It's made me try to be more understanding.'

'Well, I think that's very big of you.'

'I don't have a choice,' said Susan, softly, wondering why he didn't see the irony. Hadn't he understood how hard it had been for her, too, to accept June, who was so different from her mother? Thank heavens she'd been grown up when the pair had got married. The thought of being brought up by her father's wife made her shudder. But Tabitha wasn't grown-up. Tabitha never would be really grown-up. So it was up to her – Susan – to mend fences between herself and Josh.

Besides, if something awful happened to her, she had to have someone as a stand-by to care for Tabitha. The thought of Josh and Steff taking over was agony, but in her position some things just had to be faced.

Amazingly, it was warm on the day of the march – despite what the weather forecasters and June had glumly predicted.

'Thanks, Dad,' said Susan, as he heaved Tabitha's chair out of the boot.

'It's a pleasure, love,' he said, kissing her cheek. 'I'm really proud of you, you know. We both are.'

Joy came rushing up, resplendent in a bright orange anorak. 'We've got a fantastic turnout!'

Susan looked around, amazed. Joy was right. All the parents from the centre were there, as well as several others whom she didn't recognise. It looked as though someone had brought in the Hire-a-Wheelchair mob. Those who were able to held placards and banners reading, 'SAVE OUR CENTRE'. There was even a BBC van, and reporters from the local paper, who, Joy told her excitedly, had already taken pictures of her.

And there were Josh and Steff. To her ex-husband's credit, he didn't shy away from his former father-in-law. 'Hello, George and June.' He stepped forward boldly and shook Susan's father's hand. 'Can I introduce my wife, Steff?'

Steff beamed. She was wearing a short red and yellow tartan skirt with thick black leggings, a yellow jumper and matching scarf. If she went missing, thought Susan, naughtily, she'd soon be found. 'Nice to meet you, George.' She crouched down. 'Hiya, Tabs! How are you doing?'

Tabitha grinned and put out her hand to touch Steff's scarf. Immediately Steff whipped it off. 'You have it, love. Suits you. It's real cashmere. Your daddy got it for me from Scotland. We'll take you there one day. You'd like it.'

Entranced, Tabitha stroked the soft wool and Susan felt her throat constrict. 'Come on, Joy's waving. We're off.'

Susan had never been on a march before. It didn't take as long as she'd thought but maybe that was because so much was going on. In the time it took to reach the end of the precinct – the only safe place to walk in town with the wheelchairs – and back, they had already been asked for comments by both a BBC man (regional, not national, to Joy's disappointment) and Bekki Adams, the local-paper journalist.

By lunchtime it was all over. They had handed out the leaflets to shoppers, most of whom seemed to support them, and walked

Tabitha and Joy's Danny back to the car park. After all the excitement, Susan felt strangely flat.

Steff fell into step beside her and they walked behind Josh, who was pushing Tabitha. 'Sue, I wonder if I could ask a *big* favour. Could we take Tabitha back with us for the night?'

'Now?' Susan's heartbeat quickened.

'If that's OK with you. We'd bring her back tomorrow.'

'No. Sorry. It's too much. She'll be tired after today.'

'Would next weekend be all right, then? We could pick her up on Saturday morning and have her back by Sunday lunchtime.'

Susan felt the tears pricking her eyes. Tabitha needed time with her dad. But she'd never been away from her mother for a night.

'You can have her for a whole day but not the night as well,' she said gruffly. 'Please don't rush me, Stephanie.'

'Steff, please . . .' To her annoyance, the girl brushed her arm in what she presumably considered a girly friendly gesture. 'I understand. We'll start off slowly. Thanks, Sue. Thanks a million.'

Every morning after the march when Susan woke up, she counted the days. Six days until Josh had Tabitha. Five. Four. She didn't get much sympathy at the centre. 'I thought Steff seemed really nice,' said Joy, as they sat watching Tabitha with her jigsaw. 'If I were you, I'd be grateful they're giving you a break. It'll give you a chance to do something for yourself.'

'I've forgotten how to,' said Susan, fingering a Bourbon biscuit. Someone, thank heavens, had bought a fresh packet.

'Join the gym,' said Joy, pointedly. 'Or have driving lessons. I don't know how you manage without a car and it would do you good to get out.'

'I had some lessons before Josh left,' admitted Susan, 'but then I couldn't afford any more.'

'Wouldn't your dad lend you the money?'

He might, but he'd have to talk to June first and Susan didn't like the idea of that. Driving was just another dream she'd have to file away for the future.

Before she knew it, it was Saturday. After Josh and Steff had wheeled Tabitha out to the car, amid Susan's last repeated dos and don'ts, the house was so silent that she felt like screaming. Well, why not?

Her yell resounded in the room like someone else's and, embarrassed, she turned up the telly so that next door might think it had been that. Strangely, she felt better afterwards. Maybe, she thought, with a flash, that was how Tabitha felt when she shrieked with frustration. But now what? Tidy up? She'd already done that before Josh and Steff arrived. Tackle those weeds? Get a life. Go for a walk.

She'd forgotten how fast she could go without having to push the chair. She'd been holding out against an electric model because the consultant had said that Tabitha's arms would get less exercise. But it was tough on the pusher. Now she could swing her arms, feel the wind in her hair, get into town in fifteen minutes instead of thirty. Yet something was missing.

'I've got a child!' Susan wanted to say, every time she walked past a mother with a pushchair. 'I'm a mother too!'

The high street was full of autumn fashions but there was no point in trying anything on even if she'd had the money or the figure. What was the logic in looking nice when someone was only going to slop food over you?

A lovely house, the kind she could only dream of, caught her eye in the window of an estate agent on her left. It was Green & Co, the same firm, noticed Susan, her pulse quickening, that had advertised in the local paper for a weekend salesperson.

Susan glanced down at herself. Well-presented. For once her skirt was clean and she was wearing a jumper that matched. It wasn't going to be a one-off, this thing with Josh and Steff. They would want Tabitha again, then again. If she stayed in the house alone, she'd go mad.

Susan smoothed back her hair, wishing she had put a brush in her bag, took a deep breath, pushed open the door and went in.

Ten minutes later, she came out, breathless with excitement and fear. Fumbling for her mobile, she keyed in her dad's number. To her disappointment, there was no answer. It was still ringing, without any reply, when she got home.

Still burning to tell someone, Susan switched on the computer.

From Rainbow to Mums@Home: I've just done something really brave – for me, anyway! I saw an ad for a part-time job in an estate agent and I walked in off the street. I've got an interview next week! What shall I wear? What shall I say? I haven't worked for over twelve years. If anyone's got some advice out there, I'd really appreciate it!!!!!

25

For two pins Lisa would have called in sick again today. But she had to do lunch duty at the handicapped centre next door – they all had to do it as part of their job description for the council – and something made her feel she should go. If she didn't, maybe something would go wrong with Rose, like it had for those poor kids.

'Hiya, Tabs, how're you doing?'

She liked Tabitha and her mum, who always had a cheery smile, and never failed to ask how she was and what had happened at her last antenatal check. And she'd never once – since the last time – mentioned that embarrassing incident in the shop.

'We're fine, thanks, Lisa,' said Susan. 'How are *you* doing? Still got that nice neat bump, I see. I bet it's a boy. Girls are bigger usually and spread out all over you from the behind.'

'Someone told me it was the other way round,' said Lisa, handing Tabitha a plate of ham salad. The food didn't seem so bad today. She felt sorry for them when it was a sloppy mess of grey sliced meat and gravy. 'I did this test I got from a pregnancy website,' she added. 'You swing a ring above you, from a bit of string, like, and if it goes clockwise – it did – you're having a girl.'

'I thought you could only tell that when you're almost full term,' said Joy. 'Didn't you ask at the scan what sex it was going to be?'

Lisa finished unloading the tray. 'I'd rather have a surprise.'

Joy laughed. 'Oh, you'll get that when you're a mother, all right. Life will never be the same again.'

Lisa felt a prickle of unease.

'Don't worry,' said Susan, reassuringly, patting her hand. 'It'll be fine once you've got that baby in your arms. No point in worrying about anything until it happens. That's what my dad says. Actually, I was having a clear-out the other day and I came across some maternity clothes and baby books. The clothes are a bit out of date, but the books might be interesting. Do you want me to bring them in next time?'

'Ta.' She began loading the tray with plates, most of which had leftovers on them.

'Sure you're all right with those?' asked Susan, concerned. 'We could take them if they're too heavy.'

She was so nice, she really was. Briefly, Lisa felt tempted to confide that she hadn't had a scan at all because that American site had warned they might be dangerous. There was also quite a lot of other stuff she'd like to tell her. No. Second thoughts, Tabitha's mum might tell someone and then it would all get out.

'It's OK, thanks. I can cope.'

The bus was full, going back to the estate after work, but she made a big show of puffing out her stomach and a bloke (that was a first!) gave her his seat. Her stomach was beginning to drag with that familiar pulling-down feeling and she couldn't wait to get home. Nearly there now. Off the bus, across the car park, up the steps, one at a time. Don't tread on the cracks, whatever you do, or something will go wrong again.

'Hiya, Lees!'

Kiki was mopping something sticky off the concrete in front of her door. 'Those bloody kids,' she said, squatting on her haunches. 'Treacle. That's what they've put down. It's a bugger to get off. Careful you don't slip.'

Lisa looked at her suspiciously, wondering why she was being so nice.

'How are you doing, anyway? You'll be giving up work soon, won't you?'

Lisa mumbled something about not being sure of her dates and Kiki nodded. 'I understand, especially after the last time.'

'It would help if I could get a bit more sleep,' said Lisa.

'Still making too much noise, are we?' Kiki grinned wickedly. 'Sorry about that.'

Lisa closed the door behind her, pushing it three times to make sure it was really shut, and switched on the computer. After that conversation with Kiki, she needed to talk to someone who would *really* understand.

From Expectent Mum to Mums@Home: Has anyone lost a baby?

I lost my first daughter when I was neerly sixteen weeks. Its ment to be all right after twelve weeks but it wasnt for me. I woke up with this dragging pain and when I got to the toilet, all this stuff oosed out of me like thik slices of liver that my mum used to make us eat cos it was cheep and good for us. I yelled out for Kevin who was my partner then. But blood scares him. So Kiki – she's my naybour – she got the ambulunse. The nurses said it mihgt be all right. It happens, sometimes, they said. But then they strapped me to this machine and the doctor told me my baby's hart wasn't beeting any more. He said he was going to give me a general anesthetic but that I could see the baby if I wanted, afterwards.

It had been so long since she'd allowed herself to think about this but now she'd started, she couldn't stop.

I didnt because I was two scared and cos Kevin said it was sick. Afterwards, they told me it was a girl. I'd been hoping for a girl. Later, I wished Id seen her. I'm stil not sure if I shoud have done. I rekon she'd have looked like me. I've never told anyone any of this stuff. My mum lives miles away, in Totnes, and my best freind isn't my best freind any more.

Thanks for listning out there. Must go now. Luv Lisa.
PS I called her Hayley. It made her sound happy.

Send.

*

Hiya mum. Its Lisa. Just testing that my Outlook Express is working because I haven't heard from you.

CV
Susan Patricia Thomas
Age: 33
Previous experience: telesales worker; carer.

Dear Kari,
How's everything? I really miss you and school. The new one sucks. Guess what? I've STARTED! Have you? There's something I want to tell you about Mum too but not here. I'll ring you tonight. OK?

Dear Janie,
Just a quickie before I do supper. Something really weird happened the other day. Nice weird, that is. I met someone I'd been emailing and didn't know it was the same person. Not 'met' as in 'met', of course – it was strictly work but quite a coincidence, isn't it?

Mums@Home.co.uk
JOIN OUR ONLINE DISCUSSIONS ON
Affairs. More and more women are doing it. Could you?
Going back to work. Advice needed, please!
TIP FROM SINGLE MUM
Odd socks? Keep them in a pile and get the kids to sort them out on a rainy day.

CHUCKLE CORNER FROM MAD MUM

Why don't women blink during sex? Because there isn't time!

THOUGHT TO KEEP YOU SANE FROM MELINDA OF SOUTHSEA

When did you last hear of a man asking for advice on how to juggle a career *and* a marriage?

PARENTING NEWS

Keep Your Child Safe on the Internet is a free booklet produced by the Home Office. Top tips include remembering that everyone you meet online is a stranger, even though they might seem like a friend.

Get your copy from www.keepkidssafeonthenet.co.uk.

26

She should have been working but she'd just had to log on to Mums@Home during her coffee break. The current discussion was frighteningly riveting: 'Affairs. More and more women are doing it. Could you?'

So far, Fran 3 was the only one who'd responded:

> To be honest – and I've never told anyone this before – I was
> on the edge of an affair once with this bloke at work. But
> when he suggested going away for the night, I chickened out.
> I knew my marriage was pretty bad but I couldn't risk the kids
> hating me. It also made me realise what I could be throwing
> away: the house, the routine, and silly things like the neat,
> ordered comfort of my linen cupboard.

Caroline could identify with that. When she'd first found out about Roger's affair, she had briefly considered having a fling – not that she had anyone in mind – as a way of getting back at him. She had dismissed the idea, knowing she wasn't the kind of person who could cope with the deceit.

'Hi.' Zelda breezed in, scattering carrier-bags – a dead give-away that she'd stopped in Covent Garden *en route*. That reminded her. She ought to get a dress for the charity ball at the Savoy that was coming up: the editor had asked her to rep-resent the magazine this year. She needed to get Roger a new pair of cufflinks too: his favourites had gone missing. It was little things like that, to which she wouldn't have given a second thought before, that disturbed her peace of mind – made her imagination run riot. It wasn't inconceivable that he had taken *her* somewhere nice and left his cufflinks behind, along with God knows what else . . .

'Sorry I'm late, Caro.' Zelda's voice jolted her sharply to the present. 'Did you get those ideas for conference I emailed over?'

'No. I thought you'd forgotten so I came up with some of my own.'

Zelda checked her face in her powder compact. 'Don't worry. Mine weren't up to much anyway. And my server's playing up so I wasn't sure if they'd gone through. God, what do I have to do to make Aurora sleep?' She turned to Caroline. 'You look pretty knackered yourself, if you don't mind me saying so. How's everything?'

Caroline poured herself a glass of water. 'Not brilliant.'

Zelda raised her eyebrows. 'Want to tell me?'

Caroline hesitated. There were times when she regretted having told Zelda anything about Roger. Although not a day went by without her thinking of it – it was like a black cloud hanging over everything she thought or did – there were times now when she needed to be able to forget, which was difficult when the person you worked alongside knew your history.

'Maybe later. I've got to catch up on something first.'

'Me too.' Zelda clicked her compact shut. 'By the way, apologies about the EFT bloke last week. I'd forgotten he was coming.'

'That's OK.' Caroline finished her water to cool the flush creeping up her face at the mention of Mark. 'He had some good stuff, actually. I've almost finished the feature.'

'Fantastic.' Zelda looked at her. 'And the affairs piece?'

Her eyes, which were brimming with sympathy, made Caroline wince. 'That singles group came up with a case history who'll be ID'd. And a freelancer found two non-ID'd.'

'Probably made them up.'

'No. I checked them out with a phone call. They just don't want their names in the magazine.'

Zelda smiled ruefully. 'Understandable.'

'Yes. Anyway, I've written my bit and edited theirs so it's gone to Karen.'

'Brilliant!' Zelda leaned back in her chair. 'Looks like I'll have an easy day or two. Thanks.'

Job-sharing could be like that. Sometimes, you did more work than your partner and at others they did. It was a bit like a marriage that functioned well.

The phone rang.

'I'll get it.'

'Thanks.' Caroline was scrolling through her emails.

Zelda held her hand over the mouthpiece. 'It's that PR chap from EFT. What's-his-name – Mike someone.'

'Mark,' corrected Caroline. Her hand shook slightly on the mouse. Maybe he was ringing to cancel lunch. Or just to talk. She wanted to talk to him too, but every nerve in her body told her it was dangerous. Think children. Think safety. Think ordered linen cupboard with labelled shelves for sheets and towels, and a life that didn't tumble on to the floor in an unsortable mess. 'Can you ask him to email me?' she said crisply. 'I'm a bit tied up at the moment.'

Seconds later, a message popped up on her screen.

Just wanted to confirm lunch next week. Looking forward to it.
Best, Mark

She'd reply later. It would give her time to concoct an excuse, if that was what she decided to do.

The following week, she found herself clothes-shopping for the first time in months. She hadn't intended to but a rather nice jersey top had caught her eye in Next's window. It was perfect for a lunch although, as she told herself firmly, not necessarily the one on Friday. And no, she added, Mark *wasn't* the reason for her rediscovered shopping zest.

Meanwhile Georgie had settled into the school term, although it was still a nightly battle between homework and MSN. Ben was even less easy to deal with. Even though his A-level grades had come through satisfactorily, he continued to lie in bed, much to Roger's disapproval – 'At his age, I was working.'

Caroline agreed, and did her best to make Ben see sense but it wasn't easy: Roger's lengthy hours meant she had to discipline him and Georgie single-handedly. You could punish a younger child by withdrawing pocket money, but what could you do with a boy who was almost a man and who, just when you lost patience with him, put his arms round you and said he loved you?

Ben had already planned a gap year but, unlike Annabel's, it involved hanging around London, practising with his band – made up of exhausted post-A-level friends – and sending off CDs to record companies. He also spent hours on MSN, 'talking' to friends, and wrote lyrics for his guitar. She'd seen some, when she was tidying his room. One, in particular, had haunted her. 'It's so easy to get hard but so hard to find a girl.' Lewd, but poignant.

Sometimes she felt jealous of Roger and that woman. At least he had known what it was like to experience true passion. Would she ever have that or was she stuck with the pebbledash of life because she took her family responsibilities seriously? And how ironic that both she and her eldest son needed love – or should that be sex? – as badly as each other.

She waited until Ben had sloped off to the pub with his mates before logging on. Supper was in the oven. Roger was going to be late. Georgie was glued to *EastEnders*. The house was blissfully peaceful.

From mark@marksummerspr.com to Part Time Mum: Didn't hear back from you about Friday. Is it still OK?

Yes. No. Don't know.

Fine at the moment unless something happens. How's your week been? My husband's home late – again – so I've actually got some time to catch up. Unbelievably, Ben has got

out of bed and Georgie is improving her vocabulary courtesy
of Albert Square. Work has been mad. I'm going to have to go
in for an extra day this week. So much for working 'part time'!

Her reply, which she'd intended to be light but which, after
she'd sent it, seemed to say more than she'd meant to, elicited an
immediate response.

My week crazy too. Not just work. Florrie's missing her mother
big-time *and* she started her periods – in the school outfitters
of all places. Probably shouldn't be telling you this but, believe
me, it's quite something for a man to cope with.

She was taken aback but also impressed by the way he could
mention such an intimate subject. Roger would rather die than
say 'periods'.

She probably knows more about it than we did at her age. The
other day Georgie announced that if I ever needed the
morning-after pill, I could buy it over the counter at the chemist.

She hadn't meant to say that either but somehow she knew he'd
empathise with her dismay, and admiration, at how street-wise
kids were.

Ed tells me there are condom machines in the loos at
Hamleys.

Sometimes I think they have far more fun than we do. The
other week Ben caught me dancing in the kitchen on my own,
Jean-Brodie style. Sad, isn't it?

The delay of ten minutes was long enough to confirm the
answer. When it finally came, she was overwhelmingly relieved.

Not sad at all! I'm always singing in the car which really embarrasses the kids, especially when the roof's down.

Roof down? So he had an open-top. That was on her dream list, with walking along a white-sand beach.

How's the pushing and kicking?

Still going strong. Am thinking of wearing a label round my neck saying, 'Dysfunctional dad. Please make allowances for my offspring.'

'Mum. *Mum?*' Georgie yelled up the stairs. 'When's dinner? I'm starving.'

Got to go. Or, as the kids would say on MSN, gt2go. Maybe we should try MSN ourselves except I'm not sure how to do it.

She waited for a reply but none came. Maybe the server was busy. Or perhaps he was.

After dinner, when Roger still wasn't home, she checked again. Yes, he'd replied.

MSN is quite simple, really. Explain when I see you. Remind me to tell you about a very rude teen site that keeps popping up when I don't ask for it. Ed swears he's not responsible but I don't believe him.

I'll swap it for an anecdote about Ben.

Done.

'Mum, I need the computer. You've been on it for ages.' Georgie squinted at the screen. 'Who's Mark?'
'Someone from work,' said Caroline, logging off.

Her daughter gave her a hard look. 'If it's work, why were you talking about Ben? And who's Ed?'

'Mark's son,' said Caroline, lightly. She busied herself with papers on the desk to give herself time to think. 'It was just chit-chat. And move that glass. If you spill your drink on the key-board, it can ruin the computer. It happened to someone at work.'

She was aware that she was babbling, talking rubbish to hide her confusion. 'By the way, Georgie, can you tell me how to go on MSN?'

'Why? You're being really strange at the moment. What's wrong?'

A picture of the bed at the hotel after David's party flitted through her head, followed by an open-top car zooming over a white-sand beach. 'Nothing,' she said, getting up and stretching. 'Nothing at all.'

27

When did you last hear of a man asking for advice on how to juggle a career and a marriage?

Sometimes Mums@Home was just too sexist. He could do with some advice right now. But it wasn't something he wanted to advertise online and he didn't feel he could keep bothering Caroline. He'd have liked to have told her about the terrible argument with Florrie and how he'd finally convinced her that Hilary had been moved to a different part of the bank in New York, which was why it had been hard to find her.

In reality, he had succeeded in getting a message to Hilary, impressing on her the urgency of ringing home. She did so – but not for some days – and he'd allowed the children to talk to her first, desperately hoping she would be more communicative this time.

Judging from the children's voices, she was sounding reasonably normal. Fingers crossed, Florrie might be fooled.

'When are you coming back, Mum? Really? I can't wait.' Florrie dropped her voice. 'And I've started. You know, *started*. Yes, Dad got some stuff in but I wish you were here too. Ed's still kicking me and Dad gets really mad at him.'

'Shut up, Florrie. Let me talk to her.'

Mark allowed Ed to take the phone and then it was his turn. She sounded brighter. Thank God. 'How's school going?'

'Seems all right.'

'Is Florrie OK?'

'I think so.' She was like the old Hilary as they ran through domestic details, like whether Ed should go on the too-expensive school skiing trip and Daphne's forthcoming cruise – a week up the Norwegian coast with Saga. By the end, they were almost chatty.

'Can you ring later this week?'

'I'll try. Love you, Mark.'

That took him by surprise. She hadn't said it for months.

'And you.'

Slowly he put down the phone, realising with a horrible slow dawning that it wasn't true. Not any more.

It was a busy week. EFT was a demanding client, always wanting to know which magazines were planning a write-up. Somehow he had to make sure his other clients didn't feel neglected. Since he had turned freelance after Hilary's departure, so that he could be at home for the kids, Mark had built up a diverse range of clients, ranging from a kitchenware manufacturer to a company that produced nursery goods. The latter wanted to see him on Friday and the meeting made him ten minutes late for lunch with Caroline.

She was already at the table – bottle green to match the restaurant's botanical colour scheme – when he arrived. He spotted her immediately but she was flicking through a magazine and didn't see him at first. A chap at a neighbouring table was eyeing her, he noticed. Not surprising. She really was very pretty – slim, blonde . . . Intelligent . . . and sexy too.

Stop right there.

'Hi. Sorry I'm late. I had a meeting that overran.' He shook her hand, wondering if that was the right thing to do, and the warmth of her skin shot up his arm.

'Don't worry. This is a comfortable place to wait. Love the plants over there. Besides, I brought something to read.' Her eyes smiled. 'I never go anywhere without a magazine or a book just in case.'

'Me too. I once got stuck on a train for three hours without anything. It was so boring.' He patted his briefcase. 'I've got Alexander McCall Smith's latest in here. Have you read it?'

'It's on my list. Any good?'

She was so easy to talk to that the waiter had to come back twice before they paused to inspect the menu. He learned that she had gone up to read English at Oxford a year before he'd gone to Cambridge. They both adored the theatre. He talked about his family, and his mother who had gone back to Sri Lanka after his English father had died, some fifteen years ago.

'My mother must have died at about the same time,' she said quietly. 'Annabel and Ben, our older two, were little.'

'That must have been hard.'

She nodded. 'It was. Especially as my father had died when I was a teenager. My parents had a fantastic marriage. They showed me how important it was to provide a solid family base.' She looked away, awkward now.

He floundered for the right words to put her at her ease. 'You don't—'

'I shouldn't—'

They laughed. 'You first,' said Mark.

Caroline played with the menu. 'All right. Thank you. What I was going to say was that I still feel really embarrassed about what I said on Mums@Home about . . . well, about my marriage and husband.'

'Long forgotten,' said Mark, promptly. 'I'm good at that.'

She smiled sadly. 'I wish I was. When I wrote that email I wanted to know if it was possible to start again, but I'm still none the wiser.'

'Do you want to talk about it?'

'I'm not sure. I've already discussed it with a friend but he's also a friend of my husband so I'm not sure how biased he is.'

'Try me. I don't know you very well, or your husband at all, so I can be objective.'

She picked up her napkin and put it down again. 'OK, then. Roger and I had a good marriage. Well, I thought it was. But it's different when you have children . . .'

He nodded.

'I described – on the site – how that woman telephoned me.'

He could see how difficult it was for her to talk about it. 'When I had it out with Roger, he said it was a physical thing. 'I never found out who the woman who originally rang me was. But I suspect she was a friend of that woman – I still find it hard to say her name – who was either trying to help me or make me chuck him out.'

'But you didn't.'

'No.' She was speaking so quietly now that he could barely hear her. 'It scared us both because we discovered how much we had to lose. And the children . . .' She lifted her lovely face. 'I couldn't bear them to have just one resident parent.'

Something must have flickered in his face. 'I'm sorry.' She put a hand on his arm. 'I didn't mean to be so thoughtless.'

'No. It's all right.' He took a gulp of Chardonnay. 'I feel the same about the family-unit thing. My family was very close, even though I didn't have any brothers or sisters. When I met Hilary at university, I knew I wanted children. I couldn't believe she was interested in me. Everyone loved her. She was bright, funny, intelligent, motivated . . . and,' he hesitated, playing with his knife '. . . extremely beautiful.'

He shouldn't have said that: her eyes were wary now, as she waited for him to go on. 'It was a kind of opposites-attract thing. She was – is – very blonde. We made a striking couple and we knew it. We were immature too, and we liked the idea of shocking our parents. Sounds pathetic now, but when you're only nineteen, you see the world differently.'

'What went wrong?'

Mark laughed. 'Apart from marrying too young? I'm still trying to work it out. She'd always wanted to make money because there hadn't been much when she was growing up and it had made her feel insecure. She went into the bank's graduate-training scheme and was determined to get as high as she could.

'For years, she insisted she didn't want kids and I had to beg her in the end. After Florrie was born, we had a full-time nanny.

You know how much that costs, and we were both working all hours to meet our outgoings and also to get the kind of lifestyle she wanted. Our mortgage was crazy and we had huge rows about it because I wanted to sell and live more within our means.'

He took a gulp of water. 'At the time I was working all hours for a big PR firm in London so we hardly saw each other. I knew things weren't great but then, earlier this year, she announced she'd got a promotion in New York and was going to America for five months.'

'Hadn't she told you she'd applied?'

'No. I told her it wasn't practical and she said I was holding her back.'

Caroline was wide-eyed. 'But how could she leave the children?'

'Exactly. But since Ed's birth, she'd changed. She was distant with the kids and they picked up on it. When they woke up in the night, they often called for me instead of her.'

'Was she depressed?'

'I thought of that. But she wouldn't see anyone. So I thought, OK. Let her get it out of her system. Does that sound pathetic to you?'

'No. It must have been very difficult to handle.'

He shifted his position. 'That's not all, to be honest. I suppose I always felt she'd done me a huge favour in marrying me.'

'Why?'

'I'm not as bright as her. And I guess I'm . . . from a different background.'

'People don't worry about that kind of thing any more.'

'I wouldn't be so sure of it. Ed gets teased at school. And other parents, particularly mothers, make comments about how different he looks from Florrie because she's so much paler.'

'That's terrible.'

He nodded. 'There are times, too, when I wonder if I really know my wife . . .'

'I know exactly what you mean. That's how I feel about Roger.' She took a sip of sparkling water, which moistened her lips. He felt an insane urge to dab them with a napkin. 'So when are you seeing her – Hilary – next?'

'Not sure.'

'You ought to go out there at half-term.' Caroline put out her hand briefly to touch his arm. 'Be assertive. Tell her how much you miss her.'

'Maybe. Except that . . .'

'Yes?'

'I'm not sure I do miss her any more.'

Silence. Should he have said that?

She looked beyond him at the wall. 'It's only when Roger goes out of the door in the morning that I can be myself.'

The significance of the words hung in the air. He was about to say something when the waiter arrived, bearing a pudding menu, which they both declined. 'I suppose we ought to talk work,' said Caroline, getting out her notepad. 'Did you know that EFT has paid for an advertorial? We don't do many – our editor's very careful about what she promotes – but she's into educational toys in a big way. So, I need to know about your new spring range.'

She was professional, thought Mark, getting out his brochures. Professional and warm. He wondered what it would be like to kiss her. For God's sake! Just because he hadn't had sex for months it didn't mean he had to fancy every woman he came across. But Caroline was the first woman for whom he had felt something since Hilary. And he was deeply uncomfortable about it.

He just had time to nip home and put dinner in the oven before he had to dash out again to collect the kids from the after-school club. No sooner had he bunged in the Marks and Spencer pie than the phone rang.

'Mr Summers? This is Bernard Roberts speaking.'

The headteacher. Visions of Ed falling off the playground slide crashed into his head. 'Are the children all right?'

'I'm afraid we have a bit of a problem. Edward has been caught downloading unsuitable sites on the school computer and sending them to friends.'

'Unsuitable sites?' Relief that they were still in one piece was swiftly followed by disbelief. 'What kind of sites?'

'Perhaps you'd better see for yourself. He told me that he sent them to his home computer.'

Mark tried to think clearly. 'But we have a filter system. And so must the school.'

The head sighed. 'Sadly, they don't catch everything. I'm afraid that's not all. Ed has also been designing a website which we are not at all happy about. May I suggest that you look at the evidence, then come in to see me on Thursday morning?'

He had an EFT meeting then but he'd have to postpone it. He put down the phone and ran upstairs to switch on the computer. Come on, come on. On to Ed's file. He knew the password unless his son had changed it. Then on to History. In his day, it had been a subject, not a way of checking up on what the kids had been doing online.

Mark stared at the images on the screen. They weren't by any means pornographic, as the head had implied. But they were suggestive. Very suggestive. This time, Ed had gone too far.

28

From Scummy Mummy to Mums@Home: Just wanted to add
my own tip on going back to work. Get your kids to help
choose the clothes you're going to wear. It makes them feel
more involved – and their enthusiasm will give you confidence.

Susan had almost cried when she'd read the message. If only
Tabitha had been capable of choosing her an outfit!

Crazily, she had tried: 'What do you think of this, Tabs?'
she'd asked, doing a mock-twirl in her only serviceable skirt, a
rather dull navy blue. But Tabitha hadn't been interested: all
she'd wanted to do was look out of the window for her father's
arrival.

And now Susan was sitting in a real office, shaking like a leaf,
convinced that any minute now the rather nice-looking man on
the other side of the desk would explain that there'd been a mistake; she didn't have nearly the right qualifications; and would
she mind leaving now?

Simon Wright, whose name was on his desk, picked up his pen.
Real ink, observed Susan. Posh handwriting. 'Your application
was rather fortuitous, actually.' His warm, friendly eyes reminded
her of Josh when she'd first met him. 'In fact, we had filled the
position but the lady in question had to back out for domestic
reasons.' He sighed. 'That's the problem – no one wants to work
at weekends any more.'

'And do you blame us?' asked a perky woman, who was sitting
on the other side of him. 'We do have lives to lead, you know.'
She winked at Susan, who wasn't sure how to respond.

'Do you mind, Fiona?' asked Simon pleasantly. 'I'm meant to

be doing an interview. Don't try to put our lovely new applicant off before she starts!'

Lovely new applicant? Susan glowed even though she knew he didn't mean it. 'Actually, weekends are the best time for me. My husband, I mean ex-husband, has our daughter every other weekend. I want something to do.'

Too late, she realised how pathetic that had sounded. But both were nodding. 'Absolutely. I can understand that,' said Simon. 'My mother went back to work a few years ago, also for an estate agent, and hasn't looked back.'

His mother? Was that how he saw her? Susan shifted uncomfortably. He was younger than her, definitely, but only by a few years, surely. It was her weight that made her look older, thanks to those flipping Bourbons.

Simon was leafing through the file again. 'Every other weekend, you say. I know the ad said once a month but it would be useful to have someone a bit more often.'

'That would be fine.'

Odd. He seemed more interested in her availability than in talking about her previous jobs. They must need someone badly.

'Now, what about experience?' Simon tapped his pen on the sheet. 'Have you worked for an estate agent before?'

'No.' Susan was shaking again with nerves and had to steel herself to sound calm. 'But your ad did say no experience was necessary. Besides, I'm good with people. Before . . . I mean some years ago, I worked in telesales and I've been doing voluntary work at a day centre for the past six years.'

Voluntary work! She winced with guilt.

'Very good.' Simon's hand flew across the page. 'Basically, the job involves showing people round an estate of new houses, which we're handling for a local builder. You might know it. Blackthorne Walk.'

She had watched them going up over the last year – she and Tabitha had to pass them on the bus. They were big and a bit brassy, with small front gardens and large black electric gates at the main entrance. Not really her taste . . .

'Of course, it goes without saying that we need our sales team to be well dressed.' He glanced at her elasticated-waist skirt and cable-knit jumper, which, to her dismay, she now saw that she was wearing inside out *and* the label showed.

'Nothing dramatic. Just reasonably stylish. Like the lovely Fiona, here.' His eyes twinkled wickedly, making Susan feel frumpily uncomfortable.

'Simon,' said Fiona, warningly. She grinned at Susan. 'Don't worry about him. He's just trying to impress you.'

'We pay five pounds fifty an hour and thirty-five pence a mile for petrol. How does that sound to you?'

Petrol? Her heart sank. 'I'm afraid I don't drive. I've had some lessons but haven't passed my test yet.'

He clucked. 'Oh dear.'

'I can get the bus there,' she added quickly.

'Really?' He sucked his pen again. 'Normally our salespeople have to be drivers but in this case, as it's just the one location, you won't need to drive to appointments.'

She held her breath. 'Does that mean you're offering me the job?'

He smiled, revealing a web of crinkly laughter lines beside his eyes. 'Do I take it you're interested?'

Susan nodded. 'Yes, please. When would you like me to start?'

'I don't suppose you're free today? We've got several people who want to view Blackthorne and no one to take them round.'

She thought of her empty home and the weeds poking through the paving slabs. 'Today would be fine.'

Simon picked up the phone. 'In that case, I'll arrange the viewings. I'll drop you off myself to show you round so that you know what you're talking about.' He stood up, revealing himself to be much taller than she'd thought. 'The car's out the back. After you, Susie.'

She didn't like to point out she was 'Susan'. It seemed so staid.

''Bye,' called Fiona, chummily. 'See you soon.'

'Yes,' said Susan, still nervous although everyone was much

nicer than she'd imagined. She allowed Simon to hold open the door for her and walked self-consciously beside him towards the car park, her heart singing. She had got the job!

By mid-afternoon, Susan felt as though she was on intimate terms with each house on Blackthorne Walk. Each was, as she explained to prospective buyers, slightly different from the others, to give them individuality, but the floors were all wooden and the swagged curtains were included. As Susan had guessed, the back gardens were pitifully small, given the astonishing asking price, but only one couple remarked on that. Not one of the houses would have suited her and Tabitha. She found it hard enough to cope with the stairs at home, but these spiral staircases were lethal. And there were so many split levels between rooms! Why hadn't the architects thought about it?

'We love it but I'm scared of falling,' said an elegant woman, who held her husband's arm as they walked round. She wasn't that old – early sixties – but they'd told Susan they were looking for a retirement home. In ten years' time, it might be totally unsuitable.

'I know exactly what you mean. My friend has a daughter who can't walk very well. She would have liked a house like this, but without the steps or stairs. But have you considered the plot next to number four? That house is being built next year and I believe it's still possible to put in design alterations.'

'Really?' The woman glanced up at her husband questioningly. 'Can you give us more details?'

Susan rang Simon from her mobile and arranged for the couple to speak to the builders.

'Well done, Susie,' he said, when he arrived unexpectedly at the end of the day to see how she'd got on. 'The Fairhursts seem genuinely interested. You did a good job. But how did you know the house could still be altered?'

Susan flushed. 'I didn't. It was a lucky guess. But my dad used to be a builder and I knew there's only outline planning for that particular plot – I saw it in the local paper. So I reckoned there was still time for changes.'

'You saw it in the local paper?'

She reddened further. 'I usually read it quite thoroughly.' No need to say that it helped pass the time when she was feeding Tabitha or watching her do jigsaws.

'You've done fantastically well for your first day.' He started the engine. 'Two of the viewers rang to make second appointments and both said how helpful you'd been. Looks as though you've got a knack.'

It had been so long since someone had paid her a compliment that she'd forgotten how nice it felt. 'Thanks.'

'I don't suppose you fancy a bite, do you? An early supper? I'm starving and the Stag is meant to be rather good.'

His suggestion took her by surprise and her first instinct was to decline: she was unused to going out. A bite? Was this a date? No, don't be stupid. He was just being friendly. Probably felt sorry for her or wanted to talk work. And the Stag had always looked nice from the outside. Besides, Tabitha wasn't coming back until nine, since Josh and Steff were taking her to the cinema, and the only thing waiting for Susan was an empty house and a nearly empty fridge. Still, she ought to let Steff know where she was, just in case.

'That would be nice. Only thing is that I ought to ring my ex just to check my daughter's all right.'

He raised his eyebrows. 'Sure. How old is she again?'

'Twelve,' said Susan quickly. She knew he thought she was fussing, but let him. She didn't want him to know about Tabitha (not yet, anyway) because he might feel her domestic responsibilities would make her unreliable. 'Do you mind if I borrow your mobile, Simon? My battery's running low.'

'Course not. Here.' He passed it to her and their hands brushed briefly. She flushed.

'Steff, it's me.'

'Sue? Didn't recognise your number.'

'No, my battery's out,' she glanced at Simon, 'and I had to borrow someone's. How's Tabitha?'

'Happy as Larry. We're just off now to the Odeon.'

Briefly, Susan explained she was going out to supper but would still be back for nine.

'Have a lovely time. With someone nice, are you?'

Steff had read the wrong thing into the mobile number. 'No. I mean, yes. See you later.'

'Everything all right?' asked Simon, as she handed back the phone.

'Yes, thanks. Do you have children?'

'Me?' He seemed bemused, as though the idea had never occurred to him. 'No, not yet. Too much else going on to think about settling down, despite all the hints my mother started dropping from the minute I was thirty.'

So he wasn't that much younger than her, she thought, as he swung sharply left into the pub car park, then leaped out to open her door before she had time to do it herself.

'Thanks.'

'Susie?' His eyes held hers for a second.

'Yes?'

'You don't have to keep thanking me all the time, you know. Believe me, it's me who should be thanking you. We were desperate for an extra pair of hands and you seem to fit the bill exactly.'

The pub was nice. It had dark wooden tables with candles in the middle. There was so much on the menu and on the blackboard that, after years of not going out apart from the odd birthday treat with her dad, June and Tabitha, she floundered, unable to make up her mind.

'The lasagne's very good,' suggested Simon. 'Do you prefer red or white?'

She meant to say red but somehow white came out, which was stupid because white wine always gave her headaches. But then it seemed too late to take it back and somehow she found herself sipping a rather large glass of Chardonnay and smoothing down her navy skirt, which was riding up.

'So, tell me about yourself, Susie. How long have you been on your own?'

Was it that obvious? She'd mentioned her ex but she might have had someone else. Then again, if she did, she probably wouldn't have been free for supper on Saturday night. 'Nearly eleven years.'

He whistled beneath his breath. 'Too scared to take the plunge again?'

This was getting a bit too intimate for a conversation with someone she'd only just met. If she'd known him better, she would have explained that it was because, first, she hadn't met the right person and, second, only a very special man would take on Tabitha. Instead she said, 'Something like that,' and tried to laugh it off, steering the conversation back to work. 'Have you been at Green and Co long?'

'About a year.' He didn't want to discuss it, thought Susan, desperately searching for another subject. Luckily, he took the lead. 'Have you seen that new drama on Monday nights? It's a serialisation of Martina Cole's latest.'

She breathed a sigh of relief. She was hooked on it, and also on Martina Cole's books, which she got from the library. From then on, they talked and talked, about books, television programmes and films, although Susan was only familiar with those that had been released on DVD.

'I can't believe you haven't seen the new Tom Cruise.'

For a second, she was almost tempted to come clean about Tabitha and how difficult it was to leave her. 'I can't afford to go out much,' she said lamely. 'The cinema isn't expensive, I know, but it all adds up.'

He nodded understandingly. 'I've often thought how hard it must be for single mothers on their own.'

'It has its advantages,' said Susan, hastily, not wanting him to feel sorry for her. 'You can do as you like when you like.'

'Apart from going out,' he teased.

'Well, the new going out is staying in,' she pointed out.

'Very true.' He grinned and, for a second, she felt quite pleased with herself. Then he glanced at his watch. 'Sorry, but I have to go. I promised to pick up my mother and take her to a friend's.'

So he was caring, too. 'Can I go halves?' She opened her purse.

Simon waved it away. He had sounded slightly slurred and she tried to remember how much he had drunk. Too much to drive her home? But she couldn't say something or it would look rude. 'No, the pleasure's mine. Besides, it's on the company. We can say we talked shop, can't we?'

To her relief he drove steadily, even though she could smell the drink on his breath from the passenger seat. She couldn't help thinking that if this was work it was much more fun than people made out. 'Thanks for a lovely evening,' she said, as Simon dropped her off outside the house. Getting out of the car, she felt shamefully glad it was dusk so that he couldn't see the handrails running up the sides of the garden path.

'Thanks for coming with me.' His eyes held hers for a second, until embarrassed, she fumbled in her handbag for her key. 'See you,' he called.

Susan waved back. As she slid the key into the lock, she realised she should have gone back to work a long time ago. For the first time in years, she felt useful – no, more than that. She almost felt good about herself.

Within a few minutes Tabitha was back so it was lucky she hadn't been any later. One glance at her daughter's animated face and she had no need to ask how the cinema trip had gone.

'We saw the new Tom Cruise film,' Steff said excitedly, 'and don't worry, it was a twelve. Seen it, have you?'

'No,' said Susan. 'I don't get out often.'

Josh put his arm round Steff. 'I can't tell you how much this has meant to us. Steff said you might consider letting her come to us overnight next time.'

'I said I'd think about it.'

'It would be great if you could. I know I haven't been much help in the past but I want to make up for it now. I really do.'

No need to tell him about the job yet and the promise she'd made to work every other weekend, an arrangement that depended on him having Tabitha.

'Did you enjoy your dinner?' asked Steff, eyes glittering with curiosity.

'Yes, it was fun.'

'Out with a friend, were you?'

'That's right. Come along, Tabitha, let's get you to bed. It's past your usual bedtime, isn't it?'

'See you, then.' Josh clearly didn't want to go.

'Yes. Better get on now.' Susan made to shut the door.

'You're doing a great job, Sue.'

Steff's teeth would fall out if she didn't stop nodding like that. Funny. She'd never have put her down as Josh's type. Still, people could change. Or they might be completely different from the kind of person you had them down as in the first place. It was enough to make you wonder if you ever really knew someone at all.

29

Keep your child safe on the Internet.

Lisa kept thinking about that one. When Rose was older, she wouldn't let her go on it at all. Far too dangerous. She'd also make sure she said ta nicely, went to mass every now and then and washed her hands after going to the toilet. These days, parents let their kids get away with anything.

'Mrs Smith, can you help me write my name?'

Lisa crouched next to Daisy, breathing in her smell: fabric-conditioner mixed with glue. 'Put your hand over mine while I trace the letters. Good girl.' Lisa tried to sound positive but there was no escaping the fact that Daisy's letters were all wonky. If her mum was at home, instead of working, she could have helped her. That was another reason why Lisa was determined not to work after Rose was born. Besides, the baby's dad ought to help with maintenance. 'Now do it on your own. Hold the pencil like this. Cool!'

Daisy's face lit up. 'Can I do some painting now?'

'Why not?' Lisa spread out an old newspaper sheet on the table, carefully covering the vinyl surface in the way that Mrs Perkins insisted. As she did so, something caught her eye at the top of the page:

MATERNITY UNIT CRITICISED FOR CAMERA THAT DIDN'T WORK.

'Can I have the orange paint, Mrs Smith?'

'Hang on a minute, Daisy. I just want to read this.'

Lisa had never been a fast reader. She'd only just got to the bit about the technicians not mending the security cameras – luckily, no baby was snatched, but the point was that one could have been – when Mrs Perkins loomed up. 'Lisa, I've told you before. Daisy's group is on the painting rota after lunch. She can't do what she wants when she wants.'

Daisy made a face. Luckily, Mrs Perkins's back was turned by then.

'Never mind.' Lisa took her hand quickly before anyone saw this display of affection. 'Let's go and play in the sandpit, shall we?'

Whoops, the old bat was coming back. 'Lisa, can I have a word? Daisy, go to the slide, please.'

Lisa stood there, arms folded, bracing herself for what was coming.

'Lisa, I know you're fond of Daisy but we can't afford to have favourites. I've told you before, we can't show physical affection, like holding hands, in today's age of litigation. Besides, you're here for all the children, not just the ones you like. Now, I want you to help Aaron with his colours. Oh, and, Lisa?'

What now?

'Next week, I'd like you to be in the baby room for a few days while Annie's on holiday. I'll run over your duties with you but it's mainly changing nappies and making up bottles. You did that in your last job, didn't you?'

Lisa nodded, feeling a glow of excitement creeping over her. The baby room! No one could stop her picking one up there: it was part of her job. No one could stop her breathing them in and holding them to her, feeling their little chests rise and fall against her own.

It would be almost like having a baby of her own.

Oh, Sky and Hayley. Where are you?

Tears pricked her eyes. It got her like that, when she was least expecting it. It would help if she could talk to Earth Mother or one of the others. Lisa wiped her eyes and blew her nose on a square of loo paper up her sleeve. Maybe, she'd nip in to the special-needs centre next door in her dinner hour. With any luck, one of the computers might be free.

No one minded when she asked if she could log on for a bit. Lisa waved to a couple of mums she knew and found a computer in the corner where no one else was sitting.

From Expectent Mum to Mums@Home: I've had a really bad day today. I can't stop thinking about Sky. She's the baby I lost after Hayley. Id got to thirteen weeks when one night I had a terible dream. I was in the dentist's chair and he was pulling a tooth out. But it wasnt from my mouth. It was from my other end, if you know what I mean. I woke up and it was like I had the cramps. So I went to the toilet and there was all this bright red stuff in my knickers. When I wiped myself, something like a plastic bubel came out with the paper. I squezd it and it was all soft and squigy. Kiki, my neybur, said I ouhgt to put it in a bag and take it with me to the hospital.

I saw this ginger doctor – right know-all, he was. He sent me for a scan and then said that there was nothing left. Their didn't seem much point in giving him the stuff I'd broght in the bag. So I put it in a bin outside in the coridor. Later, after they'd given me a D and C to clear me out, I told one of the nurses about the bubel.

'That might have been the sack, love,' she said. 'You know, the sack that the baby's in.'

I screamed then. Screamed the ward down and demanded that the nurse went to get it out of the bin. But it had been emptied. I HAD THROWN MY BABY AWAY!

'You all right, love?'

Through a blur of tears, Lisa made out Tabitha's mum. She was frowning anxiously.

Hurriedly, she pressed Send and logged off. 'I think I've got a cold coming.'

Susan patted her shoulder. 'Better go home, then, don't you think? Specially in your condition.'

Lisa nodded. Why not? She'd tell Mrs Perkins she was sick and go and have a lie-down. She stroked her stomach tenderly, three times to the left; three times to the right. Positive thinking. That's what Earth Mother was always saying. Lisa took a deep breath. It was going to be all right. It was going to be all right. Keep saying it and it would work.

*

'Hi, Dad! Thanks for your message. My first day at work went brilliantly, I think. And Tabs was fine. Will ring again soon for a proper chat.'

Dear Lisa,

Thank you for your interest in our new website, MAKE YOUR OWN LUCK!, as featured in the *Sun*. Ever wondered why some people are luckier than others? It's because they BELIEVE they will be successful. Want to know more? All you have to do is send your credit-card details to the following address.

www.thesiteyourparentswouldn'tlike.com

Dear Kari,

Check this out! Dad caught Ed on this and now he's in real trouble!

'Janie – I desperately need some sisterly advice. Can't email in case anyone sees it at your end. I'll ring again tomorrow night at about ten p.m. your time.'

Mums@Home.co.uk

OUR ONLINE DEBATE ABOUT WOMEN AND AFFAIRS IS REALLY HEATING UP!

From Scummy Mummy: My friend had an affair with a married man who said he'd leave his family for her. He did and they've been together for ten years. So affairs aren't always wrong.

From Lawyer Mum: Take it from me, both professionally and personally, it's not worth it.

TIP FROM FRAN 3

Get the kids to show you how the Net works. It makes them feel grown-up – and it's free tuition!

CHUCKLE CORNER FROM ANON OF ALDERSHOT

Q: Do you ever wake up grumpy?

A: No, I just tiptoe past him in the mornings . . .

THOUGHT TO KEEP YOU SANE FROM ALI OF SLOUGH

One day, the kids will leave home. But if you've treated them nice, they might just come back.

PARENTING NEWS

A new survey has shown that fish oil can definitely improve concentration in a child but only if it's the right kind.

30

She hadn't realised how much fun emails could be when they weren't work-related.

From mark@marksummerspr.com to CarolineCrawford@beauti-fulyou.com: Thanks for lunch. I really enjoyed it. And don't worry about Part Time Mum confessions. It's between you and me.

Well-mannered. Funny. Warm. Sexy. *Stop right there*. As Janie had said, she was playing a very dangerous game.

I enjoyed it too. It was such a relief to talk to someone who really understood.

She felt a bit guilty writing that. Jeff had tried to understand but he was Roger's friend.
He was sending another message.

No easy answers, are there?

Spot on, again.

I married Hilary because I was flattered that she needed me.

When you think about it, most of us marry for reasons that seem illogical, with hindsight.

Very true. Sorry but got 2 go. Daphne's just arrived.

Daphne?

Maybe he, too, felt they'd been over-familiar because after that he sent more general emails, about the children and a book he was reading, which, funnily enough, she had just finished herself. She took care to ensure hers were equally neutral. It had been a while since their lunch and so much had happened. Georgie was heavily into the hockey season and, miraculously, Ben had got himself an evening job stacking shelves at Tesco. It meant he didn't drive back until three a.m. or even later, which meant Caroline couldn't sleep properly until she heard his key in the lock. But it was a job.

'Not much of one, is it?' Roger had said heavily. 'He'd have been better off taking the post I got him at the office. It would have looked better on his CV if and when he applies for a real job after university.'

Annabel had emailed to say she was in Queensland, on her way to Sydney. Caroline knew she had to let go of her daughter but she still woke up every morning wondering where Annabel was and if she was all right. Sometimes she confided these fears to her husband although his response was always the same: 'She'll be fine. You fuss too much.'

On top of everything else, Roger was even more distant than usual. So much for a united family front, thought Caroline, as she leafed through the pile of paper on her desk to find the one press release she needed. There it was: Educational Fun Toys.

'Ah, Caroline, I've been looking for you. Gosh, nice pics.' It was Serena, the magazine's picture editor. 'Like the toys. Good colours for a change.' Her chest, Caroline noticed jealously, was voluminous and almost heaving out of her T-shirt. 'Karen tells me you're going on the shoot tomorrow.'

'What?'

'Thought you'd be pleased. Now, look, what we need is . . .'

Seething silently, Caroline forced herself to listen to Serena's brief. Pictures always thought they were more important than Features: readers look at the pictures before they read the story, Serena was fond of saying. Caroline felt that was incorrect.

'Did you know I had to go on this wretched shoot?' Caroline asked the features secretary. 'No one told me.'

'Sorry. Maybe it's in Zelda's diary.'

There it was. Well, she hadn't told *her*. Obviously Aurora's sleep patterns were addling Zelda's brain and now she, Caroline, would pay the price – as if she hadn't enough work to get through without having to trek all the way down to Cartingdon, in Oxfordshire, where the shoot was being held. So boring too! All she had to do was check that the effect fitted in with the general features look. Would Mark be there? Probably not.

If their positions had been reversed and she had been unfaithful, mused Caroline, Roger would never have forgiven her.

'Mum, you should have changed down to second gear. We're approaching a roundabout!'

It was the longest sentence she'd heard Ben utter since the summer. But the shelf-stacking job, which Caroline would have found deadly, had stirred her son out of his lethargy. If the result was that he constantly criticised her driving – his own car was in the garage for a new gearbox – so be it. 'I've been driving much longer than you have,' she retorted.

'You can tell.' Ben flicked back his shaggy orange fringe. 'If you took your test now, you'd fail.' He smiled at her. 'Come on, take a joke. By the way, I'm finishing late tonight so I'll hitch back.'

'Don't you dare!'

'Stop fussing, Mum. Hang on, isn't that Dad?'

She didn't have time to look properly so she only just caught a glimpse of a tall man standing next to a blonde woman in a blue jacket. Too late to beep.

'Was it?'

Ben looked out of the window. 'Not sure. He doesn't normally get off here, does he?'

'No.'

For a few moments they were silent. She'd tried desperately, during that terrible time two years ago, to keep it from the children but it had proved impossible. How much Georgie knew, she still wasn't sure, and couldn't bring herself to ask. But Ben had heard more than she'd intended and he might have said something to his younger sister.

'You know,' said Ben quietly, 'it took me a long time to forgive Dad for what he did but I suppose we all do things we shouldn't, so I don't feel so mad at him now. Do you?'

Caroline was so taken aback – such philosophy was unheard-of from Ben – that she was momentarily lost for words.

'I suppose not,' she said quietly. 'But it still hurts, Ben. I can't pretend it doesn't.'

'But you do still love him, don't you?'

How could she say no?

'That woman back there,' Ben began. 'He wouldn't do anything again. I know he wouldn't.'

He reached across and squeezed her hand.

'I know,' said Caroline, her throat tight. 'Thanks, darling.' She pulled up too sharply in the supermarket car park. 'Have a nice time,' she said lamely.

Ben gave her a withering look. That was more like the old Ben and, in a way, it was a relief. 'Mum, I'm going to work, not a rave.'

'Sure you'll be all right walking back? I could pick you up, if you want.'

He patted her arm. 'No. You've got to be up early for work, haven't you?'

The thought of the shoot made her groan. 'I might be a bit late back tomorrow. Can you sort out tea for Georgie?'

He nodded. Fleetingly, he looked almost responsible. 'Course. 'Bye, Mum.'

She watched him lope off. Tall. Too thin. Jeans dragging on the ground. A tall woman in blue. Blonde, like the photograph. And a man who might, or might not, have been Roger.

'A bit more to the right. Not so far. Yes. Now, just a tiny bit to the left . . .'

The photographer, a nice man called Nick whom they hadn't used before, was frustratingly precise but the effect was good, judging from the Polaroids. Every now and then Harriet, his wife, came in with tea, squash and biscuits. One of the models was still a toddler but the other two had been given time off school and were understandably excited.

'Right.' Nick was unloading film and putting it into a box. 'Now for the seven-to-eight-year range.'

His assistant, a bony young man in a thin T-shirt, was rifling through the boxes. 'Can't see anything. Sure they're here?'

'You checked them before the shoot.'

'Thought so. Can't see them now.'

Caroline went to double-check. 'I definitely asked the PR to send them.'

Nick groaned. 'I thought things were going too smoothly. Can you ring him to bring some more?'

Had she got Mark's number? No, but a quick call to the features secretary produced it. There was only a voice message on his office line but he picked up his mobile promptly. 'Mark? It's Caroline. Look, I'm really sorry but we've got a problem.' She outlined it briefly, trying to talk over the children who were using the break to play noisily with the toys. 'You're sure? . . . Great. How long will it take you? . . . See you then.'

Nick was watching her expectantly. 'Mark, the PR, is bringing them over. He's only about twenty minutes away and he's got some in the office.'

Nick's face relaxed. 'Good. We might as well have a cuppa. You OK, Caroline? You're a bit flushed.'

'I'm fine. I'd just like some water.'

'Come into the kitchen.'

He led the way down a wonderfully long, rambling corridor with bumpy plaster walls suggesting centuries of history. Harriet was making drop scones on the Aga. She was a pretty woman with warm laughter lines round her eyes; Nick put an arm round her and she leaned her head against his shoulder. Caroline felt a stab of envy.

SOPHIE KING

'We're having an enforced break while some more boxes arrive. Poor Caroline's gasping for some water.'

'Hard work, isn't it?' Harriet gave her a glass. 'It wasn't until I married Nick that I realised how much effort went into taking pictures.'

She spoke as if they hadn't been married long, yet there were photographs on a board on the kitchen wall that showed a stunning young woman wearing a graduation robe and two grinning, lanky teenagers in shorts, both a bit older than Georgie but younger than Ben. Harriet caught her looking. 'The children are mine and that lovely girl is Julie, Nick's daughter from his first marriage.'

Which explained the clinch, more suited to early love. 'Have you been married long?' She didn't want to be nosy but something inside her needed to know.

'Nearly three years.' Nick gave his wife an intimate smile, which made Caroline want to cry. She wanted to ask more. How long had Harriet been married the first time? How had they met? Was it really possible to start again? Of course, people did it all the time but it would be nice to have some reassurance.

When Mark arrived with the right toys, Nick promptly got the children into position before they lost interest.

'I'm so glad you were in,' said Caroline, quietly, while they watched.

'Me too. It gave me an excuse to get away from Daphne, my mother-in-law. She treats our house as if it were an extension of her own.'

So Daphne was his mother-in-law! For some unknown reason, she felt hugely relieved.

'Quiet, everyone. Laura, what's that over there? And, John, is that a spider on Amy's arm? Great. Now, what do you call an egg that gets lost in the jungle?'

'An eggsplorer,' muttered Mark.

'An eggsplorer!' crowed Nick exultantly.

'How did you know that?' demanded Caroline.

'It's on the back of my son's favourite cereal packet.'

'How's he doing?' she asked, very quietly.

'Not great. We've got another problem now. I've got to see the head next week because Ed's been downloading dubious sites from the Net.'

'Ben's done that. Most of them do at some stage.'

'Well, the head seems pretty mad. I'll tell you how it goes when I see you next.'

Next? Was that an indefinite or a definite 'next'? Caroline tried to focus on the shoot but her heart would not stop thumping with anticipation. They were standing near the umbrella lighting, so close that if she put her hand out she could have touched him. The temptation was so great that she had to make an excuse and find the loo.

Later, when Nick had called it a day and the children had run into the den next door to watch television, Mark asked, 'Have you got time for a drink or are you rushing back?'

She'd been hoping for this but now she wavered. 'I'm not sure. I need to make a phone call first.'

'To see if Ben's surfaced in time for his job?'

How funny that he already knew her family's habits, albeit sketchily, through their brief emails and chat. 'Something like that.'

For a change Ben answered promptly. Yes, he'd made pasta for Georgie and now she was doing homework. Dad had called to say he'd be late.

Roger was going to be late? His mobile was off and his office answerphone on. Maybe he'd already left for the meeting – if, indeed, there was a meeting. Ben didn't have to work tonight. He'd stay in until she got back. So it didn't matter if she was late, too.

She walked to the car where he was waiting. 'I don't need to rush home,' she said casually.

'Nor me. My kids are staying late for an after-school play

rehearsal.' He glanced at her, then turned on the engine. 'I thought we could walk along the river and maybe have a bite at Brown's. I'll drop you at the station afterwards.'

A walk. She'd love that, especially if they went down by the botanical gardens and Magdalen Bridge. She hadn't been there for years.

He cleared his throat. 'I was wondering about the botanical gardens. The ones by Magdalen Bridge . . .'

'That's amazing.' She laughed, relaxing into the comfortable leather front seat. 'I was thinking exactly the same thing.'

'Really?' His dark brown eyes were boring into her.

'Really.' Her eyes held his. Considering how short a time she had known Mark, she felt incredibly at ease with him.

So much so that it was almost scary.

'It must have been wonderful being here, as a student.'

They were walking just past the spot where she could vividly remember Roger pretending to push her out of the punt some twenty-five years ago. When had he lost his sense of humour?

'It was', she said 'But Cambridge must have been the same.' His hand brushed hers – she thought, by accident because then he put it quickly into his pocket.

'It all seems so long ago now,' she said, to hide her confusion.

'Doesn't it? If you could change one thing about your past, what would it be?'

'Easy! I'd have had a gap year like my daughter, before I started work.'

He nodded. 'Anything else?'

'I'd have married later,' said Caroline, shocked by her own candour, 'after I'd had a chance to discover myself and made sure my husband had too. What about you?'

'At the risk of being accused of plagiarism, I'd go for your answers.' He sat down on the bank. 'Come on. It's quite dry.'

Hesitantly, she joined him.

'Do you have people to talk to, Caroline?'

She thought of Jeff, and Janie in Australia. 'Sort of. But there's talking and talking, isn't there?'

'I know exactly what you mean.' He gazed across the river. 'I seem to have lost touch with my university friends. There isn't enough time when you're working and bringing up kids.'

She smiled ruefully. 'Tell me about it.'

He leaned back on the bank. 'OK.' His eyes held hers. 'I really feel I can talk to you, Caroline. In fact, I feel as though I've known you for ages.'

She tried to concentrate on the river – some students were messing around on a punt. One, in a bright orange T-shirt, was larking around with another. They were so free, just as she had been once. 'I feel the same.'

'You do?'

She nodded.

'Caroline,' he said softly.

Are affairs always wrong?

Take it from me, personally and professionally, it's not worth it . . .

His arm stole round her and he leaned towards her. Later she wondered how she'd known instinctively which way to go, or at which point she'd closed her eyes. His lips felt soft but at the same time firm. Sweet. So sweet. So natural that she couldn't understand why they hadn't been doing this every day since they'd met.

They broke off slowly. His eyes were dancing and she could feel her body burning, lit up in a way it hadn't been for years. Not since she was a teenager.

'My God, Caroline,' he whispered, 'you're amazing. Do you know that?'

And then he moved towards her again.

31

There was still no news of a reprieve for the centre, despite the big spread in the local newspaper. Not surprisingly, the atmosphere was tense: the staff were worried about their jobs and the mums about their children being swallowed up in the bigger, more impersonal centre that they'd be moved to.

'Apparently, they discourage mums from going in to help out,' hissed Joy.

The other mothers tutted.

'I mean, I wouldn't want to go in *every* day, like we have to in the holidays here, but I'm quite happy to do my bit on the rota during term-time to see what's going on,' she said, adjusting one of her earrings.

'I heard that the nursery next door will take over the space here,' said another mother.

'Yeah, it's doing well with so many mums going out to work now,' said Joy, disapprovingly. 'Some people just don't think . . .'

Susan got up to look out of the window near the computer corner. Until she'd started at Green & Co, she hadn't minded doing her bit at the centre. But that day at the Blackthorne development last week had made her unusually restless. She had enjoyed showing people around, had heard herself using words she hadn't uttered for years.

'Hi!' Susan waved at Lisa, who was sitting at the end of the row, using one of the computers. 'Do they have Broadband here? I've been thinking about getting it myself.' She couldn't help glancing at the screen. Gosh! Mums@Home! 'I belong . . . I mean, I've heard of that site,' she said. 'Sorry, I wasn't meaning to be nosy.' She tried to cover her confusion. 'It was advertised on our noticeboard, wasn't it? Any good?'

''S OK.' Lisa spoke sullenly.

'I'll leave you to it.' Horribly aware that she'd intruded on the girl's privacy, Susan moved away and, in her rush, knocked into the flat screen. It wavered on the edge of the desk but she caught it. This time it was difficult not to look.

Susan's skin tingled. So Lisa was 'Expectent' Mum! What an amazing coincidence – except it wasn't because they'd both got the website's name from the board.

Still, it made you realise that these sites weren't as private as you thought. Perhaps she ought to be more careful in future in case she was recognised too . . .

'Heard you'd got yourself a little job, Susan,' Joy said, almost accusingly, as she got back to the group. The other mothers were looking at her.

Susan flushed. She hadn't said anything about it to Joy in case the job didn't work out. 'That's right. It's not much. Just an assistant at an estate agent in town.'

'I used to work for an estate agent,' said one of the other women, wistfully. 'I was meant to be a temp but I stayed on. That was before the kids, of course. Now . . .'

Her voice trailed off but everyone knew what she meant. It was hard enough finding a job that fitted in with children, but when you had one with special needs it was even harder.

Susan couldn't wait for the weekend to arrive. Although she still felt the usual tug at her heartstrings when she kissed Tabitha goodbye before Josh and Steff took her out to the car, she was tingling with excitement when she waited to catch the bus to work.

Work! So exciting to be able to say it. During the week, she had spotted a smart suit in the window of the Oxfam shop and it had actually fitted. It looked good, too: she could tell that from Simon's approving expression when he popped into the

Blackthorne development to see how she was getting on. 'The Fairhursts have signed now,' he told her. 'And that couple with the stroppy teenager have committed to number two. Only numbers one and three left now.'

'Does that mean you won't need me any more?' She'd been too efficient for her own good.

'On the contrary, Susie.' Simon loosened his canary-yellow tie. 'We've been instructed to take on another development, nearer town.'

Susan adjusted one of the swag curtains, which had been pulled by an enthusiastic boy accompanying his parents that morning. 'I was wondering, Simon, whether you needed anyone during the week as well. My daughter's at school then, and I wouldn't mind increasing my hours.'

He made a face. 'Problem is that you don't drive. It would be all right if it was just the show houses, but during the week we need someone with wheels who can take people round the rest of our properties. They're all over the place.'

'I was hoping you might need someone in the office.'

'I'll let you know if we do. You've certainly proved worth your weight in gold so far.'

'Really?'

He chucked her playfully under the chin. His touch made her jump and, for a minute, she thought he was going to do more. 'Really.'

He turned away and she felt flat, which was daft because he wasn't her type – if, indeed, she still had a type. Simon was too worldly, too confident and brash. On the other hand, it was nice to be admired even if he was only doing with her what he did with all the other women in the office – very charming and always full of compliments.

That evening, she leafed carefully through the local paper, then rang Joy and her dad. By the morning – still quiet without Tabitha although she seemed to be getting used to it – she'd made up her mind. The first company had an answerphone on, presumably because it was Sunday, but the second, who ran his own business and came highly recommended by Joy's neighbour, answered. She explained the situation, put down the relevant dates in her diary and came off the phone on a high.

Her good mood lasted right through the morning and she could hardly wait for Tabitha to come back. She might even tell Steff and Josh. Here they were now, coming up the path. 'Guess what? I've booked a course of driving lessons!'

Steff's face was grim as she dumped Tabitha's bag in the hall. Josh, coming up behind with Tabitha in her chair, glared at her. 'What the hell do you think you were doing?'

'What?'

Tabitha began to cry. She hated noise.

'What are you talking about? And stop shouting – you're upsetting Tabitha.'

'It's you who's upset her – and us,' hissed Steff. 'I don't know how you could, Susan. And we've tried so hard.'

'Would you please explain what I've done?'

'The radio programme you were on.' Josh looked as though he was going to grab her arms.

She felt cold. 'About the centre closing?'

'It was on air this morning. Josh and I couldn't believe it, could we? There you were, rattling on about yourself and how hard life's been. Well, fair enough. But why on earth did you say what you did?'

'What?' whispered Susan. Had the journalist actually been recording her when they were talking? She'd thought she'd just been taking notes.

Steff had tears in her eyes. 'You said Tabitha was disabled because Josh insisted on her having the MMR jab.'

'Well, it's true, isn't it?' retorted Susan. Tabitha began to cry again and she knelt down to comfort her. 'OK, I'm sorry. I probably shouldn't have said it but she *was* all right before, wasn't she?'

Josh's eyes were bright with anger. 'If I wanted, I could get joint custody of Tabitha.'

'You? An ex-junkie?' hissed Susan.

'Stop it, both of you – you're upsetting her.' Steff knelt down beside Susan. 'It's all right, Tabs.'

Susan pushed Steff out of the way. 'I can sort out my own daughter, thank you very much.'

Steff rubbed her shoulder exaggeratedly, as though Susan had bruised her. 'I think we'd better go now, Josh.'

'All right. But I warn you, Susan, you haven't heard the last of this.' His eyes flashed dangerously, reminding her of what he had been like before. But there was something else, too . . . Hurt. Sod him. Why did he make her feel so guilty when it had been *his* fault?

32

PCCILLIN HAS DETECTED A VIRUS.

Blow that. His bloody computer could find all the viruses it wanted but nothing would be as important as this.

Mark rubbed his eyes, trying to think clearly.

It was only a kiss, for God's sake, but it had been a kiss like no other. The kind he hadn't had since he was nineteen and even then it hadn't been like that. To call it an electric thunderbolt sounded like one of those crap press releases he had to write, but it was the nearest he could get to describing the incandescent charge between his body and hers.

And, God, she'd smelt incredible. A mixture of rose cream and Chanel No. 5.

When he'd driven her to the station, he hadn't wanted to let her go, and he was certain she'd felt the same. But now a whole bloody week had gone by and she hadn't returned his calls.

'Dad, I can't find my rugby boot.'

Mark groaned. He'd been up early to try to do some work before the school run but found himself unable to concentrate because of Caroline. And now he had Missing-shoe Syndrome to contend with. It always happened when Ed didn't want to go to school, except that usually it was one of his black shoes. Empathise, Caroline had said, during one of her emails before the Kiss. Perhaps he should put himself in his son's eighty-nine-pound rugby boots and see what worried him.

'Tell me, Ed, why don't you want to play rugby?'

Ed scowled. 'I do. That's not why I've lost my boot.'

'It is, Dad!' Florrie was jumping up and down. 'There's a boy in his class who tries to hurt him in the scrum. He's called—'

'Piss off, Florrie.'

'Ed.' Four months ago, Mark would have been more indignant but months of bad language had worn him down. 'You'll just have to take trainers and search Lost Property at lunchtime. Buck up. I've got to see Mr Roberts again, remember?'

Ed scowled again. He looked exactly like his mother on a bad-mood day. 'You will tell him it wasn't my fault, won't you?'

'Yes.' Mark sighed. He and Ed had been over this so many times that he was convinced his son was telling the truth. A friend of his at school had emailed him the offending website. Ed had merely downloaded it, not knowing what it was about. But now Mark had to face the head and get his son out of this awful mess. The very thought brought back memories of being caned by his housemaster for reading after lights-out.

'Will he tell you off about the lift passes?' demanded Florrie, when they were finally in the car, stuck deep in Oxford morning traffic.

'What lift passes?' asked Mark.

'Nothing.'

'You're not going on the school skiing trip. I told you. We can't afford it.'

'They're lift passes for school, Dad. Shut up, Ed. Stop pushing me like that.'

'I didn't think you had lifts at school.'

'We don't.' Florrie erupted into giggles. 'But some of the boys from year eight have been telling the new boys that we do and that they need lift passes. So they sell them at twenty p each.'

Mark was torn between horror and admiration at their entrepreneurial bravado. 'What happens if you get caught?'

'Detention,' confessed Ed. 'Shit, I've just remembered. I've got one tonight.'

'*Don't* swear. What for?'

'Not tucking my shirt in. It's *so* unfair.'

Florrie, in the front seat, turned to pull a face at her brother. 'He was mucking around in biology, too, Dad. He told me. Ow, don't pinch me.'

'Serves you right for grassing me up. So was everyone else, Dad. The teacher put a detention tick against everyone's name apart from three goody-goodies. Anyway, Florrie can't talk. You know that essay she was telling you about? The geography one? Well, she downloaded it last night from www.wewriteyouressays.com.'

'Is that true, Florrie?'

'Chill out, Dad. Everyone does it. You can still learn that way, you know.'

'Stop being so rude. And it's not learning. It's plagiarism. That means nicking stuff from someone else. You shouldn't download essays because it's cheating, and if you do it again I'll tell your teacher. What about you, Ed, have you done all your homework?'

He should have checked last night, as Hilary used to. He could clearly remember her going through their homework diaries. He kept forgetting to do it.

'Course I did. We had a worksheet on pussies for biology. It was cool.'

'Pussies?' Mark almost dropped the handset he'd just picked up. 'Don't use words like that. It's disgusting.'

'Whatever.' Ed grinned. 'It's just another name for what school calls the "female reproduction system".'

'Dad,' interrupted Florrie, 'you shouldn't use the phone when you're driving. It's against the law.'

'We're not moving,' said Mark, defensively.

'It's still dangerous.'

Why wasn't she picking up? She'd be dropping her daughter off at the station by now and getting on the train. He'd caught her before at this time. Pick up, Caroline. Pick *up*.

The head's office was considerably bigger than Mark's at home. It had a large mahogany desk slanted across the diagonal of one corner and a big Sanderson sofa on the other. On the desk, there was a neat pile of papers, a picture of Mr Roberts's children, and a large glass vase of lilies. Several leather-spined books stood in the shelves surrounding the stone fireplace, their glossy sheen suggesting they had never been read.

'I'm telling you, Mr Roberts, Ed couldn't have designed that website. He couldn't even spell its name. I only wish he could.'

Mr Roberts tapped his pen on the blotting-paper in front of him. He had done this so many times since the start of their meeting that it was a mass of splodges. 'Well, one of the boys did. And the content, you must admit, is alarming. However, since you've mentioned Edward's unfortunate inability to spell, I would like to mention some other things too. The other day he was caught kicking another child during an argument, which is unacceptable for a boy of his age. And his performance in class, I'm afraid to say, has deteriorated sharply in the last term. According to the last verbal-reasoning test we conducted, he can do it if he wants.' Mr Roberts blinked furiously. 'Do you know of anything that's worrying him?'

'No.' Mark looked behind the other man to the playing-field where a group of blue and white rugby-shirted kids were kicking a ball around. 'No, I don't.'

Mr Roberts was rubbing his eyes now. 'Mr Summers, we are all aware of your unfortunate family circumstances. It can't be easy for you.'

So, he wasn't a good-enough dad.

Mr Roberts's face softened slightly. 'It's a challenge looking after the children on your own. I'm not sure I could do it. So, we'll make allowances. Normally, in situations as severe as this, I would consider temporary suspension.'

'Suspension?'

'Misuse of the Internet is a serious offence, Mr Summers. Instead, I will give Edward a Saturday detention. But I would strongly recommend that he sees a child psychologist.'

'Why? There's nothing wrong with him.'

'Hurting other children consistently, on a regular basis, at the age of eleven is not standard behaviour, wouldn't you agree?'

Mark nodded as his pocket started to vibrate. 'Excuse me, I have to take this.'

Mr Roberts's face indicated that if a parent couldn't turn off his mobile during a meeting, it was no wonder that the son logged on to dodgy websites.

'Caroline! Listen, I'm in a meeting but I'll call back. OK?'

After accepting the telephone number of a local child psychologist from the head, who probably got a commission for this, Mark ran towards his car, punching in Caroline's number as he slid into the driver's seat. She answered almost immediately, and relief overwhelmed him. It was so good to hear her voice and to tell her what he'd just been through.

'An educational psychologist sounds like a good idea to me.' Her voice echoed as though she was a long way off.

'He doesn't need a head doctor,' he protested feebly.

'They're not head doctors,' she assured him. 'They're specially trained to work out what's going wrong at school. Do you think he's being bullied again? Nasty emails and websites are forms of cyberspace bullying and the kicking could be a reaction to it.'

'Maybe.' Mark sighed. 'Parenting's such hard work. Where are you, anyway? You sound as though you're miles away.'

'I'm on a train on the way to interview someone. Luckily I've got my laptop so I can do some work too. Where are you?'

'Still in the school car park.' He took a deep breath. 'I thought it – the shoot – was wonderful.'

There was an agonising pause. 'So did I,' she said eventually. 'But I've been feeling terribly guilty.'

'Ditto.' He laughed. 'I mean, I know to some people a kiss might not be a big thing but . . .'

'It is to me.' She was whispering now.

'Me too.' He couldn't help whispering in empathy. 'When can I see you next?'

'I don't know.'

His heart thumped. 'I will see you, won't I? Caroline, can you hear me? You're breaking up.'

'Better?'

'Yes.'

'Mark, when I first saw you, something really weird happened.'

He waited, too scared to talk in case it stopped her.

Her words tumbled out: 'I felt incredibly apprehensive, almost fearful, and I couldn't work it out. But I realise now. It's because I felt this powerful attraction to you, which I knew was wrong.'

He could hardly breathe. 'That's just how I felt.'

'But now I'm really not sure . . .'

Sod it. She'd gone.

Frantically he dialled her number, which he already knew by heart. 'Hello. This is Caroline. I'm afraid I can't take your call.'

Mark's hands were so sweaty he could scarcely press Redial. Maybe she'd gone into a tunnel. Or maybe she'd hung up.

From Mimi to Mums@Home: Has anyone taken their child to an educational psychologist and did it help? Also, my son is being bullied. Any advice anyone?

From Mimi to Part Time Mum: Love you.

SHIT! He'd pressed the wrong button. Appalled, he stared helplessly at the screen. Why wasn't there a magic Retrieve button? Mark buried his face in his hands. What would Clive at EFT think?

33

One day, the kids will leave home.

Fish oil can definitely improve concentration.

Two facts that applied to all children. Except hers and every other poor kid in the same boat. Mums@Home was all very well but it lived in an ideal world. What would *they* do if they had a Josh situation? Maybe she should ask them. Maybe she should have a couple of fish-oil tablets herself, especially today.

The doorbell rang just as she'd slipped into a comfortable pair of flat shoes. That had been Joy's advice when she'd confided what she was doing. 'Mrs Thomas?'

Susan nodded. Beyond the gate, she could see the car with its 'WE AIM TO PASS' sign on top. Encouraging.

'Ready for your first lesson, then?'

'Well, it's not exactly my first,' she reminded him, 'but I think I've forgotten everything I learned before.'

'Don't worry about that.' He was a small, wiry man, who almost bounced along the path in front of her. 'It'll come back. Just you see. The name's Joe, by the way.' He waited expectantly.

'Sue,' said Susan. A vision of Steff shot into her mind. Yes, she would be Sue. A new woman. Different from Susan.

She squeezed into the driving seat, embarrassed by how much room she was taking up – she was almost touching Joe. Had she put on more weight? 'That's right. Now, Sue, I want to run through a few basics first to see what you remember.'

By the end of the first lesson (a double, which cost Susan as much as she'd earned last week at Green & Co), Joe didn't seem quite so chipper.

'We need to watch our gears, don't we, Sue?' he remarked, as they drove past the new swimming-pool. 'When you slow down, you should end up in second, not fourth. And keep watching those mirrors.'

There was so much to take in, but this time she had to do it. She needed to be able to drive for Tabitha's sake, as well as for work. Their lives had become very isolated; she could see that from the excited expression on her daughter's face when she returned from an exciting jaunt to the cinema or town with Josh and Steff. Susan wanted to be able to do that with her too, and she reproached herself for not having passed her test years ago.

She had a good half-hour to compose herself before the bus brought Tabitha home from school. She'd left the computer on – her father was always telling her not to do that – and checked to see if anyone had replied. It was too soon of course but . . . Yes!

From Earth Mother to Rainbow: Why not tell him the truth? You must have been mad at him to say what you did on the radio. Tell him you needed to get that anger out. Then sit down and tell each other how you really feel. Try to reach a compromise for the sake of your daughter. It might be too late to get you back together again. But it will make life a lot easier if you're not spitting at each other.

Sensible advice. But would Josh listen? Still, thought Susan, as she walked down the path in time to see Tabitha's bus pulling up, it was worth a try.

'Fantastic, Susie!' enthused Simon, the following weekend when she told him about the lessons. 'It will make a huge difference if you can drive. I might be able to put you up for the mid-week vacancy. It's only Wednesday mornings but we do need someone with wheels.'

'But it'll take me at least three months to get my test,' said Susan. 'I haven't even done my theory yet.'

'I'd forgotten about that – didn't have it in my day, luckily. Never mind, we'll have something we can offer you, I'm sure. You're a natural at this game. By the way, I like your hair. Just had it done, have you?'

Susan flushed. 'I wasn't sure if layers would suit me but the hairdresser talked me into it.'

'She was right.' Simon nodded approvingly.

Susan beamed. Going back to work was the best thing she'd ever done. Apart from anything else, she had more patience with Tabitha because she wasn't stuck at home all the time. And she liked the company of the other girls in the office: one of them had recommended the hairdresser.

'Ever tried to Google your own name, Susie?' Simon asked, later in the afternoon, when he'd taken her back to the office to pick something up and it was quiet.

'No – doesn't it just bring up famous people?'

'You'd be amazed. Look. If I put in my name, it shows that I'm a senior negotiator for Green and Co – see? And if I put in yours . . .'

She wanted to stop him but it was too late.

'Well, blow me!' He stared at the screen. 'It's brought up a cutting from the local rag. What's this you've been getting yourself involved in? A campaign to save the centre that's going to close down? I heard about that march – couldn't bloody well park in town because of it.'

'My daughter goes to the centre,' said Susan quietly. 'She's disabled. I don't know what we'll do if it shuts.'

'You poor girl.' He drew her to him and gave her a brief hug, patting her back. 'I had no idea. You should have told me.'

'I just wanted to be normal,' said Susan, sniffing.

Slightly to her disappointment, he let her go. 'I understand that.' His pale blue eyes held hers. 'I really do. How bad is she?'

'Well, she can't talk very clearly, or walk very well so she's in a wheelchair. But she's really bright and can use the computer, although it takes her longer than most people.'

'That's incredible.' He brushed her shoulder, as though he were flicking off a piece of fluff. 'I bet you're an amazing mum.'

'Well . . .'

'Don't argue. I can tell you are. Warm, caring and affectionate. What more could anyone ask?'

Susan didn't know what to say. He was still talking and seemed unaware of her awkwardness. 'Now, how about a quick drink?'

'Sorry.' She'd have liked to, she really would, but it was hopeless. 'I've got to get back to Tabitha.'

'Of course. Another time, then?'

She smiled. 'That would be lovely.'

The following Saturday, Josh was still distinctly off-hand and Steff cool, but without being hostile. Susan tried to say something but they whisked Tabitha away without giving her a chance. She wasn't staying the night, Susan still wasn't ready for her to do that every weekend, but she had to admit that the arrangement helped her as much as Tabitha. She spent the day showing more couples round two more new developments, both of which were within half an hour's walking distance of home. With any luck, she might lose more weight with all the exercise.

That evening, Tabitha came back, proudly clutching a drawing of geometric shapes in bright primary colours. 'Redredred,' she said, beaming. 'Blueblueblue.'

Susan was astounded. 'We've been working on her colours but she's never been as clear as that before.'

Steff was pleased. 'I got some shapes from Occupational Therapy at the hospital and we spent ages doing it, didn't we, Tabs?'

Susan felt a stab of jealousy. It wasn't fair. She, too, had spent ages trying to do the same thing but Steff had got the result.

'Listen, there's something I need to say.' She tried to remember Earth Mother's sensible words. 'I'm sorry I said what I did on the radio but I suppose it was because I was angry. And I still am.' She glowered at Josh. 'I said Tabitha shouldn't have had the

MMR, I told you I was worried about it, but you always think you know best. And if you'd listened to me, she wouldn't be like this.'

'You don't know that, Susan.' Steff's eyes flashed. 'There isn't any evidence.'

'I don't need evidence. I'm her mother. I know it.'

'I think she's right,' Josh said quietly. 'I know we can't prove anything but that was when Tabs changed – after she had the jab. And that's why I had to leave. Don't you see? I felt so terribly guilty.'

His eyes glistened with tears and somehow Susan was reaching out to touch his arm. 'Why didn't you listen to me? *Why?*'

'Dad, Dad. Mum, Mum.'

Susan gasped. She'd never before heard Tabitha say both at the same time. It was agonisingly poignant, and automatically she looked at Steff.

Steff smiled. 'Susan – and Josh – if this is going to work, we've got to put all this behind us. For Tabitha's sake. Don't you think?'

Susan sat down heavily next to her daughter. None of this was meant to have happened to her, none of it. But it had, and now it was time to deal with it, fairly and squarely. She had to stop feeling angry with Josh. He had only been trying to do his best for their daughter. And, besides, although she hated to admit it, she could see that her daughter was benefiting emotionally from having a father. And, although it made her feel terrible to acknowledge it, Joy was right. It was good for her, too, to have some time to herself.

'Yes.' She nodded, drawing Tabitha to her. 'Yes, I agree.'

'Josh?'

Susan watched with grudging admiration as Steff forced him to reply. She could handle him in a way that Susan had never been able to.

He nodded. 'So do I.'

'Good.' Steff's head bobbed up and down. 'Well we must be getting off now. We're going to the gym.' She glanced pitifully at Susan's baggy skirt.

Suddenly Susan felt fat and dowdy, wishing, too late, that she'd changed out of the skirt which hid the joyous fact she'd lost five pounds through running up and down stairs at work.

'Jimjimjim,' demanded Tabitha.

'Not us, Tabs. We can't go to the gym. But you'll see Dad and Steff next weekend.'

'You certainly will,' beamed Steff. 'By the way, how's the campaign going?'

Susan grimaced. 'Not great. We've been trying to get the paper to run another piece but they don't want to do anything until there's a new angle, apparently. The council are meeting before Christmas to make their final decision.'

'Well, I'll keep my fingers crossed. Now we must get going or the gym will be shut. See you soon!'

Tabitha spent the rest of the evening, saying, 'Jimjim,' plaintively. I'd like to go to the gym too, thought Susan, ruefully, if I could afford the membership fee. But what about swimming? When she'd browsed through the Weight Watchers site the other day, she was struck by how much weight some women had lost through exercise. She passed the new pool during almost every driving lesson. It was on the bus route and she could go when Tabitha was at school. Until now it had seemed self-centred to do something for herself when Tabitha's life was so messed up. But that pitying look on Steff's face had triggered something. Losing a mere five pounds wasn't enough. It was time to re-evaluate her life.

The following week, Susan had been at the Acacia Grove show houses all day when she heard Simon's car draw up outside. Good, she thought. She could do with some company. Now it was almost autumn, there were fewer viewers, and she'd switched all the office lights on at four o'clock, nearly two hours ago. She was in no rush to get home: this weekend, Tabitha was staying over with Josh and Steff and the thought of her empty house was intimidating, as was the walk back, even though she'd brought a torch. She was cold too; the new blouse she'd bought for work was thin and a bit lower at the neck than she'd thought.

'Hi.' Simon walked in. 'There you are, Susie! Thought you might like a lift.'

'Thanks.' Susan picked up her coat and slipped her mobile, which had run out of battery again, into her bag. 'It's been very quiet, I'm afraid.'

'Not your fault. Or mine. The market's slowing down for Christmas – but our MD doesn't like it.'

Susan felt concerned. She'd heard Simon and a couple of the others talking about how bad the market was and that there were bound to be cutbacks. She hoped she wouldn't be one of them.

'What about the Jones'? They came in twice today and said they were going to the office to see you.'

He shook his head ruefully and she became aware of a stale alcohol smell that she remembered from the early Josh days. 'Never showed up. None of us will get our bonuses this Christmas if things don't improve. Here, let me help you with your coat.'

'It's all right.'

His hand brushed her right breast (a mistake, surely?) and she edged away. 'Simon, I said I can manage.'

'You're a lovely woman, Susie. Do you know that?'

Oh, God, he *was* drunk.

She stepped backwards and fell over a Regency-striped chair. 'Please, Simon, don't. I'm not ready for that kind of thing.'

'Not ready?' He grinned. 'I think you are. I think you're gagging for it. A woman like you on your own for – how many years? I'm doing you a favour.'

He lunged at her, ripping her blouse. The shock took her by surprise. Simon fancied her? Surely not. In a blur, she recalled the flirty way he had talked to her in the office and the way he put his hand on her back when she went through a door in front of him. But that didn't mean anything, did it? Or had she been horribly naïve?

'No – I said no!' Oh, my God – he was coming towards her! There was a heavy vase on the occasional table next to her.

'There's plenty of bedrooms upstairs.' He leered. 'I fancy the one with the striped canopy. Ow! *Ow!*'

The piercing screech of the rape alarm – which Joy had advised her to buy when she'd taken the job 'just in case' – shocked her too.

'You bitch. Turn it off. Turn it *off.*'

'Everything OK in here?'

'No.' Susan wheeled round, clutching her torn blouse. 'No, it's not.'

Thank God! It was the Jones'.

'I do apologise, Mr Jones,' said Simon, thickly. 'My colleague and I were having a discussion.'

'I think you'd better leave,' said the older man.

His wife went to Susan's side. 'Are you all right, dear?'

She nodded numbly.

Simon shook off Mr Jones' hand. 'All right, I'm going. And don't worry about your resignation letter, Susie. We'll take it as read that you won't be coming back next week.'

The Jones', who had returned on impulse for a third viewing on the off-chance that she was still there, were adamant about driving her home. They insisted that she should ring the area manager on Monday and tell him what had happened.

But who would the manager believe? Simon, who had been there for ages, or a new, inexperienced trainee? The house was dark when she went in and it was difficult to fit the key into the lock. The phone started to ring before she had turned on the hall light and she fumbled for the switch. It stopped just as she got to it, then rang again.

Susan's skin crawled. Simon had her home number. 'Yes?'

'It's me, Steff.'

She hadn't recognised the low, tearful voice. The internal bits of her chest bunched up inside her.

'What's wrong?'

'Tabitha's had a fall.' The sobs were whooping out of her. 'Can you get over to the hospital, Susan? As soon as you can.'

34

A and E! They were in A and E? The words seemed unreal and she floundered for a moment, unable to think. Then, somehow, she picked up the phone again and rang the local taxi company she used if Dad couldn't make the long drive over, and stammered that she needed someone *now*.

At the main entrance, she'd sprinted towards the reception desk, almost colliding with an empty wheelchair. 'My daughter. Tabitha Thomas.' She was gasping so much she could barely get the words out. 'Her father brought her in about an hour ago.'

'Sit down, dear. Now, let's start again, shall we? Tabitha Thomas, you say. Date of birth? Family doctor?'

'I need to see her *now*!' She was almost screaming.

The woman was tapping something into the screen. 'I understand but I need to find out where she is first. Right. Got her. She was seen by a doctor in A and E about twenty minutes ago. Let's see what's happened to her, shall we? Won't be a minute.'

Susan wanted to bang her head on the desk. She'd seen kids doing that at the centre and, for the first time, she understood why it made them feel better.

'Right. She's in X-ray. Don't panic. It seems like an arm injury. Nothing too awful.'

'What kind of arm injury?' Visions of Tabitha screaming with pain shot into her head.

'I don't know, but the department is along the corridor, past Maternity and first left. OK?'

She wanted to run but too much was going past her. A trolley with someone grey poking out from a white blanket. A wheelchair

234

with a youngish woman in it being pushed by an older man. Past Maternity and first left, then through heavy doors.

'Tabitha!' She flew towards her. 'Darling, it's all right. Mummy's here.'

Tabitha's thin right arm – the left was in a sling – reached round her neck. 'Mummummum.'

Gently, Susan mopped her daughter's face, which was streaked with tears. Then she confronted her ex. 'What happened?' she demanded.

Josh was sitting with his head in his hands on the other side of the wheelchair, Steff next to him, pinched and pale. 'We were getting her out of the car. We'd had a lovely evening at the cinema and everything was going great. But when we got back to the house, the light wasn't good in the street – one of the lamp-posts must have gone out—'

'I said, what happened?'

'Josh was trying to help her out of the car and I was putting up the chair and she slipped.'

'So you dropped her,' she spat. 'You *dropped* her.'

'She slipped, Susan.' Josh raised his head and his eyes were raw with agony. 'She's so heavy. She just slipped. It's her wrist that seems to hurt and part of her arm.'

'She's had the X-ray,' said Steff, 'and we've got to wait for a few minutes – look, here's the radiographer.'

'Tabitha Thomas?'

Susan leaped up. The radiographer was looking at her and then Steff. Had Steff passed herself off as Tabitha's mother? 'I'll take those. This is *my* daughter. Can you tell me if her wrist is broken?'

'I'm sorry. The doctor needs to see you first. Can you take your daughter and the X-rays back to A and E? Do you remember where to go?'

They walked down the corridor, Susan pushing Tabitha, who had stopped weeping now.

'They didn't want to give her a drink until they'd taken the

X-ray in case they had to operate,' whispered Steff. 'Such a brave soul, isn't she? You know, Sue, I could probably tell you if it's broken if I peep at those X-rays.'

'No.' Susan clasped the large brown envelope firmly under her arm. 'No. You've done enough already.'

The doctor had been quite clear. The wrist was badly swollen but it wasn't broken and neither was the arm. There was no need to plaster it, although Tabitha should wear a splint support. He also recommended anti-inflammatory tablets. If it still hurt in a few days, they were to come back.

'He was certain there wasn't a crack?' Steff kept asking, as they went back to the car. 'X-rays don't always pick things up. When I was on Orthopaedics, we used to do a scan to make sure.'

'He seemed definite enough.' Susan gritted her teeth as she lifted her daughter into the back. 'No, Steff, I can manage. I do it every day. He said her wrist was badly swollen . . .'

'Oedema,' said Steff, smartly.

The woman could be *so* infuriating! In contrast, Josh was still very quiet, slumped in the passenger seat as Steff took the wheel. The relief that Tabitha hadn't broken anything almost made Susan sorry for him. 'It's OK, Josh.' She lowered her voice before she got in to join her daughter in the back. 'She is heavy. I find it difficult too.'

'It still shouldn't have happened.'

'Well, it did and she's OK.'

'We'll take you home.'

'All right.'

No mention of next weekend. Would she trust them to have Tabitha again? *No.* On the other hand, her daughter needed to see her father regularly. And – such a selfish thought – she'd then need to ask her own father to have Tabitha if she wanted to find another job.

Simon! She'd almost forgotten about him during the panic over

Tabitha. But as Josh drew nearer the house, the reality of what might have happened began to sink in. Should she complain? He was so much more senior that they might not take her seriously. Better, surely, not to go back at all.

35

Lisa only just had time to finish her dinner duty at the special-needs centre before her baby-room shift. The 'Oh, Lisa, what *would* we do without you?' chorus from the centre mums made the rush worthwhile, even though Mandy, Mrs Perkins's deputy, was a right old cow when she got back to the nursery a few minutes late.

'Ah, there you are, Lisa. Hurry up. I haven't got much time and this is important. This one, Scarlett, has just started on solids. But it's essential, absolutely *essential*, that you don't give her any packet baby food that contains milk. She's allergic. See the notice at the end of the cot?'

Lisa nodded, listening carefully to Mandy, the nurse in charge of the baby room. Her qualification always impressed parents looking round Acorn House, although Mandy and Mrs Perkins never let on that Mandy hadn't worked in a hospital for years and had only just started at the nursery after an eight-year career gap.

She probably knew more than Mandy did, thought Lisa, thanks to the new-babies section on Mums@Home.

'When you make up the bottles, make sure you only use the ones that have been in the steriliser. And follow the instructions carefully on the milk tin. When it says three scoops, that's three level scoops, not heaped ones.'

She wasn't that daft.

'You don't have children of your own, do you, Lisa?'

What was that supposed to mean? That she didn't know what to do? Lisa could have screamed with frustration. The parents were the same. When she told them their son – it was always boys – had been naughty that day, or had refused to eat his lunch, they would nod as though it was the norm and then ask if she had kids of her own. Well, she did. Two, to be precise. And a third on the way.

Mandy's double chin wobbled. 'You need lots of patience in the baby room, Lisa. Even when we're busy, you have to pretend you've got all the time in the world. Babies pick up on tension. Now, do you know how to change a nappy?'

'Course I do. It was in my training.'

They had practised on a doll with rosebud lips. She could still remember it clearly. She had just turned sixteen. The course had been her school's idea when she'd said she wanted to work with children. The careers teacher had found it for her: a nursery-assistant course that didn't need GCSEs.

'Good. The nappies are kept over there in the cupboard. We change them every two hours and more if they soil them. Here's the cream for nappy rash but never use the same finger twice or it can infect the rest of the cream in the tube. And always wash your hands afterwards.'

'I know that.'

Mandy glared at her. 'You probably know quite a lot of what I'm telling you but it doesn't hurt to go over it again. This room carries more responsibility than any other room in the nursery.'

Lisa thought longingly of Daisy. 'I don't think you can say that. Surely every child is important.'

'Yes, you're right. But babies are particularly vulnerable. Last year a nursery not far from here was prosecuted because a baby with a rare allergy was given the wrong kind of powdered milk. The nursery had to pay thousands of pounds in compensation and was forced to close.'

'And the baby?' She could hardly bear to ask.

'It died. Now, let me tell you where we keep clean liner . . .'

The baby died. The words lumbered heavily round her head as she followed Mandy to the linen cupboard. Mandy might have kids, but she didn't know what it was like to lose one.

*

'Mrs Smith! I didn't see you today. Where were you?'

Daisy ran up as Lisa was putting on her jacket to go home. 'I missed you. Joe pushed me off the slide and Mrs Perkins wouldn't let me paint.'

Lisa bent down and put her arms round the little girl. 'I was in the baby room, Daisy, but next week I'll be back with you. I missed you too.'

She stroked her curls. 'What a pretty hair-slide. I used to have one like that when I was your age.'

'You must be Mrs Smith.'

Lisa looked up to see a large woman with slightly greasy hair tied back with a rubber band. She was puffing as though she'd been running or walking fast. 'Daisy's always talking about you. I'm her mum. You usually see my husband, don't you?'

Lisa nodded. Daisy's dad was a smallish man who dropped off his daughter without hanging around and was always on time to pick her up. Not the type to stop for a chat, like most of the other parents.

Then she saw Daisy's mum's bump.

'Sorry I'm late.' The woman sat on a chair to catch her breath. 'It was my last day at work.' She pointed at her belly ruefully. 'Not long to go now.'

'That's nice,' Lisa heard herself say. 'Daisy, you didn't tell me your mum was having a baby.'

'She's not. She's not.' Daisy flung her anorak on the floor.

The woman sighed. 'Now, duck, we've been through this before. You know I'm having a brother or sister for you. We've felt it move. Look, it's kicking now to say hello to you.'

'No. Tell the stupid baby to go away.'

Daisy's mum smiled awkwardly. 'We're hoping she'll change her mind when it gets here. Trouble is, she's the youngest. I've got two others and she's used to being spoilt.'

Four? How could this woman have four while Lisa had none?

The woman yawned, revealing large silver and black fillings that made Lisa wince. 'God knows how we'll manage. I've got to keep on working with the mortgage, so when it's three months old it's coming here like Daisy did.'

'Don't want the baby coming here.' Daisy jumped up and down, pulling at her mother's coat.

'Stop it now, Daisy, you're hurting me. Well, nice meeting you at last, Lisa. Come on now, duck. Let's get back for tea.'

No one likes you at school. Face it.

Hi Mum. Your probably wondring how I'm getting on. Not long now and you'll be a nan. It would be nice to see you sometime.

Dear Hilary,
I thought you might like these photographs of the kids . . .

Dear Mark,
Thank you for your explanation. However, I am deeply concerned that if you send wrong messages to me, you might do so to others. Please ensure such mistakes do not happen again.
Yours (please do not take this literally),
Clive

CV – DRAFT ONLY
Susan Thomas
Age: 36
Experience: Telesales, Voluntary care worker, estate agent assistant
Now looking for similar post. Flexible hours, if possible.

. . . so you see, I feel as though I've lost a kind of 22-year marital no-claims-bonus but, at the same time, found something I never knew was out there. Does that make sense? I wish you weren't so far away, Janie. And make sure you tear up this letter before anyone else reads it.

OCTOBER

Mums@Home.co.uk

JOIN OUR ONLINE DISCUSSIONS ON

Should couples stay together for the sake of the children?
The best Internet filters for kids.

CHUCKLE CORNER FROM PUSHY PRINCESS:

Why does it take one million sperm to fertilise one egg? Because
the sperm refuse to stop and ask for directions!

TIP FROM MESSY MUM

Don't clean up until the end of the day or it will get messed
up before your bloke gets back.

THOUGHT TO KEEP YOU SANE FROM BIG MUM

If you don't like what someone is doing to you, change your
reaction to them.

ONLINE DISCUSSION ON BULLYING

From Earth Mother To Mimi: Educational psychologists talk
twaddle. Trust me. I was married to one. Your gut instincts are
more reliable – and cheaper.

From Expectent Mum To Mimi: Your the one who shud see
someone. You must be doing something wrong if your kid is
STILL being a dick. No wonder hes being bullied.

36

Accept it. She wasn't returning his calls because she didn't want to see him any more. And she was right. They were both married, for crying out loud. But it hurt so much – it was a real physical pain, not being able to talk to her, touch her, be with her, ask her what she thought about the hurtful reply from that stupid woman on Mums@Home, which served him right for asking advice from strangers.

Supper. Starving children – well, irritable ones, anyway. *Concentrate*. Mark examined the circle of sliced gammon suspiciously: 'Peel back for cooking instructions.'

Peel back? Mark tore at the unyielding plastic with his fingers and then his teeth. The pain momentarily relieved the ache in his chest. Blast! The label had torn and the instructions were illegible. He'd head for a compromise and grill them on medium.

There was time to do a bit more work until school pick-up . . . or he could try ringing her just once more. Second thoughts, maybe it was better to email. Less invasive. Less like stalking. Allowing her to reply, if she wanted to.

From mark@marksummerspr.com to CarolineCrawford@beautiful-you.com: Please ring. Urgent.

RECEIVING MAIL

He waited, heart pounding, as a message pinged up but it wasn't from Caroline: it was another brief from a client and . . . what was this?

From CBX Baby Nests to mark@marksummerspr.com: As from
November, we will no longer be requiring your services.

He stared at it, stunned. Then, galvanised into action, he
reached for the phone, which, unlike emails, couldn't be ignored.
'Mark, I'm sorry.' The girl at CBX sounded genuinely regretful.
'They instructed us to use that wording. You know we've been
taken over by that American firm?'

'But you said it wasn't going to change your marketing strategy.'

'That's what we were told. But now they want us to use a
London PR firm they've used before.'

So they wanted a glossy flagship rather than a one-man band
in Oxford. 'To be honest –' she dropped her voice '– lots of us
aren't happy about the changes. I've got an interview next week
and – sorry, Mark, got to go.'

He sat still for a while, staring at the email. He'd need to find
more clients if Ed and Florrie were going to stay at Coneywood.

The phone! Grateful for an interruption to his dilemma, he
seized it, hoping it was Caroline. 'Mark. Clive here from EFT.
Have you seen the magazine?'

It took him a second to register.

'Not yet.'

'They've got a price wrong.' Clive's voice was clipped. 'We've
already had two retailers ringing in to complain. I want you to
get the magazine to print an apology, making the price clear. And
I want another photograph too. We've just paid a huge amount
of money for an advertorial. They'd better not have messed that
up too – unless, of course, it was your fault.'

The implication was that because he'd sent one email to the
wrong place he might make another mistake. Mark felt sick.
Dimly, he could remember Caroline ringing him in Boots when
he'd been sorting Florrie out. Had he been so flummoxed that
he'd given her the wrong price or had the mistake been hers? 'I'll
sort it,' he said firmly, glancing at the clock. He needed to leave
for the school pick-up but this was more urgent. Now, too, he

had a bona-fide excuse for getting hold of Caroline. Hastily he dialled her number.

'Editorial.'

It wasn't Caroline's voice.

'Zelda? This is Mark Summers.' Briefly, he outlined the problem.

'Oh dear. Hang on a minute and I'll check her copy.' He waited tersely, watching the clock hands move round. Already he was ten minutes late for school. He'd have to ring the kids on the mobile to say he was coming.

'Looks like she's put the wrong price, I'm afraid. I'll send an email to the editor.'

'My client wants an apology showing the correct price. He also wants a picture.'

'A picture?' Zelda sounded bemused. 'I'm not sure about that, but I'll let you know.'

And that was that. No proper 'sorry'. Funny. Caroline seemed too organised to make a gaffe – although everyone did from time to time: his life was full of them.

'Clive? It's Mark Summers. They've made a mistake their end.' He took a deep breath. 'They're probably going to print an apology.'

'When?'

'I'm not sure yet.'

'I want to know by the close of tomorrow. Otherwise, Mark, I may have to consider terminating our contract.'

Shit. *Shit!* 'I'll sort it. Don't worry.'

Without bothering to shut the windows or check that the back door was locked, Mark raced to the car. He was twenty minutes late. In just a month, he had been unfaithful (if not technically) to his wife and lost two clients. How bad could it get?

37

'Doing anything nice today?'

Caroline glanced up from the computer at Roger, who was about to set off for work. 'Tennis with the girls.'

'How nice,' he said.

'What about you?'

'The usual. Meetings all morning and video conference this afternoon. I'll probably be late. Enjoy the tennis.'

They'd had these conversations before and they were so wearying. The more frenetic Roger's life at work became, the more he envied her own, more flexible schedule. In the past, she'd felt guilty about this but, somehow, Mark's attentions had made her stronger.

'I will.' She glared at him. 'I work too, you know. And it's not as though you haven't had your share of fun in the past.'

He stared at her stonily. 'If you can't put it behind you, Caroline, we don't stand a chance.'

'If you hadn't done it in the first place, we wouldn't be in this bloody situation,' she said testily.

'Goodbye, Caroline.' For a moment, he looked as though he was about to move forward and peck her cheek, but she turned back to the screen.

'Do try to keep Georgie off the computer tonight, will you?' he said tersely from the doorway. 'I've told you before, it's interfering with her homework. You ought to be more strict. If we get another report like the last one, she should be banned altogether.'

'If you were at home more,' she said, 'you could help me enforce the rules. It's not easy, you know.'

'The reason I'm *not* at home more is because I'm the poor sod who's out there earning the money.'

'So do I!'

'But you're at home more than me so it's up to you to make Georgie work.'

She could have argued back but there was no point. He always got the better of her, always made her feel inadequate. 'Fine.'

He picked up his briefcase. 'There's no need to be sarcastic, Caroline.'

She clenched her teeth. *Just go.*

She waited until the door had slammed before breathing a sigh of relief. Right. She was nearly ready. Put on trainers. Grab a bottle of water. Extra jumper because it was sharp outside. Find racquet. Go to loo.

Afterwords, the soap made her wedding ring rise up her finger. How odd. It had never done that before. Caroline looked at the thin gold band. She had never once removed it – that might have brought bad luck – yet suddenly she had an overwhelming desire to take it off and see how it felt.

Don't be daft. Dry hands. Set burglar alarm. Get out of house before she did something completely mad. What had come over her? she wondered, as she walked briskly down the road to the club. It was just as well that she had one of her weekly tennis sessions: they made her feel alive, just like the kiss that she couldn't get out of her head.

Stop right there. The price of breaking up the family was too great. After all, wasn't that why she had begged Roger to stay?

The other three were on court already, even though this time she wasn't late. 'Hi.'

Ginny, whose girls were at boarding-school and who passed most of her time at the tennis club, glanced at her watch. 'We're going to have a quick run round the outside to warm up.'

Caroline's heart sank. Normally she arrived too late for this. She hated jogging, but there was no escape. Conscious that she was trailing behind, her breasts thumped up and down. *And* she'd forgotten to wear a panty-liner. She gritted her teeth and clenched her pelvic floor muscles as she ran.

'Right!' Ginny's face was glowing with the wind. 'Mind if I partner Laura? It will give us some practice for the tournament next week. Rough or smooth?'

It was rough. Just her luck. 'Want to serve, Caro?' asked her partner Jill, a thin, wiry girl who ran the local branch of the Twins' & Multiple Births' Association. 'I've still got problems with my wrist.'

She always said this but it seemed to work a lot better than Caroline's when it came to backhand. Caroline got her first serve in but then her mind wandered. She hadn't slept with Mark – and she wouldn't. She'd make sure that Zelda dealt with him in future. And she'd continue to ignore his mobile messages.

'Out,' called Ginny, triumphantly.

Caroline cast an apologetic look at Jill. That was the trouble with doubles. You were responsible for someone else's points. Just like marriage. When the other failed, you were dragged down with them . . .

'Isn't that your phone?'

They were swigging water after the third game, which Caroline and Jill miraculously won, despite Caroline's inability to concentrate. Each had placed her mobile on the bench in case a child's school needed her.

'Sorry. Hello, Caroline speaking.'

'Caroline, it's Mark Summers.'

Why the formality, unless he, too, regretted the kiss?

'Sorry to bother you but I've got a problem.'

She listened, perplexed. 'But I rang you to check the price. I remember.'

'I know. I remember too.'

'I don't get things wrong.' She felt cross.

'Well, one of us has.' He sounded polite but firm. 'I'm afraid EFT wants an apology.'

'Karen won't like that. Look, Mark, I have to go. I'll talk to Zelda in the office and get back to you.'

'Thanks. And, Caroline?'

'Yes?'

'When will I see you again?'

'I'm not sure.' She was aware that three pairs of eyes were on her. 'Look, must go. 'Bye.'

She *had* been right. She knew it. The price in the copy was the same as she had written in her notebook when Mark gave it to her on the phone.

'Look at this!' She thrust the page in front of Zelda. 'That EFT chap's moaning because he says I put the wrong price for one of his toys in the educational-toys piece. He wants an apology, can you believe it, when it was his mistake?'

Zelda made a little face. 'Actually, I'm afraid it might be my fault. I rang to double-check the price just before it went to Production and the EFT salespeople told me it had changed. I thought I'd corrected it but it looks as though I didn't.'

'Oh, no! Karen will go mad.'

'I'm really going to get it this time. I'm so bloody exhausted that I just can't think straight about anything.'

She *did* look shattered, poor thing. 'Look, we'll say it was both of us. Make up something about a muddle when one of us was off.'

'Can we really?' Zelda brightened. 'I'd be so grateful. Karen's always on the warpath – *no*, not the phone again!'

'I'll get it.'

'Caroline, it's me.'

Mark's assumption that she knew who 'me' was both annoyed and delighted her. 'I've just found out something that might clarify matters. We were both wrong. The price of that toy had changed but they hadn't told me. They did, however, tell your colleague Zelda when she rang to check.'

'So I gather,' said Caroline, grimly. 'Unfortunately, it didn't get altered.'

'So can I tell my client we'll get an apology?'

SOPHIE KING

'I can't promise anything until I've spoken to the editor. I'll get back to you.'

'All right. Look, Caroline, I really need to see you. Can I take you out to lunch next week?'

Her hand shook. For the first time she could, ironically, appreciate how Roger had been carried away by his feelings for that woman. But could she do what he had done? Before, it had all seemed romantic, unreal and flattering. But now it was getting serious and her knees were knocking. How could she throw away her children's security because this man could turn her insides to water?

'I must go, Mark. 'Bye.'

Zelda watched her closely as she sat down. 'He sounded persistent. I can't stand pushy PRs.'

'Nor me,' said Caroline firmly.

Should couples stay together for the sake of the children?

Yes. At least, that's what she'd thought two years ago. Why blow it now?

Before she changed her mind, she picked up the phone. 'Roger? It's Caroline.'

Not 'me'. Not since that time, towards the end of his affair when he had hesitated because he hadn't known if it was her voice or the other woman's when she had called.

'Ben's working and Georgie's staying late for another play rehearsal. I wondered if you felt like dinner in town tonight before we pick her up.'

No one, thought Caroline, searching for something to say, could accuse her of not trying. Dinner with her husband had seemed like an olive branch at a time when Mark's voice had sparked off all that guilt. But they had exhausted their usual topics – children, work – and hadn't even finished the first course. It was an uneasy silence – the silence of an ill-fitting date or an uncomfortable marriage.

My marriage is running on the wrong fuel, she thought suddenly.

It would be a good coverline if it wasn't so painful.

Everyone around her seemed to be chatting, just as she and Mark had during their London lunch and then again in Oxford. What was it that someone had said recently in an interview on *Woman's Hour*? That was it. Wordplay to women is what foreplay is to men.

'Are you tired?' she asked, watching her husband pick at his chicken curry.

'Not really.'

Another silence.

'Are you?'

'Sort of.' She explained about the price problem that day but he didn't seem to grasp the gravity of the situation. His work was so different from hers – at least the magazine world was relatively easy to understand but accountancy was a mysterious world of figures.

'What was yours like?' He nodded at her prawn soufflé.

'Quite nice. Yours?'

'OK. Look, Caroline . . .'

Her heart pounded. She'd learned to dread those words. Two years ago, they had prefaced a confession she had never thought to hear. As Jeff had said, if you lined up all the men in the world, Roger was the last you'd expect to be unfaithful.

'Yes?' she whispered.

'I am tired, actually. More so than I realised. Do you mind if we go home?'

'Fine.'

Instead of being filled with relief that Roger's coolness was merely down to tiredness – and perhaps boredom with her company – she felt angry. Why couldn't he make an effort? A vision of Mark swam into her head and she didn't try to push it away.

They paid the bill and walked towards the station. 'By the way,' said Roger, fishing in his pocket for his season ticket, 'I've got to go away next weekend – another wretched conference. In Leicester, this time.'

There had been conferences before, which he had later confessed had been something different. Yet this time she knew from the way his eyes met hers that he was telling the truth. 'Next weekend? You won't be able to go to the ball, then.'

'What ball?'

'I told you ages ago. That charity ball I have to go to, a week on Friday, for the magazine.'

He slipped his ticket into the machine. 'Sorry, but I can't get out of it. And before you ask, no, she won't be there.'

'I wasn't going to,' said Caroline, following him down on the escalator. A youngish man, somewhat the worse for drink, knocked into her as he pushed past but Roger failed to offer her his arm.

'No, but you thought it.'

They stood in icy silence on the platform. Caroline felt eerily calm. If he wouldn't go to the ball with her, she'd go on her own, although she didn't relish the prospect: it was very much a do for couples. She stared at a poster as a breeze ruffled her hair, the railway line began to throb and the tube appeared. Roger got on in front of her, leaving her to fend for herself in the crowd of late commuters with briefcases.

It was then that she decided she wouldn't go alone. She'd take someone else.

38

Susan had kept Tabitha at home for a few days to make sure she was all right. Their family doctor had checked her over and confirmed that the wrist was only bruised. Even so, Susan followed Tabitha around all day, applying copious amounts of arnica cream. By tea-time, she was fed up with the phone. Josh had rung twice from work and Steff three times.

'She's better,' she had reassured them. 'She's got to be if she can still do her jigsaws.'

At the back of her mind, too, she was wondering about Simon. He had been way out of order . . . but had he mistaken her enthusiasm for the job as 'leading him on'?

Now, though, she was exhausted. Having Tabitha at home all day without a break made her snappy. Every time she told her off, she'd say, 'Daddaddad.' She'd heard about kids playing off one parent against the other but this was the first time Tabitha had done it. She'd send her to school tomorrow, and on Saturday she could go to Josh and Steff as usual. But then what?

> From Rainbow to Mums@Home: Someone at work made a
> pass at me and then fired me when I rebuffed him. Should I
> report him or accept I've been fired? It was only a Saturday
> job but it was important to me.

It was worth a try. If she'd asked Joy, she'd never have heard the end of it. She'd want to know if Simon was good-looking and whether she secretly fancied him after years of not having it. Joy was frank about sex and had quizzed Susan on more than one occasion about how frustrated she felt.

The following day when Tabitha had gone off on the bus, she checked her inbox.

Just one reply.

From Expectent Mum to Rainbow: Wheres your sense of pride? Hes the one who should be ashamed. Get in their on Saturday and make a stink about it.

Funny. She'd always thought Expectent Mum was a bit bonkers even before she knew it was that rather strange girl, Lisa, at the centre. But this time she had voiced the quiet feeling inside Susan. Simon *was* the one who should be ashamed. She would go in on Saturday, although she might not make a stink. Why should that man deprive her of the first job she'd had for years?

Tabitha had gone off with Josh and Steff, waving her good arm and beaming. Steff in particular had been full of 'We'll be careful's and 'Don't worry's. Josh had still been quiet but had said they'd be back by seven p.m. and was that all right? When had he changed? Was it Steff or maturity? If she hadn't blamed Josh for Tabitha's condition, would they have been all right?

All these thoughts, and more, pounded through her head as she walked to work – for the exercise – instead of catching the bus. To her amazement, she'd lost half a stone when she'd weighed herself that morning. Whether it was the swimming, the walking or the worry over Tabitha's arm, she wasn't sure. Maybe she'd have time for another swim this afternoon, before Tabitha came home. She could also deliver more of the flyers that she and the other centre parents had had printed to put through people's doors. They simply had to keep the campaign going.

Cripes. She was at the office already, and she still hadn't worked out exactly what to say. Should she ask Simon if he really meant it about her being tired? Or should she go above him and complain? Fiona looked up brightly. 'Morning, Susan. Glad you're early. It's going to be hectic today – we're one down – and Mike wants you to be in the office.'

Susan took off her coat. 'One down?'

'Yup. Simon's gone. He left a message on the answerphone, can you believe? He was meant to give four weeks' notice but he said he's owed holiday and is using his entitlement. Cheek! You can have his desk today. Don't look so worried. We'll just get you to take down new-applicant details and book viewings. It's not difficult.'

It wasn't. It was surprisingly pleasant. Whether it was the relief at not having to face Simon or whether it was because she had a natural manner on the phone, as Fiona told her, she began to enjoy herself. She could sympathise with Mrs Cross, who didn't want anyone round today because her son was poorly, and managed to convey to the would-be viewer that it might be better to wait until next weekend in case it was catching. She discussed honestly the pros and cons of Sycamore Drive with an applicant who didn't know the area – good for the local primary but only off-road parking available. And she calmed down an irate woman who was cross with Green & Co because a seemingly enthusiastic viewer had failed to make a second appointment. There wasn't even time for a lunchtime sandwich but, funnily enough, she didn't feel hungry.

'Did Simon say why he was leaving?' she asked Fiona, at the end of the day.

Fiona rolled her eyes. 'Domestic reasons, but we all know the truth.'

Susan's heart quickened. 'What is it?'

'He was after Mike's promotion – you know he was made manager last week? It's my guess that Simon got the job that was advertised in the paper recently, same level at Haywood and Brown.'

Haywood and Brown were their major competitors, which made sense. What a relief! Now she didn't have to say anything.

'Going to the gym?' asked Fiona, pointing at her kitbag.

'Swimming, actually, then a driving lesson.'

'When's your test?' asked Fiona, kicking off her shoes and putting on boots.

'The theory's next week and then I'll apply.' She twisted her hands. 'I was hoping that if I passed I could do more hours during the week.'

'You don't need to be able to drive for that.'

'Really? Simon said I did.'

Fiona grimaced. 'Simon said a lot of things. It's an office-based position, nothing very exciting – answering the phone and making appointments like you did today. We need someone two days a week. Interested?'

'I'd have to finish at three to be back for my daughter.'

'How old is she?'

'Twelve.'

'Well, she'll be all right on her own for a bit at that age, won't she?'

Clearly Simon hadn't told her about Tabs.

'I'd rather be back.'

'Can you stay until three thirty?'

Susan nodded. If she walked home fast, she'd be in time for Tabitha's bus.

'OK, then. Start on Tuesday, if you like. Same pay as the weekend, but if it works out, there's a good career structure.'

Career structure? Susan could have hugged her. 'That's fantastic. Thank you *so* much.'

39

Mark's hand shook as he opened Caroline's message:

> Karen's agreed to print correction over price. Will also run photograph of toy as 'compensation' in next available issue. Caroline.

Caroline? Just Caroline? Not 'love' or even 'best'? Reaching across the pile of papers on his desk, he dialled her mobile number. 'You've reached Caroline, please leave . . .' If he did, there'd be no hope left when she didn't return it. But an email would give her time to think and, hopefully, reply.

> Caroline. Thanks for this. See you soon, I hope.

That would have to do. Not too pushy. But enough to say he was there if she wanted him.

EFT was not as thrilled by the proposed apology as Mark was. But at least Clive didn't mention terminating his contract. With any luck, he – or, rather, Caroline – had saved his bacon. Even so, he needed more work to replace the client he'd lost. Mark leafed through his contacts book. He'd do a ring-round until he had to pick up the kids.

'Cooee, it's only me!'

Why – *why* – couldn't she learn to ring first?

'Mark, dear, how are you?' Daphne clasped him to her ample chest. 'I got back late last night but I wanted to come over to see how you were.' She held him at arm's length and examined his face. 'I've spoken to Hilary.'

He disengaged himself gently.

'I know. We talked afterwards.'

'She sounded terribly low, poor thing.'

'I thought she was all right.'

Daphne switched on the kettle. 'That's because she's putting on a brave face. I can't tell you how hard it is for her, away from you all.'

'Then she shouldn't have—'

'Now now, Mark, please. We've been through this before. Tell me about the children. Did they miss me?'

Mark felt tempted to say that she'd only been gone a week. 'Of course. We all did. Did you have a nice time?'

'Wonderful. I hadn't realised how many nice people go on these cut-price cruises. I thought it might be a bit mixed but everyone was *so* pleasant. And the staff couldn't do enough for us. Mainly from the Philippines, they were, and *so* helpful. Perhaps it's their culture, do you think?'

Mark winced. 'Maybe.'

Daphne patted her bag. 'I've got all the pictures here – I had them developed on board. Shall I show you now?'

'Why not wait for the children to get back? Actually, Daphne, we've had a couple of hiccups.'

He told her about the website and she frowned. 'Computers are such a danger. I've said that all along. Just what we need on top of his terrible behaviour. Honestly, I don't know where he got it from. Hilary was never like that.'

Mark braced himself for the usual diatribe. He would tell her about the educational psychologist later: the website was enough for her to deal with at present. Besides, he hadn't been able to get through to the man yet. 'Computers can be helpful if they're used correctly, Daphne. And someone's just recommended a new filter, which I'm going to try out. Look, I don't want to be rude but I'm knee deep in work and I've got to collect the kids in an hour.'

'You carry on, dear. I'll have a little clean-up and then I'll fetch the children for you. Goodness, we have got into a bit of a mess, haven't we? Burnt something in the oven, did you? Smells like gammon.'

'That was ages ago.'

'I'll buy a spray-on oven-cleaner on my way to school. And I'd better get the vacuum-cleaner out too.'

Mark prickled. 'I've been doing it in the evening.'

Daphne was aghast. 'But suppose someone visits during the day?'

'Who?' He couldn't help sounding bitter. 'My wife?'

She patted his shoulder. 'Don't be too hard on Hilary, dear. We don't always know what we're doing.'

Sometimes it was easier to agree. 'Sorry. My mobile again. I'll take it upstairs, if you don't mind.'

'Of course not.' Daphne was already scrubbing the sink with a pot of white cream she had taken out of her bag. Clearly, his own cleaning materials weren't adequate. 'I've got plenty here to keep me busy.'

Only one company, with whom he had a vague connection, asked him to email a detailed proposal. The rest were happy with the PR representation they still had and one or two had gone in-house. This time last year he'd been in-house too. A regular monthly salary; people to talk to – who didn't need reminding to wash their hands after using the loo; a proper lunch hour when he could read the paper in the canteen. 'But you're a real dad, now,' said a small voice inside him. 'Not an absent one.'

True. But he still needed to earn a living.

'Dad, we're back!'

Ed thundered up the stairs and, reluctantly, Mark stopped dialling. 'Hi!' He ruffled his son's hair, which was stiff with what-ever stuff kids put on it nowadays.

'Gerroff, Dad, you'll mess it up.'

'How was your day?'

'OK.'

'What did you do?'

'Stuff.'

Mark was getting used to this. The only way to prise out information was to ask for specifics. 'What was your last lesson?'

'Maths. We're doing pubic centimetres.'

'Don't you mean cubic centimetres?'

Ed grinned. 'I know but we call them that to annoy the teachers. We started a new game too. It's called Doorknob.'

Mark listened warily. 'And what does that involve?'

'Someone farts and if someone else says, "Doorknob," before they say, "Safety," the farter has to touch a doorknob before someone gets them and beats them up,' explained Florrie, coming in.

Ed grinned again. 'Heffer farted on the rugby field this afternoon and the nearest doorknob was back at school. So we chased him down the road and got him.'

Mark winced. 'Poor Heffer. Any more problems with the other boy?'

The grin disappeared. 'No.' He turned to run downstairs.

'Hang on. You know the rules. Wash your hands and change before tea. And no television until homework's done and trumpet practice too. The homework bit applies to you too, Florrie. How was your day?'

'It was shit.'

Florrie banged the door just as Daphne huffed up the stairs in his direction. So much for the sanctity of a study.

'Those children are impossible, Mark. *Absolutely* impossible. You should have heard the language in the back of the car. If you ask me, they need to see someone.'

It looked like that was the end of work for today. 'They're tired, Daphne.' He lowered his voice. 'And, as you rightly pointed out earlier, they've got a lot to put up with. You've had a long day too, after all that travelling. I'm really grateful for everything but why don't you go home now? We'll see you for lunch on Sunday. Sorry – my mobile's ringing again. Mark Summers speaking. Caroline!' He glanced at Daphne. 'How are you?'

Daphne stiffened and began to tidy some papers on his desk. Mark, waving a hand to indicate there was no need, tried to keep his voice neutral. 'Thanks. That's really helpful. I'll check them out.'

She ended the conversation before he could say more.

'One of your clients, dear?'

He averted his eyes. 'Actually, she's a magazine journalist, someone I've been working with. She's given me details of an anti-bullying organisation that might help Ed.'

Daphne's heavily powdered face wrinkled with disbelief. 'You told someone else about it?'

'She's a mother. She understands.'

'And has she met the children?'

She thinks I'm seeing her, thought Mark. 'No, of course not. I mentioned it over a working lunch.'

'Well, it's up to you, Mark, of course, but if I were you, I'd keep things like that in the family. And I'm sure your *wife* would think the same.'

He waited until she had gone, then went to knock on Florrie's door. 'Are you OK in there? Tea's ready.'

No answer. He tried the handle. The door was locked. When they'd moved in, Florrie had insisted he put a lock on the inside of her door to stop Ed coming in. But it worked against him too. 'Florrie?'

'I'm not hungry.'

'What's wrong?'

'Piss off.'

'Florrie, you can't talk to me like that.'

'Try stopping me.' There was the sound of muffled sobbing on the other side. Mark tried the handle again. 'Please let me in.'

'I want Mum. Why did she go away?'

Mark wanted to pound his head on her door. 'She'll ring tonight – at least, she said she'd try. Please, Florrie, open up.'

'I'll get her to do it.' Mark looked down at his son. 'Go away, Dad, and let me do it.'

Reluctantly he went back to his study, which, at times like this, was a haven. He didn't understand the kids. They either hated each other or ganged up against him.

Slowly he dialled the educational psychologist's number again. Amazingly, someone was still there to make an appointment. He couldn't be fitted in for a few weeks but fixing a date made him feel better. Now he could hear muffled voices through Florrie's door so perhaps Ed was getting somewhere. Better not go out or he might mess it up.

RECEIVING MAIL.

From EFT to mark@marksummerspr.com

Mark scanned the message and groaned. Crazy! First his clients were mad at him and now they wanted to entertain him. The last thing he needed. But he couldn't afford to annoy them. Providing, of course, that Daphne could babysit.

The following week was the usual mixture of work, arguments with the children and a few stilted phone conversations with Hilary. Florrie was being nicer, although Ed had got moodier. Sometimes Mark suspected they took it in turns.

It was a relief to get out on Friday night.

'Why are you all dressed up?' asked Florrie, suspiciously.

'I told you. I've got a client do.'

He knocked on Ed's door. 'Coming down to say goodbye?' He went in. Ed was lying on his bed, cheeks flushed. 'Are you ill?' asked Mark, concerned.

'No.' He glared at Mark and sat up. 'Give me some space, Dad.'

'Come on.' Mark didn't want to leave him like this. 'Come and sit with Granny.'

Reluctantly Ed followed him downstairs. 'Florrie and I don't want you to go out. We don't want to be alone.'

'You're not, dear. I'm here!' Daphne settled herself comfortably in an armchair. 'I thought we could watch that nice auction programme.'

'You'll like that, Ed,' said Florrie, sniggering. 'Ouch. Dad – stop him!'

'Ed, please behave.' Mark heard the weariness in his voice. 'Now, you know I've got to stay over for the meeting tomorrow morning, don't you, Daphne?'

His mother-in-law shot him a knowing look. 'Don't worry about us, dear.' She began to fiddle with the remote control. 'How does this work, Ed?'

He left them to it, adjusting his bow-tie in the hall mirror as he left. An uncomfortable stranger stared back at him; he wasn't used to seeing himself in evening dress. Still, it made a change.

It took longer than he'd allowed to drive to London and find an NCP. By the time he'd entered the glittering hotel foyer, the place was teeming. It was an annual glitzy affair that he'd been to a couple of times with Hilary. In a way, he was relieved she wasn't there: the last time, she had shunned small-talk with a potential client, dismissing him later as boring. Mark hadn't got the contract.

Checking the table plan, he made his way to his hosts, who were quaffing champagne. 'Mingling, are you, Mark? Good to see you. We need as much publicity as we can get. How about some coverage in the *Telegraph*? I see they've got someone here.'

'I'll try to find them.' Grateful for the excuse, he moved into the crowd. No wonder some journalists despised PRs, he thought. At times they were no better than glorified salesmen.

'Mark.'

He swung round. 'Caroline! You look lovely.' She did. That long red dress was stunning, and so were her bare shoulders. He ached to stroke them. 'Are you with your husband?'

Something wavered in her beautiful grey-blue eyes. 'No. He's on a business trip. I'm with a friend. He's gone to get a drink.'

He touched her right arm. The feel of her flesh was electric. 'Look, I really need to talk to you.'

'Please, Mark. No.' She looked around, as if to check that

no one was listening. 'I don't want to talk about what – what happened. It shouldn't have. We both know that.'

'But you're not happy. And neither am I.'

'That's no excuse.'

'Isn't it?'

'No, it's not. Just because your wife's in America and—'

'She's not.'

'What?'

'She's not in America.'

'Then where is she?'

Sod it. He'd had enough of pretending to himself and the kids. Daphne might be able to carry it off and make excuses, but he couldn't. Not any more.

'She's in prison.' He laughed hoarsely. 'That's where she is, Caroline. In prison.'

40

'Prison?' Caroline wondered if she'd heard him correctly, with all the laughter, chattering and music around her. 'Did you say "prison"?'

An older woman next to her turned sharply at the word and Mark nodded. His eyes were feverishly bright but his face was set. 'That's right. Shall we find somewhere quieter?'

She looked round for Jeff but he was lost in a crowd at the bar. It was rude of her to disappear but this was an emergency. Clutching her still-full glass of champagne, she followed him out into the reception area and then an anteroom where there was a sofa. They sat down in unspoken agreement. 'What did she do?'

'Insider dealing.' He spoke dully to the pale green wall behind her. 'I told you she worked for an investment bank. Well, she bought some shares in another company, acting on a tip that she shouldn't have – it's complicated but there was a conflict of client interest – and she got caught.'

'You didn't know about it?'

'She told me the extra money was a bonus.' He shrugged ruefully. 'I'm not great on finance – it's not my field. In the end, she lied so much that she ended up believing herself.'

'But why? Did you need the money?'

'Not really. That was the crazy thing. But you have to know Hilary to understand. She's fiercely ambitious and she likes nice things. God knows why she married me.'

'Because you're funny and warm and charming?' suggested Caroline, softly. 'Which prison is she in?'

He named one not far from London. 'It's one of the few in the south-east for women. And it's got a good psychiatric unit, which is what Hilary needs. She's in complete denial. Says she can't remember any of it.' He rubbed his eyes. 'She's depressed, too, so they've got her on these drugs that make her all dopey.' He shuddered. 'When I visit, the noise is unbearable. You sit in a room full of tables and chairs and have to shout to make yourself heard.'

This was awful. 'But the children? Do they go?'

'We haven't told them.'

'What?'

'Hilary wouldn't let me. She was so ashamed. It was true about her getting the transfer to New York and she'd have gone, too, if she hadn't been caught. Shows how bad our relationship had got. But after she was convicted, she begged me to tell the kids she'd gone to the States for work. That was why we moved out of London to Oxford. Daphne lives there and no one else knew us, so they wouldn't be able to tell the kids about Hilary. It's a miracle we've managed to get away with it.'

He ran his fingers through his hair. 'Christ, we even buy American postcards and stamps to send to the kids, imitating Hilary's writing, to keep up the pretence. And because we can't really post them – not with American stamps – we slip them into the post pile every now and then. We can't ring her directly. In an emergency, we have to leave a message for her to call us. She's allowed to phone us but only at certain times. You can imagine how hard that is for the kids.'

Someone walked past and Caroline paused until they were out of earshot. 'Why didn't you tell me the truth sooner?'

'I didn't know you. On the way back to the station after we'd kissed, I wanted to. But it didn't seem the right time.'

Somehow her hand slipped into his. 'You poor thing.'

He stiffened. 'I don't want sympathy.'

'No, I can understand that. Do you miss her?'

Mark took his hand back. 'I miss her for the children's sake, but for me it's a relief.' He grimaced. 'Terrible confession, I know, but she's been impossible for years with awful temper tantrums or just being cold and distant.'

'That last bit sounds familiar,' murmured Caroline.

'It got worse when she moved jobs. Working in money can do that to you and Daphne says she always had to be the best. But she didn't seem like that when we got married. I think I told you she got sort of depressed after Ed. She used to get all withdrawn and say she'd never be taken seriously at work because she had two kids.'

'It's not easy when you're a mother and have a career,' said Caroline, quietly.

'I know, but—'

'Caroline! There you are. I've been looking everywhere.'

She sprang up as Jeff approached, with more drinks. 'I'm so sorry. This is Mark. We've been working together. Mark, this is Jeff, a friend of the family.'

The two men shook hands and she couldn't help appraising them. She'd always considered Jeff tall but Mark towered over him. 'I'm taking Caroline's husband's place tonight because he's at a conference,' said Jeff.

Despite what Mark had told her, she wanted to laugh. Dear old Jeff. So serious and honourable, making it clear he wasn't her date and, if she wasn't mistaken, flagging up her marital status. Then she wondered if he'd picked up on the atmosphere between her and Mark and, suddenly, felt uncomfortable.

'We had to talk work, I'm afraid, and it was too noisy in there.'

'I won't bother you, then.'

'No, it's fine.' Mark stood up abruptly. 'We'd just finished. Caroline, perhaps we can talk next week. Goodbye, Jeff. Nice to meet you.'

His table was nowhere nears hers. She spent most of the first and second courses looking around for him without success. Prison!

'You're very quiet.' Jeff topped up her glass. 'I'm sure he's all right.' It took a second to register that he was talking about Roger, not Mark. 'It *is* a conference, you know. One of our chaps has gone.'

'I'm beginning not to care,' she said lightly. 'You said to me, soon after it happened, that if I spent the rest of my life panicking about whether Roger would do it again I'd go crazy. You're right. If he does, he does. At least now I know that I wouldn't put up with it again.'

'Caroline!' A woman's shrill voice cut in on them. 'I didn't know you were coming! Almost didn't recognise you without your tennis gear! Rupert, this is Caroline.'

Caroline shook the limp hand of a short, squat man in a white dinner jacket next to Ginny, a flurry of white teeth and pink satin. 'Rupert's just taken over a PR company,' she boomed, 'haven't you, darling? That's why we had to come.' She beamed at Jeff. 'You must be Caroline's husband.'

'No,' they said together.

'Caroline's husband is away on business,' said Jeff, smoothly, 'so he asked me to accompany his lovely wife.'

'How sweet,' simpered Ginny.

Her husband linked his arm through hers. 'Better circulate, darling.'

'Absolutely, Rupee. See you next week, Caroline.'

Jeff waited until they were out of earshot. 'Doesn't seem your type of friend.'

'She's not. But we met at the tennis club and she asked me to join her doubles set. I go for the exercise rather than the company.'

Caroline watched Ginny weave through the crowds, her husband's arm round her waist. He might be short and squat with a limp handshake, but the realisation that they had more of a rapport than she and Roger could ever have made her immeasurably sad.

'Would you like to dance, Caroline?'

They'd finished dinner but she couldn't stop thinking about Mark's wife. Jeff, as always, had been an attentive dining companion and talked entertainingly about his work and the woman barrister who had been pursuing him. He was always being chased by women. Privately, Roger maintained that his friend embellished each situation to make a good story, but the rapt attention he was attracting from the pretty brunette on his right suggested otherwise.

'I'd love to.'

The music was excellent. She adored the old tunes from the seventies that made her feel young again. Looking back, as she did too often nowadays, it was the only time when she had been truly herself.

'You've got more stamina than me,' gasped Jeff, after half an hour of golden oldies. 'Where did you learn to jive like that?'

'Roger taught me. Years ago.'

'I'd forgotten how well he could dance.'

'He doesn't now. At least, not with me.'

'Don't, Caroline. You'll torment yourself.'

His sympathy irritated her and she turned to go back to their table.

'Hello again.' Mark looked up as they reached it. 'Would you like to dance?'

'We've just been on the floor,' said Jeff, pulling out Caroline's chair.

She put her bag on it. 'Actually, I'd love to.' What right had Jeff to decide what she should do? 'Thanks.'

Mark was an amazing dancer, seeming to know instinctively which way she was going to turn. Yet at first she felt inhibited. Dancing with Jeff had been like wearing a familiar pair of socks, but with Mark it was like slipping into an Agent Provocateur basque. Thrilling but unexpectedly comfortable – and so different from that terrible party in Oxford when she and Roger had been unable to look each other in the eye.

'That was great. Thanks.' He smiled at her. 'Stay for another?'

She nodded as the slow music started. Without saying anything, he drew her to him, his arm round her waist. Careful to keep some space between them, she put one hand on his shoulder and the other in his. The feel of his skin sent electric shocks through her. 'I keep thinking about what you did,' she said softly.

'And I keep thinking I shouldn't have.'

She felt headily irresponsible, all sensible decisions flying out of her head. 'I'm glad you did. I mean, *we* did.'

His hand tightened round her waist and she wished Jeff wasn't sitting at the table, waiting for her. Slowly, his hand stroked her back.

'Mark, don't.' She disengaged herself. 'I have to go. Sorry.'

The ball ended just after midnight. 'Sure you want to stay overnight?' repeated Jeff. 'I could easily drive you back.'

'I've booked a room so I can do some early Christmas shopping in town tomorrow morning. Georgie's on a sleepover so I thought it would be a good excuse. It was lovely of you to be here with me tonight.'

'It was lovely of you to ask me.' He bent forwards to kiss her cheek. 'Take care. I'll call next week.'

She went up the stairs past the framed Monet prints and along the cream corridor and into her room. Strange to be on her own in a hotel without Roger. Ironic that the noise at home drove her mad, but when she was away she missed it. She lay down on the double bed, still in her dress. She'd wanted to stay with Mark but it had been too weird with Jeff watching.

Her mobile rang.

'Mum?'

'Annabel!'

'I rang home and Ben said you were at some ball.' She sounded suspicious. 'Why isn't Dad there?'

'He's at a conference –' Caroline forced herself to speak evenly and reassuringly '– and I had to be here for work. But what about you? Is everything all right?'

'Fine. Look, I can't be long because I've run out of credit and I'm using a friend's mobile. Just to say I'll be at Auntie Janie's next week. We're having an extra week in Queensland.'

'Are you having a good time?'

'Brilliant.'

'Be safe, Bella.'

'I will. Love you. Must go. 'Bye.'

She'd gone. There had been so many questions Caroline had wanted to ask.

The phone rang by the bed. Annabel again?

'Hello?'

'Are you still awake?'

She moistened her lips. 'Very much so.'

'Look, I'm sorry but I saw you going into your room. I'm staying over too and I wondered if you wanted a nightcap. Are you still dressed?'

'Yes. Sorry. I'm a bit disoriented. My daughter's just rung from Australia.'

'That must have been reassuring.'

'It was.'

'Look, don't worry about the drink—'

'I'd like one.' The words were out of her mouth before she could snatch them back. 'I don't think I'll be able to sleep for a bit now, after hearing Annabel's voice. I'd love to go to the bar.'

'It's closed, but I'll come to you, if you like.'

He put down the phone before she could demur. Seconds later there was a knock at the door.

'Hi.' He smiled. A boyish smile.

'Night, Caroline!' Startled, she saw Ginny going past with her husband, clearly surprised to see Mark at her door. 'Maybe see you for breakfast tomorrow?' called Ginny.

'Probably,' said Caroline, flushing. When the couple were out of sight, she let him in. 'How embarrassing,' she said. 'Someone I play tennis with. Now she'll think the wrong thing.'

'Not necessarily.' Mark's bow-tie was askew and he didn't have his jacket on.

Awkwardly, she moved away to put the kettle on. 'There are

some hot-chocolate sachets, or would you prefer something from the mini bar?'

He was standing close behind her – so close that she could feel the heat from his body. 'I don't want a drink, Caroline.'

Turn round and you're lost.

Roger had done this. So why shouldn't she?

Don't turn round.

Against all her better instincts, she faced him. 'What do you want, Mark?'

'I think we both know the answer to that, Caroline.'

His lips felt the same, and she responded hungrily. So *good.* And so right. Then, before she could register what he was doing, he sank to his knees . . .

Something – someone – had taken her over, making her do things she hadn't known she could. It was like discovering a room in her body that she had never been into.

He stopped briefly. 'You're beautiful, Caroline, so beautiful.' The amazing thing was that she actually felt it, even though she knew it wasn't true. Arching her back, she heard herself cry out with pleasure. Suddenly, she saw herself from above. In just a few seconds, she had been transformed into someone she hadn't realised she could be.

And now there was no going back.

41

He had only meant to talk — kiss her at most. That was what he'd told himself last night as he'd almost run down the corridor to her room. But he'd been unable to stop himself.

He'd tried to explain that when she'd woken in his arms. He'd stroked her back — such a beautiful shape — as he'd watched her open her eyes and remember, with a start, where she was.

'It's all right,' he'd said, kissing her forehead. 'You're here. With me.'

She'd sat up, holding the sheet over her breasts. 'I shouldn't have.'

She'd started to cry then and he had held her to his chest. Pointless to say that what they had done had been inevitable, that the urge had been too strong almost from the minute they'd met. All of this was true but they had committed adultery. An old-fashioned word, which many people no longer took seriously. But it mattered to him and he knew it mattered to her.

Now guilt was sweeping over him, making him pay. Even worse, he had lied to Caroline. He hadn't stayed overnight to see his client this morning, but because he had to visit his wife.

The prison building rose before him like a massive red-brick hospital. He went into the visitors' coffee bar. This bit wasn't so bad. You could almost kid yourself that it was a normal café, except that more than the usual quota of people in hoodies, multiple earrings and trainers were around. There were lockers round the sides for bags, and a mother in front of him was trying to cram in a holdall, cursing violently because it wouldn't fit. He hadn't been here since last month at Hilary's insistence. 'Don't come next week,' she had said coldly. 'Or the one after.'

One or two people were straggling out of the room towards the visitors' centre. A man of about his age was looking around nervously. Probably new. Mark had felt like that the first time, he remembered, as he took his place in the queue. The man had two teenagers, both older than Florrie. One had a mobile glued to his ear and the other was kicking a Diet Coke can along the floor. Normal teenagers in abnormal circumstances.

Initially he hadn't been sure that Hilary was right to insist the children shouldn't know, and when he had seen other kids there, he'd wondered again if they were doing the right thing in keeping it from them.

The queue shuffled forwards. The woman with the baby was taking off its nappy in front of the prison officer.

'Why's she doing that?' asked the man with the teenagers.

'Checking for drugs,' said Mark, quietly. A woman with a very short haircut examined Mark's visitor's pass. Her hands were thick – almost like a man's.

'Get a move on, Kieran,' whined a woman behind him. A picture of Caroline floated into his head. Already, the memory of her soft skin seemed unreal. What would she say if she was here? What would Hilary say if she knew about her?

He followed the teenagers into the visitors' centre. Formica tables were placed round the room with chairs. Red for prisoners. Black for visitors. Hilary was sitting in the corner. She was staring straight ahead, lank hair tied back. She was wearing an ill-fitting blouse and loose skirt. She must have lost more weight. Her eyes stared straight ahead – had they upped her medication again? – and she didn't look at him as he brushed her cheek with his lips. As usual, she failed to respond.

Mark sat down, trying to ignore the uniformed officers who flanked the room. One was very close.

'Hilary, how are you doing?' Such a stupid question. 'Hilary, look at me, please. I've brought some pictures of the children.'

Slowly, she held out her hand to take them. She examined each one carefully, still without a word. Then she pushed them back across the table.

'Don't you want to keep them?'

She shook her head.

'Why not?'

'Someone will tear them up.' Her voice was so low, he could barely hear it. 'Or piss on them.'

She'd never used words like that before she'd come here.

'Can't you complain?'

Another shake of her head.

'I've brought you some books.'

She took them, without looking at the titles.

'It's not long now.' He tried to say 'darling' but it wouldn't come out. 'Just another two months.'

She was looking behind him again, as though she had noticed something on the blank wall.

'Please, Hilary. Please say something.'

'Go.'

At first he thought he hadn't heard her properly. 'Sorry?'

'*Go.*' She stood up, sweeping the books off the table with her arm. '*Go away, Mark. Go away.*'

Everyone was staring at them. The teenagers who'd been in front of him in the queue were at the next table. One was still fiddling with the empty can.

'Don't be silly, Hilary,' he said calmly. 'I understand you're upset but we can still talk.'

'*Go away.*'

Two officers marched over to them. 'I didn't say anything to upset her,' said Mark. 'I don't understand.'

'Back you go,' said one, holding Hilary's arm.

'But time's not up,' said Mark, panicking.

'Any disturbances and you're out. That's the rule. This way.'

''Bye, Hilary, see you next week.'

Hilary pulled away from the officer. 'No. I don't want to see you next week. I don't want to see you until I'm out of this place. Understand?'

He nodded. It was the longest sentence she had uttered since he had been there. But what would happen when she *was* out? And where would it leave him and Caroline?

42

The first thing she did after she left the hotel was find a chemist. She had never been into it before – a rather smart one off Marylebone High Street. Mark had been careful but she had felt the familiar ovulation twangs this morning, warning her that she was in her fertile period, and she wasn't taking any chances.

Deep breath. Had to be done.

'Do you sell the morning-after pill?' she had asked the young assistant, trying to sound as though she was asking for sticking plasters.

Georgie had been right. It was easy. Not cheap – how did teenagers afford it? – but straightforward.

Then she'd taken a taxi home, unable to face the early Christmas shopping she'd been intending to do. She had made love to another man. She could still feel him inside her. Why did it seem so right when it was clearly so wrong?

'I love you,' he had said at the door of her room, when he had left this morning. 'I know it sounds crazy after such a short time but I really do.'

She felt the same. It was the way they could talk about anything for ever. The way her insides were melting as she made her way up the path and into the house, glimpsing Roger's briefcase in the hall. Not home already, surely?

'Hi.' He gave her a perfunctory peck on the cheek. His touch made her recoil. 'How was the ball?'

'OK. I didn't expect you back until later.'

'One of the speakers cancelled.' Roger yawned without bothering to put up his hand. 'Quite a relief, actually, because it gives me a full day at home. Feel like going to the cinema tonight?

Georgie's announced she's got another sleepover so we don't need to find a sitter.'

'I'm not sure.' She turned her back on him so that she didn't have to see his eyes and pretended to search for something in her bag. She felt so different that it must surely be apparent in her face that something had happened.

'Well, think about it.' Roger disappeared into the kitchen. 'Want a coffee?' he called.

'Not yet.' She ran up the stairs. 'Maybe in a few minutes.'

She locked herself into the bathroom and sat down on the closed loo lid. For so long now she had made herself believe she could revive her marriage. But now that Mark had shown her what it *should* be like, she had to confront the truth. She and Roger were dead.

Hardly knowing why, she lay down on the bathroom carpet, eyes closed. Remembering. Pretending he was there. Her entire body ached for him. She wanted Mark now, inside her. She wanted to feel his skin, his tongue, his hands, which had played her body in a way no one ever had before.

It was almost amusing. Here she was, on the wrong side of forty-five, and she had only now discovered what sex was really like. How could she ever have confused it with Roger's fumbling?

There was a knock at the door. 'Ready for coffee now?'

'Coming.'

Downstairs, she began numbly to prepare lunch. The house was deathly quiet without Georgie. Did she really want to spend the rest of her life in a silent house with a man she couldn't talk to?

No. *No*. He'd brought her flowers. Stargazer lilies, lying innocently on the kitchen table, beautifully tied with pink ribbon. She picked them up. 'Thanks.'

'What?' Roger was sitting down with the paper. 'Oh, yes. Those. Well, I know you like them.'

A vision of the flower stall came back to her. 'Where did you get them?'

'The station. Why?'

'I didn't think it sold them.'

Roger turned the page. 'I've been getting off at Kentish Town recently. I like the exercise.'

The smell of the lilies made her feel heady as she snipped off the long stamens so the pollen wouldn't stain anyone's clothes.

Roger, I've slept with someone else.

That was what she ought to tell him. That was what he should have told her before she'd found out, but he'd been too scared of the consequences.

As, now, was she.

She kept her mobile with her all through the weekend in the back pocket of her jeans. If he rang, she'd tell Roger it was a work call. To his annoyance, she sometimes had to interview people at weekends. Suddenly, the connection between mobile phones and marriage break-ups, which she'd read about with a degree of moral righteousness, seemed poignantly apt.

By Sunday evening, the need to hear Mark's voice was agonising. Why hadn't he called? Did he regret what had happened? Did he assume she was the kind of woman who was accustomed to extramarital affairs?

'Can I use your mobile, Mum?'

Georgie had come up behind her stealthily. Caroline jumped. 'No. I'm expecting a call.'

'Who?'

'Annabel.'

'She'll use the house phone.'

'She can't. Ben's on it. For God's sake, Georgie, use your own.'

'I can't. I've run out of credit.'

'There's no need to snap,' said Roger. 'Use mine, if you like, Georgie. But be quick. Another glass of wine, Caro?'

'No.'

Roger was right. She was snapping just like he had in the months before she had found out about him and that woman.

'Can we go shopping during the week, Mum? You said I could get some new jeans. And there are loads of parties coming up before Christmas – I need tops too.'

Christmas? She couldn't take that. Not if she had to share it with someone she didn't love.

'I'll take you,' said Roger, smoothly.

Georgie hugged him. 'Thanks, Dad, that would be great. You're the best.'

By Tuesday, Mark still hadn't called. Caroline could hardly eat, yet had a constant craving for sweet tea. She'd been taken in, stupidly, by a man who'd had the hots for her because his own wife, poor woman, wasn't available. At tennis that week, though, she laid her own mobile beside the others. It rang as she and Jill were winning the first game.

'Sorry. Must get that. Won't be a second.'

PRIVATE NUMBER.

Her heart leaped. 'Hello?'

'It's Mark. Look, I'm sorry I haven't been able to phone. It's been manic. Hilary's been ill and I had to farm out the kids so I could go and see her.'

'What kind of ill?'

'She cut herself again. With a knife she'd stolen from the kitchen when she was on vegetable duty.'

'How awful.'

Ginny and the others were muttering by the net; Ginny in particular was talking furiously in low, hushed tones.

'Look, I just wanted to say that Friday was amazing.'

Relief washed over her as she turned away from the other women, towards the car park. 'I feel the same.'

'I need to see you again, but it's difficult with the children and Hilary.'

'I understand.'

'I'll ring as soon as I can. OK?'

'OK.'

'I love you, Caroline.'

'Me too.' The words were out of her mouth before she could take them back.

He'd gone. 'Sorry.' She walked back to the others unsteadily. 'A work call I couldn't get out of.'

In the bath that night she slipped off her wedding ring and laid it on the side. It came off easily, as though those twenty-two years counted for nothing. Only when she had dried herself, did she put it back on. But her hands were hot from the bath water and the ring stuck at her knuckle. She had to push it down. For a few seconds, it seemed as though it wouldn't go and her heart thudded at the thought of the questions Roger would ask. Then it moved back to its old place, weighing down her finger, weighing down her soul.

43

Should couples stay together for the sake of the children?

Was Mums@Home crazy? Like she'd told them, before leaving for work this morning, no one did that any more. Kevin hadn't. And neither had her mum.

Two scoops of soya-milk powder. Stir into cooled boiled water.

Scarlett was sucking greedily, her eyes fixed on Lisa. How could anyone leave their tiny baby here all day? She'd checked her notes. Both of Scarlett's parents had the same contact numbers because they worked together. So it wasn't as though the mother was on her own, and had to work.

Lisa had only ever wanted to be a mum. Funny, really, when you thought how bad her own mum was at it. Always moaning about having five mouths to feed. Always getting her to help out with the younger ones.

'Is that baby still feeding?' Mrs Perkins made her jump when she poked her sharp face round the door. 'She should be having her nap now. Otherwise the others will be late with their feeds. Look, Elton's whingeing already.'

'She's nearly finished. You love your food, don't you, Scarlett?'

Lisa held her tenderly against her shoulder, stroking her back to bring up the wind. 'That's right. Clever girl.'

'I must say, Lisa,' said Mrs Perkins, in a softer voice, 'you do have the knack.'

Flushing with pleasure, Lisa reluctantly put Scarlett into her baby chair and prepared Elton's bottle. He was yelling now; loud angry squalls that were disturbing the third baby in the nursery. Would Sky have yelled like that? No. She'd have been like Scarlett, with the same rosy lips. Petite. Popular. Clever. Everything Lisa hadn't been at school.

'You all right, Lisa?'

Mrs Perkins was giving her the evil eye again. She didn't like that woman: to her, babies were money, not little people.

Lisa stared back. 'Fine. Come on, Elton, let's give you your grub.'

Blimey, she was tired. Almost too tired to miss the cracks on the pavement on the way home. But not quite. She couldn't afford to take risks. Not when she was so close.

Sit down. Have a nice cup of tea.

'Lisa! Lees?'

Why did Kiki have to bang on the wall when she wanted something instead of coming round?

'What?'

'Lend us some sugar, can you? Just a bit.'

'I'll bring it over.'

Too late. She was at the door. 'Thanks, ever so.' Kiki was in her dressing-gown even though it was only just past six. 'Ryan's got a sweet tooth.'

Lisa could tell she was dying for her to ask about Ryan but she wasn't going to give her the pleasure. Sometimes Lisa felt mean for disliking Kiki so much. After all, if it hadn't been for Kiki, she could have bled to death. But every time she saw the woman and her kids, she was reminded of what she didn't have.

'What's that noise?'

Lisa thought the mobile had finished. 'Just a musical toy I've bought my niece.'

Kiki was trying to peer into the nursery now. 'Been decorating, have you?'

'Yes. Look, I've got to go. See you.'

'Hang on, Lees, you've got to come clean. When's this baby due?'

Lisa ran her hands over her stomach. 'I'm not sure.'

Kiki nodded. 'You don't want to say anything in case something goes wrong again. Well, you can trust me.' She tapped the side of her nose. 'I won't say nothing to anyone.' She winked. 'Who's the father, then? Not Kevin?'

Lisa pushed the door towards her. 'Like I said, I've got to go. 'Bye.'

Wait. Wait until Kiki's footsteps have finished clattering across the concrete slabs. Wait till her door shuts. Back into the nursery. Pull the mobile string once more. Sit with back to the cot, eyes closed, and listen to the music. Relax, just like Earth Mother said.

But it wasn't working this time. The memories were rolling back and, try though she might, she couldn't blank them out.

'How do I know it was mine anyway?' Kevin had raged, after Sky. 'There must be something wrong with you if you can't keep them.'

Weak cervix, the hospital had said. Next time, they could put a stitch in. Next time! Her chance of getting pregnant was slim, the ginger-haired doctor had warned her, with only one Fallopian tube. In fact, he said, it was amazing she had got pregnant twice so quickly. Besides, Kevin had walked out on her. If she wanted another baby, she had to pray for another man. And that was when it had all started to happen . . .

Hi Annabel, Where are you now? I've looked you up on my duvet cover but there's a stain over the top right bit of Australia where I spilt hot chocolate and I can't see you. Ben heard Dad on the mobile to someone and thinks he's seeing that woman again but I'm not meant to tell you so. I don't think he can be, as he and Mum are still in the same bed. What do you think?

Hi Kari. Can you ask your mum if I can come and stay for half-term? Dad's always in a bad mood and Mum wrote to say we can't go to New York now because she's too busy at work.

Dear Mum,

Still havent herd from you. R you still there?

Dear Mrs Tabitha Thomas,

I am delighted to inform you that you have won one million dollars in the United States National Lottery. Please send details of your bank account so your winnings can be transferred. DO NOT DELAY!

Mums@Home.co.uk

JOIN OUR ONLINE DISCUSSIONS ON

Do you trust YOUR man? And can he trust you?

White lies: should you always tell the kids the truth?

TIP FROM ALWAYSONADIET MUM

Buy up toys and games in the January sales and bring them out during the year to keep the kids busy.

CHUCKLE CORNER FROM RAINBOW

If a man says, 'It would take too long to explain,' he really means, 'I have no idea how it works.'

THOUGHT TO KEEP YOU SANE FROM BIG MUM

Girls grow up to be women. Boys grow up to be bigger boys.

PARENTING NEWS

Government pledges to put more money into school sports.

44

The following week was hell. He'd had to take one of his clients out for a lunch he couldn't afford, to assure them that a certain Sunday supplement was definitely going to include their new toddler stair-gate in a review. Then he had to take the journalist out to lunch to persuade him of the stair-gate's unique state-of-the-art qualities. Florrie was still moody and Ed had gone very quiet, which was worrying in itself. And Caroline wasn't returning his calls. So he'd emailed her, taking care not to send it through Mums@Home by mistake.

I know how you feel. At least, I think I do. Please ring.

He'd wait a few more days, he decided, then call again. If he still didn't get her, he'd go to her office on the pretext of EFT business. In the meantime he needed to concentrate on the kids and work.

'I've written to Hilary,' said Daphne, when she came in on Thursday evening, carrying a lamb and apricot casserole she'd made for the children's tea. Mark's mouth watered. 'You should write too. Letters are so much nicer than phone calls because you can read them over and over again. Don't look so offended, dear. If I was her, I wouldn't want people visiting me in that dreadful place either. So humiliating.'

'What's humiliating?'

Florrie had taken to sneaking into rooms so quietly that he didn't notice. Yesterday she'd almost caught him leaving a message for Caroline on her answerphone.

'Nothing, dear,' said Daphne. 'Now sit up, I've made a lovely casserole for tea.'

'What's humiliating, I said?'

Mark floundered for a substitute. 'My work. It's humiliating having to ring up journalists all the time and persuade them to run articles.'

'I don't think you were talking about that at all, Dad. I think you were—'

'Phone,' said Daphne quickly. 'Shall I get it?'

'It's all right.' Mark grabbed it, hoping against hope that it might be Caroline – she had his home number.

'What?' He frowned. 'Can you say that again?'

'Is it Mum?' demanded Florrie. 'I want to talk to her.'

'They've put the phone down.' Mark hated calls like that.

'You should dial 1471, dear.'

He was already doing so.

'You were called at five thirty p.m. The caller withheld their number.'

'How odd.' Mark stared at the phone as though it might tell him what was going on. 'Someone just rang – a boy's voice, I think, but older than you or Ed – and said, "It's me."'

'Maybe it's a prank call,' said Florrie, sitting on the edge of the table. 'We do them all the time at school.'

'What do you mean, dear?' asked Daphne, putting a plate in front of her. 'And do sit up properly, please.'

Florrie rolled her eyes. 'When we're bored, we pick random numbers and ring up with cryptic messages. And sometimes we order things. Someone in our class pretended to be a teacher and ordered ten pizzas for the staff room.'

'Didn't they get into trouble?'

'No one owned up and she gave a false name.'

'That's awful!' said Mark.

'Not as awful as the messages Ed's getting. In fact, maybe that's who rang. You said it was a boy, didn't you?'

'Yes.' Mark frowned. 'What messages *is* Ed getting?'

'Shut up, Florrie.' Ed had slunk in, still in his school uniform although Mark had told him to change.

'Didn't you tell Dad?' said Florrie. 'You promised. Ed keeps getting texts that say he's a weirdo, Dad.'

'Is that true, Ed?'

'Fuck off, Florrie.'

Daphne sucked in her breath. 'In my day, children wouldn't have dared to speak to their parents like that.'

'Ed, I won't have that kind of language,' said Mark, weakly.

Ed glowered. 'Stop me, then.'

'Right,' said Florrie. 'I'll tell Dad and Gran the other thing too.'

'What other thing?' chorused Mark and Daphne.

'He was on the computer at school, emailing some girl, and these kids – the same ones that send the texts – came in and held him down in the chair while one of the others typed that she was a slut and he never wanted to see her again. And then her father emailed back to say he was going to complain.'

'That's terrible!' spluttered Mark.

Daphne pursed her lips. 'Well, dear, you'll have to go in to see the head and tell him what happened. I must say, I don't trust computers. All this technology is creating absolute chaos. In my day, we went to see people. We didn't talk to them on a screen or with one of those horrid mobiles that are too small to reach your mouth. That reminds me, when you saw Hilary, did you tell her—'

Florrie's knife and fork clattered on to her plate. 'You saw Mum? When?'

'I meant when Dad spoke to her, of course,' said Daphne quickly. 'I'm getting old, that's my trouble. The words come out all wrong, just like your horrid computer. Now, Florrie, you are going to eat that up, aren't you?'

'No, I'm fucking not.'

'You *mustn't* use language like that. And please come back to the table. We haven't finished.'

'Something's not right,' said Florrie, from the doorway. 'I don't think you're telling me the truth about Mum. Why can't we ever ring her? Why can she only ring us?'

White lies: should you always tell the kids the truth?

He felt like shouting, Yes, Daphne, *yes*. They deserve to know.

'Sssh, dear.' Daphne bustled over to Florrie and put her arms round her. 'Mum's coming back very soon. She'll be home by Christmas. Promise. Don't we, Mark?'

He nodded, as he noticed, with dismay, that Ed's eyes were watery. Oh, God, what a mess. Why was it so difficult to be a good parent?

'Not long now, kids.' He forced himself to sound bright. 'Then we'll all be together again. In the meantime I'm going to look into those text messages. Yes, Ed, don't look at me like that. Kids can't be allowed to get away with that kind of thing.'

'But if you complain, it will be worse,' said Ed. 'Don't you see? They'll take it out on me.'

Mark remembered then how he had suffered when his father had complained once at school. But if he didn't say something, it wouldn't stop. 'Leave it to me,' he said. 'I'll sort it out.'

45

It was half-term and the shops were filling with Christmas stuff. Normally, Susan didn't bother much. Tabitha's needs weren't great and there wasn't enough money for anything extravagant. A new jumper. A couple of jigsaws, of course. And maybe a computer game. It was extraordinary how Tabitha could operate the mouse and the keyboard. But as someone at the centre had said, it was easier for kids like Tabitha to do that than it was to hold a pen. On the other hand, Susan definitely didn't want her getting into the Internet. It was all very well Steff saying it was educational but there were too many dangers, and the thought of her daughter loose in a chatroom made her feel sick.

But there was another problem this year with Christmas. 'We had a brilliant time,' said Steff, when she brought Tabitha back after her first overnighter as it was half-term. 'There's this new indoor playground that's opened up near us with equipment for kids who need a bit more help. It's even open on Boxing Day. In fact, Josh and I were wondering if you'd like to come to us for Christmas dinner and maybe stay over – both of you, that is.'

'Sorry, but we always have it with my dad and June.'

Steff's head had bobbed up and down. 'Bring them too. My dad's going to be there. He's on on his own and it'll be like a proper family.'

Susan had been so taken aback that she'd been unable to think of a good excuse. But she would. Sometimes Josh's nerve was breathtaking. But it was funny that she didn't loathe him in the way she had done before. He had changed, and she had to admit that Steff, despite her irritating ways, had to take the credit for that.

She, too, had changed. A few months ago she would never have guessed she'd have a proper job. 'You'll be on your own this afternoon,' Fiona had said to her. 'I've got a viewing and the temp's off sick again. If the Fieldings make an offer on Silver Street, ring me on the mobile. Otherwise it'll all be pretty straightforward.'

Susan enjoyed being on her own – it wasn't the first time. After Fiona had gone, she made herself a cup of coffee and went through the new property list. Years ago, when she'd been a property buyer, she had hated it when estate agents didn't seem to know anything about a house on their books. Susan knew that her attention to detail had already earned her Brownie points.

The phone rang. 'Green and Co. How can I help you?'

'Susan? It's Joy. Look, I know I shouldn't be ringing you at work but something really exciting has happened.'

'What?' Susan could see a couple looking in the window. 'I've got to be quick. Someone's about to come in.'

'The centre wants you and me to go to Number Ten.'

Susan's first thought was Silver Street, where they were expecting an offer on number ten. 'What do you mean?'

'Number Ten Downing Street! Apparently the prime minister has invited lots of representatives – ordinary people, not toffs – to join in something called a Big Conversation about services for disabled kids. Someone told his office about our campaign and we've got to go along and make our views known.'

'Are you sure?'

'Amazing, isn't it? It's not till next month but we ought to work out what to wear.'

The couple were coming in and walking expectantly up to her desk.

'That's hardly the point, Joy.'

'But they want to know if you're in or not. Yes or no.'

'Yes.' Susan put the phone down. It had to be a joke. 'Good afternoon. Can I help you?'

*

Number Ten? It didn't seem real. But, amazingly, it was. After the couple had left, armed with information on several properties to browse through, Susan broke all her rules and rang Joy back. She had read about the prime minister's Big Conversations in the Sunday broadsheet she occasionally took. Apparently he talked to various groups of people throughout the year. Facilities for disabled children and teenagers was the topic for the next meeting and their centre had been picked as a representative. Susan, who didn't normally pay much attention to politics, was impressed.

When the formal arrangements came through to the centre, it transpired they would have to make their own way there. 'Thought they might send a limo,' said Joy, disappointed. 'We've got to gather at the end of Downing Street. Apparently there's a barrier where they check your identity. Isn't it exciting?'

Luckily it wasn't one of Susan's working days. Her father had promised to pick up Tabitha from the bus after school, although he was less impressed about the outing than Joy was. 'You tell him about the centre closing and what it means to you,' he said. 'The cost of these Big Conversations, or whatever they call them, would probably pay for another term.'

He had a point. So, too, did Joy, who kept wittering on about what to wear. During one of her lunch hours, Susan gave in and bought herself a cheap but cheerful two-piece. She couldn't remember the last time she'd bought something new but she was a working woman now. It had cost her two weeks' wages but it wasn't every day you got to meet the prime minister.

From Rainbow to Mums@Home: Guess what? I've been invited to Number Ten! I belong to a local parents' group and we've been asked to give our views to the prime minister. I'm really excited.

She couldn't help it. Joy's enthusiasm was catching. Until the summer, her life had been so mundane, so samey. Now she was working, having driving lessons and about to meet one of the most famous people in the world. No need to mention that the parents' group was actually the special-needs centre. It was so nice to feel she and Tabitha were, almost, like everyone else.

46

The best bit about doing the dinner shift at the special-needs centre was that she got to use the computer when she finished before she went back to the nursery. But today she couldn't. One of the mums – the one with hoop earrings and that boy who wasn't right, poor sod – was on it. 'Sorry, won't be a minute. I just need to check something on the Net. We're going to Downing Street, you know. With any luck, we might get the prime minister to save the centre.'

That was all very well but she needed the computer too. By the time the woman had finished, Lisa only had a few minutes to log on, using her password. Still, it was worth it. Pushy Princess was really sympathetic about neighbour problems and advised her to make as much noise as she could. There wasn't time to check any more messages because another mother was hovering and she didn't want her to see her private business. Besides, she was already late for the nursery.

'Lisa, can I have a word?'

Trust Mrs Perkins to be waiting. Surprised she didn't have a stopwatch in her hand. Lisa tried to think what she'd done wrong now. She'd been really careful about sterilising the bottles and making sure little Scarlett only had soya. She even managed to keep quiet when Scarlett's mother was moaning about how tired she was.

'Lisa, we're going to move you back to the Blue Room.'

'Why?'

'Daisy's playing up now the baby's arrived and you're the only one who can handle her. Her mother had another girl, and they were so hoping for a boy. Daisy's having terrible tantrums and refusing to sit up at the activities table. You've always been good with her so I'm hoping you might be able to buck her out of this.'

Lisa snorted. You couldn't 'buck' a kid out of hating her new brother or sister. Poor Daisy. 'I'll go and find her.'

Daisy was sitting on the floor in the reading corner but she wasn't reading. Lisa squatted next to her even though it was an effort with the lump. 'Wotcha.'

Silence.

'Want to play with some toys?'

She shook her head.

Lisa didn't blame her. Toys weren't going to help her with something as traumatic as this. 'Shall I tell you a story, then?'

Daisy usually loved Lisa's stories so she took the child's silence as a 'yes'. 'Once upon a time, there was a little girl called Lisa.'

'That's your name,' said Daisy.

'That's right. Anyway, Lisa loved her mum very much until, one day, her mum had another baby.'

Daisy started to wriggle.

'Lisa hated this baby because her mum stopped giving her so many cuddles.'

She put an arm round Daisy, who leaned her head on her shoulder just like Hayley would have done. Lisa glanced round to check that Mrs Perkins wasn't looking. Not that she cared: the rules about not touching kids were ridiculous. Daisy needed a comfort cuddle just as Lisa had when her half-brother had been born. 'She tried to make it go back to where it came from.'

'Where was that?'

'Babyland. But she couldn't find the door. So then she thought that if she couldn't make it go back, she'd better be friends with it.'

'I don't want to be friends with my stupid baby.'

'That's what Lisa thought. But then she taught this baby to walk and her mother thought that was very clever. Then she taught it to talk and her mother was so pleased she said Lisa was the best big sister in the world. And all the other mothers were so impressed, they got Lisa to teach their babies to talk and walk too. And everyone thought Lisa was brilliant.'

Daisy was twisting her hair. 'Then what?'

Lisa held her closer. 'Then the nicest thing of all happened. Lisa found a new best friend.'

'Who?'

'Her baby sister. You see, she loved Lisa for helping her and that made Lisa feel all special.'

Daisy wriggled out of her grasp, stood up and flung a book hard across the room. 'I hate my baby! I wish she wasn't here! Send her back to Babyland! Now!'

Great. Here's Mrs Perkins. And there goes her tray of drinks.

'*Daisy!* Lisa, can't you control that child? And by the way, Lisa, I really will have to take disciplinary action if I see you cuddling her again. It's against the rules. And that's a warning.'

That was what she should have done. Tried being friends with her baby brother. But she'd hated him from the first day she'd seen her mother gazing down at him with more love in her eyes than she'd ever had for *her*.

She might have been little more than a kid herself but that was when she'd decided to have her own baby as soon as she could. Then she'd always have someone to love her. And she wouldn't have to go to school any more.

How old was Lee now? Four? Five? Somewhere, back in the flat, she still had the screwed-up postcard that Mum had sent months ago, with her new address. Devon was a long way off to visit. Might as well be Babyland.

It was going-home time now, and Daisy was still sitting in the corner while her mother was talking to Mrs Perkins in her office. Through the window, Lisa could see a pram by the door. She walked over, heart racing. It was difficult to see much with all the blankets but she could just about glimpse a little face and a pink crocheted hat.

Her cheek was so soft.

She could easily be Lisa's. Her very own special wish, just like the little bear on Mums@Home had promised. *This little bear can make your dreams come true by Christmas.*

The baby stirred and Lisa looked round quickly. Daisy's mother was still yapping away with Mrs Perkins, ignoring one of her other children who was grizzling at her ankles. How could she be disappointed with another girl? Some people didn't know how lucky they were.

They went soon after that and, after she had helped Mrs Perkins to tidy up, Lisa did the same. She didn't have the heart to browse round the baby-clothing shop on the way, especially as her back was killing her. Instead she'd make herself a nice cup of tea and toast before she logged on.

Mums@Home.

Bugger. The bloody computer was frozen again. She turned it off at the mains, then on again, and groaned as a message flashed up on the screen.

YOUR MODEM IS NOT CONNECTED.

Of course it was! She fiddled with some leads at the back but it still didn't work. Now what was she going to do? She certainly couldn't afford to ring the helpline, not at premium rate. And on top of everything else, her backache was even worse.

Bang, bang.

Someone was doing DIY at Kiki's. Probably Kiki's new bloke. Come to think of it, wasn't he in computers? Kiki had told her that yesterday. Ryan. That's right. Lisa didn't normally like asking anyone for anything.

But this was an emergency.

Ryan certainly knew his stuff although he would keep going on about the server and other rubbish she didn't understand. But her computer did seem to be working again.

'You all right, love?' he asked. 'You're a bit pale.'

Lisa rubbed her back. 'I've got a really bad pain.'

'Not going into labour, are you? My sister had backache with her first. You can get it that way round, you know.'

'You sure?' Lisa could hardly get the words out.

'Ask her, if you don't believe me. I think we ought to be getting you to hospital, love.'

Lisa began to shake with excitement and apprehension. It was time. It was really time! 'Hang on a minute. There's something I've got to do first.'

From Expectent Mum To Mums@Home: I think Im going into laber! My naybour's bloke has called a taxi to get me to hospital. I'll let you know what happens!

NOVEMBER

ONE MONTH NOW, EVERYONE, UNTIL OUR PRIZE DRAW!
AND DON'T FORGET THAT WISH . . .

Ed is black but his sister is white.
His mum got another man in the night.

'Ed, what *is* this? You ought to tell Dad. If you don't, I will.'

'Gosh, Tabitha, look at this! Lisa at the centre is having her baby.
Funny, I didn't think she was due yet.'

Caroline – we need to talk. Properly. Not like this.

Mums@Home.co.uk
JOIN OUR ONLINE DISCUSSIONS ON
How much do you spend on the kids at Christmas?
TIP FROM FRAZZLED MUM
Let your children fly and they'll come back.
CHUCKLE CORNER FROM ALWAYSONADIET MUM
An adolescent is an original thinker who is certain his/her
mother was never a teenager.
THOUGHT TO KEEP YOU SANE FROM EARTH MOTHER
Mistakes are gateways to the future, teaching you to take a dif-
ferent path.
PARENTING NEWS
New online bullying helpline launched by charity.

47

By conference day he still hadn't called. Again and again she went over their brief conversation on the tennis court to reassure herself. Hilary, whose name was already familiar even though they hadn't met, had self-harmed. How awful. No wonder he didn't have time to ring. And that aside, they were both married, as Janie had reminded her so clearly during their phone conversation. This was the kind of thing that drove people crazy. It was why sensible people didn't have affairs.

An email popped up on her screen:

Caroline. Please come into my office now.

'You got a summons too?'

Zelda shook her head. 'Probably wants to run through our ideas. She's getting really picky, don't you think?' She yawned. 'By the way, I'm afraid I opened one of your emails by mistake. From your friend at EFT.'

Caroline coloured. 'Really?'

'Mmmm.' Zelda eyed her quizzically. 'Don't worry. I deleted it in case anyone else saw.'

'There's nothing to see,' said Caroline, weakly.

'Sure. Better get in to Karen before she goes nuts.'

Karen was sitting at her desk, a letter in her hand. Wordlessly, she handed it to Caroline. 'A solicitor's letter on behalf of that singles organisation I interviewed for the affair piece?' said Caroline, disbelievingly.

Karen nodded grimly.

'But that's ridiculous!' Caroline felt hot and cold as she read on. 'It says I misquoted its spokesperson, Carmen. What rubbish! I used her exact words – you can see my notebook. The letter says she rang me later to say it was off the record but she didn't. I'd have remembered. Unless, of course, she rang Zelda.'

'I've already asked her. Apparently not.'

Caroline glanced through the glass wall at her colleague, who was pounding her keyboard. 'Am I allowed to talk to this woman – Carmen?'

Karen shook her head. 'Our legal department says you mustn't, in case she says we're intimidating her. They want to see you for a full comment. Did you tape the interview?'

'No. It was on the phone.'

Karen sighed. 'Pity.'

Miserably, Caroline walked back to her desk. 'Why didn't you tell me about the letter?'

Zelda looked up. 'What letter?'

'The complaint about the affair case history.'

'Oh, sorry. I forgot. Besides, you've got nothing to worry about, have you? You've got your notes.'

'She said she rang to retract her comments. Are you sure she didn't speak to you?'

Zelda flicked back her hair dismissively. 'Course I'm sure. Phone. Shall I get it?'

'It's all right. Caroline speaking.'

'It's me.'

His voice was thick and she almost didn't recognise him.

'Roger, what's wrong?'

'There's been a train crash in Queensland, near Port Douglas.'

Her right leg began to shake. 'But that's where Annabel is.'

'It's worse than that.' Roger was speaking in a detached voice, the way he did when he was upset. 'I've had a call from one of the girls she was backpacking with. She's pretty certain Annabel was on the train.'

*

TISCALI HOME PAGE

NEWS

TRAIN CRASH IN AUSTRALIA LEAVES TWELVE DEAD, INCLUDING
TWO BRITISH BACKPACKERS.

PRIME MINISTER TO HOLD NEW SERIES OF BIG CONVERSATIONS TO
'GET FEEDBACK FROM THE PEOPLE'.

48

The suit, which had seemed so perfect in the shop, clung to her bottom as she and Joy walked from Westminster tube station towards Downing Street. There hadn't been time to buy a slip and she kept smoothing it down at the back.

'Bet he doesn't realise who we're seeing,' giggled Joy, after they'd asked directions from a newspaper seller. Susan glanced at the headlines. She wished they wouldn't keep running those graphic pictures of that train crash in Australia.

'Do you think this is it?' asked Joy, doubtfully. They could see a pair of large black gates across a small side road. To the far left of them, there was a smaller one. A group of women and a couple of men were going through, showing passes to two policemen. Beyond, she could make out a line of three-storey ter-raced houses on both sides. It was a bit like a film set, not that she'd seen one.

''Scuse me, is this Downing Street?' asked Joy, importantly.

'It certainly is, madam,' said the first policeman, a young chap with a friendly smile.

'We have an appointment.' Joy produced the pass that the centre had given them.

He examined it nonchalantly. 'Through there, please, madam.'

They followed the queue into what seemed like a Portakabin. Joy and Susan put down their bags as requested and watched them go through a scanner. 'Just like the airport,' hissed Joy. No one frisked them, which Susan found surprising in view of secu-rity. They were instructed to follow a smart woman in a bouclé suit – which definitely had a slip underneath it, thought Susan ruefully – down the street.

'Look at the tourists watching us,' said Joy, gleefully, pointing backwards.

Despite the skirt, it was a good feeling. Unreal too. She mustn't forget why they were there, Susan thought. It was all very well coming somewhere grand like this but they had to tell the prime minister about the centre and why it was so crucial.

'It's not very big, is it? You'd think it would be detached,' muttered Joy, as the group stopped outside a black door. It was open but a man in a suit was standing at the entrance. 'You can leave your coats there,' he said, pointing to a rail. It seemed so ordinary, but when Susan looked around, she saw vast oil paintings on the walls and huge pieces of mahogany furniture.

'Is there a loo I could use?' she asked shyly.

'Through there to the left.'

Fancy using the lavatory at Number Ten! She went towards it, past a buggy propped against the wall. Amazing.

'Come on.' Joy was waiting impatiently outside. 'We've got to go upstairs.' They walked briskly to catch up with the others. The staircase was mahogany too, with beautiful turns. Susan tried to peep into the other rooms as they passed. They were large but cold. Museum-like. Not a place to bring up a family, surely.

The woman in the smart suit led them into a huge room, filled with tables and chairs. 'Your labels will tell you which table you're on,' she explained. 'What we want you to do is discuss the issues outlined on your own table. Then there will be an opportunity for you to raise questions and talk about your discussions with a government minister, who will be moving from table to table.'

'What about the prime minister?' said someone.

The woman nodded. 'He will come in at the end, after Prime Minister's Questions in the Commons. Hopefully, you will have a brief chance to talk to him but he won't have time for a word with everyone.'

Joy's earrings bobbed with her indignation. 'What a con.'

If the woman had heard her, she didn't give any sign of it. 'I must ask you not to talk to the press corps at the far end. They have headphones, however, so they can listen to your conversation. At the end they might ask if they can interview you but you don't have to agree.'

'We can tell them about the centre,' said Susan, quietly.

Joy nodded. 'But I hope we get to talk to the Prime Minister, don't you?'

It made Susan feel so much better to talk to the other parents at the table. One mum from Bolton had a sixteen-year-old autistic son in a residential home. 'I feel awful about it but I couldn't cope,' she said apologetically. Her marriage had broken up, too. But there was a man whose wife was at home with their daughter who had severe brain injuries after being run over by a car. 'We don't like leaving her with anyone else so we take it in turns to go out.'

So I'm comparatively lucky, thought Susan. In the last few months, she had begun to find a life of her own. But Tabitha wouldn't – unless there were more facilities.

'Hello, everyone!' A large plump woman with a beaming smile bustled up to the empty seat. She introduced herself as the minister for the family and asked if there were any issues they wanted to discuss. The man with the brain-damaged daughter leaped in promptly, and described the lack of physiotherapy at his local hospital, which meant they had a two-hour journey once a month to the large one on the edge of the county. The minister nodded sympathetically and made notes. 'Would anyone else like to say anything?'

'Yes.' Susan heard her own voice. 'My friend Joy here and I have children at a special-needs centre that's closing down. Our kids are being moved to a bigger one where there are larger classes and it's a longer journey. It's all very well the government promising more sport for schools, but that's not going to help kids who can't walk.'

'It won't be open in the holidays either, like ours,' added Joy.

The minister was still writing. 'What's the centre called?'

Susan told her, and she promised to look into it. There was a stir, and a posse of cameramen who'd been hovering on the outside of the room sprang into action. The minister stiffened. 'The prime minister's coming,' she said, getting up. 'Please excuse me. It was very nice to meet you all.'

Everyone's eyes were on the door. Susan and Joy were transfixed. 'Here he is,' said someone. He came in so fast amid the whir of cameras that Susan could hardly see him. To her disappointment, he'd sat down at a table at the opposite end and all she could make out was the back of his head – greying curly hair – and a Quality Street purple shirt collar under a navy-blue jacket.

'Will he come to us?' asked Joy, hopefully.

'Depends if he has time,' said the father of the brain-injured girl. 'That's what I was told, anyway. At least we spoke to the minister. Not everyone got her.'

Susan glanced at her watch. They'd been here for ages. Tabitha would be getting off the bus soon. Her life seemed so far removed from this room with its paintings, panelled walls and the man in the purple shirt who was getting up now, and, instead of going to another table, taking up his position by a microphone. 'I'd like to thank you all for coming and also to apologise for not being able to speak to each of you personally . . .'

Joy tutted loudly and someone said, 'Sssh.' Susan winced.

'. . . but I hope today has given you a chance to talk to my minister. It's your opinion and your experience that count – and that's what will help us get it right for you and the rest of the country.'

A man stood up. 'But what do you intend to do for us specifically, Prime Minister?'

'It would take too long to explain in detail. But, briefly, we're hoping that today will be a start.'

Susan could have wept. The platitudes meant nothing. What did the prime minister – himself a family man with a clutch of healthy children – know about undressing an almost grown woman every night, which took nearly an hour? What did he know about helping her to eat and watching her fling food on the floor if she didn't fancy it? How could he have understood Tabitha's screams when her periods had started last month? No one could. Not unless they lived that life themselves. And now it was too late. The prime minister had invited everyone to have a cup of tea before they left. Now it was being brought to the table. She could have thrown it at him.

'Excuse me?'

'Yes?'

A slim dark pretty woman, slightly older than Susan, had come up to the table. 'My name's Zelda and I write for *Beautiful You* magazine. We've been told we can talk to delegates here. I edit a Parenting page and we're doing a feature on special-needs children. The press officer told me you are trying to prevent a local day centre closing down.'

'Yes.' Joy elbowed her way in. 'We are. It's absolutely disgraceful, what they're trying to do. Let me tell you about it . . .'

It took ages to get home and Joy's babble had given her a headache. How exciting it was that this Zelda might put them in a magazine that was sold all over the country. How disappointing it had been that the prime minister hadn't made it to their table, although she supposed it would have been difficult for him to see everyone. How amazing that a man of his standing could be allowed to wear a shirt that colour. It took all of Susan's tact – recently acquired at Green & Co – for her not to tell her friend to shut up.

By the time the bus had dropped Susan at the end of the road, it had been dark for ages. Funny. Normally her spirits sank when she rounded the corner and saw the house. But after a day in London where nothing had seemed real and the so-called heart of government had offered merely a series of empty promises, she couldn't wait to get home to Tabitha.

Dad would have got the supper on by now. He was good at that. Hopefully he hadn't brought June with him and then they could have a chat while Tabitha watched telly. She could hear it through the door now as she rang the bell to save delving in her bag for the key. So nice to know that someone was going to answer, that another adult was at home instead of just her and Tabitha.

'Hi,' said Susan, as the door opened. 'Everything—'

She stopped as she took in the person standing before her.

'Good evening, Susie. Nice to see you again.'

'What are you doing here?' She was shaking now. 'And where's Tabitha and Dad?'

'Inside, of course.' Simon grinned nastily. 'Want to see them? Why don't you come in?'

49

Let your children fly and they'll come back.

But what if they crashed?

Unbelievably there was still no news. The Foreign Office had set up a helpline but, as the kindly woman at the other end had explained, the names of the injured and dead were still coming in. 'We will notify you as soon as we get any more information,' she had said.

Caroline had hoped, irrationally, that Janie could help.

'I don't know any more, Caro. I'm sorry.' Her sister was clear down the line, despite the frustrating satellite delay between Caroline's frantic questions and her sister's answers. 'I've phoned the emergency number at this end too but they're still getting names together. Now, don't freak out at this but Doug says we're more likely to get somewhere if we fly up. That's what a lot of relatives are doing. Caro, are you there?'

'Yes.' She could hardly get the word out. This couldn't be happening. It couldn't. 'But why can't they just tell us if she's one of the—' She couldn't bring herself to say the word 'dead' but Janie knew what she meant.

'Because some of them aren't carrying ID. And . . .'

There was a pause.

'And *what*?'

'Some of the casualties have been thrown quite a distance.'

Caroline let out a low moan.

'But if we can go up there, we might – I'm sorry to say this, Caro – we might be able to identify her.'

'But you haven't seen her for two years.' Caroline could feel hysteria rising. '*You might not get the right person.*'

'Don't panic.' Janie had acquired an Australian twang over the years. 'I'll recognise her. And this friend of hers might be wrong. She thought Annabel was on the train but maybe she meant someone else.'

'She'd have rung us to reassure us. She must have seen the news. I'm coming out, Janie. I've got to.'

'Hang on in there, just for a bit. We'll be up there by tonight. I'll call you. OK?'

50

'Come on in. You're letting all the heat out.'

Simon was grinning wolfishly. He was mad – he had to be! If she shut the door, he had her trapped. She could hardly breathe for panic. 'What have you done to Dad and Tabitha?'

'I told you. They're inside having tea in front of the telly. Your dad asked me to join them. More sociable than you, I must say.'

Disbelievingly, she went into the lounge. Tabitha was indeed in her chair, her eyes riveted on the news, which was showing pictures of that train crash. Totally unsuitable.

'Mummum,' she said, taking her eyes away for a second.

Susan hugged her. Furiously, she switched off the television and glared at Simon, who was watching them in bemusement. In a way this reassured her and the fear that she'd originally felt when he'd opened the door turned into anger.

'How did it go, love?' asked her dad, who was sitting in an armchair, eating toast. 'Your friend called in so I asked him to wait.' He thinks Simon's a boyfriend, thought Susan, with horror. 'He's sorted out that trouble on the computer you've been having.'

Simon grinned. 'Got rid of some viruses. Should be a bit faster now. Mind you, I wouldn't let your daughter get on the Net again, if I were you.'

'She doesn't know how to,' said Susan, indignantly.

'Actually, love,' said her dad, taking his eyes off the television, 'I'm afraid she does. No, don't look like that. It wasn't anything nasty. She was just – what do they call it? – surfing.' He dropped his voice. 'I don't think she knew what she was keying in but you still need to be careful.'

Tabitha could surf? At any other time, Susan would have been horrified by the implications. But right now there were more important things to sort out. 'Don't you think you should go now?' she said pointedly, to Simon.

'In a minute. Your dad would like some more tea. No, sir, don't get up. Susie will help me, won't you, darling?'

She followed him out to the kitchen indignantly. '"Darling"?' she spluttered. 'What the hell do you think you're doing?'

He closed the door quietly, and when he turned his eyes were narrow and mean. 'You mean how dare *you*? Getting the Fairhursts to make a complaint to my new boss! You've got a bloody cheek.'

Her face blazed and the fear crept back. '*I*'ve got a cheek? You tried to touch me up.'

'You wanted me to.'

'*I did not*. But I didn't make a complaint and I definitely didn't tell the Fairhursts to rat on you.'

'Well, they did. And if you don't tell my new boss it was a mistake, I'm out of my job.'

He was standing with his back to the door so she couldn't get out.

'And if I don't?'

His eyes travelled down her body and up again. 'I might have to come back. Nice suit, Susie. Clings to you like that low-cut blouse you wore to get me going.'

Her cheeks blazed. 'I did *not* wear it for you!'

'Try telling that to a court.'

His eyes were flashing dangerously and the terrible thought occurred to her that he might hurt Tabitha if she didn't get him out fast.

He handed her a piece of paper. 'Come on, Susie, don't make it difficult for both of us. I've brought a letter with me. All you have to do is sign it and we'll say no more.'

She scanned it. It was clumsily written, and said she did not wish to make any complaint against Simon Wright; that whatever had happened between them had been with her full consent.

'But that's not true.'

315

He put on his jacket. 'Your choice, Susie. See you later. What time's your dad going?'

She could make a run for it. Dash out and tell her father what was happening. But that wouldn't stop someone like Simon. And he had a point. She *had* been wearing a blouse that was a bit low at the front. Would a court argue that she'd led him on?

'Just go.' She signed the letter and handed it to him. 'Don't say goodbye to my father. Get out the back door.'

She locked it behind her as her father came into the kitchen. 'Your friend gone, then?'

'Yes.'

'What's wrong, love? You're crying. Hasn't hurt you, has he?'

'Oh, Dad,' she sobbed. 'I don't know what to do.'

Her father wanted her and Tabitha to go home with him. 'I feel so guilty,' he said gruffly. 'If I hadn't let him in, none of this would have happened. But he seemed so charming.'

'He can be,' said Susan, grimly. 'And devious.

'Look, love, you've got to make a complaint. It's sexual harassment at the least.'

She cupped her hands round a mug of hot chocolate. 'I can't. It would mean going to court and I couldn't take that. Besides, supposing they believed him when he said I'd led him on?'

'But you didn't, did you?' He was looking at her doubtfully.

'Course not. But if *you* have to ask me, why would someone who didn't know me believe me?'

'Come back with me, love, in case he turns up again.'

'I can't. Tabitha's asleep and it would mean moving her. Anyway, I don't think he will.'

Her father wanted to stay, and part of Susan wanted to say yes. But if she did she'd still have to cope on her own the next night and the one after that. Better to be brave from the beginning. After he'd left and she'd locked up, though, she regretted her decision. Every little sound made her jump, and when she finally got to bed, she held the cordless phone for comfort. Every now and then she got up to check on her daughter. Tabitha's breathing was heavy and regular. Supposing Simon had tried something with her? Susan felt sick. This was all her fault and now she was paying for it.

Unable to sleep, she logged on. Mums@Home.

MUMS@HOME THOUGHT FOR THE DAY
Mistakes are gateways to the future, teaching you to take a different path.

There was some logic in that.

From Rainbow to Mums@Home: Sometimes I think I've deserved all the problems I have in life. I did something terrible when my daughter was little and now I'm being punished. When she was two weeks old, I was lifting her on to the changing table and I dropped her.

Susan's fingers were shaking but she couldn't stop now.

She just sort of slithered out of my hands on to the carpet. She didn't cry and I was too scared to take her to the doctor in case they took her away. Looking back, I think I was a bit mad – I'd been so relieved to have a baby after my miscarriage that it made me over-anxious and a bit weird. I worried about everything, especially as she was a slow developer. She took ages to sit up and she bottom-shuffled instead of crawling. I kept wondering if it was because of that fall and I was terrified of doing anything else that might be wrong. There was a lot of publicity about the MMR jab at the time and I didn't want my daughter to have it, but my husband said I was worrying unnecessarily. Then, about a week after the jab, she screamed and screamed and threw a temperature. Eventually our GP sent us to a consultant who said Tabs had a form of cerebral palsy but he didn't know why. Outwardly, I blamed the jab and my husband – even though cerebral palsy has never been linked with MMR – but it was really an excuse. Inside I tormented myself that it might have been the fall. And I still don't know. Our marriage broke up soon afterwards.

The tears were coming thick and fast now. She hadn't told anyone this before, not even her father. But it was so easy, so reassuring, to come clean to people who didn't know her. Rather like a confessional box.

That's it, really. But it's so hard to cope with the guilt. Every time I look at Tabitha, I know it's my fault.

She logged off. And this time when she went back to bed she fell into one of the deepest sleeps she had ever had.

51

'I'm not doing it. I've told you.'

Ed's eyes were blazing.

Mark ran his hands through his hair. 'But you wanted to learn the trumpet. You nagged Mum and me last year. It cost a fortune to buy.'

'So? That's your problem.'

'Don't be rude.' It was so easy to lose control. He wanted to shake his son by the shoulders, force him to pick up that bloody trumpet, which made the whole house ring – as if his head wasn't ringing enough. Hilary had cut herself *again*, for God's sake. Not badly, just enough to make the pain go away, as she put it. So why did trumpet practice matter in the scheme of things? And why, in the name of God, when there was enough misery in the world – take that terrible train crash, for instance – did she need to inflict such pain on them all? 'If you don't practise, you won't remember what to do at the concert on Friday.'

Ed was halfway up the stairs. 'I don't want to play at the fucking concert. Everyone will laugh at me.'

'Don't say the F-word.' Mark could feel his voice getting hoarse. 'When I was your age, there were lots of things I didn't want to do.'

'Yes, but you didn't have to play something in front of the whole school, did you?'

Touché. He hadn't played an instrument even though his mother had tried to get him to tackle the piano. And Ed was right: it would be terrifying to play in front of the whole school, just as it was terrifying for Hilary to be in that awful place. And maybe it would make the bullying worse.

'All right, I'll write you a note.'

Relief beamed from Ed's face. 'Thanks, Dad. You're the best.'

Had he made the right decision? Or had he been weak?

'Dad, there's something I've got to tell you.'

Ed tugged at her hoodie. 'Shut up, Florrie, I told you not to.'

'But, Dad, it's important. It's about Ed—'

'Cooeee. Only me!'

Mark gritted his teeth. If he didn't get that email off, he'd have had it. He'd been hoping to ring Caroline, too, before she got home. Why couldn't he have a minute to himself?

'How are things, dear?'

She was wearing a smart checked jacket, which suggested she'd been to one of her art-appreciation groups at the Ashmolean, and brushed his cheek with hers. She waited until the children had gone out of the room. 'Any more news on Hilary?'

'I spoke to the consultant.'

'And?'

'She thinks Hilary would benefit from a home visit. Just for a weekend. Apparently it's part of a new initiative to help certain . . . offenders rehabilitate.'

Daphne's forehead wrinkled. 'But if she does that, the children will be really confused, especially when she goes back after two days. It's difficult enough to keep up the American pretence as it is . . .'

'Sssh.' Mark listened. It was all right: Florrie and Ed were arguing upstairs to the accompaniment of Ed's music. 'I told her that, and she said she'd have another discussion with her colleague.'

'I see.' The sparkle had gone out of Daphne's eyes. 'What about the bullying? Did you talk to Ed's headmaster again? And when's your appointment with the educational psychologist?'

'Soon – we're on the waiting list, apparently. And, yes, I did have a word with the head, but it didn't really help. Ed refuses to name the boys who held him down. The head's giving a general talk to the whole school about being kind to others but, if you ask me, that will embarrass Ed more than ever.'

'I heard about a bullying helpline on the Internet,' said Daphne, putting the kettle on, 'and it was in *The Times* this morning. Maybe you should log on. There's no need to look so condescending, Mark. I'm learning quite a lot in my computer class.'

'I don't know how you fit it all in.'

'Well, I need to do something at my age or the brain goes. Now, don't let me stop you. I'm sure you've got work to do upstairs. I only popped round to make the children's tea, providing you want me to.'

'That's very kind of you.' He'd offended her and he hadn't meant to. He looked up at the ceiling. 'Why are kids so noisy?'

'They're enjoying themselves, dear. It's what they're like nowadays. I've been reading up on it. Oh, and, Mark?'

'Yes?'

She handed him a newspaper. 'Here's the article with that bullying helpline.'

The helpline was being run by a children's charity, which was inviting concerned parents to email their problems. Briefly, he outlined what had happened, putting only his first name at the end. Send. Interesting to see if the expert had any solutions – he was beginning to think there weren't any. Kids could be cruel and text messages, emails and websites were natural media for abuse.

Caroline's mobile was off, which meant he'd left it too late. She'd be cooking supper now for her family, talking to her husband and, later, going to bed with him. She'd told him that she and Roger – he'd always disliked the name because it reminded him of a particularly nasty boy at school – didn't have *that* kind of relationship any more. But supposing he made her have sex?

Funny how he felt he'd known her far longer than a few months. Maybe it was those emails. He had definitely said things in them that he might not have had the courage to voice face to face.

'Well, I'm going, and that's the end of it.'

Florrie's angry voice rose up the stairs and through his study door.

His work would have to wait. He went downstairs to the kitchen and found Florrie leaning challengingly against the worktop, arms folded.

Just like Hilary used to.

'Granny says I can't go to the party tonight.'

'What party?'

'I told you! Jemma's having a few friends over. Honestly, Dad, you just don't listen.'

He truly couldn't remember.

'Well, can I go or not?'

He poured himself a glass of cranberry juice. 'I'd like a word with Jemma's parents first.'

'Why? What are you going to ask them?'

'Just directions. Nothing embarrassing.'

'You'll ask if they're going to be in, won't you?'

'Maybe.'

'God, Dad, you're *so* embarrassing! No wonder Ed doesn't tell you everything.'

'Such as?' He was hoping to find something out.

'Nothing.'

She flounced out and he could hear her running up the stairs, then slamming her bedroom door. Seconds later, loud music hurtled down to him in competition with the sound of – yes! – Ed's trumpet. He might refuse to play at the concert but at least he was practising. Win some, lose some, he thought wryly. 'Leave her,' he said to Daphne. 'She'll come round.'

'But what about their tea? It's ready and it won't keep.' Daphne was hot and flustered. 'I don't approve of these young girls going out so much. You don't know what they get up to.'

'Daphne,' he patted her shoulder, 'it's what they do. It's when they get to the rave stage you have to worry.'

Daphne shuddered. 'Don't.'

'Look, I don't want to be rude but I really need to finish off some work. You're welcome to sit down if you want but—'

'Don't mind me.' Daphne took off her apron sulkily. 'I was just off to my computer class anyway.'

He saw her out and bolted back to the sanctity of his study. Such a relief. Much as he hated to admit it, Hilary had been partly right when she'd complained in the old days about him hiding in his work. Computers didn't answer back. They didn't need nagging about teeth-cleaning. And they didn't need collecting from friends' houses when he would rather be in bed.

Mark waited in the car outside the house as instructed.

'Don't come in,' Florrie had said firmly. 'I'll be out by midnight.'

But something wasn't right. The house, a rather nice detached place at the far end of Woodstock Road, was ablaze with colour and music. A girl in a short skirt – very short – came down the path, draped round a boy who looked as though he was barely out of year nine. 'Hi, Mr Summers.' She giggled.

He did a double-take as he recognised Emma, Florrie's friend. What were her parents thinking of to let her wear that skirt or be so intimate with that boy? Mark got out of the car. Florrie had said Jemma was having a few girls over. She hadn't said anything about boys.

The door was open and, amid the smoke-filled crowd of teenagers, Mark couldn't see one adult. This was a party, not the small gathering Florrie had implied it would be. A boy was lying across the foot of the stairs, moaning.

'You all right?' asked Mark, kneeling down.

'He's been sick,' said another boy, who was mopping something off the floor. 'He'll be OK in a minute.'

'Have you seen Florrie Summers?'

'Are you joking? Do you know how many kids are here?'

Mark strode into another room. It was dark, but he could make out shapes lying on the sofa. 'Florrie? Are you there?'

It was impossible to make himself heard above the music. He fumbled by the door for the light switch.

'Oy! Who fucking did that?'

Mark stood, his arms folded. 'I did, young man. I'm looking for my daughter.'

'Dad!' A tousled Florrie emerged from a pile of bodies on the sofa. 'You're meant to be waiting outside,' she slurred.

She was squinting in the light and he could smell the drink she'd had from where he was standing.

'Get into the car, Florrie,' he said.

She lurched towards him, pushing him against the wall. 'Don't talk to me like that.'

'Now, come on . . .'

'What's going on?'

An older blonde girl came out of the kitchen. 'Are you in charge here?' asked Mark icily.

She stared at him coolly. 'Well, it's my party.'

'I was told that Jemma was having a few friends over.'

The girl lit a cigarette and blew smoke at him. 'Actually, it's my eighteenth but Mum said Jemma could ask a couple of mates.'

'Well, don't you think someone ought to be in control? These kids are drinking and some are smoking.'

Her eyebrows rose in amusement. 'So?'

Florrie clutched her stomach. 'I feel sick. That vodka jelly was weird.'

'Vodka jelly?' repeated Mark, appalled.

'Don't you dare be sick here,' said the girl, firmly, pushing her out of the room. 'Go to the loo – in there.'

Mark made to follow her and almost fell over the boy who was mopping up. The kid's eyes narrowed. 'Hey, I recognise you, don't I?'

Mark felt a cold tremor pass through him. 'I don't think so.'

The boy was sitting back now. 'Yeah, I do. You used to live in Highbury, didn't you? Off Canonbury Road.'

Apprehension gripped him.

'What a coincidence!' The boy spoke in a slightly camp tone. 'We lived opposite you until we moved here. Your wife went to prison, didn't she? I remember my mum talking about it. What did she do again? Stealing, wasn't it?'

'Piss off,' said Mark, furiously. The door opened and a green-looking Florrie appeared. 'Come on.' Mark grabbed his daughter's arm. 'Time to go.'

'Poor you,' called the boy. 'It must be hard for you.'

He marched Florrie down the path and into the car. 'What's he going on about, Dad?'

'I don't know.' He started up the engine. 'But I do know that you are never, ever to drink again like that. And if you insist on groping with boys at your age, you are not – I repeat not – to go below the waist until you are at least sixteen.'

'Dad! I'm not like that.'

He set his eyes firmly on the road ahead. 'We all do things we don't mean to.'

'Does that include you? And Mum?'

'Yes, if you really want to know.'

They drove in silence for a few minutes.

'I'm sorry, Dad.'

'OK.'

'But it's hard without Mum.'

He could sense her tears in the darkness. 'I understand that, but I'm doing my best.'

'I know.'

A small hand stole on to his as he changed gear, just as it had when she was little. The gesture was almost enough to negate the pain.

'If someone told you a secret, Dad, and you promised to keep it, do you think you should break it?'

'That depends.' He couldn't think straight. All he could see was his daughter struggling out from beneath that pile of bodies on the sofa. She was too young, far too young, for that kind of thing. 'Why?'

'Nothing.' She yawned. 'I'll tell you in the morning, when you're not so mad at me.'

*

The following morning, Florrie was back to her usual aloof self over breakfast.

'Dad made such a fuss at Jemma's sleepover. It was really embarrassing.'

Daphne, who had stayed over, put a croissant on her plate. 'I heard it was quite a party, young lady.'

'I still don't understand why that boy said it must be hard for you. What did you say to him?'

'Nothing.' Mark busied himself with the marmalade.

'You can't stop me going to parties when I'm older, you know.'

'Or me,' added Ed. 'Anyway, I'm going to live in Huntingdon Beach. You can bum around all day there and not go to school.'

'You'd get caught,' said Florrie.

'Wouldn't.'

That reminded Mark. 'Weren't you going to ask me something, Florrie? Something you mentioned in the car last night?'

'Was I? Can't remember. Ow, Ed – shut up. That *hurt*.'

'Ed, stop kicking her,' said Mark, wearily, wishing it was Monday and time to go back to school; he desperately needed some peace to chase up unpaid fees. As a freelance, he had discovered that this could take as long as it did to earn the money. Sometimes phone calls worked better than emails.

'Jenny, it's Mark Summers PR. Sorry to bother you but I've just been going through my invoices and realised you hadn't paid the last one. Can you tell me how far it's got in the system? Yes, I can hold.'

If he didn't, they might not phone him back and then he'd have to ring them again. When he'd been a staffer, dealing with freelancers, he had often instructed them to hold on, oblivious to the fact that their own phone bill was mounting as they chased money. If he ever worked for someone else again, he'd remember that.

'Next month? But you usually pay within twenty-eight days. Can you check again? Yes, I'll still hold.'

Cradling the phone between neck and shoulder, he logged on.

No point in wasting time: might as well check his emails while he waited.

RECEIVING MESSAGES.

What?

From beware@stopwritenow.co.uk to Mimi: I know what you've been doing. I know about your affair. So stop right now – before anyone else finds out.

That was it. No demand for money. And a crazy sender name. Beware? He clicked on to Properties. He wasn't a techie but he knew enough to work out some things. Not that this told him who the person was or how to track them down. He reread the message, panic gripping him.

I know about your affair. The words thundered round his head. But how in the world did this beware@stopwritenow.co.uk know anything about his life?

AOL HOME PAGE

NEWS

BODIES STILL BEING RECOVERED FROM AUSTRALIAN TRAIN CRASH.

52

'If she'd been on the train, the Foreign Office would have her name.'

Caroline could have shaken her husband if he hadn't been at the other end of the line. How could he go to work, for pity's sake?

'Because I can't do anything sitting at home. Look, I know it's a bit worrying but Australia's a big place. It's like someone assuming that we were in the Paddington crash because we live nearby.'

'But her friend thought she was on the train.'

'She wasn't certain. And I keep telling you, the Foreign Office still isn't certain they've got all the names.'

'Janie says that some of the bodies were thrown so far that it's difficult to identify them.'

'Caro, you're getting hysterical.'

'And you're so bloody calm.'

'That's because it wouldn't help if I was hysterical too. She's bound to ring soon.'

'And if she doesn't?'

'We'll go out there.'

'How do you know we can get a flight?'

'Because,' said Roger, 'as I've said before, I've already looked into it.'

She trembled violently. 'Then you *do* think something's happened.'

'That's not what I said. I'm just formulating Plan B.'

Plan B? She could have screamed. For crying out loud, this was their daughter they were talking about! What kind of man was she married to? Even more chilling, had she ever really known him?

53

On her way to work after her driving lesson, which had gone remarkably well, she opened the local paper on the bus and saw a picture of Joy staring out at her. The caption read, 'DISABLED MUMS GO TO DOWNING STREET'. She scanned the article. Yes, her name and Tabitha's were there too. Hopefully it might help the campaign but she did wish journalists could get it right sometimes. 'Disabled mums' made it sound as though the mothers were handicapped – although, in an ironic way, that was true.

'You didn't say you were going to be in the paper,' said Fiona, settling at her desk and kicking off her shoes. 'I didn't realise you had a daughter who was, er . . .'

'Disabled,' said Susan. Sometimes people needed helping out. In her view, 'special needs' was beating around the bush. 'No, well, we just try to get on with life.'

'I can understand that. My little cousin has cerebral palsy and my aunt's always moaning that people treat them differently. She has a job too – says it's a life-saver.'

Susan nodded.

'By the way, did you hear about Simon? He's been sacked already from his new job for fiddling expenses and for making a move on one of the girls in the office.'

Susan's mouth went dry. 'Where is he now?'

'South Africa, can you believe? One of the boys in the office knew someone who flat-shared with him and he did a moonlight flit without paying his rent. Then he rang from Cape Town and said he'd send the money on. It's not the first time, you know. He was almost done for sexual harassment by the woman who was here before you.'

Susan took a gulp of coffee. 'Actually, he did the same to me.'

'You?' Her expression showed that Fiona clearly considered Susan an unlikely candidate.

'Yes, I know. Crazy, isn't it?'

'I didn't mean that. What happened?'

She told her. Fiona was suitably horrified. 'That's awful. Your dad's right. You ought to complain.'

'I don't want any more fuss. Besides, if he's that far away, I don't need to worry any more, do I?'

BT HOME PAGE

NEWS

GAP-YEAR STUDENT FROM LONDON AMONG AUSTRALIAN FATALITIES.

54

From Earth Mother to Expectent Mum: How are you doing, dear? Let us know as soon as you get back from hospital. We're all here for you if you need some advice. Good luck!

It was all so embarrassing. She hadn't started labour at all. She'd had to email Earth Mother and explain that the pains had suddenly stopped and after that there'd been nothing. Probably Braxton Hicks, like Kiki said. After all, it was only the end of November and she still had some time to go, didn't she?

Earth Mother had told her to get herself checked out by her GP in the morning, but there was no way she was doing that. Doctors hadn't helped her before. She was far better off going through this pregnancy on her own. But it had all made her feel pretty low. When she got to work the next day, Daisy wasn't much better either, even when she tried to cheer her up by making Christmas decorations. 'What do you want Santa to bring you?' she asked, after Daisy had screwed up yet another paper chain.

The little girl shook her head.

'Nothing at all?'

'I want him to take something away.'

No prizes for guessing what that was.

'Now, Daisy, you know he can't do that. Why don't we make your sister a Christmas card? No, don't do that. Oh, Daisy, now look what you've done.'

The crash sent Mrs Perkins running in. 'Not again! If that child doesn't start to behave, we'll have to ban her.'

The woman had no patience! 'You can't do that. She needs time, that's all.'

Mrs Perkins sent Daisy a filthy look. 'I'll have to talk to your mother, this afternoon, young lady. Now, go and play in the sandpit. Lisa, you can see that Joel needs some help with his writing *and* we've got the storybook group waiting.'

Nag, nag, nag. Jealous, that was what she was. Just because Lisa had the knack. Everyone said so, even Mrs Perkins. 'You're a natural, Lisa,' the mothers were always saying. 'You'll be a brilliant mum.' And she would. She really would.

Daisy's mother was late. Lisa could hear her apologising to Mrs Perkins. Meanwhile, she and Daisy were making dough shapes with red plastic cutters. It was so nice sitting down together, being so close. She could pretend Daisy was Hayley and that they were doing normal mother-and-daughter stuff.

Then Daisy's baby sister began to cry. Little whimpers at first, which got louder. No one else seemed to notice and Lisa tried to ignore her, for Daisy's sake, but the noise reverberated in her head. She kept remembering what that baby book had said, about babies crying in the womb. Did Hayley and Sky cry before their lives had ended so suddenly?

She couldn't take it any longer. 'Just going to look at your sister.' Daisy didn't glance up from the dough shapes.

As she rocked the pram, Lisa could hear voices rising from Mrs Perkins's office. Sounded like they were having a bit of an argument; they certainly weren't paying this poor baby any attention. The baby's cheek was as soft as it had been when she'd touched it last week.

Her hands tightened on the handle. The brake release was easy to find. All she had to do was swing the pram down the ramp, push it through the car park and she'd be away.

DECEMBER

From www.amazon.co.uk to lisasmith123@hotmail.com: We confirm that *The Book of Luck* has been dispatched and should be with you within three to four working days.

Dear Mrs Thomas,

Thank you for your request for a house alarm system. We regret that the housing authority does not have a budget for installing the above.

'Annabel, are you out there? Phone home NOW if you pick up this message. Mum and Georgie are hysterical and even Dad's worried although he's not letting on. Shift yourself.'

Who didn't get into the rugby team? Loser, loser . . . Everyone else at school thinks you're a waste of space. That's why no one wants to sit next to you. My dad thinks people like you should go back to their own country.

PRIVATE. Dad, There's something you ought to know but which I promised not to tell you. So I'm writing you this note with Ed's Hotmail password and then you can say you found it yourself.

Mums@Home.co.uk
JOIN OUR ONLINE DISCUSSIONS ON
Bullying. Tactics to teach your child.
Confidence. If you don't have it in yourself, no one else will.
TIP FROM SCUMMY MUMMY
Hide the computer power lead if your kids won't log off.
THOUGHT TO KEEP YOU SANE FROM JULIE OF EASTBOURNE
If you buy next year's Christmas presents in the January sales, you'll save LOADS of money.
CHUCKLE CORNER FROM ALI OF SLOUGH
You know your kid is verbal when they can whine in words.

PARENTING NEWS

New survey shows that over-forties have become too complacent over contraception.

TISCALI HOME PAGE
NEWS
AUSTRALIAN TRAIN — BRITISH PARENTS' AGONY.
BABY SNATCHED FROM PRIVATE NURSERY.

55

Caroline was staring at the latest headlines on her screen, 'CAR-NAGE ON FAST TRAIN FROM DARWIN', when she felt a hand on her shoulder. Karen's beautifully made-up face was soft as she'd never seen it before. 'I've just heard about Annabel,' she said. Caroline felt herself being steered towards Karen's office. 'Sit down.' Her editor shut the door and went to the cupboard on the wall. 'You should have told me before.'

Caroline didn't normally drink whisky. 'It's personal stuff and, besides, you were away. I only came into the office because I had to get out of the house. I can't achieve anything by sitting at home with my husband ringing every now and then, insisting that no news is good news.'

'I might be able to do something,' said Karen, picking up the phone. 'I can call our sister magazine in Sydney. As you know, they're part of a newspaper group. They might know something.' She pushed across a notepad. 'Write down her personal details. Name. Date of birth.' She hesitated. 'Identity marks might help too.'

Caroline raised her face. 'She had a birthmark just behind her right ear. My mother had it too. When she was born, Mum was amazed.' She wiped away a tear.

'It's all right to cry. Is there anyone you'd like me to call?'

Mark. He was the only person she wanted to talk to. Not Roger, the man with whom she had made Annabel. And not Jeff.

'No.' Her voice was scratchy with grief. And then she began to howl.

So much was going wrong with the world. Someone had taken a baby from a nursery in Northamptonshire and there had been another terrible explosion in Jerusalem, killing a busload of schoolchildren. At any other time, Caroline would have felt distraught for their parents – Jeff had always joked that she was too soft to be a journalist – but all she could think of was her daughter. She and Roger hadn't wanted Annabel to do a gap year and now the worst had happened.

'It's not the worst,' argued Jeff, who came round that night in support. 'We don't know. And your sister's right. There's no point in flying out yet. She'll be there by now. We've got to sit tight and wait for the phone to ring.'

'She'd have called if she was OK,' sniffed Georgie.

Jeff gave her a cuddle. 'You teenagers don't always have the sense of responsibility that we do.'

Ben was lighting a cigarette, which wasn't normally allowed in the kitchen. 'I've sent her a text and emailed. She'll pick it up when she gets to a cybercafé. Look, I've got my shift now. See you later, OK?'

Caroline gathered up their mugs from the dining-table. She needed to do something or she'd get hysterical again, like she had in Karen's office. Once, she'd interviewed a psychologist who had admitted that after her divorce she had spent hours scrubbing the kitchen floor because it made her feel in control of her life. Carefully, Caroline put her mug on the left-hand side of the dishwasher and Roger's opposite. As she did so, she felt his hand on her shoulder and moved away angrily. 'I can't believe you're so calm.'

'There's no point in freaking out until you know for certain.' He pressed his head against the kitchen counter and, for a second, Caroline detected fear in his eyes. 'Maybe it's the way I cope, Caro. A kind of self-protection, if you like.'

'It's not how I work,' she said acidly, no longer caring that Georgie was in listening range.

He nodded. 'Part of our problem, isn't it?'

She put on the dishwasher; its calm, rhythmic sound belonged to another world. 'Come on, Georgie, it's bedtime.'

'I'm not going, Mum. Not until we know something.'

'Georgie.' Jeff's voice was calm. 'Mum's right. And Dad. It might take a while to find out where your sister is. And you've got school tomorrow. If you go up now, I'll see if I can get those tickets you wanted for the Darkness.'

Georgie brightened. 'Really?'

'Really. Up you go now.'

She clattered up the stairs as Caroline's mobile reverberated in her back pocket. Fumbling, she dropped it on to the floor, then retrieved it. 'Hello?'

'It's Mark. Look, sorry to ring you at home but there's something I need to tell you.'

Quickly, she switched it off.

'Who was that?'

'Work. I can't take it now.'

Roger eyed her mobile. 'Shouldn't you keep it on in case Annabel rings?'

'There's the house phone and your mobile.'

He shrugged. 'I never have it on.'

'Why not?' asked Jeff.

'In case his girlfriend rings and I answer it,' said Caroline, sharply.

'There's no need to be nasty, Caroline.'

'Nasty!' She almost laughed. 'You're the one who was nasty. You're the one who—'

'Stop it, both of you. It's not helping and Georgie might hear you. Look, I know this is awful but you have to pull together. We've done what we've can and—'

'Phone!' Georgie was charging downstairs but Caroline got there first.

'Janie? . . . Really? . . . You're sure? . . . But when? . . . No, I can't wait . . . I'm sorry but I can't. Roger said he'd try and book tickets, but I'm getting on the first available flight . . . Yes, speak in the morning.'

They were all looking at her. 'She wasn't there. Not in the –

the morgue. Or the hospital. But they're still bringing in bodies. I want to be with her, Roger.' Her eyes filled with tears again. 'And if you don't want to come with me, I'll go on my own.'

Her husband stared at her. 'You're not the only one affected, you know.'

He went out of the room. Seconds later, she heard the front door slam.

'He's not leaving us again, is he?' Georgie was white and pinched.

Again? How much had she been aware of the first time?

'No, he's getting some air. Jeff, I'll see you out.' She paused at the door. 'Thanks for being here,' she said quietly.

'Roger's doing his best, you know. He just finds it hard to show his feelings. Always has done.'

'Well, he didn't have any problems showing his feelings to that woman, did he?'

'Caro, this isn't the time to think about that.'

'Isn't it?' Her eyes pricked with hot tears. 'Actually, I think it is. It's only when you go through this sort of thing that you can see everything else in a real light.'

Something flickered in his eyes and she knew she'd struck a chord. 'I can see what you mean, but don't do anything rash. Let's get through this first.'

'What are you doing here?' asked Karen, when she went into the office the following day.

Briefly, Caroline gave her an update. 'Roger's at home. He'll tell me if something happens and I had to do something or I thought I'd go mad.' She hesitated. 'To be honest, I couldn't bear being near him. He's really getting on my nerves.'

Karen nodded. 'I felt like that when my marriage ended.'

Caroline flushed. 'I don't mean that—'

'Look, you don't have to explain. Actually, I'm glad you're here because something's happened. That case history who's threatening legal action?'

Caroline groaned.

'I spoke to her.'

'I thought you said we weren't allowed to do that.'

'We're not.' Karen tapped her elegant nails on the desk. 'I chose to take the risk. And it paid off. She told me she'd definitely called you at the office and said she wanted to retract her comments.'

'She didn't speak to me.'

'No. She spoke to Zelda.'

Caroline's mind reeled. 'I don't understand.'

Karen sighed. 'I called Zelda in yesterday and forced her to come clean. I think she was so shocked by what's going on with your daughter that she confessed everything. When your case history, this Carmen, said she wanted to speak to you to make an urgent change, Zelda pretended to be you – it was one of your days off. She knew it would get you into trouble when she failed to put through the change.'

'But why would she want to do that?'

Karen shook her head. 'Caroline, this isn't easy to say and I was hoping to hold off for a bit. You know the company's having to make cutbacks? Well, Zelda saw an email on my desk about having to reassess your job-share arrangement. We can't afford to keep both of you on, and it hasn't been as smooth as we'd hoped, has it?'

'That's because Zelda's made mistakes. She's tired with the baby and I've tried to cover for her.'

'She knows, and that's why she tried to make her own position secure.'

Caroline covered her face with her hands. 'By doing the dirty on me?'

'Well, she's failed. She's handed in her notice and will be leaving by Christmas. We've agreed to print an apology and pay Carmen compensation. It's not a lot because, as our lawyer told hers, she has to take some blame for having been open in the first place.'

Caroline felt numb. It all felt so irrelevant and unreal compared with the Annabel situation. That was all that mattered. Her family.

Not her work, which for so many years, she had tried to keep going, with her ailing marriage.

'Thanks.'

Karen nodded. 'I'm sorry it's come at such a bad time. Now, are you sure you're up to working?'

'I want to, but maybe I could leave early.'

'Keep me posted.'

During the afternoon, Caroline forced herself to concentrate on the Tried and Tested page she was editing for the March issue, but every time the phone went or an email popped up, her chest pinged. By mid-afternoon, she was ready to go home when her mobile vibrated.

'Why are you avoiding me?'

His voice was like a liferaft. 'Mark, something's happened.' Briefly she explained. 'That was why I couldn't take your call.' She lowered her voice. 'Besides, you mustn't ring me at home.'

'I know, but I had to hear you.'

She rubbed her eyes. 'I feel the same. But I can't think of anything except Annabel. You must understand that?'

'Of course. Can I do anything?'

'Not really.'

'I'm here. I want you to know that. And I don't regret anything.'

She shivered, remembering the way his mouth had sought hers. 'Neither do I.'

56

'PRIVATE.' Mark opened the envelope next to his computer, with Florrie's writing on the front. Then, following his daughter's instructions, he logged on to his son's Hotmail account, feeling slightly guilty at invading his privacy.

> . . . Everyone else at school thinks you're a waste of space.
> That's why no one wants to sit next to you. My dad thinks
> people like you should go back to their own country.

Stunned, he read the message twice, then picked up the phone to the headmaster of Coneywood. Then he went downstairs to find his son and tell him exactly what he'd done.

'You read my emails and texts?' Ed pushed him away fiercely. 'You wanker! You had no right.'

'Don't call me that, Ed.' He tried drawing his son to him. 'There are times when we all do things we shouldn't because we're trying to help. Why didn't you tell me things had got so bad?'

Ed was almost spitting with fury. 'Because you'd have thought I was a wimp. Like you did at the pool.'

'But I didn't. And I don't.' Mark pulled his son into a bear-hug. 'Bullies like this kid at school have got to be sorted. Otherwise they'll go on picking on others. I've talked to your head – no, don't look like that. I had to. And if he doesn't put an end to it, we'll go to the governors.'

'I don't want to go back to school.' Ed was pulling away from him. 'They'll get me, now you've told.'

Mark felt a prickle of alarm. 'I won't let them.'

'Really? How are you going to stop them?'

57

If something had happened to Annabel, Caroline told herself, as she got off the tube, the family would break up. She couldn't pretend any more. She would divorce Roger and make a new start with Georgie. Ben would be gone soon so it would be just the two of them.

Annabel. Oh, Lord, Annabel, where *are* you?

Roger was sitting by the phone. He looked up expectantly. 'Any news?'

'You're the one who's been at home.'

'Have you rung your sister?'

'Yes. Nothing. But Karen says the *Morning Herald* will run a piece tomorrow.'

'Right.'

He might have been talking about the weather – she wanted to kick him into admitting his feelings.

'Where's Georgie?'

'Upstairs, doing her homework. Ben's online.'

Caroline went upstairs. As usual, Ben was on MSN. 'Have you checked our messages?'

'Nothing. Chill out, Mum. She's probably stopped off somewhere with friends.'

'Please get off, Ben. *Now.* I want to look for myself.'

Stretching, he got off the seat languidly. He seemed thinner than usual, and spottier. 'You're seriously stressy, Mum. It's not good for you. Is dinner ready? I'm starving.'

'How can you think of dinner when—'

'*Caro!*' Roger was pounding up the stairs. 'It's Annabel.' He held out his mobile.

She took it. 'Where have you been? Are you all right?'

Her daughter's voice faded in and out. A bad line or was she ill?

'Oh, Mum, it's so good to hear you. We were on a bus that broke down and my new mobile ran out of battery. We were going to get the train but missed it. That's why we got the bus. I didn't know about the crash until I rang Auntie Janie on her mobile. Mum, I'm so sorry.'

Caroline tried to talk but her throat was dry and nothing would come out.

'Mum? You still there? Don't be angry. The bus was stuck in a rainforest for nearly five days until someone drove past and gave us a lift.'

'Did you have any food?' she managed.

'Not much. We were starving. Luckily, we had a few water-bottles between us. But, Mum, it's so awful. I knew some of those people on the train. We'd met them in the hostel in Darwin. I can't believe they're dead . . .'

Gulping sobs came down the line and it was all Caroline could do to hold back her own tears. 'Darling, I know it's terrible and I'm so sorry, but thank God you're safe. Where are you now?'

'Getting another bus with some friends I met on the first one. Auntie Janie's flying back to Sydney from Queensland. I'm dying for a bath.'

Caroline was shaking with relief. 'I love you, darling. Here's your dad. And Georgie. Stop it, Georgie. You can talk in a minute. She's been really worried about you, Bella. We all have . . .'

The tears were gushing out now and she sank down on to the computer chair, unable to stop. Roger was taking the phone downstairs, followed by Georgie. Annabel was safe. Her daughter was alive. They wouldn't be going to Australia now but so what if they lost the money for the tickets? The relief was agonising. How would the parents of those poor gap-year kids cope when they didn't come home?

*

It took her a while to compose herself. Lifting her head to turn off the computer, she froze. The message must have popped up during the phone call because it certainly hadn't been there before.

From beware@stopwritenow.co.uk to Part Time Mum: I know what you've been doing. I know about your affair. And if you don't stop now, I'll tell your family.

Caroline stared at the message, frozen, unable to move. How could anyone know? Jeff? He'd helped her with her computer the other month. He knew her password. But surely not. Ginny? She might have suspected something after the ball. One of the children? Forward.

From Part Time Mum to mark@marksummerspr.com: Have just got this. What shall we do?

58

> From Lawyer Mum to Mums@Home: There's only one way to treat bullies. Send their parents a letter, declaring you're taking legal action.

'I tried to ring you to say I'd got the same message,' said Mark.

They were sitting on a bench in the gardens outside the Savoy. It was cold and not as private as he had hoped but she'd suggested it as a place where, hopefully, they wouldn't be spotted. He reached into his jacket pocket and handed her the email printout.

She scanned it, shivering. 'Who could know about us? We've been so careful.'

'Someone must have hacked into our systems.'

'But why bother with us? And what do they want? They haven't mentioned money.'

Mark put his arm round her and, to his relief, she leaned into him.

'I wondered if it was anything to do with Mums@Home, so I emailed them to see if anyone else has had problems,' he said. 'You'll never guess who it's run by?'

'Who?' she asked.

'Earth Mother.'

He loved it when she smiled like that. 'No wonder she dominates the Message Board. I suppose she's a bored mother of three.'

'Actually, she's an ex-midwife with four kids and two grandchildren. Highly intelligent. She sent me her personal email address to "talk"; and she was as shocked as I was.'

She was worried now. 'You didn't tell her the exact content of the message?'

'No. I just said we had both been threatened by someone who had clearly logged into some of our personal stuff. She also said something rather interesting.'

'What?' Caroline frowned.

He stroked her hair, nuzzling it at the same time and breathing in her scent.

'She's concerned about that strange woman who calls herself "Expectent" Mum. Did you read that email about her going into labour? No, of course you didn't with everything that's been happening. Earth Mother says she's been concerned about the girl – presuming it *is* a girl – for some time. And she also pointed out that no one's found that missing baby from Northampton yet.'

'Sounds a bit far-fetched to me.'

'Maybe. Anyway, she suggested, and I agree, that we ignore our blackmailer's messages and see if they're a one-off. If they continue, we'll have to do something about it.'

'Like what?'

Mark was rubbing his nose against hers. The action seemed so natural – childlike yet grown-up. 'Not sure. Get expert advice, that sort of thing. God, Caroline, what do you do to me? I've never felt like this before.'

'Nor me. But I can tell you that when Annabel was missing, nothing else seemed important.' She sat up and a chill went through him. 'I've got to put the kids first, Mark. I can't do anything stupid.'

'I'm not asking you to.'

'And I don't do meaningless affairs either.' Her eyes were serious. 'For me, it's all or nothing.'

'I'm the same.' He spoke so quietly that he could barely hear himself.

'Then what are we going to do?'

Suddenly, all his excitement at being with her left him. 'I don't know.' He looked away. 'There's something else. Something I need to tell you. They want Hilary to come home next weekend to see how she copes.'

'But the children think she's in America.'

'I know. We – that's my mother-in-law and I – have concocted some story about her coming back for a visit.'

'I see.'

'Don't be like that.' He took her hand. 'I don't want her back, but what else can I do? If you could see that place, you'd realise how awful it is for her.'

She squeezed his knee. 'Awful for you, too. And what about the knife business? Aren't they scared she'll do it again if she's at home?'

'Exactly what I asked. But they think it was a reaction to being away.' Mark scratched his chin. 'God, it's too much sometimes. I've got to get Ed to this educational psychologist tomorrow – we've had to wait ages for the appointment. In the meantime, I've kept him off school and he's with Daphne. A cop-out, I know, but he was scared of going back after I complained. This kid who bullied him . . . From what the head said, he's very mixed-up and it reminded me of my own experiences.'

She brushed his lips with hers. Just feeling her body against his dispelled all the pain and angst over Ed. Suddenly he was filled with a childish desire to grasp her round the waist, lift her into the air, and twirl her round like a 1950s starlet.

'Mark!'

Gently, he lowered her to the ground.

She was panting, eyes shining, laughing breathlessly. 'Do you always take people by surprise like that?'

'No.' He smiled down at her. 'Only very special ones.'

'And am I?'

'You know you are.'

'I don't remember the last time I laughed like that.'

'Me neither.' He felt young, lightheaded – despite the worry over that awful email. Like a grown-up Ed. So this was what love was like. And to think it had taken him more than forty years to find it . . .

*

The educational psychologist was a short, squat man who rocked back and forth in his chair and charged a monstrous £350 for a two-hour session and a written report. For his part Ed had to fill in a chart and answer several questions while Mark sat outside. He was brought in while Ed had squash and biscuits in reception.

'In my opinion, Mr Summers, your son kicks other children because he misses his mother and is being bullied.'

'I know that.'

'So, what are you going to do about it?'

'I thought that was what you were here to tell me.'

'Mr Summers, we can only advise. You say you've been to see the head and he's failed to resolve the situation, even though this bullying has been going on for several months. On top of this, you tell me Ed and his sister think their mother is in America while in fact she's in prison. No, don't worry. Your son cannot hear me. Do you know what I'd do, if I were you?'

This had better be worth £350.

'First I'd consider a change of school. Clearly the new one isn't working for Ed. And I'd tell the children the truth about their mother because they're picking up vibes that indicate you're hiding something. Children are often stronger than you think but they feel insecure if they suspect they're being lied to.'

'That's what Caroline said,' murmured Mark.

'Well, I don't know who Caroline is but she's obviously thinking along the same lines. One more thing, Mr Summers.' He leaned towards Mark. 'I know we're here about your son but here's a bit of psychological advice for you. When your wife is finally released, don't feel you have to be a martyr for the rest of your life. People change. And sometimes you have to do things you didn't think you were capable of.'

*

The message was waiting in his inbox when he returned.

> From Beware to Mimi: If you don't stop seeing Caroline now,
> I'll tell her husband and your wife.

He rang her mobile immediately.

'I've got one too.' Caroline sounded choked. 'Can't we *do* something?'

He tried to think. 'I don't want to bring the police into this. Leave it with me. I'll think of something.'

'I'm going to tell Roger.' Her voice was scared, uncertain. 'I can't stand the deceit anyway.'

'Wait. Don't do anything until we've talked about this a bit more.'

'Cooeee! It's only me.'

'Caroline, I've got to go – Daphne's arrived. I'll call. Soon.'

'Hello, dear.' His mother-in-law didn't normally come into his study. He closed down his inbox as she puffed her way past the files on the floor.

'Daphne, this computer class you've been going to, have you got the tutor's number?'

'Somewhere.' She fished in her handbag. 'Ah, here's the brochure. That's him at the bottom. Peter Greaves. Thinking of doing one yourself, dear?'

'No. I want to ask him something.'

'Everything ready for Hilary?'

'Sort of. I'm collecting her tomorrow afternoon. Listen, Daphne, we should tell the kids. They're not stupid – if we don't they'll want to see her off at the airport.'

Daphne frowned. 'I don't think that's a good idea. Let's see how the weekend goes, shall we?'

Peter Greaves was very helpful even though he was too busy to come round in person. 'You need to contact the server that this Beware person is with. Each PC is issued with a personal number and they have ways of tracing them. Don't ask me how it works because I'm still learning myself, but it's worth a bash.'

And it might be if he could get through, but after nearly an hour of hanging on for customer relations, Mark had to give up or he'd be late for collecting the kids. He emailed instead, without giving details, and left his mobile number. For the moment, that would have to do.

He picked up Hilary on Friday afternoon. It seemed weird, taking her away with him, instead of saying goodbye in the visitors' centre. She said nothing all the way home, just stared out of the window as though she had never seen streets and shops before. Her eyes were huge, the pupils black. In his jacket pocket, he had her pills with instructions on what to give her and when.

'Mum! When did you get back? We wanted to meet you at the airport but Dad wouldn't let us.' Florrie flew into her arms. Ed hung back until Hilary, her face white, stretched out a hand to him.

'Mum's really tired, dears. Let her sit down. Would you like a nice cup of tea?'

Hilary disentangled herself from her daughter's embrace. 'Thank you.' Her eyes never left the children as they moved away from her and sat at the table.

'Go on, then,' said Daphne, producing a plate of teacakes. 'Tell your mum what's been happening.'

'I'm going to a party next weekend,' said Florrie, excitedly. 'Yes, I *am*, Ed. Dad said I could as long as there was an adult there. And Ed's still pushing other kids around because he's being bullied.'

'Why is he being bullied?' Hilary's voice sounded different: thin, wobbly and permanently alarmed.

'Nothing in particular.' Mark forced himself to lay a hand reassuringly on hers. 'You know what kids are like.'

'It's because he's black, isn't it, Ed?'

'Of course it's not, dear,' butted in Daphne. 'Now, you're not to worry about any of this, Hilary. Mark's sorting it out with the head, aren't you?'

Later, they spent the evening trying to watch television like a normal family. Hilary was glued to the screen as though she hadn't seen it before and, perhaps because he'd given her one of the tablets, was almost oblivious to the children. He'd been dreading bedtime but, to his relief, when she came out of the bathroom she was already in her pyjamas – a shapeless grey pair he hadn't seen before. He took care to take his own into the bathroom with him, and when he finally clambered into bed she was asleep.

What was it that the educational psychologist had said? Don't be a martyr. But weren't there times when you had to be? Eventually Mark fell into an uneasy sleep with thoughts of Hilary and Beware whirling around in his mind.

During the night, he woke. He could feel Hilary's breath on his face. 'Mark?' She sounded more coherent than she had last night.

'Yes?'

He could feel her hand stroking his pyjamas.

'Mark, make love to me.'

Every bone in his body recoiled. Forcing himself, he put his arm round her shoulders, drawing her to him, feeling her hand creeping downwards. This was awful.

When she reached him, he heard her sigh. 'You don't want me.'

'It's not that. I'm tired.'

'You're soft,' she spat accusingly, just as she had before she'd gone away.

Why pretend any more? 'Yes, I am.'

'Which means you don't want me.'

She rolled away from him.

'Let's just give it time, Hilary, shall we?'

A low, ironic, empty laugh. 'Exactly what I have been doing. Good night, Mark.'

When he woke the following morning, she wasn't next to him. His first reaction was relief, the second panic.

It was early and still dark outside so he padded barefoot along the landing looking for her, not wanting to disturb the children, who were still asleep.

There were sounds coming from his study. Heck, she was on his computer! Her face was grim and set as she started at the screen. To his horror, he saw she was logged on to the Message Board of Mums@Home.

'What on earth possessed you to join this?' she asked, in the disdainful manner he had become used to before she had gone to prison.

'I haven't.'

'Then why are your password and user name on the noticeboard?'

She glanced up at the cork squares he had pinned behind his computer to display vital information like his computer helpline number.

'Mimi,' she sneered. 'Quite a memorable user name. I suppose you chat up other women to get your thrills while I'm away.'

'No.' Mark wanted to lunge forwards and drag her away. 'It's not like that at all. I needed some advice about the children.'

'And these women like Part Time Mum and Rainbow have been holding your hand.' She stood up, pushing the computer screen so it fell over. 'Nice to know you're missing me, Mark.' She looked at him nastily, eyes narrowing. 'Did you ever wonder why Florrie is so much lighter-skinned than Ed?'

'Because she takes after my father,' he said unsteadily.

Hilary threw back her head and laughed. 'Poor Mark. You always were gullible, weren't you?'

Bile rose into his throat. 'What the fuck do you mean?'

She threw him a look of pure hate, pushed back her chair and stumbled to her feet.

'Wait. Hilary, wait!'

He ran after her into the corridor but she had dived into the bathroom, locking the door. Seconds later, he heard the shower. Furiously, he hammered on the door. 'Open this door! Open it at once and explain exactly what you meant!'

The shower continued to hum. Bitch! Tears pricked his eyes and he sank to the ground, his head between his knees. Of course Florrie was his. She had to be. She simply *had* to be.

Lunch was a terse affair, during which Hilary, who'd perked up enough to put on some makeup and a pair of smart black trousers, picked at the spaghetti Bolognese Mark had made. There had been no time to tackle her on the Florrie question since she'd stayed locked in the bathroom until lunchtime. Now the children were around and it was impossible to say anything. He'd have to wait until they were alone.

'I'm impressed,' said Hilary, acidly. 'Before I went, you didn't even know where the spaghetti was kept, let alone how to cook it.'

The effects of the morning's medication, thought Mark, were clearly wearing off or she wouldn't be so acidly lucid. But he didn't dare give her any more until this evening; the prescribed time.

Florrie's face crumpled. 'Don't row, you two. I hate it when you and Dad argue.'

Hilary smiled, unkindly. 'Your *father*,' she said, tilting her head at Mark provocatively, 'isn't the argumentative type. In fact, he's a perfect gentleman.'

The double-entendre was intentional; she was trying to make him believe she was referring to a different man as being Florrie's father. But Mark, who would have loved to say something, bit his tongue for the kids' sake. Christ, he almost preferred the dopey, drugged-up Hilary instead of this tight-lipped unpleasant woman who was criticising everything he did, just as she had before she'd gone away. Worse, there was more than a nugget of truth in what she'd said about the spaghetti, even though it meant nothing in the scheme of things. He *had* been hopeless at finding things and helping generally. But the insinuations she was making about Florrie's parentage . . . Mark felt sick. She *had* to be his, didn't she? Surely this was one of Hilary's little games.

'Did I tell you,' interrupted Daphne brightly, clearly keen to restore order to the table, 'that my computer tutor has suggested I entered Silver Surfer of the Year? It's an award for anyone over fifty who's learned to use a computer recently.'

'Really, Mother?' said Hilary, sharply. 'Fascinating.' She pushed back her chair so it scraped on the tiles. 'I'm going shopping. Just me and the children.'

He almost laughed. 'You *are* joking, aren't you?'

She stared back, Florrie-style. 'What do you think?'

'I want to go shopping with Mum,' said Ed. 'Why can't we?'

Because it had been stipulated that she wasn't allowed out of the house unaccompanied by an adult during the weekend visit.

'I just thought it would be nice if I came with you,' said Mark, quickly, 'but I've got to finish a press release first. It will only take me half an hour. But first I'd like a word in private.'

'Not yet,' said Hilary, lying back on the sofa and kicking off her shoes. 'You go and do your work. We'll wait or maybe go for a walk with Mum.'

He would have liked to insist but he couldn't in front of the children.

'And don't be too long,' added Hilary. 'I know what your half-hours are like once you're on that computer.'

It was true. Once he'd started working, it was easy to get carried away, despite the clock in the bottom right corner of his screen. But it was such a relief to blank everything else out. Oh, no. Not again.

From Beware to Mimi: I told you to end your affair. Or you'll be sorry.

Who was this person and did they really know how to tell Roger or Hilary? Was it possible they had somehow tracked down their addresses? This was awful. His hands shaking, Mark emailed his server's customer-relations department again. Within moments, a bland message winged back, assuring him that his message had been received and his 'query' was being looked into.

'Cooee! Only me.'

This really had to stop. Grudgingly, Mark went downstairs to meet her. The house was very quiet.

'Had a nice walk?' he asked.

Daphne frowned. 'No. I went back home for a bit. Hilary said you were taking them out when you finished work.'

'Well, I was but no one's here.'

'Do you think they went shopping after all?'

Mark reached for his car keys. 'I don't know. But their jackets aren't on the peg. And my keys have gone.'

59

She had to admit it. Whatever Dad had downloaded on to her computer had made it work a lot faster so it was easier to cope with the overwhelming response from the local paper's article. All kinds of people wrote to the centre offering support and Susan, Joy and the other mums spent hours photocopying the letters and sending them on to their local MP and Downing Street. Susan doubted that they would get as far as the prime minister's bi-focals but, as Joy said, it was worth a bash.

Slowly, over the next few nights, she stopped jumping every time she heard a crack or a creak in the dark, telling herself that even if Simon did come back from Cape Town, her house was secure.

Josh wasn't so happy. Susan's father had taken it upon himself to tell him what had happened. 'I don't like the idea of you being there on your own,' he said quietly, when he and Steff came to pick up Tabitha. It was the Christmas holidays and they were taking her to the zoo.

What a nerve! 'You should have thought of that when you left us.'

Josh twisted his hands. 'We weren't right for each other, Susan. It wasn't just Tabitha. You know that.'

It was true. Had she been unfair to him? Maybe. It wasn't a good feeling.

'What you need, love, is a man to care for you,' Steff said, as they followed Josh and Tabitha out to the car. 'No, don't look cross. I know it's none of my business and I also know you can't have many opportunities. Why don't you go out with one of your girlfriends when we have Tabs?'

Was there no limit to the woman's persistence?

'We've got a great day centre near us,' continued Steff, fringe bobbing. 'I rang them up and they said we could bring Tabitha as her dad's in catchment. They've got all kinds of things there, lessons as well as physio and the Internet too.'

'I've already had to stop Tabitha trying to go online by changing the password,' pointed out Susan. 'Can you imagine what would happen if she went into a chatroom? She's so naïve she might give out our address.'

'It's all monitored. They can't do that kind of thing. Anyway, have a think about it. OK? What are you doing today when we've gone? Anything nice?'

'Well,' said Susan slowly, 'I've been seeing someone called Joe, actually.'

'Really?' Steff's eyes glittered with curiosity. 'That's wonderful. Is he the friend you had dinner with before?'

'No, someone different.'

It was naughty of her but she couldn't help it. Susan was fed up with everyone feeling sorry for her and it wouldn't do Josh any harm to think that someone found her attractive.

'Do you think there's any future in it?' probed Steff.

Susan considered her manoeuvres, which were coming on nicely, even if she said so herself.

'I'm keeping my fingers crossed,' she said coyly.

'Check your mirrors and remember to watch that right-hand lane in the new one-way system.' Joe seemed as nervous as she felt as they drove to the centre after her hour's pre-test practice. 'You can do it, Sue. I've told you. If you don't have confidence in yourself, no one else will.'

She waited, sitting on her hands to stop them shaking, with three teenagers. In her day, there hadn't been the money for lessons at that age. If Tabitha had been different, she'd have made sure she learned.

A large man with sharp, beady eyes came into the room, calling a name. It wasn't hers and she felt a wave of relief. Then a woman entered, about her age, in a smart suit. Susan couldn't decide if she was relieved or not when the teenager next to her got up to follow her out.

'Susan Thomas?' This was it. Her examiner was a tall, lanky man with wiry hair. Would he be sympathetic or fail her at the first mistake?

Stop shaking.

Confidence. If you don't have it in yourself, no one else will.

Do this for Tabitha and all those days out. Do it for yourself.

Back home, she rang her father. To her disappointment, the answerphone was on. Joy was out too. She had to tell someone.

'Steff, it's me. I wanted to tell you something quite exciting.'

'Fire away!'

She could feel the excitement bubbling inside her: it still didn't feel real. 'I passed my driving test this morning.'

'You *what*? Sue, that's fantastic. Absolutely *fantastic*! I didn't know you were learning.'

'I didn't want to say anything in case I didn't pass.'

'I understand. Have you told your friend Joe?'

'He was the first person who knew, actually, and he's really pleased for me. Anyway, if you like, I could drive Tabitha over to you next weekend.'

'That would be brilliant. I'm so proud of you, Sue, I really am!'

Funny, she thought, replacing the phone. Four months ago she would never in a million years have thought she'd confide in her ex's new wife. But she had really seemed to understand. More so, probably, than Joy would. Now all she had to do was buy a car. She'd been saving and her dad, bless him, had offered to help out. Maybe she should look on the Internet.

She logged on. Better check her inbox first, in case there was anything from the magazine. They had promised to let her and Joy know when it was going in. Honestly, it was amazing what rubbish you got sent nowadays. Spam – the term still reminded her of the cold meat from school dinners – was a right pain even though it only took a few seconds to delete.

WHY NOT JOIN OUR DATING SERVICE?

How did they know she was single or was it just a random marketing sweep?

Automatically, she deleted it, then wondered if she'd been too hasty. She retrieved it and sat looking at it. Funny. Until now, she could honestly say she'd never missed having a man in her life. She'd had enough on her plate just concentrating on Tabitha. The episode with Simon had freaked her out but at the same time, even though she was embarrassed to admit it, it had aroused her in a way she hadn't experienced for a long time. Simon *had* found her attractive, even though he was clearly the wrong sort. Maybe, after all, it wasn't too late to find the right man . . .

Later, she went out with her dad to a garage – not far from Josh and Steff, strangely enough – to check out a Ford Fiesta he'd seen.

'I've told you,' he said, as they set off, 'I want to buy it for you. See it as an early legacy, if you like, or a gift to Tabitha.'

'Dad, I can't— Gosh, do you mind if we stop? I know that girl at the bus stop and she's pregnant. Maybe she could do with a lift.'

They pulled up and Susan wound down the window. 'Lisa, hi! Want a ride?'

She was carrying a bundle in her arms and seemed surprised and none too pleased to see Susan.

'No. I'm all right.'

It was obvious that Lisa had been crying, poor kid. 'But the bus could take ages,' she said. 'I know what it's like.'

'I said I'm all right.'

'OK. See you next week, then.'

'Didn't think much of your friend's manners,' said her father, as they drove off.

'She's not really my friend. She works at the nursery next to

Tabitha's centre. But she's normally so sweet, always kind to Tabitha and the others.'

Susan turned back. 'Dad, I know this might sound odd but Lisa was really upset. I think I should go back.'

60

This little bear can make your dreams come true by Christmas!

That was what it had said. She knew the words off by heart, had hung on to them for reassurance ever since they'd popped on to her screen.

It was nearly time now.

'Lisa?'

Tabitha's mum was leaning out of the passenger window of a car. 'Look, I'm sorry if I'm interfering, but I couldn't help wondering, is everything all right?'

Lisa looked into Susan's kindly face and burst into tears again.

'It's OK,' said Susan, getting out. 'I used to get emotional when I was pregnant too. Look, why don't I give you a lift? Where are you going?'

She tried to talk but could only sob.

'Tell you what, love, why don't we go to a friend of mine? She only lives round the corner. She might not be in, but if she is she'll give us a nice cup of tea.'

And somehow that was one of the nicest ideas anyone had ever suggested.

'Do you want to put those blankets down?' asked Steff, kindly.

Lisa looked alarmed. 'Only if it's somewhere safe. They're for the baby and I don't want to get them dirty.'

'You won't, duck.'

Steff spoke soothingly. Susan had to hand it to her: she'd taken in the situation at a glance when they'd arrived on the doorstep. Susan had only been able to explain briefly what had happened but her dad had understood and gone home, promising to defer the car-buying for another day. And now Lisa was sitting on a beautiful cream leather sofa, sobbing her heart out. Luckily, Josh had taken Tabitha out. Susan wouldn't have wanted her daughter to witness this.

'I'm so scared it's going to go wrong again.' She was fiddling with a crucifix round her neck.

Steff was stroking her hand. 'I know. It's understandable to be scared when you're pregnant.'

'I'm going to call her Rose, you know.'

'Pretty name. But how far gone are you, love?'

Lisa sniffed. 'I'm nearly due. At least, I think I am. My dates might be a bit out.'

'What do the doctors say?' asked Susan.

'I dunno. I haven't had any check-ups. I'm too scared. I reckon that's what went wrong with Sky. They did an internal, the day before, and then I started to lose her . . .'

Her wails filled the room and Steff looked at Susan in alarm, signalling her to come out into the kitchen. 'She needs help,' she whispered.

'I know. But what can we do if she won't see anyone?'

'Well, I did my midwifery, you know. It was some time ago but if she let me examine her, I might be able to reassure her. Then maybe we could persuade her to go to the hospital or at least her GP.'

It was worth a try.

'Look, duck,' said Steff, 'I'm a nurse. Would it be all right if I took a look at you? Then I can tell you everything's OK.'

Wordlessly, Lisa nodded.

'I'll go outside,' offered Susan. She stood in Steff's designer kitchen, waiting. It sounded pretty quiet in there, apart from a few low murmurs. Then Steff came out, her face serious.

'Everything all right?' demanded Susan breathlessly.

Steff's mouth was set grimly and, for once, she wasn't smiling. 'I can't be certain, but I don't think your friend Lisa's pregnant at all.'

'But she's got a bump.'

'That depends on how she's standing,' said Steff, shortly. 'And, yes, her stomach is slightly distended, which might accentuate it.'

'I don't understand. What are you saying?'

'Well, I've only seen one other case like this, but I think it's a phantom pregnancy. She wants to be pregnant so much that she believes she is, poor kid.'

'Weird.'

'Usually – although, like I said, it's rare – it's because they desperately want someone to love them. And a baby, of course, gives unconditional love. She's wearing padding, too, although she tried to stop me seeing it.'

'What kind of padding?'

'Difficult to tell. Looked like layers of fabric under her pants.'

'Blimey.' Susan was shocked. 'What do we do now?'

Steff was already putting on her coat. 'Get hold of her GP or maybe take her to hospital. She needs help. And fast.'

61

The car, to his relief, was still in the drive, unlocked with the key in the ignition as though someone had thought about driving it away, then changed their mind. So where were they? Mark began to run along the pavement towards the park, heart pounding. He peered across at the swings and slides; a couple of younger children were there with their mothers.

Then he saw them, riding on the road on bikes without their helmets.

'Where's your mother?' he called.

'At home.' Florrie skidded to a halt beside him. 'She said she was going to have a lie-down.'

At home? But he'd called upstairs and no one had answered. Still, at least she hadn't gone out and broken the condition of the visit. 'I want you back now, you two, and you know you're not meant to ride your bikes without a helmet.'

'Sorry, Dad. Can't we have just a bit longer?'

'Yeah, we can ride in the park.'

Mark considered it. It would give him time to go back and talk to Hilary. 'All right. But I want you home in twenty minutes.'

He walked back to the house, wondering whether he should come clean with Hilary about Caroline. It was clear they couldn't go on like this. Or should he wait until she was released?

'Hilary?'

No answer. The kitchen was empty and so was the sitting room. He went upstairs. Their bedroom was empty too, and so were the children's rooms. He tried the bathroom door. Locked.

'Hilary? Are you all right?'

Silence.

'Hilary. You're scaring me. Just tell me you're OK.'

'What's going on, Mark?'

For once, he didn't curse his mother-in-law for letting herself in unannounced. 'She's locked herself into the bathroom.'

Daphne rattled the handle. 'Hilary, stop being silly, dear. Just tell us you're all right.' She looked at Mark with frightened eyes. 'Dear Lord, what should we do?'

He heaved his shoulder against the door.

'You can't break it down,' said Daphne, horrified.

He rubbed his arm. 'I've got to.'

He heaved again and again. There was a crack as the door gave way.

Pushing it open, he ran in. Hilary was in the bath. She was lying back, eyes closed, one arm trailing over the side. The water was pink.

Daphne called for an ambulance while Mark ripped up a towel and tried to stem the flow of blood from Hilary's wrist. A razor blade lay on the side of the bath – presumably she had used that. Miraculously, she was still breathing.

The children, thank heavens, arrived just after the ambulance had left so he was able to play it down. Mummy had fallen in the bath and gone to hospital. He was going there now to be with her and Daphne would look after them.

Florrie was shaking with fear and he pulled her towards him, holding her tight. How could Hilary have been so wicked? Of course Florrie was his.

'Is Mummy going to be all right?' she asked, her voice muffled in his jumper. He wanted to say yes, but there had been too many lies. Too many fudges. So instead he held out his other arm to Ed and drew him in too, as he had done when they were little. 'I hope so. But she's in good hands and, remember, I'm always here for you.'

*

Dear Mr Summers,

Thank you for your letter of last week, outlining the unfortunate problems with your son Edward. I can assure you that, as the chairman of the governors, I take bullying and racism very seriously. Investigations are being carried out and we will update you accordingly. In the meantime, I hope Edward will recover soon from his bout of influenza.

Yours sincerely,
Theobald Hepplethwaite

Deer Lisa, Im sory I haven't replyed but Ive been very bisy. Good luk with the baby. Ill try and cum and see you soon. Mum

www.truelovedatingservice.org.uk
Unfortunately this web page is no longer available.

'Mum? Can you hear me? The line's terrible. Yes, me too. Can't wait.'

Mums@Home.co.uk
JOIN OUR ONLINE DISCUSSIONS ON
Safety standards at nursery.
TIP FROM MELISSA2
To avoid queues for Santa, go early in the morning or just before he closes.
THOUGHT TO KEEP YOU SANE FROM PUSHY PRINCESS
You don't have to live life just for the weekend.
CHUCKLE CORNER FROM ANON OF ALDERSHOT
Hearsay is what toddlers do every time you swear.
PARENTING NEWS
Survey reveals that the average child receives £500 worth of Christmas presents.

62

From Scummy Mummy to Mums@Home: Isn't it awful about that missing kid? I think nurseries should tag them. I couldn't think of anything worse than losing a child.

Caroline and Roger waited impatiently at the tinsel-festooned barrier as a long, straggly line of travellers went past. Some looked around hopefully, presumably for loved ones or taxis to meet them. Others strode straight ahead. A father went past with a small child on his shoulders and his arm round a woman.

Caroline's chest tightened. She couldn't remember when Roger had last put his arm round her as they walked along. It seemed so long, too, since their children had been the size of that little one. Now they were a sticking plaster for their marriage, a plaster that was fast losing its grip.

'There she is!' Roger leaped forward. She hadn't seen him beam like that for ages. 'Bella, we're here.'

A tall, tanned young woman with tightly plaited hair bounded up, a grubby black haversack thumping heavily on her back. 'Mum! Dad!' She hugged Caroline first, then Roger.

'Let me look at you.' Caroline cradled her daughter's face in her hands. It had been so long since she'd seen her that she'd almost forgotten the exact shape of her nose and that mole on her chin. She hugged her tighter. 'Bella, we were so scared.'

'I know, Mum. That's why I came back early. And I'd had enough, to be honest.' Her eyes filled with tears. 'I still can't believe that Mandy and Steve are dead. I just wanted to come home.'

But home had changed, thought Caroline, as they walked to

the car. Annabel had been away for more than six months and so much had happened since then. As soon as they got back she made her starving daughter a bacon sandwich, then stole up to the study and logged on, her heart beating fast. No more from beware@stopwritenow. In one way, that was a relief. But it might mean that whoever had sent the message was about to carry out their threat and tell Roger.

She had to get in first and come clean. In a way, it was almost ironic. She had forgiven her husband for his affair. But would he forgive her, and did she want him to?

She went downstairs. Roger was sitting on the sofa, reading the paper. She wondered why people were invariably doing normal things when their world was about to be shattered.

'Can we talk?'

He looked at her, eyes cold. 'Of course.'

She closed the door behind her. 'There's something I need to tell you.'

'What?'

'I'm seeing someone else.'

'You're *what*?'

'I'm seeing someone else.' Her voice didn't belong to her.

'Is it serious?'

'Yes.'

'Do I know him?'

'No.'

'I see.'

She sank on to a chair. 'Don't you want to know anything about him? How long it's been going on? What he's like?'

Roger stood up. 'I'm not in the slightest bit interested, although, I must say, you do pick your moments. Our daughter has only just returned and you have to drop this bombshell.'

'But what do you want to do? Shall I move out? Will you?'

'I really can't think about that yet. I need to get my head round it. I suppose you've done it out of spite to pay me back.'

'No.' She shook her head vigorously. 'It's not like that. But, as a matter of interest, if I said I was sorry, would you forgive me?'

'Like you said you'd forgiven me?' Roger laughed. 'Don't you see, Caroline? You've never forgiven me. That was the problem. But, if you want, I *am* prepared to go on with our marriage for the sake of the children. Are you?'

'I don't know.' The enormity of what she had done hit her now. She stood up and made for the door. 'I really don't know,' she repeated to herself, as she shut the door behind her, with Roger on the other side, and began to walk up the stairs to the sanctity of her bedroom. She lay for a while on the bed, trying to imagine life with Roger over the next few years if she stayed. Yes, it might be better for the children, providing she was able to mask her own emotions. But she'd been doing that for the past two years and it hadn't worked. She buried her face in the pillow. 'Be honest,' she told herself. From the minute that Mark's lips had met hers, she had known that she and Roger were over for ever.

'Mum,' said a small voice beside her.

Caroline opened her eyes. Georgie had crept in and was lying next to her. 'You and Dad were rowing again, weren't you?'

'Sort of.' She stroked her daughter's hair. 'But it's normal, you know, like you fall out with your friends sometimes.'

'Sure?'

Georgie's eyes penetrated hers and Caroline flinched. 'Sure.'

All that evening, including when they lay down on opposite sides of the bed, Roger behaved as though nothing had happened, as if to prove that he really wanted to carry on. The only clue was that he was even stiffer than usual. When she woke up the following morning, he was already in the shower. It was such a terrible muddle and she still didn't know what to do. She needed to tell Mark what had happened but his answerphone was on and the mobile off. Why? Surely he had had some opportunity to make a private phone call unless he had changed his mind about her. Cold doubt spread over her body from the centre of her ribs.

'Morning,' said the cheery receptionist at work. She had red tinsel in her hair. 'How are you?'

My life is falling to bits around me, was what she wanted to say.

Zelda's desk was empty and scarily tidy.

'She's gone.' Karen was stunningly cool in beige silk. 'I had a word with HR and released her from working out her notice. I don't want anyone like that on my staff. She was lucky we didn't take disciplinary action.'

'How will she manage?' Caroline thought of the baby on the way and Aurora at home.

'I'm afraid that's her problem. How was Annabel?'

'Older and a bit shaken. She was still asleep when I left this morning. Thank you for everything.'

'You've got to do whatever you can for your kids.'

She was right. Even if it meant putting yourself last.

By the time she got home she still hadn't heard from Mark. Caroline felt extremely foolish. Had she been so desperate for love that she had fallen for the first man who showed her affection, then dropped her when she returned it?

'Mum!'

Annabel met her at the front door, decidedly cleaner than when Caroline had left. 'Thank God you're home.'

'What's happened?'

'It's Ben. No, don't go into the sitting room. He's in there, sulking. Come up to the study. There's something I've got to show you. I found it when I came out of the shower.'

A condom in Ben's room perhaps? If so, she'd found them there before and not said anything. Teenagers were trained to use condoms now in the same way they'd been trained to wash their hands after the loo.

But it wasn't that.

Caroline stared at the screen.

From Beware to Mimi: This affair has got to stop.

'I saw Ben writing it just now,' said Annabel tersely. 'It looks as though he's blackmailing someone.'

Caroline's heart pounded in her ears as Ben came up the stairs and stood quietly beside her.

'It was you,' she said. 'You sent the emails. But how did you know? Why?'

'I was trying to stop you, Mum.' Ben actually had tears in his eyes. He *never* cried. He hadn't even as a little boy. 'I read your messages to him. I know I shouldn't have but you were acting so weirdly and you were always checking your messages. When I found that – that sick stuff you were sending each other, I thought I could stop you before it went any further.'

'You were blackmailing *Mum*?' Annabel shook him by the shoulders. 'Why?'

His nose was dripping now. 'Because I wanted to scare her off so it would be all right between her and Dad.'

Something had changed in Annabel's face. 'You've been having an affair?'

Caroline's heart lurched with shame and guilt.

'Oh, darlings.' She clasped her children to her even though they were both taller. What had she done to them? This was her worst nightmare come true. They'd never forgive her. Never.

'It's over,' she babbled. 'Well, it will be. I know it's hard for you to understand but I was lonely and—'

'Do you love him?' Ben's eyes were boring into her.

He deserved the truth but it was so hard. She hesitated.

'Of course she does, Ben,' butted in Annabel, angrily. 'You know how Dad's behaved. Doesn't she deserve some happiness?'

She felt her shoulders lifting with the unexpected support. 'It's not what it looks like,' she began.

Ben was staring at her with a hard, hurt look she had never

seen before. 'So are you and Dad going to split up? I need to know.'

'Would you cope if we did?'

He didn't answer.

'Yes, we would, Ben,' said Annabel firmly.

Caroline took a deep breath. 'Then I think . . .'

She stopped at the sound of a key in the lock downstairs.

'He's home,' said Annabel. Her voice sounded different. There was something adult in it that Caroline had never heard before. 'I can't believe it. I go away for a few months and everything changes.'

'No,' said Caroline quickly. 'No, it hasn't.'

She pulled her daughter to her but Ben turned away. 'It will be all right,' she said desperately.

Ben made a sort of choking sound, as though he was trying not to cry again. 'Come off it, Mum. It's fucking finished. Isn't it?'

63

By the time he felt able to leave the children and Hilary to ring Caroline, his wife was out of danger. The razor cut had been deep but it hadn't pierced an artery. Not that she'd necessarily intended to. A cry for help, the nurses said.

He could have cried himself. 'I can't leave her now,' he said.

'I can see that.'

'Maybe later,' he added. There was a leaden silence. 'I love you, Caro.'

Her voice was hesitant. 'We hardly know each other.'

'Maybe not in terms of years but we have something very special. You know that, don't you?'

Her voice was almost inaudibly soft. 'Yes.'

'And what are you doing about Ben? It's almost unbelievable. He must have been desperate.'

She sighed. 'He was, but I couldn't tell him off because I felt so guilty about the pain I must have caused him. I've told Roger.'

'About us?'

'Yes.'

A sharp thrill pulsed through him. That meant he was as important to her as she was to him.

'He wants us to try again.'

His heart sank again. 'And will you?'

'I'm thinking about it. For the children.'

'But what about us?'

'Is there an "us"?'

'There could be, one day. If Hilary is ever able to cope on her own.'

'Mark, I need to think about it.'

Of course she did. 'Me too.'

He hadn't realised it until the words were out of his mouth. His initial reaction on hearing her voice had been to run to her, make her his. But it was too soon. They both needed to adjust. He might not love Hilary any more but she was still his responsibility, as were the kids. And Caroline wouldn't feel right if she came straight from one relationship into another.

'Do you want a break?'

He cleared his throat. 'Maybe we should.'

'OK.'

'I'll call you some time.'

'Right.' She put the phone down before he could say any more. But he'd done the right thing. Hadn't he?

FROM BULLYING ONLINE

Due to an unexpectedly high number of queries, we are no longer able to take any more individual problems. Please log on to our site for general advice. Tips include:

*   Siting the computer in a general family area so you can see what the children are doing
*   Warning the children never to give out personal details such as names and addresses
*   Avoiding chatrooms
*   Installing a good filtering service.

FROM GOOD PUBLICITY

PR CONSULTANT REQUIRED FOR BUSY COMPANY SPECIALISING IN BABY PRODUCTS. BASED IN LONDON.

64

ONLINE NEWS: BABY STILL MISSING. HOSPITAL DOCTOR CLAIMS THE KIDNAPPER MIGHT BE A FORMER PATIENT WHO LOST A BABY.

'I see, Steff. Thanks for letting me know.'

Susan put down the office phone. In one way, the call was a relief but in another it made her feel guilty. But what else could she have done? Steff had been right. They had had to contact Lisa's GP – she'd grudgingly given them his name – and Lisa was in a psychiatric ward. The poor kid was still convinced she was pregnant.

Steff had added that, according to the GP, Lisa was settled and 'comfortable', whatever that meant. She wasn't ready for visitors but maybe next week. 'She should have been given more help after the miscarriages and then she might have coped,' said Susan.

'Maybe you're right.' Steff had sounded thoughtful. 'Listen, there's something else. No, actually, don't worry. I'll save it for later.'

'OK,' said Susan, bemused. Nowadays Steff was acting more like her best friend than her ex-husband's new wife but, in a funny way, it was all right.

Even so, it was difficult to get Lisa out of her head, although being in the office helped. Sometimes she could hardly believe how much she loved her job. And now she had wheels, her prospects were even better.

The door opened and Susan sat up straight, ready to take a new client's details. 'Steff!'

'I'm sorry.' She flicked back her fringe. 'I know I shouldn't barge in when you're working, and I nearly told you on the mobile, but I was passing and I wanted to talk face to face.' She pulled up a chair, uninvited. 'Listen, Josh doesn't know I'm here but I wanted to have a girl-to-girl chat.'

Just as well no one else was in the office to hear. 'Go on.'

'I've found out more about that centre near us.' Steff's eyes shone. 'They're adding an extra building for teenagers – not just any age – with special needs. There's computers and gym equipment and a coffee bar and loads of other stuff.'

Susan felt herself going cold. 'So?'

'It would be perfect for Tabs, don't you see?'

'If you think Tabitha's going to come and live with you, I'll fight you every inch of the way. Get out of here right now.'

'Not *with* us, Sue.' Steff grabbed her hands pleadingly. 'Just *near* us. Both of you. Josh said you'd never consider it but it would be great. Tabs could see more of her dad and she'd get the stimulation she needs. You could have more time with your friend Joe, too. Please, Sue. Just say you'll think about it.'

She couldn't. Or could she? She still couldn't sleep properly at night, scared stiff in case Simon returned. And Tabitha did need more than she was getting at the moment. She'd have to leave the centre when she was sixteen and then what? Susan had found out a bit more about this new place on the Net and it wasn't just for teenagers: it was for young people too, in their twenties and thirties.

Funnily enough, the idea of being near Josh and Steff wasn't unappealing. She felt nothing for her ex, but she had a grudging affection for Steff, who was like a puppy that wouldn't take no for an answer. She would also be nearer her dad.

But what about work? She'd tried so hard – and done well too. It would be wrong to give it up. On the other hand, she might be able to get transferred. Steff had pointed out that Green & Co had a branch in their town. She'd looked it up. From the picture and staff description, it was about the same size and the manager was quite dishy. Not that she had time to think about *that* kind of thing.

'Hiya,' said Fiona. 'Anyone been in?'

'No one who seemed seriously interested in buying,' said Susan, truthfully. 'Actually, have you got a second? There's something I want to run past you.'

'Fire away.'

'I wondered if I could have the sixteenth off next month. It's a Tuesday.'

Fiona was slipping into her office shoes. 'I'll need to check the rota. Doing something special, are you?'

Susan coloured. 'It's a big lunch, actually, at some swanky hotel in London. I've been shortlisted for a magazine award – well, my friend Joy and I have – for trying to save the centre.'

'Well done you! Course you can have the day off. What are you going to wear?'

'I'm not sure. Actually, there was something else I wanted to ask you.'

The door opened and a woman came in, clutching some brochures. 'Tell me later,' hissed Fiona. 'Can I help you, madam?'

65

'Scary, isn't it?' said Daisy's mum to Mrs Perkins. 'You wouldn't think they'd take a baby from a nursery, would you? What's your security like, by the way?'

'Very good,' said Mrs Perkins, who'd already arranged to have the centre's alarm updated. 'But I was going to say to you the other day that, if I were you, I wouldn't leave the pram outside when you come in to collect Daisy. You never know.'

'So you see,' said Mark slowly, at the end of what seemed like a very long confessional, 'that's why your gran and I told you she was in America. Mum didn't want you knowing she was in prison. Now it's got her depressed and made her act strangely. That's why she cut herself.'

'But she hasn't killed anyone?' demanded Ed.

'No, silly. Dad told you. She stole some money.'

'Well, not exactly,' began Mark. 'She bought some shares she shouldn't have.'

'What are shares?'

'A kind of money,' said Florrie, impatiently. 'But what will happen when she gets out? Will you two split up?'

She seemed so calm about it. He'd heard that kids were much better at dealing with this kind of thing than they used to be but Florrie's matter-of-fact air was unnerving.

'Possibly,' he said slowly.

'Who will we live with?'

'Well, that depends on a lot of things. Like who you want to be with.'

'You,' they both chorused.

Mark breathed a sigh of relief. 'Come here, both of you.'

He drew them on to his knees. 'I know this is difficult, with Mum and me splitting up.'

'Not really,' interrupted Florrie. 'We knew you two didn't get on, didn't we, Ed?'

His son nodded.

'It was worse not knowing what was happening,' continued Florrie. 'It's horrible when you suspect people are keeping things from you. I knew something was wrong when I rang that bank in America and no one knew about her. Anyway, loads of my friends have divorced parents, and I'd rather you were both happy.'

He was so astounded, he could hardly find the words. 'You're amazing, you know that?'

Florrie gave him a big hug. 'We get it from you, don't we, Ed?' She dropped her voice. 'I know we've been difficult but that's because we missed Mum. But now she's back, well, she's different. And a bit scary. Suppose she cuts herself when we're there – I wouldn't know what to do.'

'She wouldn't,' soothed Mark.

'Yes, but suppose she did?' interrupted Ed. 'She stole, didn't she? It makes me feel I don't know what she's really like.'

Exactly how he felt, thought Mark. 'Mum needs help,' he said slowly, 'and when she's better, we'll see how it goes. OK?'

Florrie buried her head on his shoulder and he could feel her weeping silently. He put his arms round her reassuringly. Damn Hilary. Damn her for everything.

Florrie raised her tearstained face. Her eyes were so like his own mother's, he'd always thought. Of *course* she was his. So why did he have that niggling uncertainty on top of everything else he had to cope with?

'Mum won't be coming back for a while, will she?' Florrie said.

'No,' said Mark, firmly. 'I don't think she will.'

∗

Hi, Kari, Just had a weird time with mum. She wasn't in New York at all. I'll tell you more when I see you.

'Janie, it's me. Sorry it's so late but I wanted to ring instead of emailing. Something's happened . . .'

GREEN & CO: TRANSFER REQUEST
Applicant: Susan Thomas
Age: 34
Experience: four months at Hazlewood branch
Reference (from Fiona Sterling): I have no hesitation in recommending Susan Thomas for this position. She is reliable, trustworthy and conscientious.

ONLINE NEWS: TEENAGERS PROSECUTED FOR DOWNLOADING MUSIC ILLEGALLY.

Mums@Home.co.uk
JOIN OUR ONLINE DISCUSSIONS ON
Is it acceptable for kids to email Christmas thank-you letters or should they still write them?
TIP FROM CELLULITE MUM OF LITTLEHAMPTON
Keep the kids quiet in the holidays by getting them to ice fairy cakes like mini Christmas cakes.
THOUGHT TO KEEP YOU SANE FROM LAWYER MUM
You can't change others. But you can change yourself.
CHUCKLE CORNER FROM SLEEPY MUM
Mother's definition of 'full name': what you call your child when you're mad at him.
PARENTING NEWS
Don't forget our Mums@Home Christmas Party at the community centre, Lambeth Road, on 9 December at 2.30 p.m. Nearest tube Lambeth North. Hope this is central enough for everyone who lives out of town. Do come along and put a face to your name!

66

'If you don't leave him, Caro, you'll always regret it.'

Her sister was saying all the things she felt inside. If only Janie wasn't so far away. 'And even if this Mark chap doesn't work out, at least you've tried. Otherwise you'll always wonder what would have happened.'

'But what about the children?'

'They're more resilient than you think. Annabel had already said to me she thought something was wrong. Besides, what are you getting out of being with Roger? Does he make you laugh or giggle or feel as though you're the only woman in the world for him?'

'No.'

'And how will you feel in ten years' time if you're still with him?'

'I'll wish I'd gone.'

'There you are, then, Caro. You've got your answer.'

Telling him wasn't so easy. In fact, it was horrible.

'So you want us to break up.'

His voice was solid with coldness as though it was her fault. She'd have preferred him to be angry. 'Yes.'

'Fine. We'll sell the house and take half each.'

So matter-of-fact. So practical.

'It's not as simple as that, Roger.'

They were lying in bed, with the lights off. It was much easier to talk when she didn't have to look at him.

He turned over, his back to her. 'Seems simple enough to me. You say you're not happy.'

'No.' She sat up in bed. 'I'm not.'

He moved away from her. 'I've tried my best and it isn't working. All right, I did something wrong. But I've got the rest of my life to live.'

'So have I.'

She wanted to tell him more, to explain that her marriage had died the minute she had found out about his affair but panic had made her pretend she could keep going.

'I'll move out. You stay here with the children for the time being.'

His words made it real. It was no longer some vague scenario in her head.

'Where will you live?'

'I'll find a flat somewhere.'

'With that woman?'

He sighed in the darkness. 'I told you. I'm not seeing her any—'

'Roger, I saw you both at the station. So did Ben. And he's heard you on the phone.'

Part of her still wanted him to deny it but his silence spoke louder than any words could have done.

'The man I've been seeing . . .' she began, and felt his body stiffen. 'Well, it's over. Not that it makes a difference to us. But he made me feel cherished, made me realise I need to be loved. And I don't think you really love me, do you, Roger?'

'I used to.'

Used to? The pain of what she'd lost seared through her as she felt him get out of bed. 'Where are you going?' She was scared now, not sure that she wanted him to go.

'To the spare room.'

'Can't we talk?'

'There's nothing else to say.' He shut their bedroom door quietly behind him. He still hadn't even asked Mark's name or where he lived or if he was married or any of the other questions she had asked when she'd found out about Elaine.

'Elaine.' There. She had said it out loud. For years, she had been an unable to do so. But now it was an agonising relief. Caroline felt hot tears trickle into the pillow. It was so very hard. But at the same time she felt something else, something that had eluded her for so long. The knowledge that finally, by breaking up with a man who had been so painfully unfaithful, she had been true to herself.

She leaned over to turn on the bedside light. Slowly, deliberately, she propped up the pillows behind her and spread out both hands in front of her. Her wedding ring gleamed dully as if it, too, felt the inevitable pull. She slid it off and examined it on the palm of her left hand, which now felt light without it. Something inside her made her spin it carelessly on to the bedside table; it twirled perilously close to the edge. Then, switching off the light, she turned over and fell asleep.

The next day Georgie cried when she told her after school. It was the hardest thing she'd ever had to do. It wasn't fair. If only she hadn't hung on after Roger's affair, no one could have blamed her. 'I'm sorry, darling, but you'll still see Daddy.'

'Not every day.' She was sitting on the sofa, tears pouring down her cheeks.

Thank God for Annabel who had her arm round her little sister. 'Mum and Dad haven't been happy for ages, Georgie. It'll be better this way.'

'Not for me.' Georgie leaped to her feet, dashed out of the room, slammed the door and ran upstairs.

'Leave her.' Annabel seemed so mature, as though she was the mother. 'I'll go up in a minute.'

'Where's Ben?'

'Working. I'm not meant to tell you this yet but he's rung Auntie Janie to ask if she can find him a job in Australia until he starts his course next year.'

Caroline blew her nose. 'That's not a bad idea.'

'I think he needs the structure.'

'So, you'll both be away.'

'You'll be all right, won't you?'

Caroline nodded. Annabel had coped with so much abroad – perhaps she didn't need her mother as much as Caroline had assumed. And if she did, well, she'd still be there for her, Ben and Georgie. 'Course I will, darling.'

The same cleaning urge that had hit her before when she was upset compelled her to scour the house now from top to bottom. To wash the corners of floors that hadn't seen a mop for months – maybe Roger had been right about Mrs B. Clear out under beds. Empty bins.

She stopped. A tube ticket was stuck to the bottom of the bathroom bin in a splodge of toothpaste that had leaked out of a discarded pump. An ordinary tube ticket; the kind they all used every day.

Caroline prised it out, heart pounding, as she read it. It was a train ticket from Wembley. Dated yesterday.

Somehow, she got herself into the office the next day. She felt drained from having cried so much and her bare left hand seemed like someone else's. But otherwise life seemed impossibly normal. The office was busy and her inbox was teeming. For once, however, she was grateful for the distraction.

CHECK OUT THIS NEW WEBSITE FROM SINGLE AGAIN.

How apt! Single Again was for newly separated men and women. It wasn't, it assured her earnestly, a dating agency but a group that gave support. And it was hoping she would be interested enough to add it to the Family page which the editor had asked her to take on. She put it among the possibles.

The phone. Roger? Part of her wanted it to be and yet . . .

'Hi. It's Jeff.'

'Hello.'

He was distant. Almost suspicious-sounding. 'Roger's just rung me. He's told me everything.'

'Was he all right?'

'Not great. Caro, why didn't you tell me?'

'It all happened so suddenly.'

'He says you have someone else.'

'Yes. No. There was someone but that's not why.'

'Was he the man I met at the ball?'

'Jeff, please. I'm at work.'

'Well, when can we meet?'

'I don't know. There's so much going on. Maybe in a couple of weeks.'

'That's when I'm seeing you at your magazine's awards cere-mony. Remember?'

She'd forgotten she'd asked him, ages ago, when Roger had said he couldn't make it.

'Of course. See you, then.'

67

Last reminder for our Mums@Home Christmas Party.

He reached in his pocket for the printout to check he'd got the right address. A small, barrel-shaped woman with frizzy hair pushed past him. 'Hi, I'm Cellulite Mum of Littlehampton,' he heard her saying to a tall woman with orange (orange?) hair.

'And I'm Going Grey of Manchester.' Orange Hair clapped the other lady on the shoulder. The two fell about, screeching with laughter like schoolgirls.

He looked around. Would she be there? It wasn't her sort of thing or his, but he'd had to come in the hope she might turn up.

Do you want a break?

Maybe we should. Again and again he had regretted those words. It might be the sensible option but he had a terrible feeling he might have done something very stupid. Like losing the love of his life, which seemed far more important than not knowing if his daughter was his. He'd worked the last bit out in his mind and was pretty certain now of where he stood.

'Hi. Come on in!'

A large, bubbly woman with Christmas-tree earrings dragged him in, pressing a plastic cup into his hands. 'I'm Earth Mother.' She indicated the label on her chest. 'Which one is your wife?'

'Sorry?'

She grinned at him. 'Duchess or Scummy Mummy or Sleepy Mum?' She glanced at her list. 'There are a few more, too, who we're still waiting for.'

He took a swig. 'Actually, I'm Mimi.'

Her eyes widened. 'Mimi? But you're a man.'

387

'I know. I pretended to be a woman. I'm sorry. It's a long story. Actually, I was wondering if you'd seen—'

'You know it's against the rules, don't you?' The piggy, mascara-less eyes were distinctly hostile. 'If you read the small print when you registered, you'd see that you're not allowed to give false details.'

'False details?' An extremely tall, curly-haired woman stopped, slopping warm mulled wine over his trousers. 'Sorry about that.' She eyed Mark suspiciously. 'Who's been giving false details?'

Mark drained his cup – he loathed mulled wine but anything to numb the embarrassment – while Earth Mother explained the situation. 'I used to specialise in that part of the law before I had my career break,' remarked Lawyer Mum, fixing beady eyes on him.

'Moral support.' He returned her gaze steadily. 'My wife is in prison for insider-dealing and I'm bringing up our two children whose behaviour, both at school and home, has been challenging. Most of the women I know offline are reluctant to befriend a single dad in case their friends or husbands think they're trying to have it off with me, so I thought I'd find some mates online instead. Obviously I was mistaken.'

'Please.' Earth Mother caught his arm. 'I didn't mean to be unkind. It's just that we have to be careful. You get some real freaks, you know.'

Lawyer Mum nodded. 'How long did your wife get?'

'Six months. Listen, I'm sorry to be rude – again – but I wanted to meet someone here. Someone called Part Time Mum. Have you seen her?'

Earth Mother shook her head. 'Know of her, of course. But she's not on my acceptance list. Maybe she isn't coming. Oh, look, here are some more!'

Mark swivelled round hopefully.

'I'm Melinda of Southsea,' said a woman in a pink tracksuit and a baby sling with, inexplicably, no baby inside. 'My husband's parking the car. I've got to go back in a minute to feed Garth but I wanted to say hello first.'

'Welcome!' Earth Mother beamed. 'How incredible. You're exactly as I imagined you!'

'Really?' Lawyer Mum frowned. 'I want to meet Ali of Slough.'

Melinda flushed. 'Actually, that's me too. I enjoyed saying things so much that I sort of doubled up.'

'Interesting.' Earth Mother nodded. 'They say that each one of us has two sides, don't they?'

He couldn't bear this. Small-talk was not what he had come for. Maybe Caroline was hovering outside. 'Excuse me,' he said, easing his way past.

'You'll never guess who *that* was?' he heard Lawyer Mum say. Oh, sod it.

Just as well there were labels. She'd never have guessed half of them. Single Mum had a wedding ring on – she'd taken the plunge last week she was telling everyone excitedly – and Mad Mum was perfectly normal in a jacket and skirt, uttering intelligent sentences, which she managed to finish unlike most of the people there who were too busy screaming with laughter and hugging each other as though they were old friends.

'Mulled wine?' said a woman in scruffy jeans, a tattoo on her bare arm (wasn't she cold?) and long jade earrings. Susan peered at her label. Bad Mum. 'No, thanks. I'm driving. Is there anything soft?'

'Over there. By the counter,' said Bad Mum, pityingly.

Susan hesitated, not wanting to leave Tabitha in her chair while she threaded her way through the crowd.

'I'll get you a drink,' said a small woman. Her hair was scrunched back into a bun and worry lines were etched on her forehead. 'I'm Frazzled Mum. But I'm getting better, thanks to the site.'

Susan relaxed. 'I know what you mean. Water would be great, thanks.'

There were, she thought, surprisingly few kids here, even though the invitation had said they were welcome. Anyway, she hadn't been able to leave Tabitha with anyone. Her dad had flu, and Josh and Steff had gone on a weekend break to Paris. Besides, she'd had enough of pretending. She was who she was. And so was Tabitha.

'Hi, I'm Earth Mother. Welcome!' A large, bustling woman with Christmas-tree earrings beamed down at Tabitha. 'Is this your daughter?'

'Yes. Tabitha, say, "Hello."'

It was one of her new words from the last Steff-and-Josh weekend.

'Hallhalhall.'

Susan wiped away the dribble. 'I'm Rainbow, by the way.'

'Rainbow!' A woman with a baby sling stopped beside her. 'I love your messages. They're so sensible and not judgemental like some of them. I'm Scummy Mummy, because I can never seem to keep my clothes clean – not with this one in my arms all day.' She glanced down at Tabitha's chair. 'Did you sort out the access stuff with your ex?'

'It's working out much better than I thought.'

'Was that your wish?'

'Sorry?'

'You know, your wish. The one with that funny little bear when the website got started.'

'Oh, that was just a bit of fun,' said Earth Mother. 'We thought it might catch people's attention.'

Scummy Mummy looked annoyed. 'Well, I happen to believe in things like that and it worked for me. I wished for a girl because I've got three boys already and I had her.'

'And I wished that life would get better for both me and my daughter,' said Susan, slowly.

'And has it?'

'Yes.' She reached down for Tabitha's hand. 'I think it has.'

Earth Mother clapped. 'That's wonderful! It's so amazing to see everyone together.'

'What gave you the idea to start it?' asked Susan.

'Well, I had six children of my own and then my husband left me. 'Two years ago I joined a computing class and married the man who ran it. He had four teenagers of his own and now we have thirty-two grandchildren and stepgrandchildren between us!'

She dropped her voice. 'I wanted to write a book about my experiences but no one seemed interested, so Greg, my husband, helped me set up a website so I could share my thoughts with others. It's been a lot more work than I realised but so inspirational! Here's Greg now.'

Susan tried to hide her surprise as a man who had to be considerably younger than Earth Mother joined the group. 'Everyone enjoying themselves? Great. Nice to see it's working out.'

He bent down and planted an affectionate kiss on Earth Mother's cheek. Flushing, she kissed him back and Susan felt a pang of loneliness.

'Juice anyone?' asked someone, who was handing round a tray.

'Thanks.' Grateful for the interruption, Susan fished a straw out of her bag for Tabitha. It fell to the floor and a good-looking man – he must be brave to have come – picked it up. 'Thanks.'

'No trouble.' He handed it to her awkwardly. 'You haven't come across someone called Part Time Mum, have you?'

'No. Sorry.' He had dark circles under his eyes as though he hadn't slept. And she knew what that felt like. 'All right, love?' she asked Tabitha.

Her daughter grinned. She'd been right to bring her. If there was one thing she'd learned in the last few months, it was the importance of being yourself.

'I've been looking for "Expectent" Mum,' said Earth Mother, returning to the group. 'I do hope she comes. I've been quite worried about her.'

Susan hesitated. If she told her what had happened, it was like breaking a confidence.

'Maybe she's had her baby,' prattled on Earth Mother. 'Did you read her posting the other week about her false alarm? Poor love. I've had a few of those myself.'

Susan smiled ruefully. 'Me too.'

He was here! Now what? She hadn't been going to come but Roger was coming to the house for some more clothes and she hadn't wanted to be in when he arrived. No, it was more than that. She'd wanted to see Mark. She needed closure before she could go on.

'Hi.'

The surprise in his eyes made her heart flutter.

'I didn't think you were coming.'

'I wasn't.'

Gently, he took her elbow. 'Let's go outside to talk.'

A woman with a label declaring herself to be Pushy Princess stared at him with undisguised interest as they made their way out of the hall. Outside they found a playground with animal-shaped rides.

'Bags the giraffe!'

She laughed.

'Caroline, I've missed you.'

'You're the one who broke it off.'

He held both her hands, looking into her eyes. 'No. I said I thought we needed a break. But I was wrong.'

Suddenly she couldn't breathe.

'I can't live without you. Sounds corny but it's true. And I'm filing for divorce.'

'Not because of me?' She didn't want that burden.

'No. Hilary and I would have broken up even without what happened to her. But I don't want to lose you.'

He drew her to him and she laid her head on his shoulder. 'I don't want to lose you, either.'

He kissed her briefly on the lips. Soft. Yet hard at the same time.

She gazed up at him.

'When you smile like that, it's as though the entire world has been switched on,' he said.

He made her feel so good. 'Really?'

'Really.'

She buried her face in his chest. He smelt different from Roger. A clean start. 'My husband and I are splitting up, but not because of you. Our marriage had been dead for years. I'd just refused to accept it.'

He dropped a series of little kisses all over her face. 'I'm thinking of moving back to London but I need to talk it over with the kids.'

'It would make it easier for you to see Hilary.'

He nodded. 'I can't abandon her completely.'

She had to say it: 'It wouldn't be right for us to move in together immediately.'

'I know.' He kissed her again. 'But we can see each other, can't we?'

His words wrapped her up like a duvet. Warm. Cosy. Exciting.

'Yes.' She tried to say something else but his mouth came down on hers and the ground below her fell away.

'I love you, Part Time Mum,' he said eventually.

She sparkled up at him, feeling more alive than she had ever felt before. 'And I love you too.' Laughingly, she traced the outline of his mouth. 'Even if you are called Mimi!'

Later he told her of Hilary's unkind taunts about Florrie's parentage. 'I've tried asking her for the truth but they've got her on a new medication, which seems to have doped her up,' he said sadly. 'I'm not sure if she'll ever tell me now.'

'Would it make a big difference to you if Florrie wasn't yours?' asked Caroline, snuggling up to him on the giraffe.

'Yes and no. Yes, because I'd feel cheated, and no, because I've brought her up and love her as my own.' He paused for a while, reflecting. 'I suppose that's the important bit, isn't it?'

Caroline nodded. 'I'd say so.' She lifted her face for one more kiss.

*

'Right, everyone. Time for the Christmas draw!' Earth Mother, whose real name, Susan had discovered, was Priscilla, juggled a white plastic potty that contained scraps of paper. 'Who's going to win the trip for two to Paris? Each paper contains the name of someone who entered the draw in August.'

'Trip for two to Paris.' The girl next to Susan, with twins in her arms and a name badge declaring her to be Big Mum, rolled her eyes. 'No good me winning it. Who'd have this lot?'

'I'm going to ask the only man in the room – other than my lovely husband of course – to draw,' trilled Priscilla/Earth Mother. 'It's his penance for being naughty enough to pretend he was a woman!'

A titter ran round the room. 'Mimi? Alias Mark Summers? Where are you? Not there?' Priscilla grinned, revealing surprisingly uneven teeth. 'Maybe he's gone home. Well, would you like to do the honours?'

She thrust the potty at the twins' mother. 'Don't worry. Even if you pick your own, we'll allow it. Want me to hold one so you have a free hand?'

'You can keep him, if you want.' Big Mum pulled out a piece of paper. 'Shall I read it?'

'Yes, please.'

'Susan Thomas.'

Susan gasped. 'Are you sure?'

'That's what it says.'

She had never won anything before. This was amazing. And totally impractical. Who would she go with?

'Mummummum.' Tabitha pulled at her sleeve, her face creased with a frown. She didn't like noise when she couldn't understand what was going on.

Susan knelt beside her. It might be difficult to arrange but surely it could be done. 'We're going to Paris, Tabs,' she said, smiling. 'We'll see all those wonderful places that were on the jigsaw you did. Remember? Won't that be fantastic?'

68

HOME PAGE
Mother of babysnatcher has given an exclusive interview to
the *Daily Mail*. Click here.

Mark clicked. He was still job-hunting online but he needed a break
before Daphne brought the kids back and the house went mad again.

My daughter has never been right since she got sterilised after
her second baby. She kept wanting another but I never thought
she'd take someone else's.

'Dad, it's my turn on the computer. You said.'
'I've just got to finish this.'
'What?'
Florrie had come in and was looking over his shoulder. 'Are
you writing to Mum?'
'No. She can't get emails.'
'But we are allowed to see her?'
'Yes. I promised, didn't I? Next weekend.'
He wasn't looking forward to it. How would the kids react
when they saw Hilary in that horrible visitors' centre. On the
other hand, the psychologist he had spoken to at the prison had
explained it would help both her and them.
WICKED HAS JUST SIGNED ON.
He hated it when their MSN messages popped up.
'Who's Wicked?'
'He's from Ed's old school,' said Florrie. 'Gary. Remember? He
came over once.'

A nice boy, Mark recalled. 'Why's he Wicked?' he asked dubiously.

'It means "cool", Dad,' added Ed, joining them. 'He's really nice.'

That was a relief. 'Would you like to go back to your old school?'

'Yes,' said Ed and Florrie together.

'Well,' said Mark slowly, 'I'm thinking of applying for a job in London, and if I get it, we could move back.'

'Great.' Ed was thumping the keys. '"Hey, Dad says we might be coming back,"' he had typed.

Mark was appalled. 'Don't tell him yet.'

'Why not?'

'Because it hasn't happened.'

'But it might, mightn't it?' said Florrie, excitedly. 'And if we're in London again, we'll be nearer Mum.'

'Remember what I said. Mum's not been well. It's going to take her a long time to get better.'

'Yes, but she will, won't she?'

'Sure.' Mark got up, leaving Ed to it. 'Just one more thing. Remember the rule about no chatrooms.'

'Get a life, Dad. I told you MSN's OK. You only talk to people you let in the group. You can check if you want.'

'No. I trust you.' Mark resolved to go down to PC World tomorrow and make sure his filter was still up to date. It was so confusing, and despite the earlier vow he had made to himself, he couldn't help thinking about Florrie. Things changed all the time. Including life.

'Hang on,' said Ed. 'If we go to London, what about Gran?'

'Don't worry about me,' said a familiar chirpy voice behind him. 'I'd love to come too. Would that be all right, Mark?'

He turned round. For once, his mother-in-law seemed uncertain, almost frightened. He held out his arms. 'Daphne, I wouldn't dream of going anywhere without you. And with all the courses available there, you'll be spoilt for choice. Actually, talking of going somewhere has given me an idea. But there's something I need to run past you first. Privately, if that's all right.'

When he explained Daphne looked shocked. Older too, he thought, with a pang. It wasn't until these last few months that he'd realised how fond he was of his mother-in-law.

'Mark, I'm almost a hundred per cent certain that Florrie's yours. I'm sure Hilary would have said something to me if she wasn't and, anyway, she has so many of your mannerisms.'

'They're not genetic,' he said.

Daphne pulled him to her: the feel of her arms round him was surprisingly comforting. 'You could always have a test.'

'I don't want one,' he heard himself say. 'I couldn't cope if she wasn't mine. But at least this way there's hope. Besides, it doesn't seem so important any more.'

Daphne moved away, still holding his hands. 'Then that's your answer, isn't it, dear? Now, what's your other idea? The one about going away?' Her eyes sparkled. 'You know how I like to travel!'

It was bloody freezing. Much colder than if they'd gone in September. But, as Daphne said, these were the kind of memories they'd relive when they were 'getting on'. Mark's lips had twitched at that. It would be a long time before his youthful-minded mother-in-law classified herself as being in that category.

'See up there?' He pointed up into the night sky. 'That's Orion's belt. You can tell because it's a row of stars in a line. And over there, that's the Plough. If you drew a line from one star to another, you'd have the outline of a saucepan or old-fashioned plough-shape.'

Ed stared upwards. He was still quiet and withdrawn after all the bullying but, as Daphne said, he'd be all right when they moved on to a fresh start.

'Right, everyone,' said Daphne, emerging from the canvas. 'It's not quite as nice as the tent we had in the Galapagos but it'll do.'

'I think it's great,' said Florrie, snuggling happily into her sleeping-bag.

'You do?' asked Mark, surprised.

'Yeah, cool,' agreed Ed.

Mark was filled with a wonderful sense of contentment. Maybe, if he could persuade his kids to taste the occasional old-fashioned childhood experience, he wasn't doing too badly as a parent after all.

69

The awards ceremony was at the Apothecaries' Hall in London, according to the invitation. It sounded very smart. Some big corporation was sponsoring the event with *Beautiful You* magazine, which had invited Susan and Joy because of the interview about the campaign. There were ramps, which was useful – and so many people who had done amazing things that she felt a bit of a fraud. There was a grandmother who had brought up her grandchildren after her daughter had died of cancer. There was a nine-year-old girl who had been horribly injured in a car crash: she had lost her leg but now had an artificial one. And there was a dad who had brought up eight children single-handed after his wife had left.

'We do it every year,' explained a nice woman called Caroline, who had introduced herself as one of *Beautiful You*'s feature editors. Susan could have sworn she'd seen her before but she couldn't think where. Tabitha slurped her orange juice noisily through a straw, and grinned happily at everyone. 'We select the case histories of people we've interviewed and whose stories are particularly touching. Triumphs Over Tragedy, we call them, or TOTs.'

Susan wasn't sure how she felt about being a Tot. It all seemed unreal, from the dress she was wearing – H&M, which Steff had encouraged her to buy – to moving house next month. To her amazement, the woman at the council had been sympathetic about the transfer and it was all happening much faster than she had thought possible. So, too, had the transfer to Green & Co's local branch.

'Hello. I believe I'm sitting here.'

Susan glanced up to see a tall man with a kind face examining his place card. 'I'm Jeff Golding.'

Her heart skipped a beat for no reason she could fathom. Don't be daft, she told herself. He's far too posh for you. 'Susan Thomas. Nice to meet you.'

'Aren't you on the shortlist with someone else for the award? I saw your name and picture on the board outside.'

She nodded. 'My friend Joy and I were nominated.' She nodded towards the side of the room. 'Joy is talking to the BBC. We've brought our children too.'

'Then you must be Tabitha. Hello.' He held out his hand to her daughter, who was sitting on Susan's other side in her wheelchair.

No condescension. Just normal. She was grateful for that. 'Do you work for the magazine?' she asked him.

'No, but a friend of mine does, and I'm on the board of Kids On Wheels, a charity that's here.'

'I've heard of them. They do some good stuff,' she said, with interest. 'Why did you get involved with them?'

'Well,' he seemed to be weighing up the question, 'I'm a solicitor and specialise in medical negligence so quite a lot of my clients have special needs. I also had a sister with cerebral palsy.'

Had? She didn't want to pry but she immediately felt a connection with him.

Susan took a sip of white wine. 'What kind of medical negligence do you come across?'

'All kinds. One of my clients, who's here for the ceremony, brought an action against the hospital where his son was born, because he was deprived of oxygen at birth.'

'But how do you know the parents weren't responsible?'

The words were out of her mouth before she could take them back.

He nodded. 'It happens sometimes. Not in this case, but you're quite right. Parents do sometimes pretend that their children have been hurt by a hospital or member of staff when in fact they are to blame. Gosh, are you all right? You've gone terribly pale.'

Susan stood up. 'I feel rather faint.'

He took her arm. 'It's very hot in here.' He caught the eye of an older woman opposite. 'I'm just taking Tabitha's mother outside for some air. If Tabitha needs something, would you kindly hand it to her?'

He leaned back against the stone wall while she let it all out. He was a good listener, Susan found herself thinking, didn't interrupt, just directed her gently when she faltered.

'So, you think it's your fault?'

'It had to be either because I dropped her or because I gave in about the MMR.'

'Susan, all the evidence we have so far suggests that the MMR is safe. But I'll tell you one thing. Nearly every parent I act for has the same fear. Could they have done something that contributed to their child's condition? The answer is usually no. It's a psychological thing. They need to find a reason, and they also feel guilty because they are healthy and their children are not. It's natural. Just as, in the same way, some parents feel they have brought it on themselves for some previous mistake they've made. They see it as their penance.'

She nodded. 'I can understand that.'

'But it doesn't help anyone, neither the parent nor the child. Do you want my advice? Go back to your GP. Get him to refer you to a consultant. Ask him to go through the notes. Yes it's a gamble in case they say the MMR or the fall might have contributed. But if not, you'll have peace of mind.'

He smiled kindly at her. 'It's an awful lot to take in, isn't it? Have you got any questions?'

Her mind was still churning. 'A few.'

'Tell you what, how about a light supper later? I don't know about you but I didn't have time for lunch and I'd rather hoped there'd be something more substantial than nibbles now.'

'I'd love to but I can't with Tabitha.'

'Why not? I know a great Italian near here and I'm not bad

with children. I've got various godchildren who will vouch for me.'

'Thank you.' She flushed. 'That would be really nice.'

She and Joy didn't get the award, which went to the single dad of eight but Susan wasn't as disappointed as Joy, partly because she was more preoccupied about telling Josh. She was really scared, but as Jeff had said, the sooner she got it over with, the better she would feel.

'You dropped her?' Josh demanded, the veins standing out on his forehead with fury. 'Why didn't you tell me?'

She was hot with fear, apprehension, guilt and all the other emotions whirling through her body. 'Because I was scared. I thought they'd take her away from me. It sounds crazy now but—'

'No.' Steff put her hand on hers. 'I understand. You'd gone through so much that it was hard to see things clearly. We all know that feeling, don't we, Josh? Besides, does it matter now? Surely the important thing is to give Tabitha as much support as possible.'

'Thank you.' Susan could almost have hugged her even though Josh's brows were still knitted with anger. 'But I want to see the consultant. I need to tell him everything.'

Two weeks later, she went with Steff and Josh to see a Mr Sussex. It was a private appointment and Josh insisted on paying. 'We should have done this years ago,' he said, as they sat in the pale blue waiting room with copies of Pre-Raphaelite paintings on the wall. Thankfully, he seemed calmer now. No doubt Steff had been working on him.

Steff linked her arm in his. 'Better late than never.' She glanced at Susan. 'I thought you might bring Joe with you for support.'

Susan shrugged. 'We're not seeing each other any more.'

'That's a shame.'

'Not really. We sort of outgrew each other.'

A nurse called their names and they went in. Mr Sussex was older than Susan had expected; she was glad of that because it suggested experience. Falteringly, she explained why they were there. He spent some time looking at Tabitha's notes and talking to them.

'So, you see, there's no reason to believe that either the fall or the MMR could have caused Tabitha's condition. From the earlier symptoms you describe, it's far more likely that it was a birth complication. Your notes indicate that you had a very fast labour for a first baby.' He smiled sympathetically. 'As the previous consultant said, sometimes a quick birth can cause bleeding in the brain that isn't always detected until later. This might fit in with the other symptoms such as Tabitha not crying when she was born and being slightly blue. The Apgar score wasn't particularly high either, although not low enough to raise concern at the time.' He looked again at the notes. 'I see that you haven't had any more children.'

'We're divorced,' said Susan.

'Well, if either of you has any more children, it might be a good idea to consider genetic counselling.'

Some hope, thought Susan, wistfully.

'There's just one other thing,' said Josh suddenly. 'My wife – I mean ex-wife – has been campaigning to keep the centre open where Tabitha goes in the holidays. The local authority wants to close it.'

Mr Sussex sighed. 'More cutbacks . . .'

'I was just wondering if you'd mind signing our petition?'

'I'll do more than that,' said Mr Sussex, reaching for his pen. 'I'll make a couple of phone calls. I know a few people who might be able to help.'

Susan left the hospital feeling as though an enormous load had been lifted from her shoulders. 'You're right. We should have gone before.'

'Too bloody true,' said Steff.

She'd never heard Steff swear before.

'What's wrong? Steff, you're crying!'

'I'm pregnant. At least, I think I am. That's why I'm flipping crying. Yes, Josh, I know I should have told you, but I was waiting until I was certain. And I don't mean to hurt your feelings, Sue, but suppose it's like Tabs?'

Mums@Home.co.uk
This page is no longer available.

From Earth Mother to Mimi: Thanks for your email. Yes, I'm sorry too but I had to shut up shop. To be honest, the website was taking over my life so I've given it up and Greg and I are moving to Spain. We'll send you our new email address when we get there. Have a good life!

Dads@Work.co.uk. Click here to find out more about our campaign to help working fathers negotiate more family-friendly hours. Or ring Mark Summers on 07789 6060.

'Tabitha, look at my new screen saver. Recognise it? Good girl. It's the Eiffel Tower, isn't it? Only six weeks to go now.'

From caroline.crawford@yahoo.com to annabel@hotmail.com: Hope the new term is going all right. Don't spend your loan all at once. Looking forward to seeing you when I come up next weekend.

'Steff, it's me – Susan. I've just been to see poor Lisa. She seems to have accepted that she wasn't pregnant but she's convinced she's expecting again. She says the father is a computer engineer called Ryan.'

From georgie@hotmail.com to bencrawford17@hotmail.co.uk: B gd and don't get into more trouble. Guess what? I'm in the girls' rugby team. We're going to slaughter EVERYONE!

'Sue? It's me, Jeff. Listen, I was just wondering if you felt like Sunday lunch tomorrow? With Tabitha, of course.'

For the attention of Mark Summers
I'm sorry you have turned down the offer of a new contract
with us but wish you all the best in your new job. Please
treat the Send button with extreme caution.

> *Yours sincerely,*
> *Clive*

Dear Mum,
Do you get apple-flavoured condoms in prison? My new
friend Sam says they sell them everywhere. I just wondered
because I'd like to see what they look like and Dad won't
let me buy one. Last weekend, Dad, Florrie and I went
camping. We thought it would be boring but it was fun.

> *Love Ed*

From bekki.adams@thegazette.co.uk to susan.thomas@aol.com:
Congratulations on saving the centre! Would you be prepared to
be interviewed about it?

ONLINE NEWS: BRITISH MAN JAILED FOR TEN YEARS IN
CAPE TOWN FOR RAPE. SIMON WRIGHT, FORMERLY FROM
BEDFORDSHIRE, WAS FOUND GUILTY OF RAPING A 35-YEAR-
OLD WOMAN ON A BLIND DATE . . .

From steffandjosh@btworld to susan.thomas@aol.com: Just
had to send you our first scan picture! Aren't they sweet?
Definitely both boys!!!!!! And the consultant says they look
healthy which is a huge relief. To be honest, don't think I could
cope as well as you do. Looking forward to seeing you all for
Christmas dinner. Do you dad and stepmum like turkey?
PS Please feel free to bring your new friend.

From mark@marksummerspr.com to caroline.crawford@yahoo.com:
Xxxxxxxx

This is a magic frog. It will grant you one wish and only one wish if you decide to send it to others. You can wish for anything.

If you send it to

three people – your wish will come true eventually.

five people – your wish will come true in three months.

ten people – your wish will come true in five weeks.

fifteen people – your wish will come true in one week.

COMPUTER IS SHUTTING DOWN